Stephen Booth is the internationally bestselling, CWA Dagger-winning author of the acclaimed thrillers featuring Cooper and Fry. The series is in development as a TV programme. Booth lives in Nottingham.

STEPHEN BOOTH

FALL DOWN DEAD

sphere

SPHERE

First published in Great Britain in 2018 by Sphere

1 3 5 7 9 10 8 6 4 2

Copyright © Stephen Booth 2018

Rotherham MBC		
B54 027 114 7		
Askews & Holts	29-Aug-2018	
AF	£20.00	
WAT		

Hardback ISBN 978-0-7515-6761-8
Trade Paperback ISBN 978-0-7515-6762-5

Typeset by Palimpsest Book Production Limited, Falkirk, Stirlingshire
Printed and bound in Great Britain by Clays Ltd, Elcograf S.p.A.

Papers used by Sphere are from well-managed forests
and other responsible sources.

Sphere
An imprint of
Little, Brown Book Group
Carmelite House
50 Victoria Embankment
London
EC4Y 0DZ

An Hachette UK Company

www.hachette.co.uk
www.littlebrown.co.uk

To Lesley, as always

The world is full of obvious things which nobody ever observes.

Sherlock Holmes in *The Hound of the Baskervilles*, Sir Arthur Conan Doyle

1

For one second, she was floating. Sailing out into grey nothingness like a bird released from its cage. Cold, damp air wrapped round her body as she flung out her arms and kicked her feet in a desperate attempt to find solid rock.

She tried to scream, but the breath was torn from her throat as she fell. All she could hear was a faint, distant cry, the mewl of a terrified animal, bouncing back from the muffling curtain, drowned by the crashing of water. Her waterproof rattled against her shoulders like battered wings; her hair blew free and smothered her face. She could see nothing, feel nothing, taste only the bitter tang of fear in her mouth.

It happened so fast that her brain wasn't quick enough to work out what was going on. The fall was too quick, too short and too sudden. The impact killed her instantly.

As she lay on the rock, with her blood dripping between the gritstone slabs, a bird called from the plateau. It was a long, mournful shriek like the voice of a spirit, a phantom that haunted Kinder Downfall.

Almost before she'd stopped breathing, a swirl of mist snaked across her legs and settled in her hair, clutching her in its chilly embrace, hiding her body from view. It would be hours before she was found, a day before they carried her down.

But hers wasn't the first death on the mountain. Another woman had lain here, decades before. She'd left the memory of herself on this rock, though not her name. The Downfall had seen more than its share of blood.

And that was why they called this place Dead Woman's Drop.

2

Sunday

Detective Inspector Ben Cooper knew he was in the right place when he saw the tape. The way some officers strung it up at a crime scene made it look so untidy, as if a puppy had run amok with a roll of toilet paper and trailed it all over the street.

At the far end of Haddon Close, he found blue-and-white coils tied in unsightly knots round lamp posts, fluttering in strands from a fence and lying in sodden heaps on the pavement. Someone had managed to get every horizontal length of it upside down too – quite an achievement considering how often it had been twisted. The message POLICE LINE – DO NOT CROSS was illegible to anyone not standing on their head.

But it seemed to have worked its magic. That or the bored scene guard staring into the distance with his arms folded across his chest had special powers of some kind. Inquisitive members of the public were noticeably absent for such an open and vulnerable crime scene.

'No, *Strictly Come Dancing* is on the telly,' said the guard when Cooper stopped to ask him. 'It's the start of a new season.'

'Oh, I see.'

'There were plenty of folk around earlier on, though. And there'll be a few drunks later, when the pubs shut. I'm due to be relieved by then.'

'Anyone else on scene?'

'DC Hurst and the CSIs. And DS Fry is still here from the Major Crime Unit.'

'OK, thanks.'

The guard noted Cooper's identity and the time of his arrival on a clipboard and lifted a strand of the tape for him to duck under.

The house was a fairly unremarkable semi-detached property sitting in a quiet corner of an Edendale housing estate. It looked as though it had been built sometime in the last twenty years, with stone cladding to blend in with the traditional building style of the Peak District.

Cooper stopped at the Forensic Investigation van and struggled into a scene suit before he entered the inner cordon. Stepping plates had been laid on the drive, and he could see a trail of splattered blood leading from the open front door.

He already knew some of the story. For once, this murder inquiry was almost cleared up before he arrived. Some cases had no mystery about them at all. The killing of Danielle Atherton required hardly any investigation or the identification of a suspect, just the collection and analysis of evidence, and the building of a watertight case for the Crown Prosecution Service.

Because there hardly seemed any doubt, did there? Not only had Danielle's husband still been standing over her body when the first response officers arrived, but he was also the person who made the 999 call. Most people who committed murder had no idea what to do next. For many,

4

their first instinct was to phone the police, or call for an ambulance.

So that was what Gary Atherton had done. On the recording of the emergency call Cooper had listened to, Atherton could be heard saying, 'You'd better come. I think I've just killed my wife.'

Case closed? Well, almost.

Unfortunately, people had been known to make false confessions, to pick up a knife and say they'd done it, perhaps to protect someone else. Or they might even convince themselves they *had* done it. A confession wasn't enough on its own. The evidence had to support it, and be convincing.

In the hallway, Cooper found Detective Constable Becky Hurst on duty, taking charge of the evidence. She'd been in his team at Edendale CID for a while now, and was one of his most valuable assets. She was efficient and cool under pressure, and she didn't suffer fools, as DC Luke Irvine and his civilian investigator, Gavin Murfin, had often found out.

'What do we know so far, Becky?' Cooper asked her.

'It's pretty straightforward,' she said. 'The victim was stabbed several times in the neck and shoulder, and once in the palm of the hand.'

'A defensive wound?'

'Just the one,' said Hurst.

'Have we a confirmed time of death?'

'An emergency call was made from a mobile phone located at this address at ten thirty-two a.m. The caller identified himself as Gary Atherton, and he told the call handler that he'd killed his wife.'

5

'Yes, I've heard it.'

'Well, the first response officers arrived at ten forty-four a.m. and confirmed the victim showed no signs of life. Paramedics were on scene shortly afterwards and verified death.'

'It looks as though she lost a substantial amount of blood.'

'And it seems Mr Atherton had made no attempt to control the bleeding either.'

'What about the phone?'

'Bagged up. It had bloodstains on it and some nice clear prints.'

Cooper nodded. 'And Mr Atherton himself?'

'He went quietly. He's in custody now being processed.'

'Good.'

'Dev Sharma has only just left,' said Hurst.

'I'm sure everything is being done according to the book,' said Cooper. 'I'll catch up with DS Sharma when I get back to West Street.'

'And Luke has talked to some of the neighbours. They say they heard shouting from the Athertons' property. A violent argument. By all accounts, Mr and Mrs Atherton had been having some problems recently.'

'Nothing out of the ordinary, then.'

'Not so far, boss. Oh, and there's a teenage son, Bradley. He's no more than fourteen. Social Services are looking after him.'

'Where is DS Fry?'

Hurst pointed towards the kitchen.

'I'll go and speak to her,' said Cooper.

Most of the Major Crime Unit from the East Midlands Special Operations had been and gone from Haddon Close, leaving only Detective Sergeant Diane Fry on liaison. The task of putting the evidence together would be left to Divisional CID.

For a few moments Cooper watched the crime scene examiners working in the sitting room of the Athertons' home. Then he turned towards the kitchen, where he saw the murder weapon.

With incidents like this, the outcome was often much worse when it happened in the kitchen. There were too many weapons lying around handy. In this instance, a bloodstained carving knife had been tossed in the sink, where a trickle of water from the tap had splashed the blood into a jagged arc across the porcelain.

Sophie Pullen had been the first to see the danger that day. Its approach was slow and inevitable. And still they'd walked right into it.

The hike onto Kinder Scout had started the same way as it always did. The group had met at the Bowden Bridge car park outside Hayfield and stood for a moment to examine the memorial plaque on the rock wall, as if it was some kind of shrine. Darius Roth made a point of it, and they followed his lead, as always.

The Mass Trespass onto Kinder Scout started from this quarry 24th April 1932.

To Sophie, the group of walkers depicted on the plaque looked much like their own group, a leader striding ahead, a slightly disorganised rabble following behind. The sun cast the skeletal shadows of an oak tree onto the plaque, the remains of a few leaves now brown and withered. There was a wooden bench, too, inscribed with a poem that began:

As I trudge through the peat at a pace so slow
There is time to remember the debt we owe . . .

They called themselves the New Trespassers Walking Club. That was Darius's idea, of course. A homage to the original Kinder Mass Trespass. And he made sure they would never forget it, with these little rituals at the start and finish. This was Sophie's fifth annual walk onto Kinder. But for some of the group, it was their first, which gave Darius the opportunity to explain the significance of the event all over again.

Sophie had said hello to the Warburtons, the middle-aged couple who'd booked a pitch for their caravan on the camp-site, only a few yards from the car park. For her, they seemed to be the only normal people in the group, the ones she could have a reasonable conversation with, a chat on a subject that didn't make either of them sound obsessive.

'It's a nice day for it,' Pat Warburton had said, straightening her hat on her grey curls. 'Let's hope the sun lasts.'

'I'm not sure it will,' said Sophie.

Sam Warburton chuckled. 'You're always looking on the dark side,' he said. 'It will be a wonderful day. I can't wait to get up on the moors.'

'If he makes it that far,' said Pat with an anxious frown. 'He's not as strong as he used to be.'

'I'm sorry to hear that.'

Sophie wasn't sure how old the Warburtons were, but certainly in their sixties at least. They'd been coming on the walk for longer than anyone else, apart from the Gould brothers. Sam and Pat both carried hiking poles and wore matching orange Regatta shell jackets with cotton bucket hats. They walked at their own pace, never racing to get

8

ahead of the others, the way some did. Yet the couple were also the most cheerful, enjoying every moment of their day without complaint or argument. That was why Sophie liked to talk to them. It was a refreshing change from Nick and Darius, and some of the others, who seemed to regard the walk as a competition.

Darius was waving his arms overhead like a tour guide to collect the group together. He wasn't wearing a hat at all, probably so that his expensively coiffed blond hair could stir gently in the breeze. He was the tallest of the group anyway, so it was hard to miss him. Yet he always seemed to want to make himself bigger, and even more noticeable.

'All right, guys and gals, it's time for the off,' he called.

Guys and gals? The phrase jarred with Sophie. That seemed to have echoes of the famous DJ who turned out to be a paedophile. Wasn't that one of his catchphrases? Could Darius be ignorant of that, or didn't he care?

But the two students cheered. Sophie glanced at them sourly, their eager faces grating on her. They were both wearing white Columbia Eco jackets, which they claimed were made from recycled water bottles and were free from chemical dyes. Sophie hadn't worked out yet which of the students Darius was trying to impress. The short, dark one called Millie, or Karina, the taller blonde? Perhaps it was both. In their eagerness to please Darius, they might as well be identical.

Sophie supposed she ought to try to get a chance to talk to them, to find out more about them. There must surely be more. What were they studying at Manchester Metropolitan University, for a start? How had they come to be connected with this group? And how did they know Darius Roth? But Sophie had never asked.

Then her boyfriend, Nick, appeared at her elbow, smiling in anticipation. He looked flushed, his normally tanned skin slightly pinker than usual. He was very fit, exercised regularly at the gym and went for a run every day. Climbing to the top of Kinder Scout was effortless for him. Sophie already knew he would leave her behind before they reached the summit.

Nick hadn't even bothered with a waterproof but had tossed on a leather bomber jacket, as if he was just strolling down to the pub. He'd bought a peaked Russian Army cap from Amazon, with a red hammer and sickle badge, and earflaps tied over the top. It was a personal jibe aimed at Darius, who so far had pretended not to notice it.

'Ready, Soph?' said Nick.

'Of course.'

'Hey, have you seen Liam Sharpe? He's put weight on since last time.'

'He's got a new relationship,' said Sophie. 'A Hungarian chef.'

'Oh really? I hope he can keep up. Darius will kick him out of the group otherwise.'

'Darius doesn't have the right to kick anyone out. We haven't appointed him as our dictator.'

Nick laughed. 'Trying telling *him* that. Darius does whatever he wants.'

The group were moving off, with Darius at the head. He turned to beam at his followers, flashing startling white teeth, which seemed to catch the sunlight. His wife, Elsa Roth, was close by as usual, but walking slightly behind him, fitting into his shadow, like a small boat catching the slipstream of a much larger vessel. She was dark and very pretty, with masses of wavy black hair tucked under the brim of her hat. She rarely smiled at anyone else. But when Elsa looked at Darius, Sophie saw something special, an expression beyond mere admiration.

Even Elsa's choice of a burgundy monogrammed Gucci windbreaker seemed to say something about her relationship with Darius next to his Dubarry shooting jacket with a long royal-blue lambswool scarf tossed casually round his neck. Sophie estimated they were wearing the best part of fifteen hundred pounds between them just in their coats. Elsa's Harris tweed Tilley hat alone had probably cost more than Sophie's entire outfit.

A burst of laughter came from Theo and Duncan Gould. They looked almost like twins, though Sophie knew there were about five years between them in age. They had the same receding hairlines, similar greying beards and ancient Barbour waxed jackets. They were the only members of the group who wore gaiters, with elasticated ankles and stirrup straps that passed under the soles of their walking boots. They looked like experienced hikers, which was more than some of the group did. And the brothers never split up, but walked shoulder to shoulder, bulky shapes tramping steadily onwards.

The Goulds ran a plant nursery in Chinley and did a bit of landscape-gardening work. Sophie gathered that neither of them had ever married. She wondered what they talked about to each other as they walked, and what had made them both laugh out loud just now. If she could get closer, she might try to listen in.

The group turned left out of the car park onto Kinder Road and passed the hamlet of Booth, with its ancient sheep wash on the River Kinder.

As they made their way up the road, Faith Matthew

slipped in alongside Sophie and Nick in her bright red Berghaus and red woollen hat. Nick fell silent as she approached and it was left to Sophie to make small talk as usual. She found it awkward. Suddenly, she didn't really know what to say.

'Here we are again,' said Faith cheerfully. 'How have you been, Sophie?'

'Fine.'

'The job going well? You're still teaching at that primary school in Buxton?'

'Yes, I'm enjoying it.'

'Good.'

'You haven't brought Greg with you this time?' said Sophie.

Faith looked uncomfortable now.

'Oh, Greg? No.'

'He's still, you know . . . in the picture?'

'Well, he's around,' said Faith vaguely.

Sophie nodded, trying to watch Faith's expression as she turned away to look up at the hills. She was aware of Nick stomping along silently beside her. He'd put a bit of distance between them, as if he wanted no part of the conversation. He hadn't spoken to Faith, and she hadn't uttered a word to him either.

'I hope there's nothing wrong,' said Sophie.

'No,' said Faith. 'Everything's fine.'

Then abruptly Faith dropped back to talk to the Warburtons. They were just a few yards behind. Sophie could hear their hiking poles tap-tapping on the road surface.

Sophie caught up with Nick and touched his arm.

'What?' he said.

'You don't like her, do you?'

'Who?'

'Faith, of course.'

He shrugged. 'I suppose she's OK. She's one of the group, isn't she?'

'I wouldn't have thought so, the way you reacted to her.'

'I'm just not interested in gossip about someone's boyfriend,' he said, a bit too tetchily.

'All right, all right. But there's one funny thing, Nick.'

'What?'

'I haven't seen Faith since last year, and I only started working at St Anselm's this term. How did she know I was teaching there?'

'No idea.'

They walked on in silence. The path entered water-company property before diverting at a second set of gates onto a steep cobbled track that led up onto White Brow. Below, Sophie could see the old water-treatment plant, which had been abandoned years ago. The building was extensive and had glass skylights running along its roofs. But it was rapidly falling into dilapidation, and many of the panes of glass were smashed.

Beyond the dam, they walked along the edge of Kinder Reservoir, crossing a couple of streams. The dark slopes of Kinder itself loomed across the water. At one point, they reached a muddy section, where they had to divert and go round a gnarled hawthorn tree leaning almost horizontally towards the path. Darius sat astride a branch as if riding a horse and grinned at the rest of the group.

'Take a photo,' he said.

Elsa obliged him, as she always did.

Past the furthest arm of the reservoir, Sophie looked up at the mottled slopes of Kinder, with patches of purple heather still clinging to their flowers. She could already see low cloud sitting on Ashop Head, like steam rising from a giant cowpat.

They could have worked their way up William Clough and crossed the rocky stream, but instead they veered off to the right and began to climb a steep, muddy path up towards the summit of Sandy Heys.

The group paused just below the ridge for a breather, and to enjoy the spectacular view over the reservoir towards Chinley Head and the hills on the Cheshire border, with the lower slopes of Kinder a series of green humps below them until the darker woodland encroached. The High Peak looked bright and peaceful from here, with shafts of sunlight breaking through the cloud to bathe the landscape.

Sophie turned back to the hill. Over the next rise, wisps of cloud swirled as if waiting for their arrival.

'All right,' called Darius. 'Let's keep going, folks.'

Without a word, they stood up, adjusted their rucksacks and began to climb again. Within a few yards they were out of the sunlight. The rocks at the top of the slope were wet, the clumps of tussocky grass sodden underfoot.

Striated lumps of stone lay along the edge of the plateau like unearthed graves, battered into eroded slabs. Deeper in, the outcrops had become gnarled and twisted into menacing shapes, protrusions bulging like eyes, sharp slivers of rock reaching towards the path like the beaks of prehistoric birds. Even in daylight, Kinder was populated by monsters. In the complete darkness of a High Peak night, primitive superstitions must have run riot here.

Sophie felt uneasy. Her instincts told her hundreds of eyes were watching her from among those scattered stones.

3

Diane Fry had barely exchanged a word with Ben Cooper since the last time they'd met. Now, he saw her standing in the Athertons' kitchen. Even in the unflattering scene suit and hood, he recognised the angle of her head and stiffness of her shoulders.

Cooper watched her for a moment from the doorway. He was expecting an announcement at any time about her promotion to DI in Major Crime at the East Midlands Special Operations Unit, but it hadn't come yet. They would be back at the same rank again, the way they were when they first met as DCs in Edendale after Fry transferred from the West Midlands.

He wanted to ask someone about the promotion, but there was no one he felt able to approach. It didn't seem appropriate, though curiosity was consuming him.

But something *was* going to happen. Cooper could feel it in the air, sense it in that unacknowledged network of signals that constantly flowed through a large organisation like the police force. You grew attuned to their sound after a while in the job. The change in tone of emails on a particular subject, the sudden absence of someone's name on the list of recipients or the warnings to watch out for some kind of professional misconduct that he'd never even thought of but that someone, somewhere in the organisation must have committed.

And then there were the ominous mutterings about spending reviews, which always led to doom-laden speculation about whose budget would be cut next. Sometimes the tone could be unintentionally disturbing. A flow of vague information created a hotbed for rumour.

Of course, it was possible that Fry wouldn't get the DI vacancy at EMSOU even if she was promoted. Like Cooper himself, she was still employed by Derbyshire Constabulary and was only on assignment to the regional unit. She could be redeployed to anywhere in the county, even back into uniform or to a desk job at Ripley.

That thought made Cooper laugh. The image of Diane Fry sitting at a desk in an office at headquarters sending out memos and chairing meetings was just too incongruous.

Just at that moment, Fry turned and saw him. Her eyes narrowed.

'What are you smiling at?' she said.

'Good to see you too.'

Her expression didn't change. 'I'm busy here, as you can see.'

'I know. I came to ask if you needed any assistance. Your colleagues from EMSOU seem to have left you on your own.'

'I can manage, thank you.'

She made it sound as if he'd insulted her. Cooper shrugged inside his scene suit. Fry had always been stubborn and independent. But a refusal to accept help when it was offered seemed to Cooper like a weakness, not a strength.

'I don't doubt it, Diane.'

Fry suddenly softened under his gaze.

'So how are you?' she said.

Well, that was almost human. She'd apparently remembered how to greet people she knew.

'I'm fine, thanks. Busy, as always. What about you? Anything new?'

'Not really.'

Cooper moved closer to where she was standing. The sleeves of their scene suits rustled against each other, a papery whisper in the silence of the Athertons' kitchen.

He looked down to see what Fry had been examining so closely when he came in. A book lay open on the kitchen table, a bloody thumbprint left clear and distinct on the edge of a page.

'A recipe book?' he said.

'Mary Berry's *Fast Cakes*,' said Fry.

'Is this what the argument was over?'

Fry nodded. 'Maybe they just weren't fast enough,' she said.

Cooper leaned a little nearer to peer at the book. Pineapple upside-down cake. It sounded good. But it would never be made now.

A crime scene examiner entered the kitchen and they backed away to allow him to dust for more fingerprints.

'This should be an easy one anyway,' said Cooper.

'Maybe. Most of them are hard going.'

Hard going. That was exactly how he thought of making conversation with Diane Fry. She gave so little, though he knew she had a lot more she could give if she wanted to. But that was the way she was, and she would probably never change. Fry would always be hard work.

17

'Your colleagues from St Ann's have abandoned you, then?' said Cooper.

'They aren't in St Ann's any more. They've moved somewhere else.'

'Oh yes. Their secret base. The one everybody knows about.'

'They have other priorities,' said Fry.

'Anything I should be aware of?'

Fry didn't bother to answer this time, and Cooper wasn't surprised.

The noise going on around them hardly mattered. They had nothing else to say to each other, and it might as well have been silence.

Outside, Cooper looked up and saw the first signs of mist slowly rolling down from the hills above Edendale.

The danger arrived slowly, settling on the higher slopes of Kinder Scout and creeping into the cloughs like tendrils of smoke. A blanket of it had descended from the sky, deadening the Peak District air. The rest of Derbyshire withdrew into the distance, beyond a dank grey wall. Sophie Pullen watched her companions vanish into a tide of invisible menace. They were entering fog.

Sophie said nothing at first. The group had been winding its way across the plateau in single file, trying to stick to the narrow track. She was bringing up the rear, her feet squelching in her boots after she'd stepped onto boggy ground half a mile back. She was tired and uncomfortable, but she didn't want to be the one who started complaining.

So she followed on behind Liam Sharpe, who looked out of condition and was struggling on the uphill stretches. Sophie could see him panting and wiping a hand round the neck of his lime-green Craghopper as if he was sweating despite the cool breeze.

Only the Warburtons were further back. Sam had trouble with the steep ascent because of his bad knee and had stopped several times with his wife, both of them leaning on their hiking poles.

As usual, Sophie's partner, Nick, was out at the front with their leader, Darius Roth. She could hear Darius's voice drifting back to her, though she couldn't hear what he was saying. Boasting about his knowledge of the moors probably. She saw Nick turn to the two young women immediately behind him as Darius gestured at the horizon. He didn't look Sophie's way at all. She scowled at the back of his head, covered in that ridiculous Russian Army cap. He hadn't even noticed that she'd dropped back.

The ascent of Sandy Heys had been arduous enough for some of the group. Sophie could see them already tiring and stopping to take drinks from their water bottles. Everyone was taking photographs on their mobile phones, except the Warburtons, who'd brought an actual digital camera.

'Come on, folks, this way,' said Darius.

He was wearing an oilcloth safari fedora now, which he must have been carrying in one of the vast pockets of his shooting jacket.

'Are you sure?' called Sam Warburton.

'Yes, we're going to cross the plateau.'

Nick leaned towards Sophie as she drew alongside him.

'The original mass trespassers didn't do that,' he said.

'Yes, you've told us that before. It's just some obsession of Darius's.'

'And we know Darius's obsessions have to be respected.'

19

The Gould brothers were striding ahead, looking for signs of the restoration project, Moors for the Future. Dams had been built to hold back water so that the peat wasn't scoured away. Vegetation was growing back on that part of the plateau, they said. Sphagnum moss returning to the moor.

But there was no vegetation here. Just the wet, black morass of treacherous bog and outcrops of bare rock.

Sophie lowered her eyes to watch her footing on the uneven ground. When she looked up again, she suddenly couldn't see how many people were walking ahead of her. Nick and Darius had disappeared in the fog, and so had the two young women. The Gould brothers, Duncan and Theo, were about to vanish too, marching shoulder to shoulder like soldiers bent under their backpacks.

For some reason, Faith Matthew and her brother, Jonathan, had strayed off the path and were vague shapes away to the left. Jonathan's outline was distinctive – very tall and thin, his shoulders slightly hunched, his hair long and untidy. He'd been singing quietly to himself, some song that his band were rehearsing. But his voice was muffled now by the fog.

'I don't like this,' said Sophie.

Liam looked over his shoulder. 'What?'

She realised he looked quite ill. His expression was distracted, and his forehead creased in puzzlement. He'd been thinking about something else and he hadn't heard a word she'd said.

'Haven't you noticed the weather?'

He stopped and gazed around as if he were seeing the plateau for the first time.

'There's a bit of cloud coming down,' he said.

'A bit? I can't even make out Nick and the others now.'

Liam hitched his rucksack up onto his shoulders.

'We'd better catch up, then.'

They redoubled their pace and within a couple of minutes they could see the leading group again. Jonathan was still wandering several yards away from the path, looking stooped and dejected, kicking irritably at a clump of coarse grass. His sister seemed to have rejoined the lead group. Her red hat bobbed among the figures around Darius.

Darius turned and looked back, ignoring the chattering of the students for a few seconds, as if even he was concerned. But the moment passed and he smiled again, tossing back a lock of hair as he called to Jonathan, or perhaps to Faith. It was hard to tell.

Ahead of them, the murk was getting thicker, swallowing whole rock formations, reducing visibility to no more than a few feet.

'We ought to warn them,' said Sophie.

'They must have seen it for themselves by now,' said Liam. 'Darius doesn't seem too bothered, though.'

'When is Darius ever bothered about anything? He loves taking risks.'

Sophie jumped in surprise as a motionless crowd of spectators seemed to emerge from the mist on her right. But these weren't people. They were only the twisted rocks of the Kinder plateau, sculpted by the centuries into the shapes of monsters and demons.

Half of the group might have been miles away but for disjointed fragments of conversation reaching her through a surge of fog.

Sophie shook her head, feeling the moisture slide across

her face and drip from her hair, and shivered at the first stab of a damp chill. Even the faintest warmth of the October sun had been left far behind now, blotted out by that dense grey blanket.

It was only later that Sophie heard the noises and saw the lights, and the monstrous figure on the hillside that she would never forget. And then the first cries of pain came out of the fog. And finally, she was there when death reduced their party from thirteen to twelve.

But Sophie Pullen had been the first to see the danger that day.

At least, that was what she told everyone afterwards.

4

Patiently Diane Fry waited until long after Ben Cooper had left the crime scene and driven out of Haddon Close. She watched from the window of the Athertons' sitting room as Cooper's red Toyota disappeared round the corner on its way back to the local police station in Edendale's West Street.

Then Fry got out of the town as quickly as she could. She found it hard to believe that she'd once lived in this backwater. Yes, Edendale was changing, but very slowly. In a few decades' time, it might reach the twenty-first century. There were still villages around the Eden Valley where you couldn't get a mobile-phone signal, where the erratic broadband connection was slower than one megabit per second at best. There were Third World countries with better facilities than that.

Yet each year a large proportion of the Peak District's twenty-two million visitors found their way to Edendale. Even today, in late October, the market square was choked by the volume of traffic, either passing through or looking for parking spaces. Most of them clustered by the bridge over the River Eden or strolled along steep cobbled alleys with names like Nimble John's Gate and Nick I'th Tor. Pubs and tearooms and craft shops jostled for space in the alleys, attracted by the influx of tourists. Fry had seen enough of them during her time in Edendale.

Beyond the town centre, the road climbed steadily out of the valley. Residential streets spiralled up the hillsides, with houses lining narrow, winding lanes that twisted and turned to follow the undulating landscape.

And that was another problem. The older houses hadn't been built for people who owned cars and as a result vehicles were parked nose to tail along the kerb, making driving on those lanes like tackling an obstacle course.

On the edge of Edendale, she passed a series of small council estates, which petered out into farmland. In some places, it was difficult to see where the town became country, with fields full of sheep lying side by side with unused farm buildings converted into designer homes. For now, Edendale was constrained in its hollow by the barrier of the surrounding hills. But eventually, the pressure for more housing would force up the price of land and the town would continue to spread. Fry hoped she wouldn't be around to see it.

After half an hour, she left the gathering mist behind her as the hills began to level out. She was on the Flying Mile, a flat, straight stretch of the A632 between Chesterfield and Matlock, when Fry took a call from her boss at the Major Crime Unit, DCI Alistair Mackenzie.

'DS Fry?' he said. 'Are you on your way back from Derbyshire?'

'I'm en route now. I'll be there in thirty minutes.'

He grunted, and she pictured Mackenzie checking his watch. It was an automatic reaction, something he always did when anybody mentioned an interval of time, as if he had to confirm for himself that thirty minutes was a genuine measurement on the clock. Some of the staff at EMSOU called him the Time Lord, though only ever behind his back, of course.

'We'll wait for you,' he said.

'Wait for me why?' said Fry. 'What's happening, sir?'

'We've got an operation on this afternoon. We're all ready to go, but I want you to be part of it.'

Fry felt her foot press down on the accelerator instinctively.

'I'll be there in twenty.'

'Great stuff.'

He didn't even pause to look at his watch this time, just ended the call. There would probably be a room full of officers somewhere kicking their heels and waiting for him to give the word.

Feeling the catch of excitement in her chest, Fry swung the Audi out of Matlock and up the hill through Tansley towards the motorway. The Major Crime Unit had moved from its offices at St Ann's Police Station in Nottingham, and now she had to drive to the northern outskirts of the city every morning to reach the new EMSOU base just off junction 27 of the M1.

It was actually twenty-five minutes before she drew into the car park and keyed in the security code. She could feel the buzz as soon as she entered the building. Detective Constable Jamie Callaghan greeted her as she walked into the office.

'Just in time,' he said. 'I think the boss is starting to get itchy.'

'What's up?'

'We're raiding an illegal firearms dealer.'

'A dealer? Or the customers?'

'West Midlands are rounding up the gangs. But the dealer is on our patch.'

Callaghan led her straight to the briefing room, where a photo of a man in his fifties with a short grey beard was being projected onto a screen.

'This is Mark Brentnall,' DCI Mackenzie was saying. 'He's a registered firearms dealer with a legitimate business, but he has a much more lucrative illegitimate trade on the side. We believe Mr Brentnall is a crucial link in an underground network supplying sawn-off shotguns to organised crime groups. His particular expertise is in shortening barrels and removing serial numbers.'

He turned and nodded at Fry and Callaghan as they entered the room.

'Today we'll be carrying out simultaneous raids on his business premises and his home address. Our colleagues in Birmingham are targeting the individuals believed to be sourcing the weapons and distributing them to criminal associates across the West Midlands. This is the culmination of a complex investigation that we hope will lead to significant prison sentences and to illegally held guns and drugs being removed from the streets. OK, let's get ready.'

Fry collected a bulletproof vest and joined the rest of the team as they piled into a convoy of vehicles and headed back onto the M1.

She found herself sitting with two other EMSOU officers, a DS and a DC seconded from Nottinghamshire Police. She said hello but got barely a murmur in return from either of them. The DS turned away as if he didn't even want to acknowledge her presence. Fry frowned. That seemed rude. Perhaps he was just that sort of person, though. She looked at the DC, who was staring at her as if she were an alien visitor. She stared back until he blinked and lowered his head in embarrassment.

What was the matter with these people? They made her feel like an unwanted interloper. She wondered for a moment what had been said in the briefing before she arrived. She didn't enjoy the feeling that people had been talking about her behind her back.

Mark Brentnall's home was deep in the countryside south of Nottingham, verging on the border with Leicestershire near the River Soar. When they got close to the address, many of the road signs pointed towards Loughborough or Melton Mowbray.

A vanload of officers from the task force went in first, smashing open the front door with the ram. Then they crowded into the house with shouts of 'Police!'

But Mr Brentnall wasn't there. In the sitting room, they found a woman standing open-mouthed at the sight of the police officers in her home. For a moment, Fry and the woman stared at each other as the team moved on to clear the rest of the rooms.

'Mrs Brentnall?' she said.

'Yes. What . . . ?'

'Where is your husband?'

'He's out in his car.'

'Where is he going?'

'I don't know. Business.'

The woman began to reach for something hidden behind a chair. Fry lunged forward and grabbed her hand.

'What are you doing?' she said. 'Let me see what you're reaching for.'

But it was only a mobile phone. Mrs Brentnall's instinct

had been like anyone else's – to phone her husband to tell him what was happening.

'Please don't do that,' said Fry. 'Just sit down quietly or we'll have to arrest you.'

She left a uniformed officer to watch over the woman and joined the search. In an extension to the rear of the house, they found a workshop full of equipment used for shortening shotgun barrels and stocks. Scores of well-worn hand tools hung in racks on a breezeblock wall over a cluttered workbench fitted with a vice and a bright lamp. The air was thick with the smell of dust and metal filings. A number of freshly cut barrels lay on a table, and a locked cabinet contained several handguns and boxes of ammunition.

Fry reflected on the moment Mrs Brentnall had reached for her phone. This was a house full of guns. It could have ended much worse.

She turned to make a comment to the Nottinghamshire DS, who was also in the workshop examining a handgun. But he turned away again and wouldn't meet her eye as he replaced the handgun in the cabinet.

Something was going on. Fry was sure about it now.

5

And then the walking group had reached the Downfall.
Sophie Pullen shuddered as the air began to grow chill on
Kinder Scout, the atmosphere even colder, the sense of
foreboding stronger and stronger.

The Downfall was the tallest waterfall in the Peak District,
with a hundred-foot drop where the River Kinder tumbled
off the edge of the plateau. The rocks below looked like
the debris of a massive explosion, hurled across a cleft in
the hillside. The path had become a long streak of exposed
ground scoured by rainfall. Pools of water lay stained red
by the peat.

Yet this was part of the Pennine Way, the national
walking trail that ran two hundred and sixty-seven miles
all the way to the Scottish border, rerouted from its original path across the plateau because of the erosion from
thousands of hiking boots.

On a clear day, the outline of Madwoman's Stones would
stand out clear on the horizon at the eastern edge of the
plateau. But it wasn't clear today. There were no landmarks, no points of reference on the plateau and no way
of navigating a route across the featureless moor without
a compass.

The track they'd been following seemed to have disappeared, too, and was no more than a flattened trail of soggy ground, barely a sheep track. Everyone's feet would be wet now.

Sophie broke into a trot and overtook Liam, who grumbled in protest. She was determined to catch up with Nick and the others before she lost contact completely. The burly shoulders of the Goulds came into view, but there was no sign of Faith or Jonathan. Faith was sensible, though. She wouldn't stray too far. She'd probably only veered away to shepherd her younger brother back to the route. He had a tendency to wander off, as if following a route and destination of his own.

She could hear Darius again now. He was laughing at the fog and calling to Elsa as if he couldn't see her. The poor woman would be distraught. She stuck to Darius like glue and hated to be parted from him. His joke wouldn't go down well.

Then she saw Darius and Nick. They'd stopped and were looking vaguely around them.

'We're lost, aren't we?' she said.

'Completely,' agreed Nick.

'Well, that's just great.'

'If we keep walking, we'll find our way eventually,' said Darius.

'Eventually?' said Sophie. 'I'd like to get off this mountain today, if you don't mind.'

Faith Matthew's red hat and jacket appeared again through the fog. Nick peered over his shoulder towards Sophie and waited for her to reach him. Faith stopped too, and they were both watching her as she stumbled over a rock and splashed into a patch of boggy ground, the peaty water leaking instantly into her boots and soaking her socks.

'Damn,' she said.

Sophie felt her cheeks burn, even as her feet became cold and wet. Nick said nothing about her stumble as she shook a clump of mud off her boot.

'What do you think?' said Faith, gesturing at the surrounding plateau.

She was speaking to Nick, but he turned away as if he hadn't heard her.

'I think there could be anything out there in this fog,' said Sophie. 'Or anyone.'

'I know. It's a bit scary, isn't it? I wouldn't want to be up here on my own.'

'Sometimes there are worse things than being on your own,' said Sophie.

They were silent for a moment, listening. The only sound Sophie could hear was the distant crash of water at Kinder Downfall.

Faith had heard it too.

'If we follow the sound and make our way to the water-fall, surely we'll know where we are,' she said.

'Perhaps you're right,' said Sophie.

'Have you seen those rocks?' broke in Nick. 'Did you notice the drop? Do you want to risk wandering off the edge? You'd only need to get a couple of feet too close and you'd be gone.'

Sophie looked at him in surprise. He seemed to be genuinely worried.

'It's hard to tell the direction of sound in these conditions anyway,' he said more calmly. 'You get an echo. We could be completely misled.'

'I suppose we could just keep going, then,' said Faith, and walked away with a glance back over her shoulder.

A few moments later, Sophie heard a distant, echoing yelp and pictured a fox somewhere out there on the desolate moor. Or perhaps it was a pheasant, calling to its mate.

She'd stopped again for a minute to try to get her bearings and suddenly she found herself alone. She looked around, straining her eyes to see through the mist. It swirled around her, forming unrecognisable shapes from the rocks, suggesting movements that didn't exist, breaking to allow the occasional shaft of sunlight through, then closing into an impenetrable wall again.

Sophie made out a tall figure. Was that Jonathan Matthew? Jonathan was unsuitably dressed for the moors. He was wearing black jeans and a grey jacket with a hood pulled close around his face, almost concealing his blue slouch beanie. They were the wrong colours for these conditions. When he was only a few yards away from her, he merged into the fog and became invisible. But she could see a red jacket standing out brightly in the fog. Who was wearing red? Faith Matthew, of course.

The silence was eerie now, every sound deadened by the blanketing mist. But it wasn't peaceful. It was a threatening silence.

When Darius appeared from the fog ahead, he was followed closely by Elsa and the two students, Millie and Karina, gleaming ghosts in their white Eco jackets.

'Hold on,' he said. 'Where are the others? Liam Sharpe and the Warburtons. And Jonathan too.'

'Jonathan went that way.' Sophie pointed, but Jonathan had vanished from sight. 'And the rest were just behind us.'

'No, they weren't. They dropped back.'

'They'll catch up in a minute.'

The group of walkers clustered together now for the first time. Nick and Faith and the Goulds stood around Sophie, while Millie and Karina fidgeted anxiously in the background as they waited behind Darius and Elsa. Even Jonathan had emerged from the mist, watching with a wry smile. But there were still three members missing.

'They must have got separated. Go back and look for them,' said Darius finally, looking at Nick.

'Oh yeah. Then I'll get lost too. Is that what you want?'

'Shout for them, then.'

'We should all shout,' said Nick. 'Then they can follow our voices.'

'Right.'

For a long moment, no one shouted. Sophie could see that none of them wanted to be the first person to break that eerie quietness. It felt like a sacrilege, a violation of the silence that nature had imposed on them.

Sophie took a deep breath and felt a draught of cold, moist air enter her lungs as if she was drowning in a rain-cloud. Some of the others turned to look at her, Darius with a smile, Nick with an expression of shock or perhaps admiration.

'Liam!' she called, her voice cracking on the second syllable. 'Pat! Sam! This way! We're over here!'

And then the others began to shout too. The taboo had been broken, the inviolable stillness already shattered by her nervous, wavering cry.

Was that an answering call from deep in the mist? A male voice, she felt sure. Then a second shout, getting nearer. The group redoubled their efforts.

'This way! Over here!'

The group around Sophie shifted uneasily as a muffled, rhythmic thudding penetrated the silence. Something was coming towards them and getting closer. A curious rustling and a deep panting, like a mysterious beast that existed only in the fog.

At last a figure erupted from the mist, a burst of vibrant orange like a warning signal. Sam Warburton, hobbling up the path as fast as he could go, his rucksack bouncing awkwardly on his shoulders. Sophie could hear his breath rasping in his chest before he got within fifty yards.

'Sam, what's wrong? Where's Pat?' said Sophie.

Warburton couldn't get his breath. He staggered as he reached them, and Sophie stretched out a hand to support him. His eyes were panicky, and his chest rose and fell under his waterproof jacket. He was sweating despite the chill in the air, a sheen of perspiration on his forehead and trickling in glittering beads from his temples. His waterproof gleamed with water too. It was as if the mist had settled on him, soaking him with its insidious dankness.

Sophie glanced at the rest of the group. All of them were wet. She'd underestimated the degree of moisture in the atmosphere. This wasn't just a light mist. They were actually walking through a raincloud.

'He fell,' gasped Sam. 'Liam – he had an accident. He slipped on a wet rock. He's sprained his ankle, I think, or maybe it's broken. I can't tell. He's in a lot of pain, though.'

Sophie realised that the yelp she'd heard a few minutes ago must have been human. She'd pictured an animal, but instead she'd heard a man's cry of pain as he became a victim of the moor.

'Can you lead us back to where he is?' asked Darius.

Sam looked over his shoulder, an expression of doubt crossing his face.

'Of course,' he said, trying to sound confident. 'We just have to go downhill, don't we?'

'What are we going to do when we get there if he's injured?' said Nick.

'Well, I don't think he'll be able to walk,' said Sam.

'We need to call for help, then.'

'I've tried my phone. I've got no signal.'

'Me neither,' said Faith, tapping at her phone. 'We must be in a dead spot.'

After a few minutes of almost aimless stumbling among the rocks, they found an anxious-looking Pat Warburton standing over Liam Sharpe. He lay between two boulders, clutching his leg, his face twisted in pain.

Sophie gazed around the faces of the group, seeking some sign of initiative but seeing only uncertainty. They stood helplessly, their clothes glistening with moisture from the fog, as useless as just one more rock formation frozen in the landscape.

'Someone should go for help,' said Darius. He turned to Nick. 'Find a place on the moor where there's a signal and call 999 for an ambulance.'

'How the hell is an ambulance going to get all the way up here?' said Nick.

'I don't know. There must be ways of getting casualties off the moors. A helicopter or something. Go and call.'

'A helicopter won't land in these conditions. They won't be able to see anything. The visibility is too bad.'

'Why are you still talking about it?' demanded Darius, glaring at Nick. 'Just go.'

Nick looked around for support. His eyes met Sophie's.

For a moment, she felt the old closeness between them, which had been drifting away in the chilly air.

'I'll come with you, Nick,' said Sophie. 'You shouldn't be on your own out there, in case something else happens.'

Nick nodded and smiled, and held out his hand to support her as she moved towards him over the muddy ground.

Then Theo Gould stepped forward. 'And we'll come too. Strength in numbers and all that.'

'Good,' said Nick. 'Besides, we might have different networks on our phones. I'm EE.'

'My brother and I are both on Vodafone,' said Gould.

'I think—' began Faith doubtfully.

'Never mind,' interrupted Sophie. 'The sooner we get going the better.'

'Should we go downhill, then? Towards the valley?'

'Since we're lost, we won't know whether we're going down into the valley or just into another clough with an even bigger hill on the other side.'

'We'll just have to try.'

The four of them stood up to leave.

'And we'll go another way,' said Darius.

Nick stared at him. 'What?'

'Well, if we're splitting it up anyway, it would give us a better chance of getting help if we try both directions.'

'What do you mean, "both directions"? We're in the middle of the plateau. There are dozens of directions to take.'

Darius looked unfazed. 'We could try that way.'

He pointed into the fog as if he knew what lay out there, beyond the few feet of visibility.

'I don't think it's a good idea, Darius,' said Faith.

'There haven't been any good ideas from anyone so far, except me.'

Duncan Gould turned towards him.

'If you find yourself heading onto the plateau, watch out for the lighter-green patches of vegetation,' he said. 'That's wet bog.'

'We'll bear it in mind. Elsa will come with me, of course. And Millie and Karina?'

The two girls moved to stand with Darius. The Warburtons hesitated for a moment, then looked at each other and joined Sophie's party, physically splitting the group into two factions.

'I'm staying with Liam anyway,' said Faith.

'Of course.' Darius sounded unreasonably relieved, as if that solved everything. 'You're a nurse, aren't you?'

'It just makes sense for me to be the one who stays.'

In the background, Jonathan had been leaning idly against a rock, as if he'd just paused for a rest or to admire the scenery. He began to sing quietly to himself.

'Will you shut up, idiot?' snapped Nick.

Sophie stared at him in surprise. He was in such a bad mood today. It was becoming more and more common. What was making him so tetchy?

'Whoa,' said Darius, raising a hand like an Old Testament prophet. 'Let's not get agitated, folks. We're in this together, and we'll sort it out together. One big family, right?'

He laughed, and Nick scowled at him.

'You know, I'm not sure it's a good idea for us to split up,' said Sam Warburton.

Darius snorted. 'We're a bit past that now. You should have thought of it before you trailed behind and lost contact with the group.'

'It wasn't our fault,' said Sam. 'You left us behind.'

'I said we should wait for you,' muttered Nick.

Darius threw back his head and stamped on a lump of peat, which splatted with a loud squelch. 'Will you all stop arguing about it? Are we going to go for help or not?'

A groan of pain from Liam seemed to settle the discussion. The Goulds and Warburtons began to move away, heading for small tracks that seemed to lead down through the groughs. To Sophie's amazement, Nick didn't move.

'What is it?' she said.

He didn't meet her eye. 'I think I'd better go with Darius's group.'

She stared at him. What had happened during the last few minutes to change his mind? She couldn't imagine. It wasn't the time to argue, though.

'Whatever you think best.'

Pat Warburton was calling back to her.

'I'm coming,' she said.

With a sense of despair, Sophie turned and watched Nick and the rest of the party disappear into the mist behind Darius as he strode in the opposite direction. It seemed to her that instead of going for help they were walking towards trouble.

For a moment, a break in the fog let through a burst of sunlight. And it was then she saw it. Below her on the hillside, a huge grey figure was silhouetted, far bigger than anything human. A rainbow of coloured light seemed to hover round its head like a halo.

Its appearance made Sophie's breath catch in her throat.

'What the . . . ?'

But no one else seemed to have noticed it. And the figure was there only for a few seconds before it disappeared in a blur of motion and was gone.

6

Ben Cooper called back at his office in Edendale Police Station on West Street. He checked the latest bulletins and noticed a report of a group of walkers lost on Kinder Scout.

Everyone's heart sank when there was news of people missing on the wildest moors of the Dark Peak. There had already been too many deaths. Only a couple of years previously, a leading Mountain Rescue volunteer had died on a call-out to help a teenage girl in distress on Kinder, and a mountain biker had been killed after falling eighty feet at Laddow Rocks.

So another incident was no great surprise. Even from Edendale, Cooper could see the weather deteriorating over the moors, the cloud layer getting lower and heavier.

Kinder was the highest point in the Peak District at more than two thousand feet, a windswept gritstone plateau rising steeply from the surrounding landscape, its edges punctuated with crags and rocky outcrops. The visibility would be poor up there, the conditions cold and damp.

It was an easy place to get lost at the best of times. The surface had been suffering serious erosion from overgrazing by sheep and the boots of so many walkers, particularly along the Pennine Way. Many people had no idea about the lethal bogs they might be facing, where they could find themselves stuck in mud up to the knees.

Stranded walkers having to be rescued was a familiar story. One of the Peak District Mountain Rescue Organisation teams would be dealing with it, probably more than one if the location of the party was unclear. The reports said that the walkers had set off from the direction of Hayfield. Kinder MRT was the Mountain Rescue team based on that side of the moor.

Cooper reached for his phone. One of his DCs, Carol Villiers, had recently volunteered as a member of Kinder MRT. Surely Carol had mentioned that she was on exercise with them this weekend? She might be out there right now. It was always good to have someone on the ground.

'Carol?' he said when he got through. 'Where are you right now?'

'On the edge of Kinder, near the reservoir.'

'You're with the MRT?'

'Right.'

'Do we know any more about the missing walkers?'

'Not at the moment, Ben. The team are on the job, though. They were already in the area when the call-out came and deployed straight away. The first report was of an injured walker. His party had walked up towards the Downfall but got lost in the fog after straying from the path on the plateau. Visibility is really poor up there. Too bad for a helicopter to operate.'

'What about SARLOC?' asked Cooper.

'No luck so far,' said Villiers. 'A SARLOC text was sent but failed to reach them. The phone signal is very poor. The controller has just said they're going to activate the Kinder Plan.'

'OK. Can you keep me informed?'

'It's not a CID job, Ben. It's a bunch of lost walkers. I just happened to be here.'

'I know. But Kinder . . . well, it's a special case.'

'Will do, then. As soon as I know anything.'

Cooper ended the call. He knew the MRT would do a good job. They did it week after week. They were on call twenty-four hours a day, three hundred and sixty-five days a year, and entirely on a voluntary basis. It was a task that called for skill and dedication. But Kinder – that mountain carried its own legends.

The formation of the Peak District Mountain Rescue Organisation itself had happened after a tragedy in the 1960s when three young Rover Scouts had lost their lives on Kinder Scout during the gruelling Four Inns Walk. Their forty-mile hike had started in West Yorkshire, hitting checkpoints at the Snake Pass Inn, the Nag's Head and the Cat and Fiddle – a route that could take more than twenty hours to complete. The weather had deteriorated rapidly during the day, and eventually volunteers had gone out in blizzard conditions armed only with torches and whistles to search for the missing youngsters. But by then the mountain and treacherous weather had already claimed their lives.

That incident came only a short time after the deaths of two children from Glossop who went missing on the hills, and two climbers' deaths in an avalanche in Wilderness Gully.

Cooper gazed out of his office window at the distant hills. It seemed wrong to him that lives should be left in the hands of volunteers, no matter how skilled and dedicated they were. This morning, he and his officers had arrived at the Athertons' home in Edendale too late to

41

prevent a death. All he seemed to do was clean up the consequences. It was the most frustrating part of his job.

Right now, he didn't want to hear about another death. He envied Carol Villiers for being involved in the rescue operation. She was part of a team out there on Kinder doing their best to save someone's life.

At a rendezvous point near Hayfield, Kinder MRT had called in three other Mountain Rescue teams to divide the search area between them. Triggering the Kinder Plan carved up the plateau into four areas, each allocated to one of the teams. It was a well-proven method for managing a search on the almost featureless expanse of Kinder.

Carol Villiers went back to the mobile control vehicle and found the MRT's duty controller. When the location of the missing walkers couldn't be accurately determined, a link to the SARLOC website had been sent to the phone of the person who'd called 999. If they were able to click on the link, their location would be transmitted with an accuracy of twelve metres, allowing the rescue team to log the grid reference on their GPS and walk straight to the spot.

But in this case they were only able to make outgoing 999 calls via another network. They had no idea where they were, and SARLOC had failed to reach them.

'We've had a description of a rock formation,' said the controller. 'They say it looks like an upside-down ice cream. Some of the blokes reckon they're near Fairbrook Naze. The trouble is, the party seems to have split up. There are at least three separate groups now in different locations, including one known injury.'

With minimal details received and being unable to

re-contact the group, teams were being mobilised in the pre-planned search patterns. Colleagues from Glossop Mountain Rescue Team were already deployed following a couple having reported themselves lost on the hills to the north. With visibility down to fifty feet on the plateau, the decision was taken to call in the other teams in order to cover the whole area more quickly.

Villiers knew that the longer the search took, the more anxious the searchers would become. It was October and the days were getting shorter. Darkness was only a couple of hours away. Even in the summer, hypothermia could be a real danger on these hills. Mountain Rescue teams had been called out to assist hypothermic casualties on a rainy weekend in August.

'The SARDA dogs have arrived,' said the controller. 'They're our best chance now.'

Villiers peered at the patchy fog on the slopes of Kinder. The Search and Rescue dogs were making their way up the hillside to the plateau. They didn't need an item of clothing from a missing person but worked on air scent to locate a casualty. They could cover much more ground than human search teams. And it didn't matter if visibility was poor – a dog could search as well as on a clear day.

There was very little wind today, though, so human scent particles wouldn't carry far before they were recognised by a dog. The handlers would have to compensate by shortening their sweeps. The search would take more time.

'That was a good result,' said DCI Mackenzie. He glanced at his watch. 'A nice couple of hours' work there. We have Mark Brentnall in custody for questioning. In due course he'll be charged with conspiracy to supply firearms and ammunition.'

Fry had taken off her bulletproof vest. They were always uncomfortable to wear for any length of time. It reminded her of when she was in uniform. None of her kit ever seemed to fit her, from the tunic to the utility belt. It was as if everything had been designed for a fifteen-stone male.

'What about the other teams, sir?' she asked.

'Great news there too.'

Mackenzie reported that a search conducted at Mark Brentnall's business premises had resulted in the recovery of component parts, including sawn-off barrels and ammunition. Meanwhile, armed officers had stopped Brentnall's Range Rover on a slip road of the M1 and recovered eight more sawn-off shotguns and two hundred cartridges from the boot.

In Birmingham, the Serious and Organised Crime Squad had arrested several people, including an individual named Michael Rafiq, believed to be the head of a drug-dealing network distributing Class-A drugs across the region.

Rafiq had been arrested in possession of wraps of crack cocaine and heroin, five mobile phones and more than two thousand pounds in cash. Officers searched his home address and found another eight kilos of drugs. Their haul also comprised twelve sawn-off shotguns linked to dozens of crime scenes, including two killings. Four more individuals had been arrested in the West Midlands – drug runners responsible for the distribution of Class-A substances from Birmingham to towns and villages outside the city.

Fry nodded to herself when Mackenzie had finished. It was definitely a good result. So why was she feeling so uneasy, as if something had gone badly wrong?

At the end of her shift, Diane Fry drove out of the secure car park and headed down the A611 to face the traffic on Western Boulevard.

To her surprise, another call came through from DCI Mackenzie before she'd passed Queen's Medical Centre. She answered straight away. It had to be something urgent.

'DS Fry?' he said.

'Yes, sir?'

'Tomorrow morning. Don't come into the office here.'

'Why not?' said Fry. 'Where do you need me? Not back in Edendale?'

'No.'

Mackenzie sounded less than his usual confident self. Fry began to sense that something might be wrong.

'Sir? What is it?'

'They want you at Ripley,' he said.

'Derbyshire HQ?'

'Right. You've to report to your force's Professional Standards Department at nine thirty a.m. for an interview.'

Fry stared at the traffic around her as she came into Matlock and stopped at the traffic lights before turning towards the M1.

'What is it about?'

'I don't know,' said Mackenzie. 'That's all they've told me.'

'All right, then.'

She thought he'd gone, just put the phone down at his end without saying goodbye, but Mackenzie was still there. He seemed to have been thinking about what else he should say to her.

'Diane,' he said finally. 'I'm sorry.'

*   *   *

The news came through that search dog Dolly from Kinder MRT had located human scent. Dolly soon found the first group of walkers. They were cold and wet and miserable, and one of them had lost a shoe in the mud. The MRT carried spare boots, since it wasn't unusual for walkers to leave theirs behind in the peat bogs.

The rest of the party soon followed. The injured man was treated by a team doctor before being stretchered down to a waiting ambulance and transferred to Stepping Hill Hospital in Stockport. There had been no need on this occasion to call in the air ambulance, Helimed 54.

As the lost walkers gradually emerged from the fog, Villiers could see a couple of figures wrapped in emergency foil blankets. Others seemed unsteady on their feet or were suffering from cramp and needed assistance in walking. They were all covered in mud from falls in the groughs.

Eventually, a group of a dozen or so were gathered at the rendezvous point and were given hot drinks by their rescuers. They'd been out on the hill so long that their skin and hair were wet and they were shivering with cold.

'It seems they became disorientated in the deteriorating conditions,' said the controller. 'They'd been walking round and round in circles instead of in straight lines, though at least one of them had an Ordnance Survey map they might have used.'

'If they knew how to read it,' said Villiers.

The controller sighed. 'At least they weren't high on cannabis, like that group in the Lake District last year. This lot were sober, but unprepared and reckless. Still, our first priority is people's safety, no matter what ill-judged decisions they might make to put themselves in a situation like that.'

Villiers called Ben Cooper. He'd asked to be kept up to date, and she knew Cooper well enough to realise that he'd be calling her himself if she didn't.

'We've located a party of twelve,' she said. 'One casualty has been transported to hospital with a suspected broken ankle. One treated in situ with glucose for low blood sugar.'

'Where are the rest of them now?' he asked.

'Having a warm-up before we return them to their vehicles at Bowden Bridge. They have no real injuries, but they're cold and wet, and suffering from exhaustion in some cases.'

Villiers noticed that one of the walkers nearby was shaking his head when he overheard her call.

'Hold on,' he said when she came off the phone.

'Yes, sir? What's your name?'

'Haslam. I'm Nick Haslam.'

'What's the problem?'

'We're a party of thirteen, not twelve.'

Villiers frowned. 'Are you sure? We've counted. One casualty has been sent to hospital. The rest of you are here.'

Members of the walking group stared at each other. They were scattered across yards of ground. Some were standing, some sitting. Villiers saw one man with wavy blond hair perched on a rock, another had lain out flat on the ground to rest, while an older couple had been given folding chairs to sit on. Was anyone missing, apart from Liam Sharpe, now in the ambulance on his way to Stockport?

'Oh God,' said Nick as he looked around. 'Where's Faith?'

7

Ben Cooper's house in Foolow was in the heart of White Peak country, surrounded by fields and a tracery of white limestone walls so complex and intricate that it seemed to hold the landscape together. He sometimes thought that if you followed the right lines in that imaginary web, you could discover any story, find the clues to any mystery hiding in the Derbyshire countryside. All the answers he sought might be contained within that gleaming web.

It was one of the main differences between the White Peak and the Dark Peak areas to the north. There was no such form and structure on the vast bogs of Kinder Scout. Like so much of the Dark Peak, it kept its secrets to itself. It sucked them in and refused to let them go.

Cooper knew he was arriving in Foolow when he saw a rusty bowser standing in a field, feeding water into an old bath. One day, he'd come across an offering on a field gate near the village – a ball carefully formed from stalks of straw. In the White Peak, offerings could often be found hanging from trees, placed on stones, hidden in walls. The surviving connections with a pagan past existed more strongly here than in many other parts of the country.

Strangely, St Hugh's Mission Church in the village was

named after some French saint, depicted with a swan. There were no swans in Foolow, but visitors passed a duck warning sign before they caught sight of the village pond.

After years spent in Edendale, this was home for Cooper now. Once he was behind the centuries-old walls of his cottage, he was insulated from the rest of the world. It was a house intended to last several lifetimes, and it already had. It was built of solid stone, not timber and plasterboard. With the doors and windows closed, he could hear nothing from outside.

Tollhouse Cottage sat on the hillside as if it had grown there organically. Beneath the house was a keeping cellar, a damp and chilly reminder of the earth the house was built on, a place where he could experience a connection with the landscape without even going outside.

Mobile-phone reception in Foolow was unpredictable, though, especially behind the thick stone walls of his cottage. So Cooper stopped for a few minutes by the pond on the village green to phone Chloe Young.

'Hi. What are you up to?' she said.

'Just arriving home. What about you?'

'Working late again.'

'That's a shame.'

'That's the life of a pathologist. People will keep on dying.'

'So I won't get chance to see you, then?'

'Not tonight.'

Cooper sighed. He looked forward to speaking to her every evening, but it was so much better to actually see her face to face. There was something missing from his life when he couldn't be with her. But he was in no position to question Chloe Young's workload. He'd been forced to skip dates himself when he was called out to a crime scene. Some weeks they were in danger of becoming strangers.

Chloe heard his sigh.

'I know, Ben,' she said. 'But it will get better. I'm free later in the week.'

'That will have to do, I suppose.'

'Come on, look on the bright side,' she said cheerily.

He knew she was probably in her office, but he always pictured Chloe in the mortuary, with a dead body on the stainless-steel table and a scalpel in her hand as she smiled at him from behind a surgical mask. That was the way she'd looked when they'd first met. It was a difficult image to get out of his mind, even now.

'Oh yes, the bright side,' he said. 'I guess there must be one.'

'Of course,' she said. 'I mean, you *are* the man who owns a cat called Hope.'

Cooper laughed. 'It was probably a bad choice,' he said. 'It's just, when I picked her up from the rescue centre . . .' He trailed off.

'Yes, she must have been given a name at the centre. You could have kept that if you really weren't able to think of anything else.'

He shook his head. 'No, I couldn't.'

Then he heard someone speaking to Chloe in the background, a colleague calling her away from the phone.

'I've got to go,' she said hastily.

'I'll speak to you tomorrow, then?'

'Of course.'

Cooper stood for a moment on the village green. He saw that some of the notices behind the glass in the village noticeboard had faded completely. What might they have been announcing? He could see a date for a parish meeting at Burdekin Hall, a planning application for a caravan park, an advert for the Silence heritage site on the old lead workings at Hucklow Edge. The rest were . . . well, a mystery.

He unlocked the front door of his house and waited for the familiar bang of the cat flap as Hope came home. He didn't know where her vantage point was, but she always spotted his car returning.

She fussed around his legs while he opened a tin and changed her water. Then he watched her eating for a while. It was strangely calming and reassuring after a day at work. It was nice to stand in a kitchen where the floor wasn't splattered with blood.

'Hi, Hopes. We were talking about you just now.'

The cat didn't look impressed. But then, she never did. His life outside the house was totally irrelevant to her. As far as she was concerned, he ceased to exist once he walked out of the front door. And yet he always found her waiting patiently for him to reappear each evening. Was it just the prospect of food that kept her interested, or did she feel more affection than she was able to show, because she was a cat?

Cooper glanced out of the window and saw all his neighbours had their wheelie bins out for collection next day. That was how he remembered to do it. He wondered if it was how everyone else remembered too. Perhaps there was someone in the village who was frighteningly efficient and always put their bin out first, with everyone else following their example. It only needed one person to get it wrong and the system would fall apart.

He wasn't going to cook anything for himself tonight, and he had nowhere else he needed to go. The Bull's Head in Foolow was often full of dogs at lunchtime, but in the early evening he could nip in for a Peak Ales Bakewell Bitter and a bully burger with Stilton and sweet potato fries on the side.

In Foolow, the pub was also the place to buy fresh eggs, bacon, milk and postage stamps. The first time he went into the Bull's Head, Cooper remembered noticing a lethal-looking carving knife set that had been hung in a leather scabbard over the log fire as decoration. Probably no one else thought of it as a dangerous weapon. His job gave him a perspective that he couldn't always put aside. And that was especially true today, after standing in the Athertons' bloodstained kitchen in Edendale, examining the consequences of a handily placed knife.

The image of that log fire made Cooper think about the woman still out alone on Kinder Scout. The last news he'd heard from Carol Villiers was that one walker was still missing and unaccounted for. The Mountain Rescue teams and the SARDA dogs would have been stood down for the night by now. Tired team members would eventually manage to get to bed in the early hours of the morning after returning the MRT vehicles to their bases.

Cooper could think of very few places that were worse to spend a night alone than on Kinder Scout.

That decided him to make one last call to Carol Villiers.

'Sorry, Ben,' she said. 'They've had the search dogs out on Kinder for hours now.'

'And there's no sign of the missing woman?'

'No. And it's getting dark. They'll be calling off the search for tonight.'

'Let's hope she was properly equipped and had the sense to take shelter.'

'It's odd, though,' said Villiers.

'What is?'

'The casualty, Mr Sharpe, was on his own when the dog found him.'

'You mean the others left him there injured and alone?'

'That's just it. They say they didn't. The missing woman was supposed to have stayed with him. Her name is Faith Matthew.'

Cooper could picture Villiers looking up at the bulk of Kinder in the failing light. There was very little shelter up on the plateau. A night spent on Kinder in the cold could be fatal, and everyone knew it.

Diane Fry felt numb by the time she arrived at her flat in Wilford, on the southern outskirts of Nottingham. She'd been told she was due for a meeting with a police staff investigator tomorrow. 'Meeting' probably wasn't the right word, from her point of view. She was due to be interviewed, perhaps even interrogated.

The Professional Standards Department dealt with matters of gross misconduct. That meant there had either been a complaint from a member of the public or an allegation had come to them internally. Most worrying was that the PSD was able to conduct covert investigations into complaints of misconduct and corruption against police officers. The thought that someone she'd been working with might have been investigating her already was very unsettling.

For once, she wanted to tell someone about it. Normally she preferred to keep things to herself, but tonight she felt as though she would burst if she couldn't talk. She needed to get the words out at least, to make them seem real to herself. But who could she call? Who could she share something like this with?

Fry looked at the numbers on her phone for a few minutes, rejected some possibilities, then dialled.

'Jamie?' she said when the ringing was answered.

'Yes. Is that Diane? What's up? I'm not on call.'

'No, it isn't work,' she said. 'Well, not really.'

She could almost see DC Jamie Callaghan frowning. She sounded uncharacteristically uncertain, even to herself. Callaghan would never have heard that tone before. Since he was a detective constable at EMSOU's Major Crime Unit, she was his immediate supervisor.

'Are you OK?' he said.

Fry could hear voices in the background. It sounded as though Callaghan was in a bar already, perhaps just starting a night out with his mates, or maybe a date. She wondered who he was with and wished she could see him.

'I'm fine,' she said.

And then she explained to him why she wasn't. Callaghan listened to what she had to say and whistled quietly when she'd finished.

'Bad Apple?' he said.

'I don't know yet.'

She'd thought of that, of course. Derbyshire Constabulary employed a confidential system for members of staff to report suspected wrongdoing by their colleagues. No one had yet come up with a clever acronym for it. So that was how it was officially known, and the name said it plainly. Bad Apple.

On the other hand, the term 'whistle-blower' was never spoken. It had been banned under force policy because it might be offensive to those who reported wrongdoing by their colleagues. The preferred term was 'professional standards reporter'.

'If you want a friend . . .' said Callaghan tentatively.

'Thanks, Jamie,' she said.

Fry knew he didn't mean it in the usual way of friendship. 'Friend' was the technical term for a colleague or Police Federation representative who was allowed to accompany her in disciplinary interviews.

'Though you might be better with a Fed rep,' he said.

'You're probably right.'

'Let me know how it goes anyway.'

'If I'm allowed to.'

Fry ended the call. He was right: she would probably be better asking for a Police Federation representative as a friend. After all, there was no way of telling who had reported her and what for. It could be anyone, including Jamie Callaghan.

She looked at her phone and thought about calling her sister, Angie. But what would be the point? Angie might be her only blood relative, or the only one she acknowledged, but as a friend she was pretty much useless.

Fry blinked in surprise as she remembered that she now had two blood relatives since the arrival of Angie's baby, Zack. She still hadn't got used to that idea.

There wasn't much for her to do at home in the evening, except re-watch old films on Netflix. She avoided reading the papers or watching the TV news. There was too much about politics and political scandals. Politicians often lectured the police on the importance of transparency, integrity and ethics. But she supposed they were well beyond irony now.

Fry found half a bottle of Chablis in the fridge and poured herself a glass. She spent the rest of the evening wondering what it was she'd done wrong.

And she spent most of that night going over and over the incidents in her mind, trying to work out which one of them she'd been reported for.

8

Monday

Ben Cooper had heard talk of replacing the old E Division headquarters in West Street, Edendale, with a new building. In fact, people had been talking about it for the past thirty years or so.

Too many decades of mouldering paperwork, half-smoked cigarettes and junk food had left their mark, and the 1950s building was considered unfit for purpose now. Whenever he entered the CID room, the rows of computer screens looked strangely anachronistic. Downstairs, the custody suite was due to close soon. Conditions at West Street were unsuitable for prisoners, though officers and staff would have to continue tolerating them for a while longer.

Every day the same kind of reports crossed Cooper's desk. Details of some of those thousands of dysfunctional people who cluttered up the police stations and courts.

So what was new this morning? A scattering of overnight burglaries and assaults outside pubs and nightclubs. An early morning raid had been conducted on an address in Edendale, resulting in two arrests and the seizure of a quantity of Class-II drugs. And there had been several complaints from tourists over the last few days about youths throwing stones at their cars on the descent into Hartington, the latest incident resulting in a smashed windscreen and bad publicity for the tourism business.

A memo was on his desk from a team that had been set up to review recent rape convictions, in case significant evidence had been ignored or not disclosed to the defence. They were asking for files from cases his department had dealt with during the last five years. That would take time.

An operation was still ongoing to target the use of Peak District holiday homes as pop-up brothels by slave gangs. A gang master would rent a secluded property, install a group of trafficked women, then move on somewhere else after a month or so, before anyone became suspicious about what was going on. A difficult one to deal with without an early notification when a new brothel popped up.

What else was there? An email in his inbox informed him that an officer serving in Edendale Local Policing Unit had been shortlisted in the Police Twitter Awards for Best Tweeting Individual Police Officer. Apparently, there were sixteen categories, including Best Tweeting Police Horse and Best Tweeting Police Dog. Old-fashioned bobbies like his father, Sergeant Joe Cooper, would be turning in their graves at the thought of community policing by smartphone.

Cooper leaned back in his chair and fingered the lanyard with his identity badge, staring at a shelf of box files with the Derbyshire Constabulary starburst logo on them. His office was in a flat-roofed 1970s extension, with the inevitable damp stains on the polystyrene ceiling tiles.

Down in Scenes of Crime, Gary Atherton's bloodied clothes were hanging in a locker to air-dry before being packaged in paper bags. Recovery of DNA evidence was vital. The CSIs would have gathered everything from the scene, though. A flake of paint, a plant seed, a trickle of soil, a fragment of broken glass, a tiny scrap of paper. Any of them could play a crucial role in confirming the identity of a suspect.

Meanwhile, on Kinder Scout, the search for Faith Matthew had resumed at first light. Cooper expected news soon. The SARDA dogs were bound to find her.

In the CID room, Ben Cooper's team were sitting in front of their computers under diffused lighting from panels set into the ceiling. In one corner were a series of blue screens where no one was working. Half hidden by a pillar in the middle was Gavin Murfin, his civilian investigator, once a fixture in the department as an old-school DC.

Cooper's sergeant, Dev Sharma, had proved more than capable of taking responsibility and running the team of DCs. Since his arrival in Edendale from Derby, Sharma had taken on a lot of the workload and Cooper had come to rely on him heavily.

It wouldn't last, of course. Nothing ever did in this job. DS Sharma was here in North Division to gain experience and add a few paragraphs to his CV. Cooper didn't have any illusions that he'd be keeping Dev for long. His DS was destined for better things.

Cooper moved quietly into the middle of the room and was rewarded with the familiar sight of Murfin dipping his fingers into a paper bag for an Eccles cake he'd bought on the way into work. He was speaking to DC Luke Irvine, seated at the opposite desk.

'Apparently she ran a dominatrix dungeon in a disused building at the back of the old post office,' Murfin was saying between bites. 'No one knew about it until Open Gardens weekend, when people heard the screaming.'

'The dominatrix was squatting?' asked Irvine.

'I think she usually stands up,' said Murfin.

Across the room, Carol Villiers was telling Becky Hurst and Dev Sharma about a new vicar who'd arrived in her village.

'Well, when I say "arrived", you know what it's like these days – she's in charge of about seven parishes, and she's based ten miles away,' said Villiers. 'She has a team ministry, with three curates or assistant vicars scattered around. But when she did come to St Mark's, the locals didn't like her.'

'Why not?' said Hurst. 'Because she's female, I suppose?'

'No, because she's an evangelical. They're old-fashioned in our village. They want to do things the same as they always have, like they did under the old vicar before he retired. The new one wants to modernise everything. Readings aren't from the King James version any more, and she got rid of the organist and brought somebody in to play CDs through a sound system. And there was a wedding . . . One of the oldest families in the village. They had the church booked for months, all traditional style. And then the new vicar put the mockers on everything.'

'What are mockers?' asked Sharma with a puzzled frown, listening to their conversation.

'Well—'

Cooper cleared his throat. 'Morning, everyone.'

'Boss.'

'Dev, do want to bring me up to date on the Atherton murder inquiry?'

Sharma stood up and gathered some papers together.

Then a call came through and was answered by Villiers. She looked across at Cooper.

'They've found her, Ben.'

Cooper didn't need to ask who. He could tell from the tone of her voice.

'Faith Matthew? Dead?'

'Yes.'

He sighed. 'It took too long to find her. Where was she?'

'Near Kinder Downfall,' said Villiers.

He could picture the place. A narrow track between high rocks was called Kinder Gates, a landmark for walkers coming off the moors to the steep descent towards the Mermaid's Pool. The Downfall lay a few hundred yards away. There, water streamed off the gritstone edge and sprayed horizontally as the incessantly buffeting winds battled against gravity. Sometimes the wind won and the water flowed upwards, back over the edge. It was a spectacular place, but dangerous.

'She was found at the foot of one of the highest rocks,' said Villiers. 'It has its own name on the OS map.'

'A lot of them do.'

All across Kinder Scout and Bleaklow, rock formations had been given imaginative names, often due to their shape, or their connection to an old story from Derbyshire history and legend. The Woolpacks, the Seal Stones, Pym Chair, the Druid's Stone.

'Which rock?' he said.

Villiers hesitated. 'They call this one Dead Woman's Drop.'

Diane Fry left her apartment in Wilford a little later than usual that morning. She had no idea when the post came on her road, because she was always out, so she thought of checking her box outside the communal entrance. For some reason she'd never understood, the boxes were all named in German – *Briefkasten*.

There was a small pile of junk mail in there. Life insurance, a clothing catalogue, an offer of a specially minted crown coin commemorating the latest royal wedding. And three envelopes full of Christmas raffle tickets for various charities.

She felt like throwing the whole lot into the brambles that grew behind the beech hedge on the other side of the parking area. But instead she dropped them onto the passenger seat of her black Audi, where they'd sit until she could find a litter bin.

As usual, Fry called at the BP service station on Clifton Lane and bought a few supplies at the Spar shop, along with a cappuccino. Something told her she would need to stay alert today. Opposite the service station was a piece of rough ground used as a car park for the Trent River Walk. She pulled off the road to drink her coffee safely.

She'd hardly slept last night. People talked about your whole life flashing in front of you just before you died. She'd always imagined that would be horrible. She had too many incidents in her life that she might regret, if she ever had to stop and think about them. Most of the time, she managed to push them to the back of her mind, bury them in the deepest parts of her subconscious, where they never troubled her.

But the summons to Ripley had changed that. It had forced her to review the last few years of her life, to work out what in particular Professional Standards might want to interview her about. Of course, they might want to speak to her as a witness in someone else's disciplinary hearing. So why had her subconscious spent all last night pulling out incident after incident from her career for her to worry about?

Fry took a sip of her coffee as she watched the traffic passing along Clifton Lane towards the bridge. She had to accept the fact that she'd lived a charmed life in some ways. She'd got away with things she shouldn't have done, strictly speaking. But no one had reported her. Perhaps it had given her a false sense of security. That was fatal.

Well, it seemed likely that someone had reported her now, made a complaint about her behaviour. A member of the public, or a fellow officer?

The second was far worse. The public made complaints against police officers all the time, but most of them were trivial or malicious, and very few of them were ever followed through to the stage of a disciplinary hearing. Police officers, on the other hand, were reluctant to blow the whistle on their colleagues. It was a world of 'us and them' out there. No one wanted to be a grass. So it had to be something serious.

In her head, Fry ran through a list of the people she might have offended or antagonised. After a moment, she realised it was pointless. An opposite list would be a lot shorter.

She drained her coffee and poked at the junk mail on the seat, as if something there might give her a clue. So what was it to be? Misconduct or gross misconduct? Honesty, confidentiality or fitness for work? Not a criminal offence at least or she would already have been arrested, wouldn't she?

Or would she? She wasn't entirely sure how the PSD operated. Perhaps they were waiting to arrest her when she arrived at Ripley. So maybe she should make a run for it and try to disappear, like any other criminal?

She laughed to herself. As if there was any other option but to see it through.

Fry spotted a litter bin at the edge of the car park. She gathered her junk mail together and took it with her empty coffee cup to dispose of. If only she could gather up the debris of her past life and dispose of it in the same manner.

But that wasn't the way life worked, was it? Your actions had a habit of catching up with you.

9

A damp road, damp grass, damp sheep, a stone wall dripping with moisture. As Ben Cooper headed out of Edendale towards Hayfield, he could already see the mist hanging low over the moors and drifting into the valleys. Dark copses stood out against the grey background, a series of hills getting fainter and fainter into the distance.

As he left the outskirts of the town behind, the stone slates of the roofs gradually petered out along the River Eden, the deep green of the Eden Forest swarming along the opposite hillside. Beyond the limestone hills and a patchwork of fields divided by drystone walls lay the brooding, desolate moors of the Dark Peak, rising to the plateau of Kinder Scout, the highest point in the Peak District.

The route took him westwards through a series of White Peak villages. Abney, Bradwell, Hucklow, Tideswell. To Cooper, they were all places steeped in history and crime.

Turning onto the A623, he hit the A6 near Chapel-en-le-Frith and headed north over Chinley Head. He could have driven to Castleton and crossed the Winnats Pass to reach the same point, but even in October the area was likely to be busy with tourists visiting the show caves and Blue John mines.

Only ten miles north of Buxton, Hayfield was an old village, once a staging post on the packhorse route across the Pennines from Cheshire to Yorkshire. The settlement had grown with the arrival of cotton and the railways until it straggled down the valley into the basin of the River Sett.

North-east of the village lay a reservoir that controlled the flow of the River Kinder, avoiding the risk of flooding that had previously once been a serious problem in Hayfield, necessitating raising the height of the main street. The church had famously been flooded, causing corpses to rise up from their graves.

These days, it was the gateway to the west side of Kinder. An increasing number of residents were people who'd moved from Manchester and Stockport seeking a better quality of life. Hayfield was undergoing gentrification.

There was a big car park on the western side of the village, next to a now deserted visitor centre at the start of the Sett Valley Trail. But that side was mostly residential. The shops and pubs were on the eastern side, where the streets were choked with parked cars. At every corner, he found vehicles coming at him on the wrong side of the road.

A narrow road leading off to the side of the Royal Hotel passed another pub, the Sportsman, before arriving at Bowden Bridge quarry, the starting point for the famous Mass Trespass. From here, the view extended over the valley of the Sett to the high plateau of Kinder Scout, stretching across the eastern horizon like an enormous beached whale. What looked like a weeping wound in the whale's flank was Kinder Downfall.

National Trust rangers had opened an access onto the

moor for the police. Cooper met up with Carol Villiers and they got a ride up the hill in a Land Rover. They would have to walk the rest of the way when they came within reach of Kinder Gates and the Sandy Heys cliffs.

Villiers looked at him as they clambered into the back of the Land Rover.

'It is an unexplained death,' she said. 'But probably an accident.'

'We can't say that yet.'

Cooper stared out of the window at the landscape, wondering if it was Kinder itself that was raising the hackles of his suspicion.

'What do we know about the victim so far?' he said.

'Faith Matthew,' said Villiers. 'She was a nurse. Contracted to an agency, so she worked in different locations, both NHS and private hospitals. She has an address in Market Street, Hayfield. Aged thirty, unmarried, but there's a boyfriend in the picture, by the name of Greg Barrett. He's an electrician, runs his own business in the Hayfield and New Mills area.'

'Any family?'

'Not locally. Her parents live in Manchester. They're due in Hayfield today, though. And there's a younger brother, Jonathan, who was also on the walk yesterday. Luke is working on getting some information on the rest of the group. The only other thing we know is that Miss Matthew drove a silver Honda Jazz, which has been recovered from the car park at Bowden Bridge quarry.'

'Good.'

When they got out of the Land Rover, Cooper could see the fog was still lingering at this height. In places it was dense enough to reduce visibility. It also changed the sound of the voices he could hear, their tones distorted as if the upper range of human vocal chords had been suppressed.

'High-pitched sounds are muffled by fog,' said Villiers when he mentioned it. 'That's why foghorns have such a low pitch, to carry a long distance.'

'Something to do with the vibration of air on water molecules, isn't it?'

'I think so.'

Beyond the covering of fog, Kinder was basically a massive bog. No one with any sense would come walking here after a period of heavy rain. Well . . . Cooper mentally corrected himself. No one with the smallest bit of local knowledge.

In places, the peat layer was fifteen feet thick. But erosion had already set in five millennia ago. Higher rainfall had worn deep gulleys into a pattern of meandering groughs, cutting right through to the bedrock. The process had been accelerated by acid rain from the nearby industrial cities. Now a trig point on Kinder stood a couple of metres clear of the eroded surface around it.

Cooper could almost feel the connection with the past through the soles of his boots on the muddy track. Fifteen feet represented a lot of the world's history. You could walk along the groughs and pass between walls of peat representing ten thousand years of the Earth's formation. It was like walking in a channel dug directly through time.

These moors had been laid down after the retreat of the glaciers at the end of the last ice age. Within that black, sodden mass lay the remains of dead trees, grass, fungi, insects and animal carcasses, all preserved by the acidic conditions and a lack of oxygen. Occasionally, human remains were unearthed from a bog, shrivelled but intact, dried like a pickled walnut.

On the surface lurked dark gritstone outcrops, weather-beaten rocks sculpted into shapes the human eye struggled to make sense of. They'd been formed by exposure to ice, rain and wind over lengths of time he couldn't even imagine. They stood here on Kinder like reminders of the prehistoric past. Nothing that happened in the last few centuries had even touched them.

Ahead, Cooper could see uniformed officers and crime scene examiners.

'That's the top of the Downfall,' said Villiers.

Kinder Downfall flowed west over the gritstone cliffs at the edge of the plateau, barely a trickle in summer but impressive when it was in full spate. With a strong westerly wind, the water was blown back on itself, and the resulting cloud of spray could be seen from as far away as Stockport. If you were close to the Downfall, you could get wet from above and below at the same time. In cold winters the water could freeze against the rock, creating vertical sheets of ice that hung in the air like organ pipes, providing a challenge for climbers with their axes, ropes and crampons.

No wonder this was regarded as a magical place. Even on the sunniest day, that cliff of shattered rock looked like the edge of the world. He'd stood at the top many times and looked down over the valley, his eye attracted by the glint of light off a pool of water below – the legendary Mermaid's Pool.

The village of Kinder once lay on the side of the mountain. Now there was only a mythical nymph who came to bathe in the Mermaid's Pool. If you met her, she would either make you immortal or drag you to the bottom of the pool and drown you. The water was said to be so deep that it connected to the Atlantic Ocean.

Kinder was an awfully long way from the sea. But a fact like that didn't get in a storyteller's way. Inconvenient reality was never a barrier to the creation of a legend.

At the Downfall, the forensic team had cordoned off the approach to the edge of a massive gritstone slab that jutted out into space over the ravine. Dead Woman's Drop. There must be an old story to account for the name, some incident from the distant past that Cooper was unaware of.

Outdoor crime scenes often caused problems for officers trying to tape off the scene. Sometimes they could use a tree or a bush, or a gate or a wall. Here on Kinder, there were none of those things. There weren't any trees in sight across the whole of the plateau. Strong winds and rain could be problems too. They would be struggling to get tents up in this exposed position. The only answer was to work as quickly as possible and hope for the best.

Stepping plates also looked a bit futile. But Cooper followed the designated route to the edge and looked down, experiencing a momentary wave of vertigo at the sudden shift in perspective. A splash of bright red seemed to leap at him out of the fog, and he almost ducked at the sensation of something hurtling towards him.

But it was an illusion. That splash of red wasn't moving. It was Faith Matthew's body, lying spreadeagled at the foot of the Downfall, broken on the jagged and unforgiving rock. She'd fallen fifty feet from a vertical drop into the ravine. Her red jacket was spread out around her as if it had ballooned like a parachute as she fell. Her left arm and leg were thrown out at an odd angle, the bones shattered by the impact on the rock. Her right arm and leg were concealed beneath her body.

Cooper frowned. That seemed an odd way to fall. The natural instinct when you felt yourself falling face forward was to throw both your arms out to protect yourself. This looked as though Faith had been twisting her body as she fell, like a cat adjusting its position in mid-air. Could she have bounced off the side of the Downfall on the way down?

He kneeled and peered cautiously over the edge. No, the drop was sheer. There was nothing Faith could have hit before she impacted on the rock where she lay.

Thoughtfully, Cooper stood up and brushed off his knees. Damp had soaked into his trousers just in those few seconds of contact with the surface of the gritstone.

He walked back to the cordon and examined the spot Faith Matthew had fallen from. A CSI was crouched over the ground with a camera.

'What have you got there?' Cooper called.

'A few shoe marks in a layer of mud. They're not very clear.'

'Just one set of boots? Or more?'

'Just one, so far as we can tell.'

Cooper pointed at a print, set at a different angle to the others.

'Have you recorded that one?'

'Of course. Why?'

'I'd like someone to focus on analysing which direction that print is facing.'

'Will do.'

Cooper took another look at the corpse. It glittered with

moisture, and the gritstone was dark and wet all around it. A few trickles of water still dripped from the overhang onto the body. Faith's hat had fallen a few yards away and teetered on the brink of the waterfall.

But he couldn't see Faith Matthew's face from here. And that was what he needed most of all.

After a moment's hesitation, he called Chloe Young's number at the hospital in Edendale.

'Ben? What's up?' she said.

'I'd like you to take a look at a body in situ,' he said. 'Are you free?'

'Now? Yes, OK, if you want my opinion. Where is it?'

Cooper told her.

'Oh my goodness. I'd better make sure I've got the right gear.'

'I'm sure you'll have something that will do. I'll get someone to watch out for you and drive you up onto the moor.'

'Wait . . . Is this the missing hiker?' said Young.

'Yes, it is.'

'Not an accident, then? She was pushed?'

'That,' said Cooper, 'is what I need your opinion on.'

10

Detective Constable Luke Irvine looked as though he felt out of place in the Bowden Bridge car park, surrounded by the cars of walkers getting ready for an afternoon in the hills. He joined Ben Cooper and Carol Villiers in Cooper's car, leaned over from the back seat and flipped open his notebook.

'So,' said Irvine. 'This is what I've got so far. They were a party of thirteen hikers in total. They call themselves the New Trespassers Walking Club. I have no idea why.'

Cooper looked up at the looming mass of Kinder Scout. 'Well, I think I might have a good idea. You don't know the history of Kinder, Luke?'

Irvine shrugged. 'It's just a hill, isn't it? And not a very interesting one, if you ask me. It's too flat. We have better-looking hills in Yorkshire.'

'It's over two thousand feet, so strictly speaking it qualifies as a mountain.'

'It's still kind of dull.'

'No,' said Cooper. 'Not dull at all.'

Cooper had been on Kinder Scout many times over the years. He'd struggled up and down its slopes and walked across the plateau at all seasons of the year, in all kinds of weather. There had been times when he could hardly move because of the heavy peat clinging to his boots, when every step he took was an enormous effort against the grip of the sticky morass, as if Kinder was the surface of an alien planet with twice the mass of Earth.

And there had been walks in the summer, when the top few inches were dry and bouncy like a trampoline, turning his steps into an exhilarating leap as the pull of gravity suddenly halved.

At any time, stepping out onto Kinder was leaving the real world behind. And yes, there had been times when the weather changed while he was on the mountain. The cloud level came down, a mist or fog rolled in, snow began to fall, or the light began to fail. Then you weren't just in an alien landscape. You were in great danger.

'It's obvious,' said Cooper. 'They named themselves after the Kinder Mass Trespass.'

'The what?'

Cooper tapped his steering wheel impatiently.

'The Mass Trespass. It was in 1932.'

'Never heard of it,' said Irvine. 'Before my time.'

'Mine too,' said Cooper. 'But still . . .'

The Mass Trespass on Kinder Scout had been a famous act of civil disobedience that had given impetus to the campaign for access to the moors and eventually led to the Peak District becoming Britain's first national park.

That day, a large party of ramblers had clashed violently with gamekeepers and bailiffs employed by local land-owners. Several had been arrested and sent to prison. They'd become martyrs in a symbolic battle between the working classes and wealthy landowners, and Kinder Scout had been their battleground. It was a story that was taught to schoolchildren in Derbyshire, celebrated in books and TV programmes, marked by commemorative plaques.

Cooper had seen photographs of the Mass Trespass, showing troops of laughing young men with Brylcreemed hair, wearing tweed jackets and shorts, like a bunch of 1930s schoolboys on an outing.

'The trespass was eighty-six years ago,' said Villiers.

'But it never lost its symbolism, did it? It was all about the exercise of freedom, and resistance to the status quo.'

'It sounds like something I ought to know about,' said Irvine.

'Yes, you should.' Cooper looked at him, surprised at Irvine's ignorance on the subject. 'Some time. So who are the leaders of this walking group?'

'One leader,' said Irvine. 'Well, leader or founder, I don't know which – the other members of the group refer to him in both ways. A gentleman by the name of Darius Roth.'

'Gentleman?'

'That's the impression he gives,' said Irvine with a wry smile. 'He describes himself as a property developer.'

'I'll look forward to meeting him.'

'Mr Roth is aged thirty-five. I gather he's pretty well-off. Apparently he inherited a business empire built up by his father in Manchester.' Irvine checked his notebook. 'Mr Roth was accompanied by his wife, Mrs Elsa Roth. They live here in Hayfield, where the walk started from. They call their house Trespass Lodge. I guess that's also because of—'

'The Mass Trespass, yes. And the rest of them?'

'Also in the group were Sam and Pat Warburton, a retired couple from Manchester, and two brothers who run a garden centre near Chinley, Theo and Duncan Gould. The casualty is a Mr Liam Sharpe. He's a check-in supervisor at Manchester Airport. There are two students from Manchester Metropolitan University, Millie Taylor and Karina Scott, both aged nineteen. There's a Nick Haslam, an IT consultant who lives near New Mills, and his girlfriend, Sophie Pullen, a teacher in Buxton. She lives at Chapel-en-le-Frith. And that just leaves Jonathan Matthew, the dead woman's brother.'

'And Faith Matthew herself, of course.'

'Of course.'

'That's a very disparate group,' said Villiers. 'What do you imagine members of this club have in common?'

'Maybe the clue is in their name,' said Cooper.

'Well, as you know, they managed to get totally lost in the fog,' said Irvine. 'Then when Mr Sharpe was injured, they split up into three groups. They said they couldn't get a phone signal to call for help, so that's why they set off in different directions. Miss Matthew stayed with the casualty.'

Cooper frowned again. 'Did she? Just her, on her own?'

'It seems so.'

'But if the injured walker was immobilised, how did she end up at Dead Woman's Drop? She must have left him at some point.'

'True.'

'A couple of the walkers were suffering from a degree of shock after their experience,' said Irvine. 'The two youngest ones, Miss Taylor and Miss Scott.'

'What about the injured man?' asked Cooper.

'Mr Sharpe is still in hospital for X-rays,' said Irvine. 'He has a suspected broken ankle, along with exhaustion and hypothermia.'

'We need to talk to him as soon as possible. I don't like a delay in being able to ask someone questions. It gives them too much time to make up a story. Carol, can you liaise with the hospital and get access to him as soon as possible?'

'No problem.'

'If his story is different from everyone else's, we'll know there's something wrong,' suggested Irvine.

'Not necessarily,' said Cooper. 'They'll already have talked about it between themselves. They had plenty of opportunity.'

'You think there was some kind of conspiracy?'

'I don't know. It's possible.'

'They may be a very close-knit group,' said Villiers, 'no matter how disparate they appear on the surface.'

Cooper looked back towards Hayfield. The weather was completely different down in the valley, with small puffs of cloud drifting across a blue sky. As he gazed over the patchwork of fields, the sun broke through the clouds sporadically, highlighting one hillside and then another, changing the colours in the landscape as it went. It caught a white-painted farmhouse here, casting shadows from a copse of trees over there.

'What next, Ben?' asked Villiers.

'I need to start by visiting the family,' he said.

He didn't need to specify whose family. Villiers would know perfectly well. A case like this always started with the victim.

Faith Matthew's house was in the middle of a terraced row on Market Street, Hayfield, near the bottom of Fairy Bank Road. The street climbed northwards out of the village, with the tower of the parish church set against a background of moors across the valley.

Ben Cooper and Carol Villiers mounted a short flight of steps to reach the front door of the house. When they knocked, it was answered by a middle-aged woman with her hair dyed in grey streaks. She was still wearing an outdoor coat, as if she'd just arrived or was about to leave.

'Mrs Matthew?' said Cooper.

'Yes, I'm Jennifer Matthew. You must be . . .'

Cooper held up his ID. 'Detective Inspector Cooper, Edendale CID. This is Detective Constable Villiers.'

'Come on in.'

'I'm not holding you up?' he asked.

'No.' She looked down at her coat and fingered the buttons. 'Oh, I haven't been here long. And it's an odd thing, but I couldn't take my coat off. It didn't feel right without Faith being here. This was her house.'

'I understand,' said Cooper.

But he didn't really. Why would she not feel able to take her coat off in her own daughter's house? It wasn't Cooper's experience of family. When he was growing up at Bridge End, relatives walked in the back door without knocking, let alone worrying about taking their coats off, as if they were tradesmen. Mrs Matthew looked positively uncomfortable, as if she was a stranger here and had never been in Faith's home before.

Just inside the front door, a small lobby was hung with Faith's outdoor coats, scarves and hats. The sitting room was decorated in shades of red, with a magenta patterned rug in front of the fireplace.

'How long has your daughter owned this house?' asked Cooper as he followed Mrs Matthew through into the sitting room.

'Oh, a couple of years,' she said.

'Did you visit her here often?'

'Occasionally. Why do you ask that?'

'I was wondering how well you knew some of her friends.'

'I can't say we knew them at all.'

Cooper listened, registering that there was no one else in the house.

'Is Mr Matthew not here with you?'

'Jack is in Buxton at the moment. There are lots of things to sort out, you know . . . at a time like this.'

'Of course.'

At a time like this. That phrase coincided with the first crack in her exterior, a wobble of her voice. 'A time like this' meant the violent death of her daughter. Her reserve was very British.

'There should be a family liaison officer on the way,' said Villiers.

'Oh, she's been,' said Mrs Matthew. 'She's very nice. I asked her to get me a few things, so she's gone into the village.'

She looked vaguely around the house. What was she thinking? That the place wanted a good clean? The fridge needed emptying? Surely not that she had to start sifting through her daughter's possessions already.

'I just wanted to be able to make a cup of tea,' said Mrs Matthew. 'For people who come, you know. It seems so rude otherwise. And Faith doesn't appear to have any fresh milk.'

'I wouldn't worry about it, Mrs Matthew.'

'Well, sit down anyway,' she said.

'Thank you. There are some questions we need to ask you.'

'I realise that. Though I'm not sure what Jack or I can

tell you, Detective Inspector. As I said, we didn't know Faith's friends. And that's who she was with, wasn't it? Her group of "friends".'

Cooper heard the intonation clearly. She definitely said 'friends' with inverted commas.

'Your daughter mentioned the walking club to you, I suppose.'

'Yes, she did. I can't say I understood what it was all about myself.'

'The Kinder Mass Trespass,' said Cooper.

She frowned. 'Sorry.'

'It doesn't matter.'

So the Matthews lived in Manchester but had no idea of the history of the movement that had started there. It was odd, in a way, that the story was remembered so clearly here in Hayfield, where local people had come out to jeer and shout insults as six ramblers were arrested by the police on Kinder Road. The commemorative plaques were here, the plans for a visitor centre. Yet Manchester people had forgotten. Or at least, some of them.

'You must know Faith's boyfriend, though,' said Cooper.

'Greg,' she said. 'We've met him.'

Cooper exchanged glances with Villiers. Mrs Matthew had a definite knack for making her feelings clear in a simple phrase without saying out loud what she meant, or even changing her expression. It was evident to Cooper that Greg Barrett was disapproved of.

'You don't like him,' he said.

'I always thought Faith could have done better for herself.'

'I understand he has a good trade and runs his own business.'

She turned her head away so that he couldn't see her eyes. 'It's not important now, is it?'

'We'll need to speak to him all the same,' said Cooper.

'Was he with her?' asked Mrs Matthew, suddenly interested. 'Was he part of that group? We haven't been told that.'

'No. As far as we know, Mr Barrett wasn't part of the group.'

'Mmm.'

'Faith was a nurse,' said Villiers. 'Working for an agency?'

'Yes, recently.'

'She must have worked for hospitals previously. Where did she train?'

'In Manchester, at the Royal Infirmary. Then she worked at a private hospital for a while. Meadow Park. But she left there, which was a shame. I always thought a career in private medicine would have been better for her than the NHS. You can end up dealing with all kinds of people in an NHS hospital, can't you?'

Cooper wasn't surprised at that. He'd heard that kind of thing many times before. It was strange how often parents had that sort of snobbery on behalf of their children, when they would never have run their own lives along those lines, or with that kind of belief. They all wanted better for their sons and daughters, and for their grandchildren too. As if future generations could somehow avoid the unpleasant experiences, the disappointments, the crises, the contact with unsuitable people. Even if it was possible, would it be desirable? What sort of individuals would they become if they lived their lives wrapped in balls of cotton wool?

'We deal with all kinds of people in the police too,' said

Cooper. 'It's unavoidable really. We can't choose to work with only the most respectable criminals.'

Mrs Matthew looked at him suspiciously, as if she thought he was making fun of her. Cooper smiled, and she relaxed.

'I need to know whether Faith mentioned any of the group members to you, Mrs Matthew. Do you recognise any of these names?'

Villiers passed her a copy of the list Luke Irvine had printed out for him, the names of the twelve remaining members of the New Trespassers Walking Club.

'I believe she mentioned that first one,' said Mrs Matthew. 'Darius. I wouldn't have known his last name was Roth, but she did refer to a Darius somebody. He was the leader, I think.'

'That's right.'

'Oh . . .'

Mrs Matthew put a hand to her mouth as she stared at the list.

'My son, Jonathan, is on the list. But surely he wasn't a member of this club, was he?'

'He was with them on the walk,' said Cooper.

'Well, yes. But he wouldn't have joined a club. Jonathan doesn't join things.'

'Perhaps not. It isn't really clear. We just know that he was there when this tragedy happened.'

'Poor Jonathan,' she said. 'It's affecting him badly. He adored his sister.'

'Have you spoken to him since the incident?'

'Jack has. We thought we should come straight here, but we'll be seeing Jonathan later. It's been such a shock for all of us, you know.'

'I'm sorry.'

She made an unnecessary fuss of straightening some cushions on the sofa.

'I'm afraid I don't see much of my son these days,' she said. 'Jonathan has his own interests, which aren't ours. Music is very important to him.'

'Music?' said Cooper.

'Yes, he plays the guitar. He's in a band. If you can call it that. A bunch of layabouts probably. They hang around at some old mill in Manchester. Ancoats, of all places. It's hardly Didsbury.'

Cooper could almost see the phrase that was going through Mrs Matthew's mind. *Sex and drugs and rock 'n' roll.* The three went together, didn't they? Especially for a young man who felt the need to rebel against his controlling parents.

'In fact, Jonathan has been trying to get money off us for this band,' she said. 'Thousands of pounds he said he needed for equipment and promotion, and to make, I don't know . . . a demonstration of some kind.'

'A demo.'

'That's right.'

'And you refused to give him what he asked for?'

'Of course. It would have been money down the drain.'

Cooper thought about whether he would ever have asked his own parents for a large amount of money. Thousands of pounds? Almost certainly not, whatever it was for. And his relationship with his family had always been better than this one he was hearing about. Jonathan had drifted away. His parents disapproved of his musical ambitions. His mother complained they didn't see much of him, even though he lived not far away. Jonathan would have had to be desperate to come to them for money for his band. What would he have done when help was refused?

'Mrs Matthew,' said Cooper, 'do you think Jonathan might have been trying to get money from his sister?'

'Well, I suppose he might have. He always turned to Faith rather than to us. She was his big sister and she always helped him out. Always. But I doubt he'd have much luck with that.'

'Why not?'

'Faith was a nurse. She was hardly rolling in cash.' Mrs Matthew hesitated. 'But he was very insistent about it. It seems to mean an awful lot to him, though I can't understand why. He has a perfectly good job in Manchester.'

'Do you know anyone else involved in this band? Any of his friends?'

'Not friends as such. There's a man he's mentioned a few times – a musician, some kind of mentor, I think. He's a Canadian. Jonathan has talked about him getting this band together in Manchester.'

'Do you remember his name?'

'As a matter of fact, yes. We made a note of it, in case anything happened. You understand what I mean?'

'Yes.'

Mrs Matthew opened her handbag and poked about until she found a small diary. She pulled out a pair of reading glasses and turned to a back page.

'Farnley,' she said. 'His name is Farnley. I imagine he knows more about my son than I do.'

Cooper suspected that the longer he stayed talking to this woman in this cramped sitting room, the more her emotions would begin to spill out. At the moment, it was only an occasional crack in her voice, a fleeting expression, a second when she couldn't meet his eye. But soon she would fall apart, the way grieving family members did eventually. He wished the family liaison officer would get back from whatever errand she'd been sent on. This wasn't the way it should be.

'Could I go back to Darius Roth?' he said. 'What did Faith tell you about him, Mrs Matthew?'

'Nothing really. Nothing at all. She just said that she was "going on Darius's walk" or something like that. I can't remember exactly how she put it.'

'When was this? When did you last talk to her?'

'About three days ago. Yes, it would be Friday. We spoke on the phone.'

'Did she call you?'

'No, I called Faith to see how she was. And to ask if she might be coming to visit us at the weekend. It was . . . Well, it's not relevant.'

'It was what, Mrs Matthew?'

She paused for a moment.

'Well, it was my birthday yesterday,' she said.

And then there were tears, trickling down her cheeks. She hardly seemed to notice them and made no attempt to wipe them away. Cooper bit his lip. These were the worst moments to deal with. He could cope with dead bodies, and with individuals who committed violent acts. But distraught loved ones – these he could never come to terms with.

11

Where the narrow River Sett flowed under the bridge at the Royal Hotel, empty beer kegs stood in front of the war memorial, painted blue and yellow. Cooper passed Millie's tearooms and chocolatier on Church Street, and an old Co-op store on the corner of Fishers Bridge.

The Mass Trespass was quite a theme here. On New Mills Road, notices outside the Kinder Lodge Hotel said, HIKERS WELCOME, and even the pub sign had an illustration of ramblers setting off towards the mountain.

'You were very interested in the brother, Jonathan,' said Villiers as they moved to the next address on their list.

'Of all the group, he seems to be the odd one out,' said Cooper. 'Or the oddest, at least. His presence looks incongruous.'

'And he needed money badly.'

'That might explain why he went on the Kinder Scout walk.'

'Do you think he asked Faith for money yesterday and she refused him too? Would that have made him so angry that he would have reacted violently?'

'I couldn't hazard a guess until I've talked to him,' said Cooper. 'But in my experience, if someone is under enough pressure, it may only take a very trivial thing to make them cross that line. We're going to have to talk to them all further and see if we can get a coherent account.'

Villiers sighed. 'I wouldn't hold out much hope,' she said.

Greg Barrett lived with his parents in a modern semi on the Wood Gardens estate off Swallow House Lane, a development of stone cladding and bay windows, tiny patches of garden squeezed next to each drive. The Barretts' house was half stone cladding and half white render, with a front garden open to the road and paved to make space for two vehicles to park. Greg's van stood there, a white Renault Kangoo with his name and phone number on the side.

It felt as far away from the wild plateau of Kinder as it could possibly be, though it was barely a mile or two in reality, just on the other side of the A624 bypass.

'People here call it the bypass,' said Barrett, 'but it doesn't bypass anything. As you can see, it comes straight through the village and divides it in half.'

Barrett was still in jeans and work boots, a multimeter and a pair of wire strippers hanging from his tool belt. He was in his early thirties, lean and angular, with deep-set eyes darkened by a troubled frown.

'When did you last speak to Faith?' asked Cooper.

'It would have been Friday, I think. We talked on the phone a bit. She was going to meet with her group the next day, of course.'

'You didn't go on the Kinder Scout walk,' said Cooper. 'Why was that?'

'I don't fit in,' he said. 'Not with that lot. I never

understood what Faith saw in them. She couldn't have got me to go on one of their stupid walks. And now look what's happened.'

'How long had you been in a relationship?' asked Cooper.

'A year. Two years. I'm not sure.'

Cooper felt sure Faith Matthew would have known exactly. There would probably be a note in her diary marking the anniversary of the date they met. A year or two sounded much too vague.

'Were you going through any problems?' he said.

'What do you mean?'

'I was wondering whether your relationship had any difficulties. Was Faith happy?'

'Of course she was happy. We were fine. No problems at all. It's not as if she was likely to go off and do anything stupid. She was sensible. Level-headed. It was one of the things I liked about her.'

'Did she talk about Darius Roth much?'

Barrett scowled. 'Yes, quite a lot actually. She was a bit taken with him.'

'Taken with him? She admired him?'

'She said he was passionate. About what he believed in, I mean. Not, you know . . .'

'That can be attractive,' said Cooper tentatively.

But Barrett shook his head. 'I'm sure there wasn't anything like that.'

'Sure?'

'Positive. Like I said, we were fine.'

'OK. Have you spoken to Faith's family?'

'To her mother. Her parents don't like me.'

'That's often the case,' said Cooper.

'But Faith has a brother too. He's quite different.'

88

'Jonathan.'

'Yes. He might know more about Roth and that group.'
Villiers turned to Cooper as they left the Barretts' home.
'I suppose this means a trip into Manchester?' she said.

'I'm afraid so.'

The old semi-detached stood in a leafy street just off
Withington Road in Whalley Range, South Manchester,
near a Catholic grammar school and the International
Centre for Krishna Consciousness.

All the houses here were faced in pale brick with deco-
rative arches. The row of buzzers and flat names by the
door were enough to indicate it was in multi-occupancy,
even without the swarm of wheelie bins on the drive.

An aged four-wheel-drive Subaru Impreza was parked
out front. It was about fifteen years old, judging by its
registration number, but well maintained apart from some
rust on its rear wheel arches. The colour was something
quite queasy-making between blue and green, perhaps teal
or viridian.

From the names on the buzzers, Cooper saw that
Jonathan Matthew lived on the top floor of the house.
When a tall, stooped young man with long hair answered,
Cooper showed his ID.

'Oh, is it about Faith's accident?'

'Yes, sir. We'll need to get someone to take a full statement from you later. But we just have a few initial questions to help us focus our inquiries.'

'All right. Come on in.'

Jonathan showed them into a small sitting room in what
would once have been described as an attic flat but was
probably listed as a loft apartment. It had been recently

modernised, but its dramatically sloping ceilings and dormer windows gave away its origins.

'I should be at work today,' he said, 'but I've taken the day off.'

'Understandable. Your mother is at Faith's house in Hayfield, by the way.'

'Is she?' said Jonathan vaguely.

'I thought you might like to know, in case you needed to be there.'

'I've spoken to Dad this morning. I don't want to . . .'

'What?'

'To go over it all again. That's what it would be like. Over and over again. There's nothing I can do to change what happened. I can't save Faith. There's no point in trying to blame anyone, is there?'

He looked appealingly at Cooper and Villiers on the last phrase.

'I'm sure no one is trying to allocate blame,' said Cooper.

'Really? Well, you don't know my mother very well.'

Cooper glanced into the next room and saw instrument cases stacked against a wall.

'What do you do for a living, Jonathan?' he asked.

'I work as a graphic designer, but I'm really a musician,' he said. 'I'm in a band, and we're doing well. Really coming together. I reckon we could be going places before long. We have a gig next week, in fact.'

'Where at?'

'The Spinning Top in Stockport.'

'I know it.'

'You should come along. We cover some classic rock, as well as doing our own stuff. Some of the other guys are older and played in bands decades ago. But that's what people want now. Tribute bands, or old rockers still touring. You have to start off like that and get your name known.'

'Anyone I might know in your band, then?' asked Cooper.

'The guy who put it all together is Robert Farnley. He goes way back to the music scene in Manchester in the 1970s and he's met everybody who was anybody.'

'That's before my time.'

'It's all coming back, you know, that kind of stuff. The kids appreciate good music. We've all learned a lot from Rob.'

'I'm glad to hear it's going well.'

'Oh, we're doing a demo, and some proper promotion,' he said proudly. 'We'll get there.'

As Cooper watched him, Jonathan was fiddling with something metallic, turning it over and over in his hand. Cooper noticed that he had long fingers, like a lot of musicians.

'Mr Matthew, did you ask your sister for money?' he said.

Jonathan looked up. 'How did you know that?'

'It was something your mother said.'

'Oh yeah, she would. Well, I did mention to Faith that I needed some cash. She had a big nest egg put aside, you know.'

'But she said no?'

'That's right.'

'How did that make you feel?'

He flushed. 'What are you getting at? I was disappointed, that's all.'

'When did she tell you that she wouldn't give you money? Was it the day of the walk?'

'No, before that.'

'When?'

'The day before, if you must know. All right, I was a bit pissed off. I thought I could rely on her.'

'But she let you down.'

'Just this once. But she was my sister. She meant a lot to me.'

'Is that why you went on the walk?'

'Because she asked me to, yes.'

'I have a feeling you weren't impressed by Kinder Scout,' said Cooper. 'Or by the history of the Mass Trespass.'

Jonathan smiled. 'The only thing I liked about it was the alien evacuation.'

'The what?'

He put the metallic object down on a table. It was only a capo for the neck of his guitar.

'Don't you know the story?' said Jonathan. 'There was this guy back last century who said he'd been contacted by extraterrestrials. They told him the world was going to end, but they could rescue some members of the human race. He formed an organisation, the Aetherius Society, and they came up with a list of mountains around the world where the aliens would come and evacuate people at the right time. "Magic mountains", they called them.'

'And?'

'And Kinder Scout was one of those mountains. There's a rock up there with a cross painted on it and the guy's initials. GK – his name was George King. That rock is the exact spot his society said the aliens would evacuate from.'

'And when is this evacuation going to take place exactly?' asked Villiers.

'Well, they said it would be 2015.'

'That's a bit disappointing.'

'It's a good story, though.'

Jonathan went suddenly quiet, and his face darkened. He'd been enjoying himself for a moment, and now he was angry at his own apparent callousness. It was probably the words 'a good story' that had penetrated his exterior.

Cooper recognised that feeling. Sometimes you heard a phrase coming out of your mouth and it struck deep into your own heart while meaning nothing to anyone else who heard it.

Now Cooper regretted having led him down that path.

'I'm really sorry about your sister,' he said.

Jonathan looked away. 'Thanks,' he said. 'But nothing will help with the guilt.'

'You feel guilty for her death?'

'Of course I feel guilty,' said Jonathan. 'I should have been there with her. She always looked after me when we were kids – you know, the big-sister thing. But I wasn't there when she needed me. I lost sight of her in the fog and she died.'

'It wasn't your fault,' said Cooper. 'Everybody was disorientated. The group had split up. You were lost. You were all suffering from cold and exhaustion.'

Jonathan's expression didn't change.

'It doesn't matter what you say. You can make all the excuses for me you like. The fact is, I wasn't there for her. I let Faith down. I'll always feel guilty for that.'

Cooper nodded. Despite what he'd said to Jonathan Matthew, he fully understood those feelings of guilt. He'd suffered them himself, and was still experiencing them now, those sharp pangs of despair whenever he thought about what had happened to his fiancée Liz. He'd been there when the abandoned pub had been set on fire, trapping them both in the blazing building. He'd been unable to save her. He should have been able to bring Liz out alive, but he hadn't.

That kind of guilt didn't respond to logic. And he supposed it would never go away.

'Do you have any idea who might have wanted to harm your sister?' he asked after a moment.

'Harm her? Are you saying she was deliberately killed? I thought it was an accident?'

'We're not sure yet. But I have to ask. Can you think of anyone—'

'Nobody at all. Faith got on with everyone. Why would anyone want to do something like that?'

'I don't know,' said Cooper. 'That's what we'd like to find out.'

What he could have said to Jonathan Matthew was that he'd lost count of the times he'd heard friends and family members say that a victim 'got on with everyone'. Sometimes they were in denial. But often there was always a small, secretive corner of someone's life that was unknown even to the people closest to them.

Jonathan stared miserably at Cooper.

'You've got to be wrong,' he said. 'What happened to Faith – it *must* have been an accident.'

Cooper sighed. 'I wish I could tell you that, sir. But I'm not sure it would be true.'

Chloe Young had been accompanied down to the body by a crime scene examiner and was wearing a safety harness provided by the Mountain Rescue team, in case she inadvertently went too close to the edge.

Ben Cooper stood on the overhang and watched her working. Mist still surged below Dead Woman's Drop, masking the distant valley bottom and making the fall from here seem even further. He felt as though he'd be falling for ever through the cloud if he lost his footing.

Each stage of the process was photographed from every angle as Young inspected the body bit by bit, then gently began to turn it onto its side.

That was when Cooper caught his first glimpse of Faith Matthew's face, shockingly pale against the red of her jacket. There was blood around her right temple where she'd hit the rock. Young examined Faith's face and neck, then checked the limbs that had been hidden under the body.

Young turned and looked up, as if judging the distance of the fall. She caught Cooper's eye and gave a small smile and a shake of the head. Cooper wasn't sure what that meant.

'In my opinion,' said Young, when she'd returned to the top of the cliff and freed herself from the harness, 'and it's a provisional view, you understand . . .'

'Yes?'

'Well, the victim was already turning round when she fell.'

'Turning?'

'The position of the body and the location of the injuries would be consistent with that scenario.' Young twisted her own body to demonstrate a half-turn, as if looking at something over her shoulder. 'You see, one arm and leg were underneath her. She fell sideways.'

'Which means she didn't just step off the edge in the fog,' said Cooper.

95

'I think she would have fallen at an entirely different angle.'

'Perhaps she was turning because she heard something behind her.'

'Possibly.'

Cooper thought of the angled shoe mark he'd seen. If that was found to match one of Faith Matthew's boots, it would support the idea that she was turning away from the drop.

'I can see what you're thinking, Ben,' said Young. 'Obviously I can't offer an opinion on what happened up here.'

'Of course not.'

But Cooper had the certainty that Chloe Young agreed with him. Faith Matthew hadn't fallen from Dead Woman's Drop. She was pushed.

12

The room at Ripley was much more pleasant than any interview room in a custody suite that Diane Fry had ever seen. It was as if she was sitting down for a budget meeting or a staff appraisal. She must be wary not to be lulled into any false sense of security by her surroundings.

Her interviewer introduced himself as Martin Jackson, an investigator with the Professional Standards Department. He was aged around forty, with sleek brown hair, a well-fitting suit and a pair of black-rimmed glasses.

He smiled at Fry as he sat down, trying to establish a friendly relationship perhaps, the way salesmen did. She was determined it wasn't going to work.

'DS Fry,' he said, 'you're aware that you're entitled to be accompanied at these interviews by a representative of your staff association or a colleague to act as your "friend"?'

'Yes, I am.'

'And you've decided not to take up that opportunity today.'

'That's correct.'

'So is it all right with you if we make a start, then?'

'I can't wait.'

His smile was slightly crooked, she noticed, the left side of his mouth barely moving as if he might have suffered a mild stroke at some time. It undermined his demeanour, made his affability look like a disguise, a persona adopted by an actor. But then, all good interviewers were actors in one way or another.

'I take it you're familiar with the College of Policing's Code of Ethics, dated July 2014,' said Jackson. 'I have a spare copy here for you, if you're not.'

He tossed a booklet down on the table between them. The natural instinct would be to pick it up, or at least to pull it towards her side of the table. But Fry resisted the impulse. She didn't touch it, or even look at it, deliberately ignoring his gesture.

Jackson met her stare with that slightly crooked smile.

'The Code of Ethics sets out the Principles and Standards of Professional Behaviour for the Policing Profession of England and Wales,' he said.

'I'm familiar with it, of course.'

'Excellent. Well, might I draw your attention first of all to Section Three – the ten Standards of Professional Behaviour.'

'Do you want to know what they are?' said Fry. She began to count on her fingers. 'Number one, "Honesty and Integrity". Number two, "Authority, Respect and Courtesy". Number three, "Equality and Diversity". Number four—'

He held up a hand. 'We'll get to number four in due course,' he said. 'But let's take things a little more slowly. We have other matters to deal with first.'

Fry clenched her jaw to control her expression as a surge of unease ran up her spine. Number four in the Standards of Professional Behaviour was 'Use of Force'. He was deliberately making her think back over all the possible incidents in her career that might fall under that heading.

Jackson was watching her carefully. 'For your reference, DS Fry, we'll be dealing with issues under standards one, two, four, seven and nine.'

'Very well.'

She'd been thinking so hard about number four that now she couldn't remember what seven and nine were. The copy of the Code of Ethics still lay on the table between them. But having ignored it when he tossed it there, she couldn't pick it up now to check.

'Remind us of number one again,' he said.

'"Honesty and Integrity,"' she repeated. 'And you shouldn't need reminding.'

'Indeed.' Jackson looked down at his notes. 'The code offers several examples under this section for assessing your honesty and integrity. Shall we just run through a few, with regard to your personal choices?'

'If you like.'

'Would you agree with these statements, then, DS Fry? Please answer as directly as you can. Do you ensure your decisions are not influenced by improper considerations of personal gain?'

'Yes.'

'Have you knowingly made false, misleading or inaccurate statements in any professional context?'

'No.'

'Have you either solicited or accepted the offer of any gift, gratuity or hospitality that could compromise your impartiality?'

'Of course not.'

99

'And finally, have you ever used your position to inappropriately coerce any person or to settle personal grievances?'

Fry opened her mouth but found she couldn't answer. Jackson didn't look at her but kept his eyes directed down at his notes, as if he was simply waiting for a cue to read the next question. He waited what felt like an uncomfortably long time before he glanced up. He twitched an eyebrow and made a mark with his pen.

'Would you like some water, DS Fry?' he said. 'I have a feeling we might be in for quite a long session.'

Ben Cooper called his DS in Edendale and agreed that Sharma could cope without both Luke Irvine and Gavin Murfin for a while.

When Murfin came on the phone, Cooper allocated him and Irvine interviews with the Gould brothers and the Warburtons, as well as the students Millie Taylor and Karina Scott.

'Take their statements, show them a map and try to get them to pinpoint their exact positions. Oh, and ask them for any photos they took on their phones while they were on Kinder,' he said. 'Everybody does that. Gavin, I want you to go first to take statements from the victim's family. Her mother and her brother, Jonathan.'

'No problem.'

'Oh, and Gavin?'

'Yes?'

'See what you can find out about an individual called Robert Farnley and his connection to Jonathan Matthew.'

'Right you are.'

*　　*　　*

100

Gavin Murfin put his jacket on, straightened his tie, then loosened it again. He was a civilian – he didn't even have to wear a tie if he didn't want to.

He looked around for Dev Sharma. Murfin had worked under scores of different supervisors during his thirty years with Derbyshire Constabulary. When he was a young probationer, the older bobbies taught him a lot about the real world out there on the streets. As a PC, his shift sergeants had ranged from tough disciplinarians to insecure drunks who could barely hold down the job. One or two had managed to be both at the same time.

His CID career had been no different. Murfin had stayed a detective constable right up until the moment he could claim his full pension. Ben Cooper had been his DS for a while, and so had Diane Fry. He didn't really mind either of them. At least he knew where he stood, even if it was far down the scale of estimation in Fry's case. But with Dev Sharma, he just wasn't sure.

It was a feeling Murfin wasn't familiar with. He'd always prided himself on being able to sum people up pretty quickly, whether they were colleagues or suspects or members of the public. He'd have their number, get them pegged accurately before they'd even noticed him hanging around in the background. It was his talent, a skill he'd learned from his decades on the force. Yet DS Sharma evaded his assessment.

Murfin patted his jacket pockets and made sure he had supplies for the trip. If he was going to Manchester, he needed something to comfort him.

Dev Sharma nodded briskly when Murfin told him where he would be.

'Don't hang around,' said Sharma. 'There's a lot of work for you to do here.'

'Yeah, I know. I've got a little list.'

Sharma frowned. 'We're really busy, Gavin.'

Murfin sighed. He couldn't fault the way Sharma did the job. He was always efficient and fair, helped him when he needed guidance, praised him if he did something well. But it was the man behind the façade that Murfin couldn't reach. He had no idea what sort of person Sharma was on the inside. All he knew was that this DS was someone you wouldn't go down the pub for a drink with, wouldn't dare to try a risqué joke on. Murfin's wrists still stung from the number of times they'd been slapped for being politically incorrect. He was feeling uneasy and unsettled, and he didn't like it.

Ben Cooper was someone he could talk to. But Ben was a DI now, shut away in his own separate office like a proper boss. You had to knock on the door to speak to him these days. There might be others in the CID room who felt the same way, though.

Murfin looked around and caught Carol Villiers's eye. Instinctively, he smiled and winked. She raised her eyebrows and gave him a puzzled glare. Murfin switched off the smile immediately. Was he being inappropriate? He wasn't sure. He didn't really know what the word meant, but he'd heard it used a lot recently.

'Sorry,' he said.

Villiers looked even more puzzled. Murfin straightened his tie again, just for something to do with his hands, and headed out of the door.

The Roths lived just outside Hayfield, deep in a network of lanes that no one but walkers would discover. Ben Cooper and Carol Villiers passed a small hamlet halfway up Valley Road. Beyond it, the road became even narrower, bounded by a stone wall and overhung with dense trees. One property seemed to be accessible only by a footbridge over the river.

Up ahead lay a pedestrian access to the campsite where Sam and Pat Warburton had stayed. But just before a terraced row of houses, Cooper turned the Toyota onto a track and headed away from the river. A neat sign at the bottom of the track indicated that he was approaching Trespass Lodge.

After a few bends, the house came into view among the trees. From this viewpoint, it seemed enormous – a long Georgian frontage with perfectly symmetrical mullioned windows and a stone portico at the front door. An extra wing had been added at some time, tastefully designed by some previous Victorian owner. Cooper wondered what the house had been called back then. The Victorians had no idea of the Mass Trespass, and would never have approved. It was only after the First World War that the working class started to get bolshie.

Imitation gas lamps lined the drive near the house. A water feature resembling a miniature version of the Emperor Fountain at Chatsworth House stood in the middle of a neat swathe of grass, alongside a large pond that had ambitions to be a lake, with a patch of rushes but no bird life. Beyond it was a stable block and paddock, but Cooper could see no sign of horses. A range of garages looked much better used, and other outbuildings had been converted and modernised, perhaps as guest accommodation or for holiday lets.

A pair of French bulldogs scampered about on the lawn. They turned their snub noses and bat ears towards him as he approached. He could imagine what his brother would say about dogs like this. For Matt, working dogs were the only kind that mattered. These Frenchies he would dismiss as fashion accessories.

Cooper parked on the gravel and Villiers rang the bell. Elsa Roth answered the door herself. She was slim and dark-haired with bright eyes that assessed Cooper and Villiers instantly.

'Yes, please come in,' she said. 'Darius is expecting you.'

They were led into a large hallway through the porticoed entrance, which seemed out of keeping with the age and style of the house. The huge sitting room had black sofas with black cushions round a wood-burning stove and a massive flat-screen TV. Through a stable-type door the kitchen boasted a four-oven Aga and a long pine table beneath exposed beams. When Roth opened another door, Cooper got the distinctive whiff of chlorine. An indoor swimming pool somewhere.

'We'd like to talk to you too, Mrs Roth,' he said.

'Oh, I suppose you will. Though I don't know anything really.'

'I take it you know about the Kinder Mass Trespass, though? Your house is named after it.'

She looked vague. 'It's an interest of Darius's. Something one of his family was involved in.'

'Do you know when it was?'

'Oh, I'm not sure. I'm not good on historical dates.' She laughed. 'Before my time anyway.'

Cooper was struck by the womb-like silence of the lodge. Every house he entered had a different soundscape. The acoustics depended on the thickness of the walls, the depth of the carpet, the ratio of tiles to curtain, the size of the windows and the effectiveness of the double glazing. And the sounds changed, depending on the time of day, the atmospheric conditions, the number of people in the room.

Here, the sound was so different from the Athertons' semi-detached in Edendale with its rustling scene suits, the voices of busy professionals, the noise of traffic in the road outside. He might as well have been in another world, a different country.

The furnishings were expensive, he could see that. The carpets were thick, the wooden floors highly polished, the Georgian plasterwork beautifully preserved. But there was something about the furniture, the choice of pictures on the walls that suggested there wasn't the taste to go with the wealth. It was something he often noticed in stately homes. Each owner wanted to put their own mark on a property, and their tastes didn't always fit in.

'We were the founders of the New Trespassers,' said Darius. 'One of my ancestors took part in the original Kinder Trespass in 1932.'

'That must have been – what, your grandfather?'

'Yes, his name was Daniel Roth. He was only a young man at the time of the trespass. Just eighteen years old, I believe. But he was a man of strong principles, like a lot of his friends. He stood up for what he believed in, and he became a martyr. I think those are the sort of people we should be remembering, don't you?'

Roth pushed a lock of his wavy blond hair back into place. He was reclining in an armchair, his long legs stretched out on a Wilton rug. His most prominent facial feature was his nose, which Cooper thought was the type referred to as aquiline. It made him think of Roman emperors and Egyptian pharaohs, someone noble and aristocratic.

'Most of the group came from Manchester, didn't they?' said Cooper.

'Yes, they were mostly young working-class men,' said Roth with a pleased smile. 'My grandfather Daniel worked in a railway yard in Gorton. They made steam locomotives. When the weather was good, they could see the upper slopes of Kinder Scout from where they lived. It must have looked like a promised land from the back streets of Gorton.'

Cooper was examining the elegant surroundings. A lot of money had been invested here.

'You're in the property business, I believe?' he said.

'For my sins, yes. Property development. We have a substantial portfolio of properties in Greater Manchester and right across the North-West.'

'Has that always been your family concern?'

'Not at all. We used to be in textiles,' said Roth. 'We got out of that business in my father's day. It was one of the best things I persuaded him to do. No one can compete with the Chinese these days. Property is a different matter.'

'Is your father still alive?'

'Sadly, no. We lost him ten years ago. A heart attack. He was only seventy, but he pushed himself very hard all his life. You have to do that if you're going to make a success in business. So we inherited control of the business from Dad when he died.'

Cooper doubted whether Darius pushed himself so hard that he'd end up in an early grave. He treated himself too well, perhaps enjoyed the trappings of wealth without feeling the compulsion to add to it in the way his forebears had. It was often the case when money was inherited. It all came too easy. And it could disappear just as readily.

But there was only one aspect of his family history that Darius Roth really wanted to talk about.

'I've got an archive of everything published about the Mass Trespass,' he said. 'All the newspaper cuttings, everything. I employed a researcher to do a proper job for me. Look, there's a framed photograph over the fireplace. My grandfather is the one in the middle.'

Cooper dutifully studied the photograph. And there they were – five of those laughing young men with the Brylcreemed hair, the tweed jackets and shorts. They all carried heavy-looking backpacks as they linked arms ready for the expedition onto the forbidden territory of Kinder Scout.

'They called it rambling in those days,' said Darius. 'It sounds a bit too aimless for us now, doesn't it? As if there's no real purpose or destination to it. We can't stand that idea in the twenty-first century. So most of us call ourselves walkers. The more serious ones are hikers.'

'But October isn't the anniversary of the Mass Trespass, is it?' said Cooper.

Roth nodded approvingly. 'No, the original walk was in April when we began it eight years ago. But that's a bad time of year for most of us.'

Cooper looked round and noticed that Elsa Roth had disappeared. At some point she'd slipped quietly out of the room and left Darius to do all the talking.

'There's been a suggestion that Faith Matthew didn't fall but was pushed,' said Cooper.

'Who told you that?' demanded Roth. 'It's ludicrous.'

'I can't tell you where the suggestion came from, I'm afraid.'

'Pushed? I don't believe it for a second.'

'Nevertheless, we have to make inquiries.'

'Well, if it's true, there must have been someone else on the moor, then,' said Darius. 'It can't have been one of my group.'

'What? Someone followed you onto Kinder Scout to attack Faith Matthew?'

'Isn't it possible that Faith wasn't always intended to be the victim? She might just have been in the wrong place at the wrong time. It could have been any one of us.'

'Did you actually see any signs of anyone else up there?'

'Well, there were noises,' said Darius. 'I couldn't have put a name to them myself. I didn't really take any notice.'

'Did you see any lights?'

'Like a torch, you mean? They're not much use in fog, are they? The beam doesn't travel very far.'

'No, that's right.'

Roth walked to the window and gazed out at a manicured lawn. The grounds of Trespass Lodge seemed to be extensive. From here, Cooper could see nothing that resembled a boundary – only trees, flower beds and swathes of grass gently undulating towards a spectacular view of Chinley Head and the Sett Valley, with a dark copse of trees covering the southern slopes of Kinder Scout itself.

'Pushed?' said Roth again. 'It's unbelievable. Just incredible.'

As if by magic, Elsa reappeared and took Roth's arm.

'It's OK, Teddy Bear,' she said.

Reluctantly, Roth allowed himself to be led away.

'Teddy Bear?' said Villiers with a twist of her mouth as if she'd tasted something too sour. 'Really?'

Cooper shrugged. 'I've heard worse.'

'I suppose what goes in relationships can be surprising.

But they should keep that kind of intimate stuff to themselves.'

'It does rather ruin Mr Roth's image,' said Cooper.

Villiers laughed quietly. 'I'll think of it every time now when he starts getting pompous.'

Elsa came back on her own as they were leaving. Cooper had stopped at a large framed photograph in the hall. It showed a climber looking up at the camera from a dizzying height as he clung to a sheer rock face. A printed caption said the photo was taken on the Black Dog Arête at Brimham Rocks in North Yorkshire.

'Who is this, Mrs Roth?' he asked.

'That's Darius's brother, Magnus.'

'He's a rock climber?'

'He was, until the accident.'

'What happened to him?'

'He was killed climbing in the Alps,' said Elsa. 'He fell sixty feet when the edge of an arête cut his rope.'

'I'm sorry. When was that?'

'Six years ago.'

'Were he and Darius very close?'

'Very. Magnus gave Darius someone to live up to.'

Elsa walked them out to their car.

'You don't seem to know much about the history of the Mass Trespass yourself, Mrs Roth,' said Cooper.

'It doesn't mean anything to me, to be honest,' she said. 'I come on the walks because of Darius really. He likes me to be with him.'

'Where did you originally meet him?'

'Oh, some swish dinner at a hotel in Manchester. A conference, or a trade organisation that Darius was a member of. I can't remember the event exactly.'

'You can't remember? But if you were at the dinner too—'

She laughed. 'Oh no. I was a waitress working at the hotel. I must have caught Darius's eye that night. He asked for my phone number. A lot of blokes used to do that, but Darius actually rang the next day. And' – she threw out her hands as if gesturing at the elegant house around her – 'the rest is history. It's been like a fantasy for me.'

13

Sophie Pullen wore a set of gold bangles that glittered whenever she raised her hand. If she'd been his teacher, Cooper would have found that distracting. But when he was at school, any flicker of light was appealing.

'We were all so cold and exhausted,' said Sophie. 'It's hard to remember exactly what happened or who said what.'

'I understand.'

Cooper had always had a soft spot for redheads. Sophie Pullen had that pale, translucent skin that often went with her hair colour. She had blue eyes too, intense and penetrating, the sort of eyes that didn't miss very much. He imagined she might have let her hair grow long when she was younger, but now it was cropped short and business-like. A plain grey skirt with a white blouse and black cardigan only seemed to emphasise her looks.

'I'd been walking near Liam Sharpe,' she said. 'Liam is a bit slower than everyone else on a steep uphill stretch, but he always catches up eventually. He never gives in.'

Cooper considered that for a moment. Whenever he went out walking with a group himself, the fittest members always slowed down to stay together with the slowest.

They never left people behind and forced them to catch up. The Trespassers sounded more and more as if they were out to compete with each other and humiliate the weakest.

'But later on?' he said.

'There was a cry,' said Sophie. 'I thought it was from an animal of some kind. A fox, perhaps.'

'Not during the day.'

Cooper was listening intently to Sophie as she described her experience on Kinder Scout. He always tried very hard to listen to what people were saying and absorb small details. A detail was often what came back to him later, a memory of something apparently trivial that a witness had mentioned.

Sophie shrugged. 'Well, a bird, then. I don't know. It seemed to come from a long way off. Some distance across the moors.'

'All right.'

'And there were lights,' she said. 'Lights on the moor. I could see them through the mist, moving around.'

'How far away were they?'

'I couldn't tell. You know what it's like in those conditions.'

'Very difficult to judge.'

'Exactly.'

'Did they look like torches?' asked Cooper. 'Another party of walkers, perhaps?'

She shrugged. 'I really couldn't be sure. I didn't hear any voices. Besides, if that's what they were, why didn't they come over to us? Our group was making enough noise, with the argument—' She stopped suddenly and stared defiantly at Cooper as if he'd deliberately interrupted her.

'What argument?' he said.

Sophie shook her head. 'It was nothing.'

'I need to know about it.'

She sighed. 'It was Darius and Nick, as usual. They were often at each other's throats. But it's not relevant.'

'Why don't you let me decide what's relevant?' said Cooper impatiently.

She looked abashed at his tone. 'Sorry. I suppose we all seem pretty stupid to you. Getting lost on Kinder Scout, going onto the moors without being properly prepared, and then being so hopeless when things went wrong.'

Cooper opened his mouth, but she waved a hand dismissively.

'Oh, I overheard some of the Mountain Rescue team talking about us,' she said. 'I suppose they have to do that sort of thing all the time. Rescue useless people like us.'

'Perhaps not useless,' said Cooper. 'But certainly misguided.'

She sighed. 'I think it was all part of the thrill originally. A bit of an adventure, getting away from our humdrum lives. We all enjoyed the thrill of the risk. Though we never really believed, deep down, that there was much actual danger. It was more the *thought* of it. The concept. Do you know what I mean? We even used to laugh about what a reckless and foolhardy bunch we were. We thought we were taking on a challenge, flouting the rules in our own way. Just like the original mass trespassers, I suppose.'

Cooper nodded, though her explanation sounded unconvincing. If it had come from one of the others – Darius Roth, perhaps – it might have made sense. Had she just taken on someone else's beliefs, accepted the views of a more forceful personality as her own? In Cooper's mind, the New Trespassers Walking Club was beginning to sound more like a cult, with a leader being followed unquestioningly.

But that wasn't right. One of them at least had questioned the leader.

'Tell me about this argument,' he said. 'What were Darius and Nick arguing about?'

'Everything. Whether we were lost, who should do what, which of us should go in what direction . . .'

'And that was normal?'

'Yes.'

'And there was Faith,' she said.

'What?'

'Well, I think Faith was going to point out that it doesn't matter what network your phone is on – you can make an emergency 999 call through any available network.'

'Was she the only one of the group who knew that?'

'I can't say. I must admit I didn't know it myself. I've never had the occasion to dial 999 in my entire life.'

'What, never?'

'No, I don't think so.'

'You've lived a sheltered existence, Miss Pullen.'

Sophie smiled. 'I think there was always someone else there to make the call before me. People tend to fall into two groups in an emergency, don't they? There are those who know exactly what to do and get on with it, and others who stand around helplessly waiting for someone else to make a decision. I'm afraid I'm in the second group.'

'So did Darius make the decisions for the group?'

'Usually.'

'Did he, for example, make the decision about who should stay with the casualty and who should go to get help?'

'No, we all volunteered to go.' She paused. 'At least, I did and the Goulds.'

'But Nick didn't volunteer?'

'It just seemed to be understood that he would go. Darius was speaking directly to Nick when he suggested it. There was no argument from him. Not about that, anyway. Darius assumed he would go and he went. He was never given the choice.'

'But Nick didn't always jump to do what Darius wanted.'

'Nick's different,' she said. 'He doesn't see Darius in the same way as some of the others. Nick is a sceptic, you see. He scoffs at the story of the Kinder Mass Trespass, makes references to Darius's ancestor being a Communist. I don't know if you saw the hat he was wearing . . .'

'I remember one of my officers mentioning it. The Russian Army hat with the red star on it.'

'That's right. He got it purely as a joke, as a dig at Darius. It wasn't very subtle.'

'So if Mr Haslam doesn't respect the history of the Mass Trespass the way the rest of you do, why did he join the walking club?'

'He came because I asked him,' said Sophie. 'The first time, anyway. After that, I think he enjoyed it in his own way.'

'What was your view of Faith Matthew?' asked Cooper.

'Faith? I didn't know her that well. Like the others, she was brought into the group by Darius.'

'You must have spoken to her sometimes.'

'A bit.'

Cooper pictured the group. They were very diverse. But Faith Matthew and Sophie Pullen were the two who seemed to have most in common. A similar age and background at least.

'Didn't you like her?' he asked.

'I wouldn't go that far.'

That seemed to answer his question. Sophie hadn't liked Faith, but she didn't want to say so. Perhaps it was just a reluctance to speak ill of the dead.

'And what is your relationship with Darius Roth?' said Cooper.

That got quite a different response: Sophie's expression became more much animated than when he'd asked about Faith Matthew.

'I've never known anyone like him,' she said. 'He seems to have the ability to get people to do whatever he wants. It's not as if he really tries very hard. There's not much in the way of smooth talking about him, like you might imagine a used-car salesman, or an estate agent.'

Cooper hadn't been imagining Darius Roth as a used-car salesman. More as a Charles Manson or a Jim Jones, with this corner of Hayfield the equivalent of Jonestown. But perhaps his imagination was leading him too far astray.

'Is there anything else you can recall?' he asked.

She hesitated, and again his interest was piqued.

'I'm not sure about this,' she said. 'But Darius once told us he knew how to commit the perfect murder and get away with it.'

'Really?'

'He said he'd been told by a Home Office pathologist he once met that if you can get someone up onto a high place like a cliff, or to the edge of a steep drop, then as long you don't have any eyewitnesses who see you do it, it's practically impossible to prove whether a person fell or was pushed.' She gazed at Cooper. 'Is that true?'

'If it was, it wouldn't be wise for me to tell you,' said Cooper.

She nodded as if he'd confirmed the theory. 'I think it's

probably true. No forensic evidence. You might have suspicions, but you can't prove it.'

'Who else was there when he told you that, Miss Pullen?'

'Just Elsa, of course. She's always there.'

'Elsa doesn't say much, does she?'

'No, but there's a lot going on under the surface.'

'What do you mean, Sophie?'

'Well, all I can say is, she's not what she seems. She's acting a role. Perhaps some people haven't seen it, but I have. Elsa has never bothered hiding it from me. I suppose I'm not important enough in the scheme of things. There's someone else behind that façade. You need to watch her eyes and you'll see it.'

'Thank you for the observation,' he said.

'I don't suppose it's of any use.'

He didn't want her to realise how useful it might be, so he changed the subject.

'Just to go back a bit,' he said. 'That cry you heard while you were on Kinder – you said it seemed a long way off.'

She shook her hand to move the bangles back on her wrist, an oddly elegant gesture.

'Yes. Is that important?'

'It might be.'

Cooper was remembering what Carol Villiers had said about high-pitched sounds being muffled by fog. The cry of a fox or bird wouldn't have carried any distance. It must have been much closer to the group for Sophie Pullen to have heard it.

Carol Villiers had been sent to take a statement from Sophie Pullen's partner, Nick Haslam. He'd returned to work at an IT company based on a business park off the M60 orbital motorway south of Manchester.

Haslam wore black stubble a bit too long to be fashionable, but not quite a beard. It formed dark 'V's on either side of his cheeks, which moved disconcertingly when he smiled. And he seemed forever to be smiling, or on the verge of it. He gave the impression that every answer was a joke.

'I just have a couple of additional questions,' said Villiers.

'All right.'

'I wondered why the group carried on with the walk when the weather turned bad and visibility became so poor. Wasn't that a bit of a risk?'

Haslam shrugged. 'Maybe. But what's life without a bit of risk? We were all happy to carry on. Well, almost all of us.'

'Oh?'

'It was Elsa Roth,' he said. 'Elsa wanted to call it off when the fog came down. I remember her saying something about it being dangerous. We didn't take any notice of her.'

'Not even her husband?'

'Particularly not Darius.'

Villiers frowned. 'And after the accident, when the walking group split up, you went with Darius Roth's party, didn't you?'

'Yes.'

'Why didn't you stay with Miss Pullen?'

'There was only one man in Darius's group.'

'You didn't think it was more appropriate to stay with your girlfriend?'

118

'Not in the circumstances,' he said. 'I knew she would be safe. Darius was with Elsa, Millie and Karina. It made sense to me at the time. A division of responsibilities.'

'It wasn't that you didn't trust Mr Roth on his own?'

'I don't know what you mean.'

'Did he welcome you in his party?'

'Why wouldn't he?'

'From what I've heard, you didn't take Mr Roth's interests seriously,' said Villiers.

'You mean all the stuff about the Mass Trespass?'

'Yes.'

Haslam laughed. 'The leaders of the trespass,' he said. 'They were all Communists, of course.'

As she looked at Nick Haslam, Villiers remembered the Russian Army hat he was said to have worn on the walk on Sunday.

'Do you think so?' she said.

'Think so? It's not a question of me "thinking so". It's a fact. They were members of the British Workers' Sports Federation, part of the Young Communist League. By the time of the trespass, it was basically the Communist Party's sports organisation. Darius Roth doesn't like hearing that. But it's not his fault. You can't change what your ancestors were, can you?'

'I suppose not.'

'The working-class struggle for the right to roam versus the rights of the wealthy to have exclusive use of the moorlands for shooting grouse,' said Haslam.

He smiled again, an attempt to persuade Villiers not to take him too seriously. It was much too late. She'd already decided he wasn't funny at all.

119

'That sounds like a quote,' she said.

'Darius's favourite sentence,' said Haslam. 'Working class? Have you met him?'

'Yes, I have.'

'Well, you'll know what I mean. Darius Roth? If you ask me, there isn't a bigger fraud in Derbyshire.'

When he finally arrived back in his office at West Street, Ben Cooper picked up the phone to call the EMSOU base near Nottingham.

'Can I speak to Detective Sergeant Fry, please?' he said.

'Hold on.'

There was a long pause, and Cooper began to wonder if he'd called at a bad time. Perhaps there was a major operation under way at EMSOU that he didn't know about. Then the officer came back on the line.

'I'm sorry, DS Fry isn't available.'

'Do you have any idea when she'll be free?'

'No idea.'

'Well, could you give her a message, then? Ask her to call me back.'

The officer cleared his throat, and there was a muttering in the background. Cooper had a mental picture of him referring to someone else nearby, perhaps with the lift of an eyebrow. *What should I say to him?*

'DS Fry won't be available for the foreseeable future. Maybe someone else can help you. If you hang on, I'll transfer you.'

'No, it's OK,' said Cooper.

'Sorry, what was your name again?'

But Cooper had put the phone down.

'That was strange,' he said.

'Diane too busy to speak to you?' said Carol Villiers, looking up.

'She's not there. And she won't be for the foreseeable future. Or so I've just been told.'

'Perhaps she's on leave.'

'I don't think so. If she was, why wouldn't they just say that?'

'Strange.'

'Exactly what I just said.'

Cooper put it out of his mind. He could manage anyway, unless there were significant developments.

But what real evidence did he have that Faith Matthew had been deliberately killed? The witness statements coming in from Irvine and Murfin's interviews didn't offer any substantial proof. Yet there was something in them that Cooper was unsatisfied with. Perhaps more statements from the other members of the walking group would help. And of course he could pin his hopes on the results of the post-mortem examination.

Cooper found Luke Irvine and Gavin Murfin in the CID room.

'I've taken Jonathan Matthew's statement,' said Murfin when he saw Cooper. 'Did you know he plays guitar?'

'Yes, he told me. In fact, his mother had already mentioned it.'

'He plays bass with one of those bands you've never heard of. We had a good chat about guitars, actually. Guitarist to guitarist, like.'

'You're not a guitarist, Gavin,' said Irvine. 'You're just taking lessons.'

Cooper looked up in surprise.

'You're learning to play the guitar, Gavin? Do you fancy yourself as a rock star?'

'I reckon it must be part of my midlife crisis.'

'Well, at least it doesn't involve food,' said Cooper. 'So how is it going?'

'To be honest, I'm just learning chords yet,' said Murfin. 'And I'm having trouble with F. I call it "the F-ing F chord".'

'Let me have a copy of Jonathan's statement as soon as you can.'

'It's already on your desk,' said Murfin. 'Oh, and Robert Farnley . . .'

'Yes?'

Murfin looked smug as he consulted his notes.

'Mr Farnley is kind of an old 1960s rocker. Back then, he was a member of a band called the Confederates, based in Gorton. They started off as an instrumental group under the name of the Zodiacs, playing covers of Shadows hits, then moved on to Beatles and Gerry and the Pacemakers stuff. Farnley took over as manager and got them a record deal.'

'I've never heard of them.'

'Well, the band did pretty well in the mid-1960s. Built up quite a following, played at the Belle Vue Top Ten Club, the Catacombs in Oldham and Beat City in Manchester. In their publicity photos, they all wore waistcoats and ties, and they had Beatles haircuts. But they never quite hit the big time and they went their separate ways.'

'So what happened to Farnley?'

'He moved to Canada years ago, and now he lives mostly in Port Hope, Ontario. He had a career in media and advertising, including a spell working for the Government of Ontario, then started his own consultancy firm. But he still has a lot of family in Manchester, and he's a long-standing Man City fan.' Murfin shrugged. 'I suppose someone has to be. And that's why he's back in Manchester for a while.'

'You've done well, Gavin.'

Murfin smirked. 'Old skills come in useful now and then.'

'We found it all online,' put in Irvine. 'I've shown Gavin how to use the internet.'

Cooper looked at Murfin, who shuffled his feet uneasily.

'I'll go and talk to him tomorrow, should I?' said Murfin.

14

On her way home from Ripley, Diane Fry called again at the service station on Clifton Lane. She didn't really need anything, but it was always a good idea to keep her car topped up with fuel, just in case.

Besides, tonight she felt an overwhelming need for some routine activity, a bit of real-world contact with ordinary people who had no idea who she was. Paying for her petrol at the kiosk wasn't much, but the young woman who worked there did at least smile when she gave her pump number. Fry felt as though no one had smiled at her for months. It was her own fault, she supposed. No one could accuse her of being sociable and outgoing. She hardly went out of her way to make friends.

When she checked her phone in the store, she noticed an email message was waiting for her from InPost to alert her to a delivery, with a code to access her locker. The collection terminal was here at the service station, right next to the air pump.

She used the lockers because they were accessible twenty-four hours a day, seven days a week. Much more convenient for her than having to find a helpful neighbour to take in parcel deliveries if she'd made purchases from

Amazon or eBay sellers. She wasn't even sure that she had any helpful neighbours in Wilford. Not during the day at least.

A security camera pointed down at her from its position over the locker terminal as she scanned the QR code on her email to open the locker and retrieve her item. She drew out a yellow box, tucked it under her arm and returned to her car.

When she got into her flat, she shrugged off her jacket, kicked off her shoes and relaxed with a deep sigh. It was only later that she realised that the wine was finished. The empty bottle stood like a tragic reminder on the kitchen counter, along with its useless cork. She should have remembered to buy some more when she was at the service station, but her mind had been on other things. She couldn't be bothered to go out of the flat again now.

Then she remembered there was half a bottle of gin left in the kitchen cupboard. These days, she tried to keep it for emergencies. But tonight? Tonight definitely felt like an emergency.

Sophie Pullen and Nick Haslam had stopped off for a drink at the Sportsman Inn outside Hayfield.

'It's a bad business,' said Nick over her pint of Thwaites Wainwright and her glass of malt whisky. 'About Faith, I mean.'

'What do you think we should do?' said Sophie.

'Do? Why should we do anything?'

'The police . . .'

He shook his head. 'Don't tell them anything. Whatever you think you saw, the chances are you imagined it. It's much better to say nothing.'

125

He peered at her suspiciously, as if reading disagreement in her silence.

'You know that's for the best, Soph. Don't get too involved.'

'Aren't we already involved?'

He scowled. 'Not me,' he said. 'And I'd like to keep it that way. It's Darius's pigeon. His group, his idea. His responsibility for the consequences.'

Sophie had thought she would never tell anybody about what she'd seen, but the detective inspector she spoke to seemed as though he might listen to her without being too quick to leap to a judgement.

'I think I might . . .' she said.

'Soph, really?' he said. 'Your imagination . . .'

'Why would I have imagined what I saw?'

'Think about it. We were all tired. Cold and exhausted – you said that yourself. We were lost and confused. And the weather – the cloud suddenly coming down the way it did. You could barely see your hand in front of your face. None of us could be sure what we saw in that fog. There might have been anyone out there.'

'Or no one.'

'You can't be sure of anything, Soph. Why would you take a story like that to the police? Your account would fall apart as soon as they started asking questions. You'd look like an idiot.'

Sophie said nothing. She thought he'd trotted out far too many excuses. Cold, exhausted, lost, confused. And of course the weather . . .

But that last one was right. She *had* seen something out there in the fog.

*   *   *

Matt Cooper switched off the TV news and threw the remote down on the coffee table. He slumped back in his armchair in the sitting room of Bridge End Farm.

'Idiots,' he said sourly.

Ben looked at his brother. Matt was a farmer, so he complained about pretty much everything. There had been several items on the news he might have objected to. Brexit, the Budget, a disappointing football result or even the weather forecast.

'Who are?' asked Ben.

'All of them,' said Matt, with a wave of a large hand in the direction of the farmyard. 'All the fools who go up into the hills without being properly prepared and equipped. Why do they think it's OK to put other people's lives at risk rescuing them? Idiots, the lot of them. That's my opinion.'

'You're not alone.'

Matt sighed as he stretched his legs out in the tattered denim jeans he always wore. The armchair creaked under his weight. Ben's sister-in-law, Kate, and his niece Josie were somewhere in the house, but they often left him and Matt alone for a while when he visited the farm. He suspected it was because they heard enough of Matt's grumbling and thought it only right that his younger brother should put up with his share.

Now Matt looked nervous and began to fidget, as if there was something on his mind, something that he needed to say but couldn't find the words for. Ben waited patiently. He knew it would come out in the end.

'You know it's our twentieth wedding anniversary coming up?' said Matt eventually.

'Oh, of course. Twenty years, is it?'

Ben had forgotten, but he shouldn't have. The day of Matt's wedding was still a very clear memory for him. It was the last time all the family had been together, including the father and mother of the groom. Joe Cooper had been there in his new suit, with a recent haircut and a flower in his buttonhole. And there had been Isabel in her bright blue dress and enormous hat, posing with Matt and Kate and the bride's parents in the grounds of St John the Baptist Church in Tideswell.

He knew it had been October. He could remember the drifts of leaves swirling down from the trees in the church-yard and mingling with confetti strewn on the path as they stirred in the breeze that forced Isabel Cooper to hold on to her hat for the photographs. But twenty years? That was almost a lifetime ago.

Of course, Ben had been too young to act as best man, though he was sure Matt would have asked him otherwise. Instead, the role had gone to one of Matt's friends in the Young Farmers' Club, resulting in an innuendo-laden best man's speech at the reception and a stag night that had proved almost fatal for Matt. On the wedding day close-ups, you could still his pallor and the fresh bruise on his temple.

'China, isn't it?' said Ben.

'What?'

'A china anniversary. Fifteen years is crystal, twenty-five is silver, and twenty years is china.'

'China? What's the point of that?'

'I don't know. I didn't make them up.'

Matt scowled in bafflement. 'Anyway. It's our twentieth. And we're thinking about going away.'

'Really?'

'Well, more than thinking about it.'

Ben's eyebrows shot up. Now, that *was* unusual. Matt was notoriously difficult to prise away from the farm, even for a weekend. He was always terrified that he'd come back and find all the livestock dead, his crops rotting in the field, the barn burned down, his tractor stolen. Kate must have been working really hard on this one.

'Just for a break,' said Matt, almost defensively.

'You deserve it,' said Ben. 'Both of you.'

'Eric Locke and George Whittaker are going to look after what needs doing on the farm. They're good blokes. And we're past harvest, so it's as good a time as any to get away for a bit.'

Ben knew Matt got on well with his neighbours, and they always helped each other out, though this was a whole different level of trust, allowing them to care for Bridge End in his absence.

'What about the girls?'

'Amy's term has started this week, so she's at college.'

'She'll be in Sheffield, then?'

'Yes, settled into her student accommodation. And we've arranged for Josie to go and stay with Aunt Margaret and Uncle John.'

'She won't like that very much.'

'It will only be for a week,' said Matt. 'And Margaret will make sure she gets to school in the mornings.'

There was obviously more. Ben waited, but it didn't come.

'So . . . ?'

'Well, I wondered if you might keep an eye on the house,' said Matt, with an anxious frown. 'And the dog.'

'Jess?'

'I don't want to put her in kennels. She's all right on

her own most of the time, and Eric and George and their lads will be knocking about, but I want to make sure she's fed and exercised properly.'

'I'll look after her,' said Ben. 'And the house will be fine.'

'There's a bit of a leak in the back porch. If it rains too hard—'

'I'll keep an eye out.'

'And leave a light or two on. You know what it's like with thieves coming round trying to nick equipment from the yard.'

'Don't worry about it. You two just enjoy yourselves. When do you go?'

'This Saturday.'

'So you *were* more than just thinking about it, then. It's all booked.'

'Seems so.'

'Where are you going, by the way?' asked Ben.

'The Algarve.'

'Portugal?'

'I know,' said Matt. 'Europe. I've had to get a new passport. What's the odds that air traffic control will be on strike?'

Matt heaved a deep sigh, as if the prospect of a holiday depressed him enormously.

'So how's it going with the new woman, anyway?' he said.

'Chloe? Fine. It's going really well.'

Matt peered at him, trying to read his face. Ben had never been able to keep anything from his older brother. They understood each other too well, often without the need for any words.

But in this case Matt seemed reassured.

'Good,' he said. 'When are you bringing her here to meet us?'

'To Bridge End?'

'Of course.'

'What's this? Meet the in-laws?'

'Kate would like to get to know her,' said Matt a little sheepishly. 'And the girls too.'

'I see.'

So Matt had been pestered by his wife and daughters to find out about the new woman in his brother's life. Ben supposed it was inevitable. But would he want to put Chloe Young through that sort of scrutiny?

'I'll ask her if she'd like to come,' he said.

'That would be great.' Matt looked relieved. He'd done his best, as instructed. 'Kate and the girls will pitch in and cook something special. They'll look forward to it.'

'Wait. I haven't said—'

Matt put a hand on his arm. 'It'll be fine,' he said. 'Don't worry, Ben. It'll all be fine this time.'

As Ben Cooper turned the Toyota in the farmyard and drove away from Bridge End Farm, it was his brother's last phrase that kept repeating in his head. *It'll all be fine this time.*

Those two words only served to emphasise what had happened last time. Perhaps that was why he was nervous about introducing Chloe to his family. Matt hadn't meant to do it, but he'd put his finger on the most sensitive point of his brother's feelings.

Ben put his foot down as he headed back towards Foolow. And Matt was right, of course. It *would* be fine this time. Wouldn't it?

15

Tuesday

Next morning, DS Dev Sharma was waiting to brief Ben Cooper on the Danielle Atherton murder case as soon as he arrived in the office.

'There are still a few loose ends to tie up, Dev,' said Cooper when he'd reviewed Sharma's file.

'Of course. We've got a result, though.'

Cooper looked at his DS, saw the satisfaction on his face.

'It still gives you a buzz when you know you've got the right person in custody, doesn't it?'

Sharma nodded. 'And there's no doubt about this one.'

'No doubt at all.'

As soon as he uttered the words, Cooper experienced a frisson of uncertainty. It always felt wrong to say that at such an early stage in an investigation. In his experience, fate had a habit of throwing a spanner in the works, even in the most watertight of inquiries.

But Sharma was looking confident, and Cooper didn't want to dampen his enthusiasm.

'Have you spoken to DS Fry at EMSOU?' he asked. 'She's liaison with the Major Crime Unit, isn't she?'

'I tried,' said Sharma. 'But they told me to report directly to the senior investigating officer, DCI Mackenzie.'

Sharma's expression was impassive now. Cooper wondered if his DS knew something he didn't. He probably still had contacts in Derby, or even at headquarters in Ripley. He could ask, but he didn't want to push the issue. It would only cause speculation.

'OK, that's fine,' he said instead. 'Carry on, Dev. You're doing a great job.'

'Thank you.'

Cooper watched him leave, torn between envy at Sharma's confidence in what appeared to be a simple case he could help the MCU tie up and his own irresistible curiosity about what had happened to Faith Matthew on Kinder Scout. He needed to find out some answers for her. It might be hard, but somebody had to try. Nothing ever seemed to come easily.

It seemed to Cooper that he might usefully focus on what had happened *before* that walk on Kinder Scout. Did something occur that resulted in those fatal events? He could take the day before. What did the witness statements have to say about it?

Members of the New Trespassers Walking Club had met at the Roths' house outside Hayfield the night before the walk. Trespass Lodge had a guest annexe with two bedrooms. Darius Roth had stopped the self-catering business run by the previous owners and had kept the accommodation free for his friends. If 'friends' was the right word.

He called in Luke Irvine.

'So who stayed at Trespass Lodge the night before the walk?' said Cooper. 'Not all of them surely?'

Irvine consulted his notebook. 'The two young women shared one of the rooms in the guest annexe. Millie Taylor

133

and Karina Scott. They say Darius didn't want them having to pay for a hotel.'

'That's good of him.'

'Jonathan Matthew took the other room. But then there's the Warburtons.'

'That's the older couple, the ones with the caravan?'

'That's right. They brought their caravan from Didsbury and berthed it at the site off Kinder Road. They were within a couple of minutes' walk of Trespass Lodge.'

'That's quite a cosy grouping,' said Cooper. 'But what about the others? Sophie Pullen and Nick Haslam in particular?'

'They had rooms at a B and B in Hayfield. So did Mr Sharpe.'

'The same B and B?'

'Yes. They use it every year, apparently.'

'Go on.'

'Well, that only leaves the two brothers, the Goulds. They live nearby, though.'

'Oh, do they?'

Irvine flipped a page. 'Chinley.'

'About five miles south.'

'But wait a minute. Nick Haslam – didn't he say he lives in the area too?'

'Er, yes. A place called Strines. I've never heard of it.'

'There isn't much of it to hear about,' said Cooper. 'It's not far from New Mills. I'd say it's no further from Hayfield than the Goulds' place in Chinley. And Miss Pullen works in Buxton but lives in Chapel-en-le-Frith.'

'So?'

'So why did Miss Pullen and Mr Haslam choose to stay in a B and B no more than five miles from where they live?'

'I couldn't say.'

Cooper frowned. 'What really binds such a disparate group together?' he said. 'It clearly isn't an interest in the Kinder Mass Trespass. I get the feeling there's a lot more going on with this group.'

'Swingers?' said Irvine.

'What?'

'Well, it happens. A bit of partner swapping. They tell me it goes on in my village.'

'In Bamford?'

'You'd be surprised.'

'I can't imagine it,' said Cooper. 'Besides, Mr Sharpe is gay, isn't he?'

'He could be bisexual.'

'No, no. It doesn't add up.'

Irvine shrugged. 'Well, it might provide a motive. A bit of old-fashioned jealousy.'

'We'll keep it in mind.'

Carol Villiers put her head round the door.

'I've just spoken to the hospital where Liam Sharpe was admitted. They're discharging him this morning, so I've arranged to go and speak to him at his home in Bramhall.'

'Excellent.'

'Oh, and we've just taken a call from Elsa Roth,' said Villiers. 'She'd like to have a meeting.'

'Who have we got free, Carol?'

'No, she'd like to meet with you, Ben. She says she feels she can talk to you.'

'All right. At their house?'

'No, she wants to see you at the Chestnut Centre. It's not far from Hayfield.'

'I know it. The otter place.'

135

'She didn't say why she chose it. But I imagine she wanted to get away from the house – and from Darius. Don't you?'

Cooper had to acknowledge to himself that he wanted to hear what Elsa Roth might have to say when she was on her own, away from her husband. He hadn't really got a grasp of who she was yet. But then, had he got a clear picture of any of the members of that walking group?

'Let's have a conference this afternoon when I get back,' he said. 'I'd like outlines of every one of these twelve people on my desk and we can go through them all. Use the time between now and then to do a bit of research, find out their background and family connections. Carol, will you co-ordinate that, please?'

'Of course. What do you hope to find, Ben?'

'I'm not sure,' said Cooper. 'But perhaps the answers we're looking for might lie in their history.'

Gavin Murfin eased himself out of his car, careful to avoid scraping the driver's door on the brick wall of the mill. He felt protective towards his little green Skoda. It was his most valuable possession, considering that a building society still had the biggest claim on the ownership of his house.

When he arrived in Manchester, Murfin had driven up Bradford Road and turned in through an arched entrance to reach a cobbled courtyard overlooked by hundreds of windows, with fire-escape ladders snaking up the walls. Brunswick Mill was a massive nineteenth-century survivor from Manchester's cotton-manufacturing heyday. He felt as though he could almost remember those days – though maybe he'd just heard the old folk talking about them when he was a kid.

The mill stood seven storeys high, backing onto the Ashton Canal. Murfin craned his neck to look up at its top floors, where windows were boarded up and tree saplings grew out of the guttering.

He loved a bit of old industrial architecture. Perhaps he had an affinity with it. After all, he was something of an ancient brick monolith himself, designed for a practical purpose that had long since disappeared and now converted into a multi-functional community facility. Dinosaurs never did adapt very well. A meteorite struck, the climate began to change, and that was pretty much that. Extinct before you knew it. Lots of little hairy apes running around instead, ruling the world.

Murfin sighed as he locked his car and brushed the crumbs off his jacket. Recently North Division had been visited by a 'Police Now' officer from the West Midlands who'd been directly recruited as a university graduate and had just finished her two-year training scheme, complete with summer academy, skills sessions and personal development planning. She'd mentioned that she might go on to be an inspector in another two years' time if she opted for the fast-track programme.

That was when Murfin realised he'd made the wrong choice when he decided to work his way up from being a cadet. All that foot-slogging and driving about and picking up drunks from the street on a Saturday night. Getting punched and abused and working killer night shifts. He'd completely wasted all those years getting experience of front-line policing when he should just have gone to university, then sneaked in through the back door and done a personal development plan instead.

It was too late now, of course. At least he'd done his

thirty and got his pension. The trouble was, he'd got bored silly when he didn't have the job any more. He'd been desperate for something to do.

Among the occupants of Brunswick Mill now was a Thai fight club. But a large part of the building had been converted into a series of rehearsal studios, with practice rooms and a central hub where musicians could buy drinks and snacks, as well as leads and strings for their guitars.

Inside, Murfin was directed to one of the practice rooms. A tune he didn't recognise was being played as he entered. Something that sounded as though it came from the 1970s. A man's voice singing over a guitar about riding in the sky.

The room contained a drum kit, microphones and stands, amplifiers and a tangle of leads. There were psychedelic hangings on the wall, and a couch in the corner for when the band became exhausted by arguing. One of the amplifiers stood on something that looked like a giant Rubik's cube.

'Mr Farnley?' he said.

'Yes?'

Robert Farnley was a heavily built man of about seventy with glasses and a few remaining strands of grey hair. He stopped playing and stared when he saw his visitor. Murfin had noticed he had that effect on a lot of people over the years.

'What can I do for you?' said Farnley when Murfin introduced himself.

'Jonathan Matthew,' said Murfin. 'How much do you know about him?'

'Well, he doesn't talk a lot,' said Farnley. 'But he can play.'

'Sounds like the opposite of me.'

Farnley smiled, but with a puzzled frown. Murfin looked around for a chair, then began to ease his backside onto a speaker. Farnley winced as the casing creaked under his weight.

'Here, take my chair,' he said.

'Thanks.'

As Farnley perched on a stool instead, Murfin made himself comfortable.

'Jonathan plays the guitar,' he said.

'No, not really. He plays bass.'

'That's still a guitar to me.'

Farnley picked up a guitar that flashed blindingly in the overhead lights.

'*This* is a guitar,' he said. 'This is a Gretsch Country Classic. It's my favourite guitar. A birthday present from my wife, Margo.'

'Nice,' said Murfin.

'It's more than nice.'

'Of course. It's a classic, like.'

Farnley put the guitar down carefully and patted it as if to apologise for disturbing it in front of such a philistine.

'How long has Jonathan been playing with you?' asked Murfin.

'A few months. He replaced the original guy I had.'

'Why did you want to replace him?'

'No reason in particular,' said Farnley. 'He left, that's all. Bass players come and go. They're attracted to the light, like moths. I'm hoping Jonno will stay around.'

Murfin wasn't very good on accents. He had trouble with Manchester voices and couldn't distinguish Yorkshire from Lancashire. But he'd been listening to Farnley and detected the transatlantic twang.

'I've always been a Mancunian, no matter how much time I spent in Canada,' said Farnley when he asked. 'I was the oldest of four children, brought up in a two-up two-down here in the back streets of Ancoats before we moved to Gorton. My dad bought me my first guitar when I was thirteen. That was the start of my music career.'

'My dad got me a Derby County kit,' said Murfin. 'But they never signed me up to play at Pride Park.'

'I'm sorry?'

'Never mind. Go on.'

Farnley glanced at the wall. There was a photograph of him in action at a gig, sweating at the microphone, wearing a Hawaiian shirt and clutching a red Fender.

'Then I went to Johnny Roadhouse Music on Oxford Road, here in Manchester, and I got my first electric guitar,' he said. 'A Rossetti Lucky Seven cutaway. That must have been about 1960. I remember it so well – it was like a bad copy of a Gibson, seemed to be made of tea-chest plywood. I didn't know any better back then.'

'But you've been in Canada most of your life,' said Murfin.

'Yes, we live in Port Hope.'

'I don't know where that is.'

'On Lake Ontario, east of Toronto. Jonathan was interested in it because it's only thirty miles from a city called Oshawa, which is a popular movie location. He said it was used for making *X-Men* and *It*. And *The Handmaid's Tale*.'

'I suppose I must have seen it on screen, then.'

'Do you watch horror films, Mr Murfin?'

'Only the ones that aren't too scary.'

'Jonathan likes them gory,' said Farnley. 'He talked about a few of them when we had breaks from rehearsal.'

'And so you came back to Manchester,' said Murfin.

'We come back a lot. We came over right after the Manchester Arena bombing in 2017. You know, at the Ariana Grande concert?'

'Oh, aye. Terrible.'

'So while I was here, I decided to set up a new band, and Jonathan Matthew answered an advert for auditions.'

'Apparently he needs money,' said Murfin.

'No, he's got money.'

'Are you sure?'

'So he says.'

'Do you know where he's getting it from?'

'I couldn't say.'

Murfin glanced around the practice room and sniffed. He thought he could smell hippies.

'Where's the rest of the band?' he said.

'We've got rehearsals later in the week,' said Farnley.

'A gig coming up, I heard.'

'You heard right.'

Murfin stroked the neck of a guitar resting on a stand. As Farnley watched, he strummed a finger across the strings. He wasn't sure what chord that was. It definitely wasn't an 'F'.

'What was that song you were playing when I came in?' he said.

'It's called "A Rocket Ride". It's one of my own.'

Murfin sniffed again. 'Right. No wonder I didn't recognise it, like.'

16

Martin Jackson took a drink of tea and leaned back in his chair; Diane Fry had refused anything but water. She felt like a spy being interrogated by her captors, afraid that anything they gave her might be spiked with a truth drug. A ludicrous image, but that was how her mind was working.

'We'll take standards four and nine together, shall we?' said Jackson after a while. '"Use of Force" and "Discreditable Conduct".'

'I will behave in a manner, whether on or off duty, which does not bring discredit on the police service or undermine public confidence in policing,' she responded.

She could see he was surprised now. Fry was quite surprised too that the exact sentence had come into her mind without having to look at the booklet.

'Very good,' he said.

'Are we going to go all the way through the Code of Ethics, or do you have anything specific to put to me?'

He looked at his papers.

'Well, DS Fry, there is a complaint of assault on file. What do you know about that?'

'Geoff Pollitt?' said Fry in shock. 'I didn't think—' Then

she saw the puzzled expression cross his face and she stopped speaking.

'Who is Geoff Pollitt?' he said.

Fry shook her head. 'Sorry. It was nothing. What were you asking me?'

'Are you feeling all right, DS Fry? Would you like to take a break? I'm happy to finish my tea while you compose yourself.'

'I'm fine,' she said. 'Fine. You were saying . . .'

'A complaint of assault. From a fellow police officer.'

'Oh.'

She ran her mind back over the interactions with her colleagues. Some of them hadn't been friendly, it was true. But assault?

'Perhaps I could refresh your memory. An inspector with the Leicestershire force?'

'Leicestershire? But I've never . . .'

And then it came back to her. A memory of a course she'd attended at Sherwood Lodge, the Nottinghamshire Police headquarters, attended by officers from throughout the East Midlands. A session in a nearby pub afterwards. The Seven Mile Inn. She could remember the pub, but the officer's name escaped her. Mick something? Or was it Dick?

'Inspector Rick Shepherd,' said Jackson. 'Do you remember now? His nose was broken in a pub car park.'

'I'd forgotten he was an inspector,' admitted Fry.

'Yes, a senior officer. But it doesn't seem to matter to you, does it?'

'It was self-defence,' said Fry. 'A sexual assault.'

'Really? There's no complaint of that nature on file.'

'I didn't report it.'

'Why not?'

'Sometimes you just have to deal with these things yourself and move on,' said Fry.

Jackson grunted. 'That's not what we encourage, as I'm sure you're aware.'

She shrugged. How could she explain to this man? How could she tell him that she detested the thought of all the fuss and the questions and the paperwork, and the stares and whispers of other officers? She would have done anything to avoid that. But her feeling was hard to put into words. At least, not the kind of words that would make sense in this room.

'I'm sorry I didn't follow procedure,' she said. 'Sometimes it happens.'

'Noted.'

Diane Fry remembered that evening well. She'd been starting to feel suffocated – and not just by the heat, or the airlessness of the conference room. The suffocation went much deeper. It was a slow choking of her spirit, the draining of life from her innermost being. In a few more minutes, she would be brain-dead. Heart-dead, soul-dead, her spirit sapped, her energy levels at zero. It was purgatory.

She'd spent two days in Nottinghamshire Police head-quarters at Sherwood Lodge, watching someone whose name badge she couldn't read sticking Post-it notes on a sheet of brown paper that had been Blu-tacked to the wall. The Post-its were all the colours of the rainbow, which apparently had some significance.

It was called a brown-paper workshop. She was part of the Implementing Strategic Change working group, discussing co-operation between neighbouring forces. Her task after the working-group sessions was to write demand management reports on control-room processes for all five regional forces.

These working-group sessions were supposed to be inter-active. That meant she couldn't entirely escape joining in. At strategic moments, she had found herself blurting out phrases that sounded right. *Methodical workforce modernisa-tion. Greater interoperability.* She tried to say them while other people were shouting out suggestions, so that her words were swallowed in the general verbiage. The best place to hide a tree is in the forest.

She'd been sitting next to an inspector from the Leicestershire force. They'd all had to do ten-second intro-ductions at the start of the session. *Tell us who you are and what you hope to get from today.* Cue a bunch of po-faced lies.

After a lunch the first day, she'd accepted his invitation to go to the pub again when the second day's session finished, without much thought of the consequences. They'd gone to the Seven Mile Inn, close to Sherwood Lodge. Fry knew she mustn't drink and drive, so only one glass of wine would be acceptable. God forbid that she should get breath-alysed by her colleagues on her way back to Derbyshire.

She remembered waiting in the garden of the Seven Mile Inn, checking her phone and seeing she'd missed a call from Angie. There was a voicemail message. *Hi, sis. We haven't talked. We need to talk, you know? Call me.*

'A boyfriend?'

'No, my sister.'

His smile became a smirk, as if he'd just been given some kind of signal. Fry gritted her teeth. Just because the call wasn't from her boyfriend didn't mean she hadn't got one. But that was the way some men's minds worked.

They read an invitation in the slightest thing. She supposed it must be some instinct from their primitive past, sniffing the air to detect the presence of a rival, then mating anything that stood still long enough.

She'd struggled to get her companion's name right, and he'd taken off his badge when they left Sherwood Lodge.

'Rick Shepherd. I'm stationed in Leicester.'

'Of course. I remember.'

Then he was smiling at her again, one eyebrow raised. Some unspoken message was being conveyed. Fry knew what the message was. She ought to respond, knew deep down what she should do. She ought to act, before it went any further.

And yet, a great weariness had come over her. None of it really mattered, did it? Perhaps there might be a moment when she felt something, a brief response that was more than the deadly worthlessness she'd been feeling for the past few weeks. Rick Shepherd wasn't the greatest thing she'd ever met. But he was there, he was available, and she had his attention.

He took another drink, laid a hand on the table, toying with a coaster, seemed to search for a line of conversation. He didn't wear a wedding ring, but that meant nothing. People slipped them on and off like raincoats these days. And many couples chose to live together for years without bothering to marry. He could have a partner back in Leicester. Would he tell her, if she asked? Did she want to know?

But then she recognised in his conversation the exact tenor of complacency and laziness, a lack of concern about accuracy and rigour. Just the sort of qualities she hated.

Fry had finished her drink and stood up. Her companion hastily drained his beer, picked up his jacket and his phone, suddenly eager to leave. They walked back towards the pub car park together and stopped when they reached her Audi. Rick leaned casually on the roof.

'I'm sure we could work closely together, you and me,' he said. 'Don't you think? A bit of mutual assistance, Diane? I know a nice, quiet spot in Sherwood Forest where we could explore our personal merger options. I can promise you I always come up to my performance targets.'

He was standing a bit too close now. Well inside her personal space. Fry felt herself tense. It was that instinctive reaction she couldn't control, an automatic response of her muscles triggered by a suppressed memory. She always knew it would happen. But she couldn't explain the reason for it, not to someone like Rick Shepherd.

He was close enough now for her to smell the beer on his breath, the deodorant clinging to his shirt. Fry was frozen, her limbs so stiff that they hurt. A long moment passed, when neither of them spoke or breathed. Just when it seemed that nothing would happen, he made his move. And Fry felt his hand touching the base of her spine.

It was already dark when Fry drove back into Edendale and turned into Grosvenor Avenue. When she pulled out her key to enter her flat, she noticed that she had streaks of blood on her hands. Strange that she hadn't see it while she was driving back from Nottinghamshire. Her mind must have been on other things.

She'd closed the door, shrugged off her jacket and headed for the shower. Blood on her hands. That was something not everyone could cope with. But right at that moment, it felt good. For her, the sight of blood was exactly the right thing.

*   *   *

Sitting in the interview room at Ripley, it dawned on Diane Fry that Rick Shepherd must have waited. Waited until he realised she wasn't going to make a complaint, perhaps waited until he heard that she was already under investigation. And then he'd put the boot in.

'When was this complaint made?' she asked.

Jackson rustled his papers. 'A month ago.'

'But the incident referred to was – when?'

He couldn't meet her eye. 'Three years previously.'

'Why wasn't *that* reported at the time?'

'Inspector Shepherd's original version of events was that he tripped over a kerb in the pub car park and struck his face on the bonnet of his own car. You were listed as the only witness to the injury.'

'But the inspector has since changed his account for some reason?'

'Yes.'

'I see.'

It was a small moment of satisfaction. The case was weak, and Jackson knew it.

But she was certain of one other thing. He wasn't going to leave it at that.

'And of course we have to present the main issue, DS Fry,' he said.

'Which is?'

'A personal relationship. To be specific, your relationship with Angela Jane Fry.'

Fry felt a sudden sinking sensation in her stomach. 'Angela . . . ?'

'Yes,' said Jackson, smiling again. 'Your sister.'

17

At Slackhall, a small village green lay at a crossroads near the entrance to the Chestnut Centre. The remnants of an ancient chestnut tree looked as though they had been blasted by lightning, three bare, stumpy trunks stripped of bark like broken torsos. Only one side of the tree was still alive, its leaves starting to turn golden in the autumn sun.

At busy times for the wildlife park, there would be cars parked along the roadside all around this junction. But the Chestnut Centre closed at dusk during the winter months, so visitors tended to come early.

Cooper walked past the restaurant and gift shop, and crossed a deer meadow towards the aviaries, with a herd of fallow deer watching him from the hillside. There was a good view of Kinder Scout from here. He wondered if that was why Elsa had chosen it.

Signposts pointed towards polecats, pine martens and Scottish wildcats, or to the badger rehabilitation pen. There were a lot of owls here too. Barn owls, spectacled owls, snowy owls, burrowing owls and a great grey owl. He walked past the pine martens and polecats on the lower trail, sniffing the musky smell of foxes and catching the high-pitched yowl of a wildcat, until he reached the otter pools.

And there she was. He saw Elsa Roth waiting for him by a pen full of European otters, a splash of glistening bodies and inquisitive whiskery faces behind the glass as he approached. Elsa looked as out of place as he'd imagined in her Gucci windbreaker, like a model from a mail-order catalogue.

When she saw him, she pointed away from the otters towards a large cage across the pathway.

'Look, a Eurasian eagle owl,' she said. '*Bubo bubo.*'

'I know.'

Cooper recalled his first sight of an eagle owl. He'd been a child, visiting an agricultural show with his family some-where – probably Bakewell. He wasn't sure how old he would have been at the time, but the owl had stood as tall as him on its perch, and was so striking with its barred wings and ear tufts. Its amazing orange eyes had been staring directly into his, totally unblinking. The young Ben had been mesmerised by the bird, and eventually he had to be dragged away by his mother to look at the exhibits in the produce tent. The way this one gazed back at him so knowingly, it could almost be the same one.

'It says here the females can have a wingspan of more than six feet,' said Elsa. 'That's impressive.'

'Very.'

By unspoken agreement, they began to walk along the bottom path past a series of animal enclosures. Cooper turned to look at Elsa a bit more closely.

'You weren't always a waitress, were you?' he said.

She smiled. 'I was doing the waitressing to earn a bit of money. I wanted to study veterinary science. But it's a five-year course, and it's far too expensive. I was never going to achieve that, no matter how many tips I got from customers.'

'So you married Darius instead.'

'It seemed the best option. I put that ambition behind me.'

Cooper could tell from the distant look in her eyes that she hadn't put it all that far behind her. What a pity that it was an ambition Darius hadn't been willing to finance. He could certainly have afforded it, even if Elsa couldn't.

'Darius and I got married eight years ago,' she said. 'It was funny, actually. We had to postpone the wedding for six months because Darius suffered a burst appendix and was admitted for surgery.'

'Six months? That seems a long time. What hospital was he in?'

'Hospital? Oh, not on the NHS. He has private medical insurance. He went to Meadow Park in Manchester. It was his choice to go there. Treatment at a private hospital was covered by his insurance, and it's the nearest private hospital to where we live.'

Cooper waited for Elsa to get round to the subject of their meeting, but she seemed content to be quiet, a role she'd probably practised during her time with Darius Roth.

'What exactly did you want to talk to me about, Mrs Roth?' he asked eventually.

'Well, I'm not sure if it's important,' she said. 'But I know Darius was concerned about the make-up of the group on this last walk.'

'Oh? Was there something in particular he was concerned about?'

'Well, he hates the idea of illegal drugs.'

151

Cooper stopped in mid-stride near an aviary containing barn owls. 'Drugs? What do you mean?'

'Faith's brother, Jonathan, is an addict of some kind.'

'Are you sure?'

'The signs are all there. And Faith was a nurse.'

'What does that have to do with it?'

'She's worked as a staff nurse in a surgical ward. She knows how to treat wounds, to deal with infections, to control pain. That means she must have had access to prescription medications. Strong painkillers like morphine. Even in the best regulated of hospitals there can be opportunities.'

Cooper was astonished. It was an accusation completely out of the blue. What had prompted Elsa Roth to come forward with this? The quiet woman who preferred to stay in the background and hardly spoke – yet she'd called him here to blurt this out.

'Do you have any evidence for what you're saying?'

'No, none at all.'

'Then it's baseless speculation.'

Elsa brushed back a strand of hair. 'You're right. I'm sorry.' She turned to walk away from the aviary. 'It's just something that's been bothering Darius. He's very sensitive, you know.'

'Really?'

She smiled. 'I know it doesn't always show, but I understand him very well.'

'I'm sure you do, Mrs Roth. You seem extremely close.'

'Oh, we are. So I'm very aware that Darius has a horror of blood and disease. You know, Faith Matthew once told us that among all the patients with gallstones and appendixes and bladder infections on her surgical ward there was one man suffering from necrotising fasciitis. Darius was almost ill when she described it.'

'The so-called flesh-eating disease. It causes the death of the body's soft tissues. Horrible.'

They crossed a series of wooden bridges over a stream. A keeper in a green sweater passed them, riding a vehicle like a converted golf buggy.

'And now Mr Roth seems to be obsessed with the Kinder Mass Trespass,' said Cooper.

'It might seem odd to an outsider,' she said. 'But there are worse things to have as an obsession. It was a significant historical event.'

'Nick Haslam says that the ramblers who took part in the Mass Trespass were all Communists.'

'Oh yes. He never stops telling us that. He knows it infuriates Darius.'

'I don't understand why it would anger your husband.'

'Darius is quite conservative on the quiet. He worships tradition, you know. His grandfather and all those other men who took part in the Mass Trespass have become heroes in his mind. The embodiment of British-bulldog spirit, like the Charge of the Light Brigade or the Welsh Guards at Rorke's Drift.'

Cooper smiled, faintly puzzled. Both of those episodes from British history had been disastrous defeats, surely? Brave perhaps, but ultimately a lost cause.

He wondered if Elsa was mocking her husband's beliefs. If so, did she do that to his face? Was it only Nick Haslam who'd infuriated Darius Roth with his contemptuous references to the original trespassers?

With a sigh, Cooper turned back towards the exit. Supposedly, Elsa Roth had called him because she wanted to talk. But she hadn't told him anything so far, had she? Nothing useful anyway. Apart from the wild allegation against the Matthews, all she'd talked about was her husband. It seemed nothing else mattered to her except Darius.

'I talked to Faith on the Saturday, you know,' said Elsa suddenly. 'The day before the walk.'

'How was she then?'

'She was upset by the note.'

'Note?'

'Didn't you know? She'd had a note a few days before the walk. Some crank letter.'

Again she'd taken him by surprise, made him look at her differently. Was she doing this deliberately? It was as if she was playing a game, toying with him like an otter with a fish.

'What did the note say?'

'Oh, I can't remember exactly,' she said. 'Some kind of threat, I think.'

Cooper bit his lip. A threat? Why was he only finding out about it now? Hadn't Faith's mother known about this, or her brother? It was bizarre that it had been left to Elsa Roth to volunteer information that could be vital to his inquiry.

'Did Faith tell you anything else?'

'That's all I can remember. I hope I've helped.'

He sighed. 'It could be very important.'

'I'm glad.'

Was she really? Cooper couldn't be sure. He hadn't been able to figure out her motive yet. It might be a deliberate distraction, not an effort to help at all.

Cooper said goodbye to Elsa Roth in the car park. She'd

arrived in a Mini convertible in metallic electric blue. Cooper felt sure there was probably a whole selection of other vehicles available for her to use in the range of garages at Trespass Lodge.

When Elsa had gone, he called Carol Villiers and asked her to collect the key for Faith Matthew's house from her mother and meet him there.

'What are we looking for?' she said.

'A threatening note of some kind.'

'Seriously?'

'I think so.'

Cooper could smell hot soup and jacket potatoes from the Chestnut Centre café. He peered through the window of the gift shop at the books and cuddly-toy otters.

As he was about to leave the centre, he heard a noise. A wild creature calling to him from a distance. Cooper turned and looked back but saw only the orange eyes of the eagle owl in the distance. It was staring back at him, totally unblinking.

An hour later, Ben Cooper stood looking around the sitting room of Faith Matthew's house in Hayfield with Carol Villiers. There were no open fires here – not even a log burner, as there might have been in many homes in the Peak District. There was only central heating. Nowhere to dispose of a threatening note by the traditional method of burning it.

'We need to search the bins,' he said.

Cooper checked among the plants and lamps on all the surfaces, opened the drawers of a dresser, pulled out the volumes on a bookshelf, inspected a desk with a laptop computer and printer. Nothing.

'How was Liam Sharpe, Carol?' he said. 'Did you get anything useful from him?'

'No. He was too taken up with himself. Rather over-playing the injured victim, if you ask me. As a result, he's pretty vague about what happened on Kinder that day, apart from his own accident. He seems to have lain there nursing his bruises oblivious to what was going on around him.'

'He must have been aware of Faith Matthew. She stayed with him when the others went off to find help.'

'Yes, he remembers that. And he knows she left him alone at some point. He didn't see anyone else until the search dog found him. That was quite a long while, you know. I got the impression he was starting to panic by then.'

'But thinking only about his own situation.'

'He wasn't concerning himself about what had happened to Faith, anyway.'

'I suppose it's understandable.'

Upstairs, Cooper found the smallest bedroom of Faith's house had been used as a large walk-in wardrobe, with clothes hung from the picture rails and piled on the bed. In the other, a dresser top was scattered with hairbrushes and cosmetics, while a dozen teddy bears and other soft toys were arranged on a chair in the corner. Faith would probably have liked one of those stuffed otters from the Chestnut Centre for her collection.

The bathroom gleamed with white tiles, so that a pink back scrub hanging over the showerhead stood out like a splash of blood.

Villiers had gone straight to the kitchen. It wasn't a big room, with half a dozen oak-fronted units round a built-in oven and a framed Bovril poster on the wall. With a gloved hand, she pulled something out of a stack of bills and bank statements shoved behind a bread bin.

'I think this is it,' she said.

Cooper hurried into the kitchen.

'What does it say?'

'Not much. Take a look.'

She was right. The note was short and to the point, and written in block capitals. It simply read,

FALL DOWN DEAD.

18

Diane Fry stared across the table at her interviewer. The smile had gone from his face now. His eyes were sharp as he waited for her answer. He thought he'd caught her off guard.

'I don't know what you mean by my "relationship",' said Fry. 'Angie is my sister. That seems a pretty straightforward relationship to me.'

Martin Jackson remained impassive, leaning forward with his elbows on the table.

'DS Fry, you do know the rules about the business activities of a police officer's immediate family members?' he said.

'Of course.'

'And you must surely be aware of what "business" your sister has been involved in for a number of years now?'

Fry swallowed. Martin Jackson was an expert in the use of verbal quotation marks. 'Relationship' and now 'business'. His change of tone when he said those words made them sound like accusations of depravity.

'No, I know nothing about that,' she said.

Jackson raised an eyebrow. 'Really? I find that hard to believe. This *is* your sister we're talking about.'

'We lost touch for a long time,' said Fry.

'Ah yes.' Jackson shuffled papers in his file. 'That would be when you were both living with foster parents in . . . Where was it?'

'Warley, in the West Midlands.'

'But you were only teenagers then.'

'Angie ran away from our foster home. It was years before we met again.'

'Would you like to tell us how that came about?'

She frowned at Jackson. 'It involved another police officer,' she said. 'But I suppose you know that already.'

'Detective Inspector Cooper.'

'Ben was only a DC then,' said Fry.

Jackson was alert again, and she realised she'd given something away in her tone.

'It sounds as though it might be a difficult memory,' he said.

'It was a surprise.'

'And not a pleasant one?'

'It was hard, as it turned out. We were very close when we were kids. As I'm sure you know, we were both taken into care as children. I was nine, and Angie was eleven.'

'For your own protection?'

'Social Services said my parents had been abusing my sister. They said it was both of them.'

'So your childhood was spent in foster homes?'

'Yes.'

At first, they'd kept moving on to different places. So many different places that Fry couldn't remember them. It was a few years before she realised that they didn't stay anywhere long because of her sister. Angie was trouble wherever they went. Even the most well-intentioned foster

159

families couldn't cope with her. But Diane had worshipped her sister and refused to be split up from her.

'But you were separated from your sister at some point?'

'When she was sixteen, Angie disappeared from our foster home and never came back.'

The small details were impressed on Fry's mind. The last memory that she had of her sister, Angie unusually excited as she pulled on her jeans to go out that night. There was a boy who was picking her up. She was off to a rave somewhere. Diane had wanted to know where, but Angie had laughed and said it was a secret. Raves were always held in secret locations, otherwise the police would be there first and stop them. But they were doing no harm, just having fun. And Angie had gone out that night, with their foster parents making only a token attempt to find out where she was going. Angie had already been big trouble for them by then and was getting out of hand.

Looking back, Fry knew she had been unable to believe anything bad of Angie then. Every time they'd been moved from one foster home to another, it had been their foster parents' fault, not Angie's.

And when Angie had finally disappeared from her life, the young Diane had been left clutching an idealised image of her, like a final, faded photograph. The memory still brought the same feelings of anger and unresolved pain. Feelings that revolved around Angie.

'But it all fell apart,' said Diane, 'when—' She stopped, wondering exactly how much Jackson knew. He was giving very little back so far. Would he complete her sentence?

'When your sister started using heroin?' he said.

'I was going to say when she ran away from our foster home.'

160

But that was what Fry had been wondering. Jackson knew about the drugs. It suggested he probably knew an awful lot more too.

When he got back to West Street, Ben Cooper smiled with satisfaction to find the outlines on his desk. Carol could always be relied on to get the job done. Not for the first time, he wished that she was his DS. Maybe one day.

He looked at the pile in front of him, wondering who to start with. Which member of the New Trespassers Walking Club might have had a reason to send Faith Matthew that note telling her to 'fall down dead' – and perhaps even a motive to push her to her death on Kinder Scout?

The note itself had been bagged and sent for analysis, but developing fingerprints from a porous surface like paper required processing with chemicals in the lab. They used ninhydrin to react with the amino acids and inorganic salts left in print residue. It would take days to get a result back. In the meantime, he could ask for handwriting samples from all the members of the group for comparison. But that would take time too.

In the absence of any evidence, he had to make a choice. So who should he take first? It had to be Darius Roth, he supposed. He could almost hear Villiers saying that Darius would expect it. OK, then.

Darius Roth
    Mr Roth is aged thirty-five, born in Manchester from a Jewish family, though the last two generations have been non-practising. His great-grandfather originally came from Lithuania and settled in Manchester with his family. He's chairman of Roth Developments, though seems to

be fairly hands-off and leaves the day-to-day running to a management team. There's a large portfolio of properties in Manchester and throughout the North-West, mostly business units and office conversions. The company has invested a lot of money buying up derelict mills and factory premises.

Mr Roth's father died a few years ago, but his mother is still around, living in a retirement village in Cheshire. There was an older brother, Magnus, who was killed in a climbing accident in the Alps.

Darius's interests seem to be fancy cars and golf – he's a member at New Mills and Disley golf clubs. He married Elsa eight years ago. They moved into their property in Hayfield and changed the name to Trespass Lodge. Darius's obsession is with the Kinder Mass Trespass of 1932, in which his grandfather took part.

'Mmm.' Cooper nodded to himself. There must be a lot of people descended from the mass trespassers, like the number of Americans descended from the Pilgrim Fathers. Most of them didn't make a big fuss about it.

He turned to the next sheet.

Elsa Roth

Mrs Roth is aged twenty-seven. Her maiden name is Montgomery. Elsa's family are from Connah's Quay in North Wales, but she came to Manchester when she was eighteen to attend college. She holds a Level 2 Diploma in animal care from Coleg Cambria in Northop. Her ambition was to study for a degree in veterinary medicine at Manchester Metropolitan University, but she never completed her training. She met Darius Roth at a corporate event while she was working part-time as a waitress to earn some extra money to support herself in her studies. They married fairly soon afterwards, and they've been together now for eight years.

Mrs Roth is an animal lover and owns a Maine Coone cat and two pedigree French bulldogs called Buddy and Barkley.

Cooper was struck by the contrast between Darius and Elsa, even in those brief summaries. Wealth and success seemed to have come to Darius without much effort on his part, while Elsa had never achieved her ambitions. Buddy and Barkley were the last traces of her hopes of being a vet – not forgetting the Maine Coone, who didn't seem to have a name. Nor had the cat been evident on Cooper's visit to Trespass Lodge.

Jonathan Matthew

Jonathan is aged twenty-six and is a graphic designer. He works for a large advertising agency based at the Digital World Centre in Salford Quays. He was born in Stockport and educated at Kingsway School and Stockport College. His parents live in Stockport. His father, Jack Matthew, is a partner in a local firm of solicitors, and his mother, Jennifer Matthew, is a charity co-ordinator.

Jonathan rents a flat in Whalley Range, Manchester. He drives a Subaru Impreza but commutes to work in Salford Quays by bus and Metrolink tram.

He's the younger brother by four years of the victim, Faith Matthew. He was close to his sister, but not his parents.

Jonathan plays bass guitar with a band recently set

up, and he hopes to be a full-time musician, an ambition his parents disapprove of.

Cooper read through Jonathan Matthew's summary again. There was something about Jonathan that didn't ring true for him, but he couldn't put his finger on it. Perhaps it was his feeling from these first three summaries that everyone was living behind a façade, or aspiring to be something else.

But here was one he could be sure was different.

Sophie Pullen

Miss Pullen is aged twenty-eight, a teacher at St Anselm's Primary School in Buxton. She teaches year five, preparing pupils for Key Stage 2. She only started teaching there this term. Before that, she worked at a school in Stockport.

Sophie was married briefly when she was twenty-one, but divorced and reverted to her maiden name. After the divorce, she became eligible for a shared-ownership scheme with a housing association and now occupies a two-bedroom semi on a new development off Manchester Road in Chapel-en-le-Frith.

She's local, born in Buxton, where her parents still live. There are two sisters, one older and one younger, both married with families and living in the area. Her mother is also a teacher and works at Lady Manners School in Bakewell. Her father is a GP. Sophie is a volunteer at the Chapel-en-le-Frith Playhouse.

Cooper was surprised that Sophie Pullen had been married previously. But he moved straight on to the next summary.

Nick Haslam

Mr Haslam is aged twenty-nine. He works as an IT consultant with a company based on a business park off the M60 near Manchester. He helps businesses set up IT networks, so he frequently travels around the area. He lives in New Mills, where he shares a house with two other young professionals.

Mr Haslam met Sophie Pullen at a mutual friend's birthday party in Buxton, and they've been in a relationship for about two years. He faced a drink-drive charge a couple of years ago but escaped a disqualification.

So Nick Haslam was the first one of the group who had a criminal record. He didn't come across as the most responsible of people. What did Sophie Pullen see in him?

Well, that was the eternal puzzle, wasn't it? No one could analyse the mysteries of mutual attraction. Often couples seemed to be complete opposites of each other. There was no point trying to figure that out.

The next two had been grouped together.

Sam and Pat Warburton

Mr and Mrs Warburton are both retired, aged sixty-seven and sixty-four respectively. Sam was a firefighter with Greater Manchester Fire and Rescue, and retired as a station officer, while Pat was a care worker for many years in nursing homes. They're from Manchester and live in the quiet suburb of Didsbury.

They spend their time cruising, touring with their caravan and visiting grandchildren. They particularly like Scandinavian cruises – the Norwegian fjords, Icelandic glaciers, etc. They have a son and a daughter. One lives in London, and the other emigrated to Australia. There are several grandchildren. Mr and Mrs Warburton are planning to fly to Australia next year to see the daughter's family. They're keen walkers, but Sam has a history of heart problems. After the incident on Kinder Scout, he was diagnosed with low blood sugar.

Was a connection emerging? Darius Roth and the Warburtons were from Manchester, Elsa had moved there for college, and Jonathan Matthew lived there. But it was hardly significant. Manchester was the nearest big city to that side of the Peak District, a huge urban sprawl. Half of the people who lived in the Hayfield area would have a link to Manchester in one way or another. It was statistically irrelevant.

Theo and Duncan Gould

The Gould brothers are Derbyshire people from a farming family. They run a small-scale plant nursery just outside Chinley. Neither of them has ever married and they have no immediate family. They share an old farmhouse next to the nursery. It's a bit run-down, left to them by their parents, who were farmers. Most of the land was sold off when their father died and their mother went into a nursing home. They kept the land and the buildings they needed to establish the business. They also do a bit of landscape gardening on the side. But it's seasonal work, as is the nursery.

The Goulds have a Land Rover Discovery but turned up for the walk on Sunday in the Renault Trafic van they use for the business. Theo is the elder of the two by a few years. He's fifty-two, and Duncan is forty-eight. Theo has hearing loss, wears a hearing aid.

No story of wealth and success there. If the nursery was small-scale and their landscape gardening seasonal, it was hard to see how they made enough profit for the two of them to live on, even without families to support. It sounded as though the Goulds didn't live a very lavish lifestyle. In fact, their existence sounded a bit precarious.

Liam Sharpe

Mr Sharpe is aged thirty, a check-in supervisor at Manchester Airport. He recently moved into a penthouse apartment in Bramhall, close to the airport. He's in a relationship with a Hungarian chef called Tamás Horváth, who he shares the apartment with.

Mr Sharpe comes from a big Liverpool Irish family, with five siblings, but he doesn't seem to have much contact with any of them as far as we can tell. He's a graduate of Edge Hill University, Liverpool, with a BSc in business management.

Villiers had added a footnote to the reference to Bramhall. It said:

A very upmarket area where a lot of the Manchester United and Manchester City footballers live. Two-bedroom apartments go for upwards of half a million pounds. The rent on this one is two thousand five hundred pounds a month.

The unspoken inference was a question mark over how Liam Sharpe had been able to afford the expensive apartment. Check-in supervisors presumably didn't earn huge salaries. So what about the Hungarian boyfriend? Just because he was a migrant worker from the European Union, it didn't mean he was on the minimum wage or a zero-hours contract. He might be a celebrated chef in charge of the kitchen at a Michelin-starred restaurant, or from a well-off Czech family.

And finally:

Millie Taylor and Karina Scott

Miss Taylor and Miss Scott are both nineteen, students at Manchester Metropolitan University. They're in their second year studying tourism management at the School of Tourism, Hospitality and Events Management on Cavendish Street.

Millie comes from Oldham, and Karina is a Yorkshire girl from Sheffield. They met at university and became close friends. They're living in student accommodation at Daisy Bank. As part of their course, they've been studying the impact of tourism on national parks like the Peak District, hence their interest in Kinder Scout. They've done various part-time jobs working in bars and restaurants to make ends meet. They're very environmentally conscious, support the Green Party, are members of the Manchester Metropolitan Environment and Geography Society, and do volunteer work for Hulme Community Garden Centre. Millie wants to be a chartered environmentalist, and Karina plans to work in sustainable tourism.

And that was the lot. Manchester again, but that was the only evident connection. Besides, Millie Taylor and Karina Scott had the most credible motive for being on

Kinder Scout that day. It was just a pity for them they'd linked up with Darius Roth's walking group.

And yet . . . there was one among them who hadn't linked up with Darius through the walking group or through any interest in the Kinder Trespass. One individual had a link to him that was much more personal.

That interested Cooper. It was like finding the odd one out in a puzzle. And of course, personal feelings were a much more credible motive for a violent crime. If financial and emotional stability were threatened, anyone might lash out to defend their position. Even the quietest of women.

19

Diane Fry waited patiently, watching her interviewer take his time. She had no problem with awkward silences. She used them herself, and had never felt any compulsion to fill the void by blurting out information. If Martin Jackson hoped that was going to work, he was wrong.

'So, your sister,' said Jackson at last. 'She travelled to Sheffield from the West Midlands, didn't she?'

'Apparently.'

'And formed associations that were . . . shall we say . . . undesirable?'

'I don't know anything about those years Angie spent in Sheffield.'

'And you might say that those sorts of associates were inevitable, given her drug habit.'

'I didn't say that.'

'It's very relevant, though, isn't it?'

'Is it? Relevant to what?'

He didn't give her an answer. 'And how much do you know about what your sister has been doing in the mean-time?'

Now it was Fry's turn to interpret her interviewer's tone of voice. There was no doubt from his manner and the sudden tension in his posture that this was a crucial question.

'Not very much,' she said warily.

'Do please share what you can,' he said.

'She turned her life around,' said Fry. 'In fact, my sister was recruited by the National Crime Agency as an informant.'

'We know that. It was why she didn't want to be contacted by you in Sheffield. Your interference might have damaged a major operation by the NCA.'

'I wasn't aware of it at the time,' said Fry. 'I only discovered her involvement with the NCA later.'

'Your sister told you, of course.'

'Yes.'

'She shouldn't have done that.'

'Perhaps not.'

'Did she share any confidential information with you?' asked Jackson.

'No, not at all.'

'Are you sure of that, DS Fry?'

'Yes, absolutely.'

'So did you ever meet a man named Craig Reynolds?'

'I don't know the name.'

'That's not an answer to my question.'

'If I don't recognise the name, I can't tell you whether I've met him,' said Fry.

'As it happens, Craig Reynolds is the father of your nephew, Zack.'

'Oh, him. My sister mentioned him a few times, but I don't believe I ever heard his surname. And no, I never met him.'

Fry waited to be asked whether she'd had suspicions

171

about Craig, but the question didn't come. There would have been only one thing she could say. There were times when it was better not to know.

Over the past months, she'd formed an image in her mind of Angie's boyfriend, Craig, the father of her child. She knew he drove a Renault hatchback and was involved in some kind of business that brought him to Nottingham occasionally. She was sure it was dodgy, probably illegal. But she deliberately hadn't asked.

Then Craig had disappeared suddenly from Angie's life. The next time she arrived at Diane's home in Wilford, Angie was in a new relationship. *His name is Sunil Kumar. Everyone calls him Sonny.* And there was a kind of mother-in-law in the background too, referred to as Manjusha, who didn't mind looking after the baby. Free childcare was a useful extra.

Craig? Angie had said. *I couldn't have left Zack with him for the day, let alone his mother. She's a drunken old slag.*

Fry still didn't know what else was coming from Martin Jackson. But she was aware that not long ago an officer had faced allegations of breaching the Standards of Professional Behaviour in respect of 'honesty and integrity' and 'discreditable conduct' after he was found guilty of three charges of fraud.

So she decided to take the initiative.

'What exactly is it we're here for?' she said. 'Are you looking for a reason to suspend me?'

Jackson sat back in his chair and observed her like an interesting specimen in a zoo.

'As you may know, very few police officers or members of staff are suspended from duty,' he said. 'The force policy is to seek to redeploy officers to low-risk roles instead. Any decision to suspend is made by the DCC and is reviewed monthly.'

'And the tendency is for officers to resign while they're suspended.'

'That's sometimes the case. You should also be aware that if an officer is allowed to resign while suspended, the constabulary provides a reference with the words "Resigned while under investigation". All cases are taken to conclusion, even if an officer has resigned, so that the individual's details can, where appropriate, be included on the College of Policing's Disapproved Officer Register.'

'I understand all that.'

'Interesting. Very few officers have occasion in their careers to even think about the possibility of suspension, let alone look into the consequences.'

'I remember all this from my training,' said Fry.

'So it hasn't been on your mind?'

'Is there a reason why it should have been?'

Again he didn't answer, but turned a page of his notes. Fry began to feel frustrated, as she did in an interview room when a suspect deflected every question with a 'No comment'.

'So let's turn our attention back to your sister,' said Jackson, and her heart sank. 'When exactly did she tell you what she'd been involved in?'

Ben Cooper arrived at the mortuary at Edendale District General Hospital, wondering if Chloe Young could show Darius Roth's theory to be wrong. There must be some evidence, one way or the other, to establish whether Faith Matthew simply fell to her death or was pushed. If there was nothing from the post-mortem, he would be entirely dependent on forensic evidence from the scene.

At work, Young's hair was always tightly wound into a bun, two ponytails tied close together and secured with pins. She was still wearing her green mortuary coverall but had taken off the mask and cap, and was peeling off her gloves as he entered her office.

'Well, it's tricky,' she said. 'There's an extradural haematoma resulting from a skull fracture, which was the immediate cause of death.'

'I'm interested in the position of the injuries on her body,' said Cooper.

'I know. As I suspected at the scene, the victim's injuries are consistent with her falling while her body was twisting to the side. She fell with most of her weight on the right arm and leg, which were underneath her body. There are serious internal injuries, as well as the fracture of the skull, which could have caused her death on its own. But those are grouped on the right side too.'

'And on the left side?'

'The left side of her body is damaged in a relatively minor way,' she said. 'Mostly contusions from the rock, and a break in the left femur.'

'I see.'

'So cause of death is a combination of multiple trauma, internal injuries and the skull fracture. I'm not sure that really helps you.'

'Is it possible she fell in that way?' asked Cooper.

Chloe Young shrugged. 'Well, I'm afraid so. All I can say is that she was turning to the side for some reason. Inconclusive, perhaps. But that's often the way it is, Ben.'

'It's OK.'

Young looked at him with a half-smile. 'What were you hoping for, Ben?'

'To be perfectly honest,' he said, 'I was hoping for something that looks suspicious but isn't conclusive enough to confirm murder and oblige me to call in the Major Crime Unit.'

'Well, that's lucky,' she said. 'Because, as far as I'm concerned, that's exactly what you've got.'

The conversation with her sister was one Diane Fry had been hoping to forget. At her flat in Wilford, she'd shared her yuk sung chicken and vegetarian spring rolls with her unexpected visitor, conscious at first of an unusual awkwardness. Then Angie had sat back and taken a deep breath.

'There's something I should have told you a long time ago,' she'd said. 'About a part of my life I've always kept from you.'

Diane had immediately experienced the sinking feeling in her stomach that her sister was uniquely able to provoke.

'Whatever it is, it doesn't matter.'

But Angie had shaken her head firmly. 'You have to listen, sis. It's too late to do any harm now.'

'Are you sure about that?'

She'd been convinced her sister was about to tell her some shady truths about her previous boyfriend Craig, the father of Zack. But that wasn't what Angie had in mind.

'It goes back a long way,' she'd said, 'to when you first found me – or rather, when your friend Ben first found me.'

'What?'

That had been a painful part of their history. It had changed Diane's life, and not always in a good way.

'You don't need to remind me of that.'

'In all this time, you've never asked me what I was doing in Sheffield,' said Angie. 'I know you wanted to skate over all that and go back to the way things were in Warley. But that just wasn't possible, sis. Not after everything that had happened to me in the meantime. Didn't you ever wonder?'

Of course she'd wondered. Yet Angie was right – it was an aspect of her sister's life that she'd pushed determinedly to the back of her mind. She'd tried to pretend that Angie was the same person she'd lost sight of years ago, even though the truth was staring her in the face.

'It didn't seem important,' she said.

Angie had laughed then. 'Liar. You just didn't want to know, in case it compromised your principles. I kept quiet then, but it had to come out. And there are reasons I have to tell you now.'

The chicken had lost its flavour by that point in the evening. Diane had felt trapped in her own apartment, with no means of escaping whatever her sister was about to inflict on her.

'The fact is,' said Angie, 'I fell in with some very bad people in Sheffield. The worst kind you can imagine. I was an idiot, of course. I was at risk all the time. But then I did something even more dangerous – I got recruited as an informer. That was when Ben Cooper traced me. It almost caused disaster for a major operation the NCA were planning.'

'The NCA?'

'As in the National Crime Agency.'

'I know who they are. Angie—'

But her sister had held up a hand to stop her interrupting. 'I've got to tell you now, Di. Because there's a good chance I'm going to need your help.'

Fry sighed at the memory. Angie was almost her only family, and a police officer's family connections were scrutinised closely. The PSD probably knew all about her.

Jackson hadn't asked about her biological parents, though. Her mother was long since dead, or so she'd been told. Her biological father . . . now he was a different matter. If Martin Jackson didn't know about him, it was significant.

What it signified, Fry couldn't quite work out for now. She would have to puzzle it over later.

20

Cooper brought Carol Villiers, Luke Irvine and Gavin Murfin into his office. There wasn't really enough room for the four of them, and Luke had to bring in an extra chair from the CID room. The room would soon get stuffy. But it was one of those times when Cooper needed to escape all the other distractions and get a clear focus.

'All right, let's examine who we've got in this group,' he said when everyone was settled.

'Well, there are twelve of them,' said Irvine. 'All potential suspects.'

'It's too many. Let's try to whittle them down. Who had the opportunity? What were their movements at the time Faith was killed? And what motives can we dig up?'

'There's the threatening note someone sent to her house,' said Villiers.

'It's gone to the lab to be examined for fingerprints. Not much chance of getting any results back yet.'

'A note, though,' said Irvine. 'Who sends handwritten notes these days? You're much more likely to get trolled on Twitter.'

'It's low-tech,' said Cooper. 'There's a lot to be said for

that. There's no email address, no ISP, no phone number to trace a text back to. Just someone with a black marker pen and a sheet of printer paper. Much harder to trace.'

'A suspect, then?' said Villiers.

'A partner or boyfriend is always the most obvious suspect,' said Irvine.

'But Faith's boyfriend wasn't even there on the walk. Do any of the group know him?' There were blank looks from the team. 'Well, let's find out, then.'

Villiers made a note. 'He's told us he has no interest in the Mass Trespass,' she said. 'Or in Kinder Scout, or even in walking as an activity. That's why he didn't join in with the group. Faith went with her brother instead.'

'We can count the brother out, surely?' said Irvine. 'What motive could Jonathan Matthew have for killing his sister?'

'He'd promised Robert Farnley he could find the money to promote the band. But his parents had turned him down, and when he asked Faith for it, she said no too. That was disastrous for him, likely to destroy all his dreams. Though she might not have realised it at the time. He could have been angry enough.'

'There are always other possibilities too. Things go on in families that we can't imagine from the outside.'

'Jonathan Matthew's statement is with the others,' said Villiers. 'He's no more helpful as a witness than any of the others. As far as we can tell, he seems to have wandered about aimlessly on the moor. It isn't clear that he attached himself to either group when the party split up. No one else's statement refers to him being there after the point when they decided to get help. They all seem to have assumed he was with the other group. But he was brought down by the MRT at the same time, so he must have been in the area.'

Villiers shook her head. 'Not quite. I spoke to Dolly's handler.'

'Dolly?'

'The search and rescue dog. She's a German Shepherd. You'd love her.'

'What did the handler say?'

'That his dog located one walker separately and brought him to the rest of the group. From his description, that was Jonathan Matthew.'

'So Jonathan was alone, and he had the opportunity?'

'It seems so.'

'Bring him in and go over his statement again, Carol,' said Cooper. 'See if you can pin him down on his whereabouts.'

'Okay.'

'Well, even if Jonathan did decide to kill his sister, why would he choose to do it so publicly when he must have had plenty of other opportunities?' argued Irvine.

'Perhaps it wasn't what you'd call a choice. It might have been in the heat of the moment.'

But that didn't sound right to Cooper, even as he was saying it. It wasn't a heat-of-the-moment crime, an impulsive lashing-out by someone blinded with anger. It wasn't like the Danielle Atherton case. Someone had seen an opportunity in the fog and had taken it. They'd planned on having no witnesses.

Cooper turned to Murfin. 'You talked to Jonathan Matthew, Gavin. I expect you've formed your own impressions.'

'He looks like a student to me,' said Murfin. 'Acts like one too.'

180

'You've never had much time for students, have you, Gavin?'

'I never saw the need to go to university myself. And look how well I did.'

Cooper smiled. It was one thing he had in common with Murfin. Sometimes he thought he might be the last of the non-graduates in the police service. But in Gavin Murfin's day it was the norm. A couple of A levels was all you needed back then. In his years with Derbyshire Constabulary, Gavin had seen dozens of younger recruits arrive, waving their degree certificates as they overtook him on the promotion ladder.

'Why would you say Jonathan Matthew was on that Kinder Scout walk? What was his interest? Why was he a member of the New Trespassers Walking Club?'

'He's definitely not the type,' said Murfin. 'According to the reports from the Mountain Rescue guys, he wasn't even dressed right for a hike on the moors. They said he was in the early stages of hypothermia. If Jonathan had been forced to spend the night on Kinder, it's possible he would have been dead too. I don't think he has any interest in the Mass Trespass stuff.'

'So why was he there?'

'Because of his sister,' said Murfin simply. 'He worshipped her. Jonathan didn't talk much about his parents. But Big Sis was really important to him.'

'So he went to please her?'

'Or because he just wanted to spend time with her. Or . . .'

When he hesitated, Cooper looked at him more closely. He'd known Murfin a long time. Despite the flippant exterior, Gavin was always capable of surprising him. His experience could produce insights he might never get from anyone else.

'Yes? Or what, Gavin?'

'Or perhaps because he wanted to protect her,' said Murfin.

'Interesting.'

Murfin shrugged apologetically. 'I don't know why I said that really. It's just an impression, like.'

'No, that's great. Thanks, Gavin. Is there any point in me asking the obvious question, though?'

'Who he wanted to protect his sister from? No. Sorry, Ben, that I couldn't tell you.'

'We can't discount him,' said Cooper. 'So we keep him on the list for now.'

'We can count out the boyfriend,' said Murfin. He glanced at Villiers. 'Sorry.'

'I know. He wasn't with the walking group,' she said.

'Nowhere even near Kinder. He was doing a job.'

'On a Sunday?'

'He had an emergency call-out at a care home in New Mills. A broken circuit. He couldn't leave them without lighting, could he? Not a reputable tradesman like Mr Barrett. And I checked with the care home. He was there for nearly three hours. They gave him a cup of tea and a piece of cake when he'd done the job.'

'When did he find out about what happened to Faith?' asked Cooper.

'Monday morning. He couldn't get any answer from her phone, so he called at her house and found her brother there.'

'Jonathan was at Faith's house in Hayfield?'

'Apparently.'

182

'Greg Barrett and Jonathan Matthew,' said Cooper. 'Do those two get on, Gavin?'

'Now that,' said Murfin, 'is something I'm quite sure about. The answer is no.'

Impatiently, Villiers tapped a form on the pile on Cooper's desk.

'It's hard to see what Darius Roth would gain from this either,' she said. 'He's very possessive of the walking group, talks about them as if they're his family and he's responsible for all of them.'

'I thought you didn't like him, Carol,' said Cooper.

'I don't. He's creepy. But Faith Matthew's death is entirely against his interests, as far as I can see. It's likely to break up the group, and therefore frustrate his obsession with recreating this walk every year.'

'True. So who else is there?'

'Nick Haslam, Sophie Pullen's partner,' she said. 'He's the disruptive one in the group. He has no interest in the history of it, and he tries to turn everything into a joke. That gets up people's noses.'

'But what was his relationship with Faith?'

'We don't know that.'

Cooper sighed. There was going to be a lot of 'Don't know.' There were still a great many questions to ask.

'Dead Woman's Drop,' he said thoughtfully. 'Do you think one of this crowd has a really warped sense of humour?'

'Well, some of them know the area well enough,' said Villiers. 'I bet at least one or two are familiar with the names of the rock formations.'

'Which of them was it who had an OS map in his pocket?'

'Actually two of them. Nick Haslam and Liam Sharpe. But they don't seem to have used them much.'

'And Mr Sharpe was already incapacitated after his fall,' said Villiers.

'There's the older couple, the Warburtons. They're keen walkers.'

'Sam Warburton has a history of heart problems,' said Irvine. 'At the scene, he was diagnosed with low blood sugar. Once glucose was administered, he recovered well. One of the Mountain Rescue team's mobile units took him to hospital later as a precaution, because there were no more ambulances available. But they didn't keep him in. He's back in Hayfield now.'

'In Hayfield? Don't the Warburtons live in Manchester?'

'Yes, but their caravan is still on the campsite outside Hayfield.'

'On the walk, they seem to have been trailing at the back,' pointed out Villiers. 'Besides, they were always together. Practically inseparable. It's hard to imagine one of them creeping up on Faith Matthew from behind.'

'I agree.'

'So that just leaves us with the women.'

Cooper nodded. 'So it does.'

'Elsa Roth and the two students, Millie Taylor and Karina Scott.' She glanced up at Cooper. 'And not forgetting Sophie Pullen.'

'Miss Pullen has been by far our best witness to date,' said Cooper. 'She's very observant. She noticed what everyone was doing – as much as she could, in the circumstances. All the other witness statements look vague and confused compared to hers.'

Villiers looked stubborn. 'But she still can't tell us who killed Faith Matthew,' she said. 'Her statement is useful, but there's no evidence in it that helps us to identify a specific suspect.'

'All right, all right. She stays on the list too.'

'Millie Taylor and Karina Scott seem harmless,' said Irvine. 'They were the most distressed by their experience, and in a state of exhaustion when they were rescued. They don't look capable of planning something like this, let alone carrying it out and covering up their guilt.'

'So if we put the students aside, who's top of our list?' he asked.

He could already work out the answer. It was a process of elimination, as someone else had once said. There seemed to be just one name left.

'Elsa Roth,' said Villiers. 'The quiet ones are often the most dangerous.'

'But wasn't it Elsa who wanted to call the walk off when she saw the fog coming down?' asked Irvine.

'Yes, but she didn't tell us that detail, did she?' pointed out Villiers. 'It's in the statements from a couple of the others. I bet she knew no one would take any notice of her but would carry on with the walk. And she also figured that some of the others would mention it when they were questioned. She had her fellow walkers summed up accurately.'

Villiers turned to Cooper. 'And us too, perhaps,' she said.

Cooper smiled. It was always good to see Carol Villiers thinking in the same direction, even if it was for different reasons. Elsa Roth was the only one on the list who hadn't connected through the walk but had already been with Darius when the others came along one by one. What had she thought as she watched those relationships fostered by her husband, apparent evidence of his need for more approbation, and more loyalty? More love, perhaps.

And Villiers was right. That buttoned-up individual standing in the background was often the one you needed to watch out for.

21

Ben Cooper had asked both the Roths and Sophie Pullen to come into Edendale to make their formal statements. He was particularly interested in talking to Darius and Elsa Roth out of their normal environment. Being in a police station often made people think differently, or decide to tell an alternative story. It was as if the mere suggestion of being a suspect persuaded them to play a different role.

'Elsa Roth's background checks out,' said Carol Villiers as they waited to speak to the Roths.

'So why did she try to cast suspicion on Jonathan? I wonder,' said Cooper.

'And implicate Faith too.'

'Yes. I don't like that, Carol. It smells of victim-blaming.'

The Roths were shown into Cooper's office. Darius perched uncomfortably on a chair as if he found it too small. He gazed around the room, and his eyes seemed to focus on the damp patch in a corner of the ceiling that Cooper had reported weeks ago. Villiers hovered by the door, paying most of her attention to Elsa.

'No, I know nothing about a note,' said Roth when Cooper asked him. 'A threatening note sent to Faith? It's bizarre.'

Cooper didn't find him convincing. Everything about Roth was bizarre, yet when he said the word himself, it seemed to mean nothing.

'We found it at her house,' he said. 'Do you have any idea who might have sent it?'

'None.'

'Or who might have had a reason to threaten her?'

'No again.'

Cooper thought about asking him if he'd met Faith Matthew during his stay at Meadow Park Hospital, but he changed his mind. It would be revealing that Elsa had spoken to him privately.

'How dare anyone do this to one of my group?' said Roth.

'Your group?' said Cooper. 'You know, I still don't quite grasp what unites you as a group.'

'What unites us? We're united by an attraction to the moors, specifically to Kinder Scout. It has a magic that gets into people's souls.'

Cooper could understand that. He'd felt the magic himself. Kinder was a place like no other, a different universe, a world away from life in the city. But that didn't explain what kept the group together, when there was so much to be gained by experiencing the moors alone.

'It's so much safer in a group,' said Roth as if anticipating his question. 'You can easily come to grief on your own, or even with just two of you. Safety in numbers, that's what we always say. Enjoying the experience as a family.'

Cooper nodded. But it hadn't been safe, had it? And the New Trespassers Walking Club were one of the most dysfunctional families he'd ever encountered.

'What you don't understand is that we're not just

188

recreating the Mass Trespass of 1932. We're perpetuating it, moving the principles behind the trespass forward into the future. It's about the rights of the people against the will of a small, powerful minority who rule our lives. That's still happening now, as much as it was in my grandfather's time.'

Roth took a deep breath.

'And it's no longer just landed aristocracy like the Duke of Devonshire,' he said. 'Some of them are large corporations who decide where we can go, and when. Our group is small, but we're here and we're persistent. And we get attention – I make sure of that. It's a warning to all those who like to go back to the 1930s and keep the masses in their place.'

'Forgive me, but you're an odd choice for a working-class hero,' said Cooper.

Roth laughed. 'You know nothing about me. I came up the hard way. As I told you, my great-grandfather Adam worked in a railway yard in Gorton – the Beyer Peacock locomotive factory, which closed in the 1960s. My grandfather, Daniel, took all the overtime he could get in a boiler works until he'd saved enough money to open a small corner shop. My father helped him in the shop until it went bust, forced out of business by the supermarkets. He had to get a job at the Slack & Cox mineral-water factory and put his effort into supporting me, because he wanted us to do all the things he never could.'

Darius had a smooth, persuasive voice. Cooper felt he could listen to that voice all day. But he wouldn't believe a word it said.

'Didn't your family run a textiles business?' he asked.

'The business was a huge gamble, but it paid off because

of the way my father slaved day and night to make it a success. I might look affluent to you, Detective Inspector Cooper, but I'm a working-class boy. I live in Hayfield, but the back streets of Manchester are in my blood. I understand what those boys were trying to achieve when they came here to walk onto Kinder. I live the spirit of the Mass Trespass every day.'

By the time he'd finished, there was a flush in Darius's cheeks and his eyes were alight. Cooper couldn't doubt his passion. In a way, he had sympathy with it. But he was still unsure whether Darius Roth was using that passion in the right way.

Elsa was sitting quietly at his side, letting Darius do all the talking, nodding occasionally.

Her quietness reminded Cooper of Nick Haslam's statement that Elsa had wanted to call the walk off when the fog came in. It was just that nobody took any notice of her. Perhaps Elsa was one suspect he could count out. Someone had taken advantage of the conditions on the Kinder plateau to kill Faith Matthew. If Elsa Roth had wanted to turn back, it suggested she had no such intentions.

But perhaps Villiers had been right. Maybe Elsa knew perfectly well that no one would take any notice of her, because no one ever did. So she'd been safe making the suggestion, in the knowledge that it would be ignored. Was she clever enough to have planned that bluff in advance? Cooper wasn't sure. Elsa had been one of the least forthcoming – or the least talkative, anyway.

And she would have to be very clever, wouldn't she? Because Elsa hadn't volunteered that nugget of information herself when she was interviewed. It would have been the obvious thing to do, if she wanted to make herself appear innocent. But she'd left it up to one of the others to mention it. That made her look like someone who had no doubts about her own innocence and didn't feel she had to justify herself.

Cooper took a deep breath. He looked at Elsa again, remembering what Villiers had said about her earlier. The quiet ones were often the most dangerous. It was harder to tell what they were thinking. He much preferred the suspects who found themselves in the interview room and couldn't wait to spill their guts and tell their whole story. Sometimes they talked and talked and talked, and the difficulty was stopping them. It was as if they felt compelled to fill the silence of the room with all the stuff that was burning and seething inside their heads, waiting to get out.

A person who could keep secrets was rare. But it seemed there was at least one of them among the members of the New Trespassers Walking Club.

Carol Villiers was particularly unimpressed by Darius Roth. 'Darius,' she said after the Roths had left. 'A biblical name, isn't it? It makes me think of all those endless Hebrew family trees in the Old Testament. Adam begat Daniel, who begat David, et cetera.'

'Actually, I think Darius was a Persian king,' said Cooper. 'Not Hebrew at all.'

'Oh, Darius the Great?'

'Yes. He had a vast empire in his day. They say he was ruler of half the world's population.'

'Our Darius's empire is a bit smaller than that.'

'Large or small,' said Cooper, 'all empires fall apart eventually.'

'That's very cryptic. What do you mean?'

'I think we should start examining Darius Roth's business affairs,' said Cooper. 'Let's get Luke on to it.'

'Why? No one has ever mentioned his businesses.'

'That,' said Cooper, 'is exactly why.'

Sophie Pullen looked troubled. Her eyes were tired and dark-rimmed, as if she hadn't slept since the day of Faith Matthew's death.

'Is something bothering you?' asked Cooper.

'Yes,' she said. 'I've been turning it over and over in my mind since Sunday. I think I was near the place where Faith died. It's hard to be certain, of course. But the more I think about it—'

'You were with the Warburtons and the Gould brothers,' said Cooper. 'Did you separate from your party at some point?'

'Only for a short while. I was right behind Sam and Pat Warburton, but I'd stopped to tie my bootlace and the others got ahead of me. I think I headed in the wrong direction for a few yards after that. That's the reason I was there, in that particular spot. I could hear the waterfall and I got worried I was too near the drop. So that's why I think it must have been where Faith fell. I was following someone, you see.'

'Wait a minute. Who were you following?' said Cooper.

'I don't know. I saw someone in a blue jacket. But I soon realised it wasn't Sam or Pat Warburton and I turned back. Then I caught up with the others again.'

'No,' said Cooper. 'It can't have been a blue jacket.'

'What?'

'That doesn't make sense. Perhaps it was someone wearing

a blue scarf that you saw. You couldn't have been sure in the fog.'

'It was a blue jacket,' repeated Sophie firmly.

'Miss Pullen, I've been through the witness statements, the descriptions, the accounts of what everyone was wearing and all the photographs that were taken. Only one person on that walk was wearing a blue jacket – and that was you.'

She shook her head. 'I can't have been mistaken about the colour. Even in the fog. It doesn't confuse you so much that you'd mistake red for blue.'

'No, but it might have been a blue scarf you saw,' said Cooper. 'Or a blue hat, perhaps. Not a blue jacket.'

She raised an eyebrow. 'You *do* think I was mistaken.'

'Mistaken or confused,' he said. 'In the end, it always comes down to a question of interpreting what you see.'

'That's just another way of saying you don't believe me.'

Cooper paused. He was recollecting, as perhaps Sophie Pullen couldn't, that Darius Roth had been wearing a long royal-blue lambswool scarf that day.

'Was there anything else you noticed?' he asked instead.

'Yes, there's one thing I haven't described,' she said. 'But I'm not sure I want to tell you about it now. You'll say I was mistaken about this too.'

'I'm sorry,' said Cooper. 'I don't mean to dismiss anything you say. If you noticed something else, it might be very important.'

She sighed. 'Well, it was the shape of something, shining out of the fog.'

'What do you mean, a shape?'

'I can't explain it. It was like nothing I'd ever seen before.'

'A rock formation,' said Cooper. 'There are many of them on the Kinder plateau. They have weird shapes sometimes.'

'I know. I've seen them. But this . . .'

'What?'

'Well, it was the light. It shone *through* the shape, as if it wasn't entirely solid. I realise I'm not explaining it very well.'

'No, it's fine. Go on.'

'I'm calling it a shape,' she said. 'But actually it was a figure.'

'You mean a human figure?'

'Not really. Well . . . almost.'

Cooper could see she was struggling with her explanation, but he didn't know how to help her. He let her take a few moments to recreate the memory in her mind.

'The figure was huge,' she said. 'I can't explain how big it looked. I was looking down on it and it seemed enormous. It stretched in an odd manner. It was like looking at a three-dimensional shadow, rather than a two-dimensional one, if you can understand that. And there was an arc of multicoloured light round its head, like part of a rainbow. Yes, it seemed to be a shadow, but a shadow of what? I don't know. All I can tell you is that I saw it. I looked at it for a few seconds; then it moved.'

'Moved?'

'Yes, it moved. Shimmered and moved. And then it was gone.'

She looked at Cooper for his reaction. What response could he give to that?

'A trick of the fog,' he said.

Sophie smiled. 'Another one? Odd sounds, now strange shapes. It's as if you think I was having illusions and just imagined it all.'

'Kinder Scout is a strange place,' said Cooper.

He was thinking about the photographs that had been collected from the phones of the walkers. Perhaps he needed to take a second look at them. Sophie Pullen was a good observer. And now he was beginning to get the feeling that there might have been something he had missed.

Sophie was no longer smiling at his tone. Cooper could see that she felt the same about Kinder as he did. She had been there, and she knew exactly how strange it could be.

'I wouldn't go back again, anyway,' she said. 'Next time – if there is a next time – I'd definitely be voting to turn back.'

'Yes,' said Cooper. 'That would probably be wise.'

None of the photographs taken on Kinder Scout were any good. There seemed to be nothing clear or in focus. But it wasn't the fault of the photographers. Cooper could see that they'd been high enough on Kinder to be above cloud level. Mist had been lying deep in the groughs, dense against the wet mounds of peat, swirling slowly in a breeze off the mountain. Everything beyond the first few feet of foreground had faded out, as if a net curtain had been drawn over the view. In each picture, the background was nothing but a grey glimmer, mysterious and menacing.

Walkers were often tempted to continue higher and higher still to see what lay beyond the mist. Sometimes it could be a fatal mistake. Without proper equipment, there was no way of judging direction. What lay before you might be a rock formation, a cliff, a pool of icy water or a plunge into nine feet of grough. Some people couldn't find their way off Kinder Scout without help. A few never found their way off at all.

Cooper looked through the list of photos he'd been given. Many were useless, being vague landscape shots – particularly those from the Gould brothers, who'd seemed more interested in cotton grass and sphagnum moss.

Though every member of the walking club had been carrying a smartphone, none of the photos were from Darius's phone, or from Jonathan Matthew's either. Cooper imagined that Darius would have seen himself as the centre of attention, so would never be on the other side of the lens. But why hadn't Jonathan bothered? Well, perhaps that was the answer. He just wasn't bothered. Jonathan had no interest in his surroundings, or in most of the people he was with. The one exception was his sister, though.

Many of the students' photos showed Darius in his shooting jacket and fedora, often with Elsa close at his elbow in her Gucci windbreaker. Those from Elsa's phone were almost entirely of Darius, some with him grinning at the camera, others more candid shots. It was interesting to observe how his face changed when he was unaware of being photographed. His expression lost that manic energy, the sparkle in the eyes, as well as the beaming smile. Whenever he thought he was unobserved, his look became more serious. In one or two shots, his stare looked lost and desperate. Like an actor, Darius was able to put on an instant public persona when it was needed.

And there was Faith Matthew, of course. She appeared in only two photographs, both from Millie Taylor's phone. In one, Faith was walking near Liam Sharpe as the group made their way onto the Kinder plateau. The rocks along Sandy Heys ridge were visible in the background, so it must have been taken from somewhere near the Downfall.

The second showed her standing alone and pensive on a gritstone boulder while Karina Scott and Darius Roth pulled comic faces in the foreground. The fog had been closing in by then. Faith Matthew seemed like a figure posed dramatically against an artificial backdrop, a stage set lit from within to make it look more menacing.

He pulled out half a dozen shots and held each one to the light from his desk lamp as he studied them closely. These were all taken when the fog was at its thickest on Kinder. Millie and Karina had perhaps thought they could capture the atmosphere in a single digital snap. Instead, everything had washed out in a grey miasma.

He peered more closely at some of the later photographs, in which the fog was thickest. Were there lights in the murk? They might just be reflections from a flash on a phone camera, or an optical illusion caused by the fog itself. The impression meant nothing now, though he could see it might have struck someone on the moor as significant at the time.

Tales about the Devil's Bonfires went back generations. Cooper's own grandmother would have pointed towards Bleaklow and the Bronze Age mound of Torside Castle and Glossop Low and talk about 'the devil's lights' that hovered above the Devil's Elbow. Motorists has sometimes reported lights that looked like distress flares above the moors. One story said the lights were torches carried by phantom legions marching along the Devil's Dyke, a Roman road linking the fort at Glossop with the Hope Valley. Many of the folk tales focused on the Devil's Elbow, a dangerous bend in the Glossop to Woodhead road above Ogden Clough, a boundary between the inhabited valley and the desolate moor.

Even in recent years, strings of moving lights had been mistaken for ramblers lost on the mountain. A Mountain Rescue team had turned out from their base at Glossop on several occasions when lights or flares had been spotted, only to find the lights fade as they approached. Local police no longer passed on reports of mystery lights unless they felt it was a genuine sighting of a distress flare.

In his grandmother's day, these phenomena were put down to devils and witchcraft. Now, it was more likely to be attributed to aliens and UFOs. But the traditional explanation he met with most often was that the lights were mischievous spirits intent on leading travellers astray.

And yes, there were lights in the fog. Cooper could see them himself.

But then he found the most striking photograph of them and realised he was looking at quite a different phenomenon. He sat back in his chair and breathed the name to himself.

'A Brocken spectre,' he said.

Carol Villiers sat across his desk a few minutes later and looked at him as if she'd misheard what he said.

'A what?' she asked.

'You've not heard of it?' said Cooper.

'No, never.'

'It's a perfectly natural phenomenon, but it doesn't occur very often. The conditions have to be just right, so most people have never seen one. It only happens when you're looking down on a bank of mist or cloud in front of you and you have the sun directly behind you. The light projects your shadow through the mist, sometimes in a triangular shape.'

Cooper found himself standing up from his chair and gesturing as he tried to explain how it worked.

'The strange thing is, you can only see your own spectre. If someone is standing right next to you, they can't see yours, just their own.'

'What does it look like?'

'A kind of giant grey creature. They call it "the Big Grey Man" in Scotland. It's an enormous, magnified shadow figure, and the head is surrounded by glowing rings of coloured light. They call it a "glory". The magnification of the shadow is an optical illusion. The figure can even appear to move because of a shift in the cloud layer. It's caused by light refracted through suspended water droplets in the air.'

'A Brocken?'

'A Brocken spectre. The name comes from the Harz Mountains in Germany. The first climber who saw one was so frightened by it that he fell to his death. He was killed by his own shadow, Carol.'

22

When Diane Fry finally called Cooper back, it was to ask him for his help. She wanted him to do her a favour.

'What?' he said in astonishment.

'A favour,' she repeated slowly, as if she was talking to an idiot.

Cooper recalled the last occasion Diane Fry had asked him for a favour. The time she'd gone back to Birmingham to confront an incident from her past. For some reason, she hadn't felt able to trust her former colleagues from West Midlands Police. Had that all come round again? Had something she'd done in Birmingham rebounded on her? If so, it was hard to see how he could help her.

But he'd agreed to meet her, and she'd volunteered to come to Edendale instead of making him travel to Nottingham. That made him even more suspicious. She was obviously trying to soften him up. She'd be offering to pay for the drinks next.

They arranged to meet at the Wheatsheaf pub off Market Square. Across the road was Stone Bottom, the yard where the Way of the Eagle Martial Arts Centre had once occupied the basement of an old warehouse at the end of Bargate, the other three floors being filled with craft workshops, software developers, a small-scale publisher of countryside books and an employment agency. The steps down to the dojo were always bathed in the smell of freshly baked bread from the ventilators in the back wall of the baker's in Hollowgate.

It seemed a century ago that he and Diane Fry had gone there together. He'd tried to be friends with her then, when she first came to E Division. Something had gone wrong along the way, and he still wasn't quite sure what.

Cooper had a flash of recollection, back to the conversation he was having with Fry as they arrived at the dojo that day and parked their cars in the middle of an area of mud-filled potholes, with the sound of dull thumps and hoarse screams filtering through the steel grilles of the warehouse windows and that scent of baking bread.

The buildings were clustered so close together in Stone Bottom that they seemed grotesquely out of proportion from ground level as they leaned towards each other, dark and shadowy against the sky, set with long, blank rows of tiny windows. The slamming of car doors had echoed loudly against the walls and reverberated down the stone setts to the narrow bridge over the River Eden.

He and Fry had been talking about the possible motives for murder in an inquiry they were involved in, the case of a teenage girl found dead in woods outside Edendale.

'You make people sound really complicated,' she'd said. 'In my experience, their motivations are usually very simple and boring.'

'Motivations like ambition and greed?' he'd replied. 'The old favourites? They can certainly make people ruthless and selfish, can't they?'

'And sex, of course,' she said.

'But sex isn't so simple either, is it?'

'For some of us, it's very simple, I can assure you.'

The craft workshops and software developers were still there on the upper floors of the warehouse, along with an interior designer and a photographic studio. But the martial arts centre had gone now, and so had the employment agency and the publisher.

For a moment, Cooper wondered what had happened to his old flat in Welbeck Street. He hadn't driven past it for a while. The house had passed to his landlady's nephew when she died, and he'd been planning to sell both of the houses she owned. Property didn't stay on the market for long in Edendale, especially the smaller terraced houses. He was pretty sure both of them would have been snapped up and converted into family homes.

But he was happy about that. He felt no nostalgia about that first-floor flat, though it had been the first home of his own when he moved out of Bridge End Farm. Number 8 Welbeck Street had been an important part of his life for a while, but it was gone now.

Diane Fry arrived quietly. Cooper didn't notice her until she was standing over his table and putting an arm on his shoulder to make him jump. She'd never lost the ability to creep up on him like that. He wondered if she found it funny. It was hard to tell when she so rarely smiled.

'Ben,' she said simply.

'You'd better sit down. Do you want a drink?'

She held up a glass. 'I've got one.'

'So you have.'

He wondered how long she'd actually been in the pub, whether she'd been watching him from some corner while he reminisced about the past, probably baffled at his ability to be content with own company.

'Sit down, then. Tell me what it's all about.'

Fry explained what was happening to her, and he listened in silence, studying the way her demeanour changed. Behind the façade, she was genuinely worried.

'I haven't had much experience with Professional Standards,' said Cooper, when she'd finished.

'No, of course you haven't,' began Fry. 'You—' Then she stopped. Whatever she'd been about to say, she'd had second thoughts.

Cooper watched her curiously. She had never before been so reticent about saying exactly what she thought, even if it was rude or ill-mannered. Now something was different. It was as if she was worried about rubbing him up the wrong way. That made him feel more concerned about her than if she'd come here for another argument.

'So that's why I haven't been able to get hold of you,' he said.

'You've been trying to get hold of me? Why?'

'Oh, nothing important.'

'Good, because I've been a bit busy, as I just said.'

'It can't be anything too serious,' said Cooper. 'I know people make misjudgements now and then. They have unfortunate incidents. Remember when a drunk's finger was severed while he was being transferred into a caged van?'

'Officers were observing standard procedure with a non-compliant prisoner,' said Fry.

'Of course they were. But the guy still lost a finger.'

She took another drink and eyed the rest of the customers in the pub. It was still early in the evening, but it would get busy later. The empty tables would soon fill up.

Fry put her glass down with a thump.

'People talk,' she said enigmatically.

'Surely they can't believe everything they hear.'

'In my case, they probably do.'

'What makes you think that?'

'They want me to go for a psychological evaluation,' said Fry.

'A what?'

'You heard me. They want an assessment of my emotional and mental stability.'

'That's ridiculous,' said Cooper.

'Is it? I'm not so sure.'

For the first time since he'd known her, Cooper saw self-doubt in Diane Fry's eyes. Had she doubted her own stability all this time? He could sympathise with that. He'd gone through periods in his life when he felt he was out of control, or only just holding things together on the surface. Had the Diane he'd known only been on the surface all along? Was there so much more underneath that he'd never suspected?

But the moment passed. Fry took a ragged breath, and her posture changed as the old veneer of confidence returned.

'It's rubbish, of course,' she said.

'I'm glad to hear it.'

'But there are, you know . . . some incidents in my past.'

Cooper frowned. 'Nothing that they could make a case out of for gross misconduct. That's what you're worried about, isn't it?'

'Losing my job? Yes, that scares me stiff.'

'So why have you come to me?' asked Cooper.

'I need help,' said Fry simply. 'And I didn't know who else I could trust.'

'Trust hasn't always been what we had between us, Diane.'

'No, you're right. But still . . . when it comes down to it, you're the only one.'

Cooper fidgeted uncomfortably in his chair, while she watched him expectantly. She wanted an answer, but he didn't know what to say. When it involved Diane Fry, he'd rarely known what the right thing was to say.

'What exactly is it you want me to do?' he said.

'You know people,' she said. 'You've been in Derbyshire, like . . . for ever. I've always been an outsider, I know that. I bet people tell you things they would never share with me.'

'You're talking about internal organisational stuff.'

'Obviously. I need to know what's going on, who's been telling tales about me.'

'It must be someone you've worked with,' said Cooper. 'What about DC Callaghan?'

'I've thought about him. But there was one incident just recently . . .'

'What was that?'

'I shouldn't tell you. But internally, only Jamie Callaghan was aware of it.'

'So?'

'The PSD haven't mentioned it,' she said.

'So you don't think they know about it?' said Cooper. 'Whatever it was.'

'Not so far.'

Cooper stared at Fry.

'I'm still puzzled,' he said. 'What do they really want from you?'

'I don't know,' said Fry. 'I don't even know where this is all coming from, so it's hard to tell.'

'Could it be somebody in the West Midlands?'

'Setting me up, you mean?'

'I just wondered if you had information that might, well . . . compromise someone.'

Fry gave a sardonic laugh. 'Undoubtedly. How could I not have, during the course of my career here and in Birmingham? But where do I start?'

'Birmingham,' said Cooper, 'sounds like the ideal place to start.'

'I suppose so.'

'Well, go on, then. I know nothing about your time in the West Midlands.'

'There was a DI in Birmingham. Gareth Blake. We worked together in Aston years ago. He was supposed to be investigating my assault case.'

'Your case?' said Cooper. He hesitated. 'Oh, you mean *your* case. The . . .' He dried up, too uncomfortable to say it out loud.

'Yes, the rape,' said Fry. 'Blake was assigned to cold-case rape inquiries.' She jerked her head dismissively. 'Cold case? It didn't seem so cold to me.'

'I suppose not,' said Cooper. 'Though it was a long time ago.'

He knew he'd said the wrong thing. But what was there he could say that would sound right? Probably nothing. Fry had told him about her rape years ago, when she'd first transferred to Derbyshire and they found themselves working closely together. It had been an act of unusual openness on her part, which he'd never known how to respond to.

Fry gazed at him stonily, as if his reaction was no more than she expected. She would probably have given him a withering put-down. But for once she couldn't. She'd come to ask him for a favour.

Cooper remembered Fry being called back to Birmingham when the investigation into her rape was reopened. A DNA hit had presented new evidence, and she'd become the subject of a cold-case inquiry, referred to constantly as 'the victim'. How she must have hated that.

And he recalled that Fry had asked him for help then too. Was that connection what had made her come to him again?

'OK, so DI Blake was in charge of investigating your cold case. But didn't it fall through in the end?' he said.

'They lost a vital witness,' said Fry.

'And you did some investigating of your own.'

'Thank you for calling it investigating. Sometimes it seems more like digging through dirt. The whole thing was fishy from the start – a DNA hit they didn't tell me the real meaning of, a witness who changed her mind about testifying. And you do know who was at the centre of it all?'

'Yes,' said Cooper. 'Your—'

'No,' she interrupted. 'Just a corrupt lawyer.'

'William Leeson. Of course I remember.'

Cooper didn't know what else she'd done on that visit to Birmingham, apart from enlisting his assistance to get access to the dodgy solicitor, who turned out to be a major part of her past. He hadn't asked her too many questions, and he wasn't about to do so now.

'In reality, Blake and his partner were keeping tabs on me,' said Fry. 'It must have been them. They knew that I'd met with my colleague Andy Kewley before he died. Kewley was going to give me some information I needed, something that would have helped me find out what went wrong.'

'The PSD can't possibly think that you had anything to do with his death,' said Cooper.

'I don't really know what they think,' said Fry. 'They might just be throwing it all out in a fishing expedition, hoping one item will stick or I'll give something away inadvertently.'

'You mean they want you to incriminate yourself.'

'It looks that way.'

'That's not acceptable, Diane. You really should have someone with you in these interviews.'

'I've told you, I don't want that.'

'Well, be careful.'

She took a long drink, and Cooper waited. Sometimes, he felt it was what he did best.

'It's Angie,' said Fry finally. 'She seems to be the main problem.'

'Ah.'

'I've never really asked you,' said Fry. 'I mean, going back to that time when you first made contact with her.'

'No,' said Cooper. 'To be accurate, she made contact with me. I didn't want anything to do with it. It was your business. But Angie turned up at my flat one day. She told me she wanted you to stop trying to find her.'

'But you did the opposite,' said Fry. 'You fixed up a meeting. You put us back in touch with each other.'

Cooper shrugged. 'It seemed simpler than trying to stop

you looking. I don't know she expected me to do that. I never had so much influence over you.'

'What did you know about what she was doing in Sheffield?'

'Not much. I do know she was picked up by someone in a BMW with a blocked registration.'

'So you suspected.'

'It wasn't my business,' said Cooper.

'Oh, but you made it your business, didn't you?'

Cooper held out his hands. 'I was just trying to help, Diane.'

'Well, help me now.'

'What is it you want from me?'

'Just for you to be there if I need you. Someone to back me up, and give me a bit of support. And if you can use any contacts . . . well, I'd be grateful.'

He could see it was hard for her to ask. Forget that she'd made things difficult for him so often over the years. It wasn't relevant now. And it wasn't in his nature to refuse to help.

'I'll do what I can,' he said.

She breathed a sigh of relief. 'Thank you.'

They walked back out into Market Square. Fry's black Audi stood just a couple of spaces away from Cooper's Toyota, its deep red paintwork standing out among all the greys and silvers of the other vehicles.

Cooper looked at the empty spaces between their two cars. Had they been empty when Fry arrived? Did she deliberately leave that space, rather than park right next to him? It was such a small thing, yet it seemed to symbolise something about their relationship.

'Diane,' he said. 'Just one thing.'

'Yes?'

'You're not taking anything, are you?'

She stared at him. 'What?'

'Well, it happens,' he said. 'A lot of police officers . . . they can't cope with the stress day by day without a little bit of artificial support.'

'You think I'm on drugs? What, cocaine? You're suggesting I might snort a few lines of coke before I go to work in the morning?'

'No. But . . . well, there *is* the matter of your sister.'

Fry took a deep breath and seemed to calm herself down with an effort.

'You're right, Ben. Yes, you're right. Absolutely spot on. I bet that's exactly what the PSD are thinking. That's why you said it, isn't it? To make me think of the worst-case scenario. They've latched on to Angie connections and they think I will have been contaminated. That's why they're putting me through this process. They want me to reveal myself to be a junkie. A cokehead. A cocaine-sniffing cop. Jesus wept.'

'Your behaviour can be a bit . . . unpredictable.'

'I see we're going for the full-frontal honesty tonight,' she said.

'Well, if you want my help, it's best to have these things out in the open.'

She breathed quietly for a moment, and he was reassured when she refused to turn away but continued to meet his eyes.

'I'm not taking anything,' she said. 'Does that satisfy you?'

'Yes,' said Cooper.

'You believe me?'

'Absolutely.'

The tension dropped away. Fry even managed a smile.

'Have you been wondering about it all this time?'

'Not really,' said Cooper. 'Besides, it's not something you can go ahead and ask.'

'But you just did.'

'This is different.'

A group of young men passed them, talking loudly as they headed for the pubs around Market Square. Fry unlocked her car and paused with her hand on the door.

'Ben,' she said.

He turned. 'Yes?'

'You know this could get you into trouble, don't you?'

Cooper looked at her for a moment, saw in that one second everything he'd gone through with her, the times she'd been a thorn in his side and the occasions when she'd saved his life, or saved him from himself.

'You've always caused me trouble, Diane,' he said. 'But you know that, don't you?'

23

Wednesday

Detective Superintendent Branagh was based at North Division headquarters in Chesterfield now. Since Edendale was relegated to a Local Policing Unit, most of Ben Cooper's direct access to his boss was limited to phone calls.

It took a couple of attempts before he could get through to her that morning. Meetings, he supposed. One of the penalties of rank.

'This death on Kinder Scout,' she said when he was able to get through. 'Is it a murder inquiry, DI Cooper, or a suspicious death?'

Cooper hesitated. 'We're not entirely sure, ma'am. The post-mortem results are inconclusive.'

'Well, if and when you *are* sure, it'll have to be passed to the Major Crime Unit to lead the inquiry.'

'I don't think that's necessary.'

'We'll make sure you're involved. But there has to be a qualified SIO in a murder case – you know that.'

'Of course,' said Cooper. 'I'll keep everyone informed. But there's something I wanted to ask you.'

'Yes?'

'Do you know what's happening with regard to DS Fry? I understand there's an internal investigation under way.'

'There isn't much I can say about it, I'm afraid. The Professional Standards Department are handling it. They do things in their own fashion. Why does it concern you, Ben? I know you've worked with her, but—'

'I was wondering how serious it is, that's all.'

'I'm not privy to the details at this stage. In fact, I'm not sure they'll include me, even if it comes to a case conference. I'm not currently DS Fry's divisional commander.'

'No, I understand.'

'I'm sorry I can't help any more than that,' said Branagh. 'I shouldn't say this, Ben, but you could probably find out more by unofficial means.'

'I'll bear that in mind,' said Cooper. 'Thank you, ma'am.'

When Cooper had finished the call, he reflected for a moment that he was glad Detective Superintendent Branagh hadn't asked more about Faith Matthew's death. He was reluctant to let it go, and it was an advantage to have an inconclusive post-mortem result. Branagh had probably realised that. She'd covered herself but allowed him some rope. He hoped he wasn't about to hang himself with it.

Then Dev Sharma knocked on his office door. He didn't look happy.

'Ben, we've got a problem with the Atherton inquiry,' said Sharma. 'The files have been flagged up with a query.'

Cooper looked at him in surprise. 'A query from the CPS or from EMSOU?'

'Major Crime Unit have kicked some of the statements back to us. They say they're contradictory.'

'What's wrong? I thought it was an open-and-shut case.'

'Apparently not.'

'Show me what you've got again, Dev.'

'Well, the statement that causes the problem is from the

next-door neighbour. She says she saw Gary Atherton arriving home at ten thirty-eight a.m. She was sure of the time because she was waiting for a taxi to take her for a hospital appointment and it was due at ten thirty-five. She heard Mr Atherton's car pull up and thought it was the taxi, so she looked at her watch. It was ten thirty-eight.'

'And?'

'The 999 call was recorded at ten thirty-two.'

'From a mobile phone.'

'Yes. But its location was shown as the Athertons' address. The call was made from that house. And it was Mrs Atherton's phone, not her husband's. His own phone was still in his pocket when he was detained.'

'You're telling me someone else made the call, claiming to be Gary Atherton?'

'That appears to be what the evidence suggests. The CPS would say it's enough to weaken the prosecution case.'

'Who took the statement from the neighbour?' asked Cooper.

'Luke Irvine.'

'Send Becky Hurst to talk to her again. No pressure. Just let her explain it all again. She must have got something wrong.'

Sharma looked dubious. 'We could extend our door-to-door inquiries. Talk to more neighbours. They might have a different account.'

'Yes, you're right, Dev. Do that too.'

'All right.'

'And can you send DC Villiers in, please?'

Sharma disappeared, and Carol Villiers came in a few moments later.

'Dev is panicking a bit,' she said.

214

'He'll be OK. He just needs to get through this. He thought he had it all tied up, but something always catches you out. DS Sharma will be able to deal with it.'

'Isn't it a bit of a risk giving him so much responsibility?' said Villiers.

Cooper shook his head. 'It's what he's here for. Trust me.'

'So what have you got for me?'

'Here's a nugget from Darius Roth's past history,' said Cooper. 'According to his wife, he suffered appendicitis eight years ago. He was admitted to a private hospital, presumably for an appendectomy.'

'Was he in Meadow Park Hospital, by any chance?'

'Right. Can you find out if Faith Matthew was employed there at the time? And whether she worked on the same ward? I'm looking for alternative connections between these people.'

'I'll try, Ben, but you know—'

'Yes. Medical practitioners are notoriously difficult to get information out of, and not just about their patients.'

Villiers placed an interview report on his desk.

'What's this?'

'I talked to Jonathan Matthew again first thing this morning and went over his statement in detail,' she said. 'He's no clearer about where he was on Kinder Scout – except lost. He's insistent that he never saw his sister after the party split up. He says he kept his distance from both groups because he thought they were being foolhardy.'

'He had a point,' said Cooper. 'But he's managed to draw suspicion on himself nevertheless.'

Cooper had decided to talk to Sam and Pat Warburton together. He saw no reason to separate them. They didn't feature high on his list of potential suspects, and if they'd wanted to come up with a consistent story together, they'd already been given plenty of time to do it.

Their caravan was still parked up at the Hayfield campsite. The site was quiet in October and Cooper soon found the Warburtons' pitch. They had a brand-new Swift Conqueror 630, with four berths and a toilet and shower room at the end. It was nearly eight metres long, and inside it was furnished better than many homes he'd been into in Edendale. Parked alongside it was a Nissan X-Trail in vivid yellow.

'I'm surprised to find you still here,' said Cooper when he was sitting in the caravan with a mug of tea. 'I thought you might have gone back to Manchester.'

'The pitch was booked for a week, and paid for,' said Sam Warburton. 'So we thought we might as well make use of it. There are lots of things to do around here, and places for us to go. We like living in Didsbury, but the Peak District is special to us.'

'And life doesn't stop, does it?' said Pat. 'The rest of us have to carry on.'

The couple were still dressed as if they were about to go for a walk at any moment. Cooper could see their boots and hiking poles standing in an open cupboard, along with their waterproofs.

'When did you arrive in Hayfield?' he asked.

'On Saturday morning,' said Sam. 'The day before the walk.'

So the Warburtons had been there for the whole weekend. Was that a detail missed in the initial statements?

'What did you do on Saturday?' he asked.

'We visited Castleton.'

'After lunch at the No Car Café at Rushup,' added Pat. 'I know it,' said Cooper.

Pat Warburton explained that they liked it at the No Car Café because you couldn't get to it by road, though there were facilities for washing your bike or tying up your horse. Drivers had to park in the layby on Sheffield Road and walk five hundred metres down to the café. It created the feeling of remoteness they liked.

Cooper nodded. 'So you weren't in Hayfield at all?'

'Not during the day,' said Sam. 'We got the caravan on site, then unhitched the car and went off for lunch.'

'What about in the evening? I imagine you might have met up with some of the other walking-club members?'

Sam Warburton glanced at his wife. It seemed this was a subject they didn't like talking about quite so much. Pat fiddled with her glasses, as if they were uncomfortable on her face.

'We called on Darius and Elsa,' she said in the end. 'We had a bit of supper with them at their house.'

'Was anyone else there?'

'The two girls, Millie and Karina. They were staying at Trespass Lodge.'

'And there was Jonathan,' said Sam. 'Faith's brother.'

'A strange young man,' said Pat with pursed lips.

'Was he staying there too?'

'Apparently. It was very good of Darius to put him up at the lodge. None of us know him very well.'

'And he was very quiet,' said Sam. 'Hardly said a word all through supper. The girls didn't like him. They thought he was a bit creepy.'

'Did they tell you that?'

'They told me,' said Pat. 'They mentioned it as we were leaving.'

'But it was just because he was so quiet,' said Sam. 'He came over as rather sullen.'

'And no one else was there?' asked Cooper.

'No. We met the rest next morning.'

At least that was consistent with the statements made by Millie Taylor and Karina Scott, as well as Jonathan Matthew. A cosy gathering at the Roths' house the night before the walk. Jonathan seemed like the odd one out, though. Was it really just a generous gesture of Darius Roth's to offer him accommodation at Trespass Lodge?

'There was nothing very exciting about the conversation,' said Pat, as if anticipating Cooper's next question. 'It was just small talk, catching up on what people had been doing. You know the sort of thing. Millie and Karina talked a lot about their courses at MMU. They're studying tourism management. Millie mentioned a subject called "Tomorrow's Tourist".'

'And Darius?'

'Darius? He's a very good listener.'

'And that was all you did, just ate supper?'

'And had a few drinks,' said Sam. 'Since no one was driving, you understand.'

'We were very restrained,' said Pat.

'I thought there might have been some kind of meeting of the club that night,' said Cooper.

'What, like an AGM?' said Sam with a laugh. 'It's not that kind of club. We don't elect officials and vote on resolutions. It's all very informal.'

'I see.'

Cooper switched the subject and asked the Warburtons

how they'd become part of the New Trespassers Walking Club, and when they'd met the other members of the group.

'We just latched on somehow,' said Pat Warburton. 'They seemed like a nice bunch. How was it we met them, Sam?'

'It was on an official guided walk with the Peak Park rangers,' said her husband.

'Oh, that's right.'

'We did the walk on the anniversary of the Mass Trespass one year. Mind you, it wasn't this group we met.'

'It wasn't this group?' repeated Cooper, puzzled. 'What do you mean?'

'It was quite a different set-up back then. The Roths were there from the beginning, of course. Darius and Elsa. But the rest of the group has changed. Faith and her brother weren't part of the club at that time, for a start. Nor Sophie and Nick, or the students.'

'Or the young man who works at the airport,' said Pat.

'Liam. No, he wasn't there either.'

'How long ago was this exactly?' asked Cooper.

'When we joined up with the group? About six years, I suppose. Is that right, Sam?'

'I reckon so. It was a different time of year too, though. April, because it was on the anniversary of the Trespass.'

'So members of the club come and go,' said Cooper. 'I thought it was a more stable group than that.'

Sam Warburton laughed suddenly, and Cooper looked at him more closely. What had caused that reaction? Was it the word 'stable'?

'No, almost all of the present members came along after us,' said Pat, frowning at her husband.

Cooper mentally ran through the list of names in his head.

'So, apart from the Roths themselves, the only people

219

who were part of the group then and still are now would be . . . ?'

'The Gould brothers,' said Pat. 'Theo and Duncan.'

Her husband smiled. 'Very interested in the natural landscape, they are. There's more to Kinder than just the Mass Trespass, you know.'

'Have you kept in touch with any of those previous members? Do you know how we could get hold of any of them?'

The couple looked at each other.

'Why, of course not,' said Pat. 'What use would that be to you? They weren't there with us on Kinder.'

'We're just trying to cover all the angles,' said Cooper. 'If you think of anything that would help us get in contact with them, please let us know. Such as where they lived or where they worked, for example. Anything you remember might be useful.'

'All right. But people come and go, like you say. We don't always know very much about them.'

'I understand.'

'We'll be dropping out ourselves soon,' said Sam Warburton. 'Even without this tragedy, it would have been time.'

'Oh? Why?'

'We're getting a bit old for it.'

'Well, *he* is,' put in Pat, pointing at her husband.

'Getting up onto Kinder,' he continued, 'that's a young people's game, isn't it? It's a long haul from the car park at Bowden Bridge. Some of the going gets a bit rough, and the track is steep. Even that first bit up White Brow nearly kills me now. It's the knees, you know.'

'He's all right once we're up the plateau,' said Pat. 'But

getting him up there is a different matter. I told him we'd have to get a helicopter to winch him up next time. They could drop him in with the sacks of seed at the restoration project.'

Sam smiled. 'There comes a point,' he said, 'when you just can't do it any more and there's no use pretending any longer. You stop putting on a front and admit it. You have to throw in the towel. So this would have been our last trip anyway, I think.'

'Things haven't always gone smoothly for us, to be honest,' said Pat. 'We had some problems with pension funds. We withdrew a large lump sum and invested it unwisely.'

'I'm sorry to hear that.'

'We got over it.'

'You get over everything, one way or another,' said Sam.

Cooper stood up to leave. Pat was fiddling with her glasses again, sliding them back on her nose, as if to help her see more clearly.

'Previous members,' she said suddenly. 'There's only one I remember.'

Sam stared at her. 'Really?'

Cooper noted the look exchanged between them. A hint of rebellion in Pat Warburton's eyes? Sam might have preferred her not to speak, but she was taking no notice.

'What was their name?' asked Cooper quickly.

'Eavis. That was it. Julie Eavis. I think she spelled her name with an "a" in the middle.'

'Yes, she did,' agreed Sam.

He knew when he'd lost at least. Sam must be able to see the same stubbornness on his wife's face that Cooper could.

'Do you have any idea how I can get hold of her?'

'Not really.'

'Where does she live?'

They looked at each other again, an unspoken agreement this time.

'Buxton,' said Sam. 'That's all we know. But it's quite an unusual name. She shouldn't be too difficult for you to find.'

'I hope not,' said Cooper. 'But it rarely works out that way.'

As he left the site, Cooper looked back at the caravan. When he got to his car, he pulled out his phone and googled the price of a Swift Conqueror 630. Around thirty thousand pounds. With the value of the Nissan X-Trail added in, the Warburtons had around fifty grand worth of assets sitting on that campsite. You could buy a house for that in parts of Derbyshire. Though perhaps not in Didsbury.

Back in Edendale, Ben Cooper sat in his office quietly for a while after visiting the Warburtons. His impressions of the New Trespassers Walking Club were changing with every conversation. People came and people left much more often than he'd imagined. So perhaps Darius Roth didn't have that much influence over them after all. They could take their leave of the club whenever they pleased.

Or at least, most of them could.

He did a search of the phone directory. As it turned out, there were only three addresses in Buxton with the name of Eavis. Cooper hit the right one on the third attempt.

'Hello. I'm trying to contact Julie Eavis,' he said when a man's voice answered.

'Who is this?'

'Detective Inspector Cooper, Derbyshire Constabulary.'

'You're a bit late.'

'What do you mean, sir?'

'She died last year.'

'I'm sorry. Can I ask . . . ?'

'It was a car accident. Last winter. She went off the road in the snow. They say she was driving too fast for the conditions.'

There was a hint of resentment in his words. Cooper had heard it often before. When a tragedy happened, the death of a loved one, the instinct was to find someone to blame. When no one else was involved, it became the mysterious 'they'. In this case, unfortunately, 'they' was probably the police.

'Am I speaking to Mr Eavis?'

'Yes, that's me.'

'I apologise for intruding, Mr Eavis, but I wonder if you recall your wife being a member of a walking group called the New Trespassers.'

'Yes, I remember. She was a bit of a local history enthusiast and she seemed to think it was important. She dropped out of it after a while.'

'Did she say why?'

'I don't think she hit it off with some of the other members. She didn't say much about it, but that's the impression I got. Reading between the lines, like. She just dropped it one day and never went back.'

'No one specific you can recall her mentioning?' asked Cooper. 'Or a particular incident?'

'Not really. There was some meeting at the clubhouse that seemed to upset her.'

'Clubhouse?' said Cooper.

Eavis sounded unsure now. 'I think that was it.'

'You don't mean at someone's house? Trespass Lodge in Hayfield, perhaps?'

'Mmm. No. She definitely mentioned a clubhouse. I don't know any more than that. Sorry.'

'Thank you for your help, sir.'

Cooper rang through to the CID room. 'Carol, could you see if we can fix a time to speak to Theo and Duncan Gould, please?'

'The landscape gardeners? As soon as possible, I suppose?'

'You got it. Thanks. And send Luke Irvine in, will you?'

Irvine appeared almost straight away with his notebook. 'Yes, boss?'

'Can you do a bit of research for me, please, Luke?'

'Of course. Is it connected with the Faith Matthew inquiry?'

'I think so,' said Cooper. 'The Kinder Mass Trespass in April 1932.'

'Oh, that. What about it?'

'I think there were six men arrested and tried at Derby Assizes after a confrontation with gamekeepers. Can you find out who they were? Their names at least.'

'No problem,' said Irvine.

'Thanks.'

Irvine looked at Cooper with a hint of surprise at his tone. Cooper realised he probably sounded less than businesslike. That was because he wasn't entirely sure the information was relevant to the investigation. It might just be to satisfy his own curiosity.

'Also, find out if there are any derelict or abandoned buildings in that area, near Hayfield,' said Cooper. 'And check on any properties Darius Roth owns in addition to his home at Trespass Lodge.'

'I'll get straight on to it.'

When Irvine had gone, Cooper spread the witness

statements out on his desk, then separated them into three piles. The Roths, Millie Taylor, Karina Scott and Nick Haslam went into one stack, and the Goulds, the Warburtons and Sophie Pullen into another. That was the way they'd separated when they split up to get help. Then he put Liam Sharpe and Faith Matthew together in a third pile. Faith was the only one who'd stayed with the injured man when the others left.

But wait a minute. That left him with one witness statement in his hand. Jonathan Matthew's. Why was he reluctant to put it in the third pile? Hadn't Jonathan stayed with his sister? She was the only person he really knew in the walking group, certainly the one whose welfare he would have cared about. Everything else meant nothing to him.

So what was Jonathan's account? Cooper skimmed through the statement again. Jonathan said that he'd waited behind when the two groups set off. And that wasn't the same thing, was it? Jonathan seemed to have hovered in the background, not definitely part of any group. But he'd been doing that before the split, according to the statements. He'd wandered off the path, doing his own thing, disappearing in the fog for minutes at a time. Afterwards, no one could be sure where Jonathan had been at any point in the walk. And when the MRT located the walkers, he was found separately by Dolly. Jonathan definitely had the opportunity. But what could his motive have been?

Cooper sighed. So what did he know for certain? Lost on Kinder Scout in the fog, the walking group had split up. After an argument about which direction to take, they'd set off in different directions to see who could get a mobile-phone signal to call for help.

225

What had then happened in that fog was hard to tell. The accounts of the people involved varied so much that it was obvious their imaginations had come into play, sparked by the eerie silence and muffling effect of the mist. Had they heard voices? Lights? A shout? Someone screaming? None of them seemed completely sure.

And, crucially, where were they in relation to Faith Matthew when she died? Their statements taken next day didn't seem to be much help. Almost without exception, the walkers had looked at the map they'd been shown and shrugged. There was no way for them to tell by then, sitting in the bright artificial lights of an interview room. It was a totally different world from the one they'd been lost in a few hours previously. The lines and symbols of an Ordnance Survey map bore no relation to the disorienting confusion of their disastrous expedition. Probably they didn't even feel like the same people as those who'd panicked on the moor as they became wet, cold, frightened and lost.

The mind could forget so very easily. It could wipe out an experience completely, blur it into something less traumatic or even create misleading memories.

'It seems like a nightmare now,' Millie Taylor had said. 'As if it didn't really happen.'

'It was like being in a film,' said Karina Scott. 'The Blair Witch Project. All we could see was a flash of torchlight now and then. All we could hear were odd sounds we couldn't explain.'

Yes, there was a lot that couldn't explained. And that was what Cooper was missing. A coherent explanation.

24

Diane Fry was sitting in the same room at Derbyshire Constabulary headquarters, at the same table, with the same stack of files on its freshly polished surface.

Martin Jackson looked as though he enjoyed his job. He'd entered the room full of energy, fresh and pink-cheeked like someone who'd just been for a run around the grounds. And perhaps he had.

Jackson put his glasses on and spread his files out in front of him as if ready for a party game. Hangman or snakes and ladders maybe. One where someone slipped up and met an unfortunate end.

'DS Fry, do you remember a colleague of yours from West Midlands Police, Andrew Kewley?' he asked.

'Of course I remember him,' said Fry.

'He died rather suddenly.'

'I know that.'

'Naturally. You were there, weren't you?'

'To be more accurate, I found his body,' she said. 'It was very distressing for me.'

'I'm sure it was. Kewley was a friend of yours, as well as a close colleague.'

'He'd retired by then,' said Fry. 'And I hadn't seen him for some time, since I transferred to Derbyshire.'

'Really? Didn't you meet with him earlier that same week, a day or two before his death?'

Fry clenched her fists under the table, hoping he couldn't see her reaction. How did Jackson know that? Only she and Andy Kewley had been present at that meeting. Warstone Lane Cemetery, with its catacombs and broken angels, right in the heart of Birmingham's Jewellery Quarter. It had been Kewley's choice of location. Had he mentioned their meeting to someone else? Someone currently on the West Midlands force? Or had Gareth Blake already been watching Kewley by then?

'I meant I hadn't seen him before that week,' she said.

'Mmm.' Jackson made another note on his pad. 'As I understand it, you'd asked Mr Kewley for some information.'

'Yes,' admitted Fry. 'It was in connection with an old case.'

'*Your* case, in fact.'

'Yes, my case,' said Fry, momentarily irritated at hearing the same phrase Ben Cooper had used.

Jackson pursed his lips at her change of tone.

'A violent assault you suffered during the course of your duties when you were stationed in Birmingham, serving with Aston CID. I gather you were separated from your colleagues during an operation and assaulted by gang members when they discovered you were a police officer.'

'You can call it a rape,' said Fry. 'That's what it was. And of course it was obviously of concern to me.'

'As the victim, yes. We fully appreciate that. Very understandable. But as a serving police officer, you should have known better than to be conducting inquiries of your own, making unofficial contact with witnesses. Possibly even suspects?'

He made the last phrase sound like a question, which Fry avoided answering.

'Perhaps,' she said. 'But should police officers be held to much higher standards than members of the public even when they're victims themselves?'

'Ah, a much-debated question of principle. But beyond my remit, I'm afraid. We only attempt to apply the existing rules here.'

'Then perhaps you should be investigating what happened to Andy Kewley that day,' said Fry. 'It seems to me that's a more serious question to be asking.'

He looked at her over his glasses. 'You think his death was suspicious?'

'I don't have the evidence, but . . .'

Jackson switched smoothly to another file from the bottom of his pile. 'The inquest recorded a verdict of natural causes. The results of the post-mortem were fairly clear. Mr Kewley was suffering from heart disease. No doubt the result of too much alcohol, too many cigarettes and not enough exercise. Things were different in those days, I suppose.'

'I think someone was watching him,' said Fry. 'How would anyone know that we met earlier that week otherwise? Where does *your* information come from?'

'From our colleagues in the West Midlands,' said Jackson.

'Exactly.'

'I can't tell you more than that.'

'Because it might constitute evidence, I suppose.'

Fry felt herself growing angry. She'd been trying to fight it ever since she first entered this room and sat across the table from this man. She'd tried to keep the flood of rage and frustration under control, but now she was afraid she might lose the battle. The worst thing was, she knew that was exactly what Martin Jackson wanted.

He took off his glasses and laid them carefully on the table. 'DS Fry, if you have allegations to make of improper behaviour by your former colleagues, you should make them through the proper channels. This inquiry only covers your own conduct.'

'I know,' said Fry, biting her lip. 'And of course I deeply regret what happened to Andy Kewley.'

Jackson smiled.

'And so,' he asked quietly, 'do you blame yourself for his death?'

Fry was silent. There were some questions she wasn't obliged to answer. Not even to herself.

The Kinder View Nursery wasn't quite what Ben Cooper expected. He'd heard it referred to as a garden centre. But there were no fancy plant pots here, no racks of gardening tools, no bamboo trellising and not even a tearoom. Only plants. The Gould brothers were evidently growers, not retailers.

There were a few years in age between Theo and Duncan Gould, but they were so alike that they could almost be taken for twins. Cooper had to look closely at their eyes to discern that Theo was the older of the two.

The Goulds were dressed in matching olive-green fleeces today with their company logo. Despite the weather, both wore shorts, revealing powerful, hairy calves and thick woollen socks.

Cooper recalled the descriptions of what each of the walkers had been wearing on Kinder that Sunday. Surely the Goulds had dressed alike for the walk. Could it have been feasible in the fog to mistake one for the other? Of course it could. But would it also have been possible to think you'd seen both Theo and Duncan when you'd actually only seen one, because the other brother was somewhere else? That was a more difficult question.

'We didn't like the Matthews very much,' said Theo frankly.

'The Matthews? Either of them?'

The brothers looked at each other. Cooper noticed the older brother, Theo, wore a discreet hearing aid tucked among his greying strands of hair. Theo rubbed the palms of his hands on his fleece.

'Jonathan really,' he said. 'That young man doesn't belong. He has no interest in anything.'

'He just complains all the time,' said Duncan.

'And Faith?'

'Well, she insisted on bringing him,' said Theo. 'She spoiled it for us. And look what's happened now.'

'You don't blame Faith for her own death?'

Theo shuffled his feet. 'She didn't get on well with the girls,' he said. 'Millie and Karina. They laughed at Jonathan, and they called Faith "the headmistress".'

'Are you sure?' said Cooper. 'Sophie Pullen is the one who's a school teacher.'

'No, the girls liked Sophie. They called Faith that because she obviously disapproved of them. She didn't like them being around Darius all the time, for example. They made an awful fuss of him.'

'They are a bit silly,' broke in Duncan suddenly. 'To be honest.'

'So what do *you* think happened to Faith?' asked Cooper.

'Well, we have our own little theory,' said Duncan.

He looked at his brother, a bit coy now. Cooper was beginning to get irritated with them. They reminded him of Tweedledee and Tweedledum from *Through the Looking Glass*. Those characters had irritated him even as a child.

'And are you going to tell me what your theory is?' he said impatiently.

'It might be nothing,' said Theo. 'But we were talking about it today. And it's all to do with those silly girls.'

Cooper left the nursery clutching a plant the Gould brothers had given him. Its name was written on a label stuck into the pot, but it was in Latin and he couldn't remember what they'd said it was.

Theo Gould had assured him the plant would grow fine in his little patch of garden in Foolow. They might not have accounted for the fact that Hope had already claimed it as her outdoor toilet, though.

The gift hadn't eased his irritation with the brothers. After talking to the Goulds, he was no closer to getting an answer about what had happened among the members of the New Trespassers Walking Club.

Each person Cooper spoke to seemed to point a finger at one of the others.

'So the Gould brothers think it was some stupid prank by the two students?' said Carol Villiers when Ben Cooper got back to the office.

'Yes, a joke that went badly wrong. According to them, Millie Taylor and Karina Scott thought it was hilarious when Sophie Pullen fell into the bog earlier on, and they thought they'd play a trick on someone else.'

'And Faith Matthew was just the unfortunate member of the group who happened to be in the wrong place at the wrong time?' said Villiers.

Cooper recalled Theo Gould's exact words: *Those silly girls. They were only messing around, I'm sure – trying to push people into the peat bog so they'd get their feet wet. I don't think they would have realised they were pushing Faith off a drop. That was why they were so distressed afterwards.*

'So it could have been anyone who died at Dead Woman's Drop?' Villiers was saying. 'We're wasting our time examining Faith's relationships with the rest of the group?'

'Let's not be too hasty. We need to get their accounts. If Millie and Karina have been hoping so far that no one has guessed what happened, then they might be ready to spill the whole story when we ask them directly. A fatal misjudgement like that doesn't sit well in anyone's conscience for very long. It needs to come out.'

'Theo Gould is right, though. They did look pretty shaken up when the MRT retrieved them from Kinder. The doctor said they were suffering from shock.'

'It will have hit home by now. They've had plenty of time to think about it.'

'Let me and Becky interview them,' said Villiers. 'We'll get anything there is to get from them.'

Cooper considered it, and realised it was a good idea.

'Yes, all right.'

Before Villiers could leave, Luke Irvine came in to report on the results of his research.

'I'm still working on Darius Roth's business set-up,' he said. 'It's pretty complicated. But Darius Roth is definitely a busy man. He recently came up with a scheme for the old water-treatment works outside Hayfield.'

'Just below the reservoir?'

'That's it. It's been empty for twenty years since they built a new facility at Wybersley. I think United Utilities have been trying to sell it for a while. Mr Roth wanted to buy the building and develop it.'

'Into what?' asked Cooper.

'He had plans drawn up for a visitor centre telling the history of Kinder Scout and that mass trespass you were talking about. There was going to be a café and shop, and all kinds of other facilities. The main building on the site is the former filter house and there's around ten thousand square feet of floor space, as well as a couple of acres of grounds.'

'Sounds like an ideal development. What went wrong?'

'Funding,' said Irvine. 'He couldn't convince the vendors that he had the money to see the development through.'

'Seriously?' said Villiers. 'But he's supposed to be loaded.'

'That's the impression he gives.'

'Interesting,' said Cooper. 'Anything else?'

'Yes. Five years ago, Darius Roth was granted planning permission by High Peak Borough Council for the conversion of a disused church building to residential use.'

'What church?'

'It says here the former Primitive Methodist chapel.'

'In Hayfield?'

'Somewhere on the outskirts, I think,' said Irvine. 'Highgate Road?'

'Is there a site map with the planning application?'

'Yes, I've printed it out for you.'

Cooper studied the map Irvine handed him. The site of the application was small, and rather isolated from the residential part of the village, surrounded only by agricultural land and a few acres of woodland. Perhaps the Primitive Methodists were considered a bit too primitive even for Hayfield.

He compared the location to the map pinned on his wall, where the Roths' home was marked.

'Do you know what?' said Cooper. 'I think this site actually adjoins the Roths' property on its southern boundary.'

'Blimey, they must have a big garden,' said Irvine.

'I'm not sure the word "garden" really covers it,' said Cooper, recalling the gently undulating slopes, recently mowed by the Roths' gardener, with their spectacular views of Chinley Head and the Sett Valley, and the dark copse of trees covering the southern slopes at the foot of Kinder.

'If you get Google Maps up,' said Irvine, 'we'll be able to see the satellite image.'

'Good idea.'

When Cooper zoomed in on the screen, he found that Trespass Lodge looked even more impressive viewed from above. That was often the way with a large property. On the ground, you only ever saw a small portion of it all at once. A visitor might never guess the size of the house or the extent of the surrounding land.

'That must be the chapel,' said Irvine, pointing at the screen.

'Yes, I think you're right, Luke. It's very close. If Darius Roth had plans for that building, he might have intended to incorporate it into his own property.'

'But what would he do with it?' said Villiers. 'Convert it into a house, I suppose – though it looks a bit small.'

'He couldn't knock it down, because it's Grade II listed,' pointed out Irvine. 'The planning permission is quite specific about the conditions. Perhaps he could rent it out as a holiday let?'

Villiers laughed. 'What? Tourists right on his own doorstep? I don't think so. Not Mr Roth.'

'What, then?'

'What I'm thinking,' said Cooper, 'is that the old Methodist chapel might have become the clubhouse for the New Trespassers Walking Club.'

Cooper noticed that a public footpath was marked on the plan. It came off Valley Road and skirted the woodland towards the edge of Kinder. He wondered if it was possible to slip down from the path through the trees to reach the old chapel, if you knew the way. There seemed to be no other direct access, so probably the Primitive Methodists had come that way themselves, going to and from the church on foot. It looked ideal for a private location to meet in.

Diane Fry was recalling that rainy Monday morning when she'd found Detective Inspector Gareth Blake standing in her boss's office at E Division headquarters in Edendale. She hadn't recognised Blake at first, as she automatically held out her hand, seeing a man who wasn't much above her own age, his hair just starting to recede a little from his forehead, grey eyes observing her sharply from behind tiny, frameless glasses.

'Diane,' he said.

And then she'd remembered him. It was the voice that did it. She and Gareth Blake had worked together years ago, on the same uniformed shift in the West Midlands. But he'd been ambitious and got himself noticed, earning an early promotion. He was more mature now, better dressed, with a sharper hairstyle. The reek of ambition still hung in the air around him.

So what was Blake's specialty now?

Cold-case rape inquiries. Well, of course.

And then there had been Rachel Murchison, smartly dressed in a black suit and a white blouse, dark hair tied neatly back, businesslike and self-confident, but with a guarded watchfulness. A specialist counsellor, there to judge her psychological state.

Some of the phrases leaped out at her from the conversation that had followed.

'Obviously we don't want to put any pressure on you, Diane.'

That was Blake, pouring a meaningless noise in her ear.

'It's understandable that you feel a need to be in control. Perfectly normal, in the circumstances.'

Murchison's contribution. Well, Fry hadn't wanted this woman telling her whether she was behaving normally or not. She didn't want to hear it from anyone else, for that matter.

Just the sound of her name from Blake's lips had brought back the memories she'd been trying to suppress, but which would now for ever bubble up in her mind. She remembered how both of them, Blake and Murchison, had watched her carefully, trying to assess her reaction.

In the days that followed, others had seemed to be watching her in that same careful manner. But they could never comprehend the painful attempt to balance two powerful urges. The need to keep her most terrible memories safely buried now had to be set against this urge she'd suddenly discovered growing inside – the burning desire for vengeance and justice. No one could understand that.

Blake and Murchison had brought the news of a DNA hit that would enable them to reopen the inquiry in which she was the victim. All they needed was her decision, whether she wanted to go ahead with a fresh inquiry or close the book and put the whole thing behind her.

Blake's words still echoed in her mind.

'When we get a cold-case hit, we consult the CPS before we consider intruding into a victim's life. We have to take a close look at how strong a case we've got, and whether we can do something to strengthen it.'

'With the help of the victim.'

'Of course. And in this case . . .'

'This is personal. Don't try to pretend it isn't.'

But she'd said yes to a fresh inquiry. Perhaps that was it. That was her mistake. She should have closed the book on it. Instead, she'd reopened too many difficult chapters that didn't make comfortable reading.

She'd never been one to do what was expected of her. And here were the consequences, coming back to catch up with her with a vengeance.

25

Ben Cooper stood in a small clearing in the woods with Carol Villiers. The trees had encroached onto the site of the old Primitive Methodist chapel since it was abandoned, but the area immediately around it had been kept reasonably clear of weeds. Perhaps another job for the Roths' gardener?

Cooper realised he had no idea who that was. He made a mental note to find out the man's name and speak to him. Like servants, gardeners were often the people who observed small details and knew most about their employers. There was just a chance he might have noticed something useful.

In front of him stood a plain stone building. It had no fancy carvings or stained-glass windows. And certainly no spire or steeple. There was no reaching up towards God with ambitious building projects for these worshippers. At this church, each man must have had to find God within himself.

The main door of the chapel had been secured with deadbolts, and Cooper could see that some work had been done on the roof to make it watertight. Missing lead was still one of the biggest threats for old churches in rural areas, even those that were still in use. Thieves could strip a roof in a single night, leaving the interior awash with rain by the next day.

Villiers was walking round the walls of the building.

'Can you see anything through those windows?' called Cooper.

'No, they're too high.'

'Same on this side.'

The windows were small too. Not much light had penetrated this church.

'It's handy, isn't it?' said Villiers. 'Anything could be going on in there. Unless there was some reason for an official inspection, no one would know about it.'

'Can you see a water supply, or electricity?'

'No.'

'Then the last official visit might have been by a planning officer when the approval for conversion was given. It's clear there's been no attempt to convert it to residential use, anyway. The building inspectors probably lost interest after a while. They have better things to do with their time.'

'Lucky for Darius Roth, do you think?'

'I don't think anything comes to Mr Roth by luck, Carol.'

Cooper decided to call Darius Roth's mobile number.

'Mr Roth,' he said, 'we're here at the old chapel next to your property. I'd like to take a look inside, with your permission.'

'Why?'

'As part of our inquiries.'

'I don't see what relevance the old chapel can have.'

'Is there some reason you don't want us to see inside, sir?'

'Don't you need a warrant?'

'Not if we have your permission.'

Roth had sounded anxious, his voice a few notches higher than normal. But he paused, seemed to gather himself together, and his voice was back to its usual smoothness when he spoke again.

'All right,' he said. 'I'll send Will up with the key.'

'Will?'

'Will Sankey. My gardener.'

'Thank you, sir.'

When he arrived, Will Sankey wasn't as old as Cooper had imagined. For some reason, he pictured professional gardeners as middle-aged men with weathered faces and tweed jackets. Stereotypes. They always caught you out.

Sankey was dressed in a quilted body warmer and wore a baseball cap with his company logo on it. He was quietly spoken and polite, the sort of man who'd you like to come and do your gardening, who'd arrive and do the work without any fuss.

Cooper could imagine this man going practically unnoticed by the Roths as he went about his business. But if there were secrets being hidden at Trespass Lodge, Sankey might also be the man to know about them.

'Do you ever see anyone down here at the old chapel?' Cooper asked him as he produced the key.

Sankey looked shocked at the question. 'It's not for me to report on what my clients do on their own property.'

'So you do see people here?'

'Once or twice. I think they come here at night now and then.'

'And what are you doing here at night, Mr Sankey? Mowing the grass in the dark?'

241

Sankey smirked. 'No, you've got the wrong end of the stick. Of course I'm not here at night. I come early in the morning to start work. I've got a lot of jobs on, so I'm busy as soon as it gets light. Once or twice when I've made an early start at the lodge, I've seen them leaving.'

'Leaving?'

'Coming from the old chapel, like you said. I've seen them leaving early in the morning. It's pretty obvious they've spent the night in there.'

'Who?'

'Well, I can't say who they are. I don't know Mr Roth's guests. I'm only the gardener.'

'Would you recognise them if you saw them again?'

'Some of them, maybe,' said Sankey.

'I might get someone to show you a few photographs. Would that be all right?'

'I'm not sure Mr Roth would approve of that. You'll have to ask him.'

'OK.'

Sankey stood for a moment rattling his bunch of keys, choosing a large, old-fashioned key.

'What do you think they're up to, then?' he said.

'I don't know, sir. Do you?'

Sankey shrugged. 'A bit of funny business, I suppose. But my dad always told me not to ask too many questions. People don't like it, do they?'

'It depends what they have to hide,' said Cooper.

Sankey opened the door of the chapel. It swung back on his hinges with a creak and a scrape of wood against stone flags.

Inside the chapel, the wooden benches were still in place, rows of them worn and shiny from decades of use. They couldn't be called pews – they were too plain, with no ornamentation.

Cooper stepped over a pile of hymn books left on the floor. Some of them had lost their covers and pages were showing signs of mildew. They were well used in their day, but had been abandoned along with the chapel itself.

A plain wooden pulpit was raised above the body of the church, with a lectern where an enormous Bible would once have lain open. At some time, the congregation must have grown larger. A gallery had been built onto the rear wall, right over the furthest rows of benches. It was reached by a set of stairs through a trapdoor, and might have held another twenty or thirty people. Cooper wondered which of the worshippers had the privilege of looking down on the preacher from that height.

Sunlight crept in through the high windows, glittering off strands of ancient cobweb. The stonework was streaked with damp where water had come in through gaps in the roof tiles, and some of the flags in the aisle were sunken and uneven. Whatever had been Darius Roth's intention when he bought this building, he had never completed the work.

Cooper reminded himself that not everything was the way it seemed. And certainly not how Darius Roth tried to present it. His original planning application for the old Methodist chapel could have been camouflage. The condition this building was in now might have been his real intention all along. Perhaps it had been designed as a stage for Darius's ego, just as Kinder Scout was. Did he rehearse his dramas here, or invite members of his group into this sanctuary to work on them separately?

He turned back to the pulpit again. He had no trouble

243

imagining who stood there when the club had meetings here. Darius Roth had the look of an evangelist, a man with a mission and a powerful belief in himself.

And then Cooper was struck by something odd where the altar had once stood. He strode down the aisle, past the pulpit, wondering whether he could believe what he was seeing.

'Carol, look at this.'

'What is it?' asked Villiers, sensing the sudden shift of his attention.

'See for yourself.'

Villiers came to join him. 'Oh my God.'

'Exactly.'

On a bare oak table against the far wall of the chapel, an ancient teddy bear had been duct-taped to a crude wooden cross in an imitation of a crucifixion. The detail that had stood out most from the far end of the aisle was a red bow tie the teddy bear was wearing. When Cooper bent to examine it, the bear's glass eyes seemed to wink at him as they reflected the light from the high windows.

Villiers seemed to be about to reach out and touch the bear, perhaps to take it down from the cross. It was an instinctive reaction to what looked like an act of sacrilege.

'Don't touch it,' said Cooper. 'There might be latent prints on the duct tape.'

She flinched back. 'Sorry.'

Cooper turned at the sound of footsteps on the flagstones. Darius Roth himself was standing in the aisle of the chapel, a horrified expression on his face as he stared at the teddy bear.

'Who did this?' he said.

'Haven't you seen it before, Mr Roth?' asked Cooper.

'Of course not. It's horrible.'

'Perhaps one of your group has a sense of humour that's in bad taste.'

Roth looked at him, narrowing his eyes.

'You don't believe that, Detective Inspector Cooper. Just a bad joke? Really? This looks malicious to me.'

'Is there a particular significance to the teddy bear, sir?'

Cooper waited patiently for the answer. Both he and Villiers had heard Elsa Roth use that affectionate nickname for him when he was upset, as if he was a child who needed placating.

'Yes, my wife calls me that sometimes,' said Roth, slightly embarrassed.

'And who else would know that?'

'I couldn't say. Anyone who's ever seen us together, I suppose.'

'So all the members of your walking club, then.'

'Well, yes.'

'And what is this chapel used for now, Mr Roth?'

Roth dragged his gaze away from the teddy bear and narrowed his eyes as he looked at Cooper. Roth wasn't stupid. He would have worked out by now that Cooper already had the information but was asking the question to see whether he got a denial.

'We use it as a kind of clubhouse sometimes,' said Roth, evidently recognising when there was no point in evasion.

'Do you?' said Cooper. 'So who would have access to the building?'

'When the club are meeting for a walk, the chapel is left open. Anyone can come in here for a quiet moment.'

'But it was locked today,' said Cooper.

'Well, after what happened with Faith, you know . . . I

245

didn't think anyone would want to come down to the chapel. So I asked Will to lock it up.'

Cooper gestured at the bear. 'And he didn't mention this to you?'

'I don't suppose he looked round the interior.'

Cooper wondered if that was true. Sankey had left pretty quickly after unlocking the chapel for them. Did he really have so little curiosity about what was inside?

'Mr Roth, do you keep records of your members?' asked Cooper. 'I'm thinking about previous members of the club who've since left.'

He shook his head. 'We're a very informal group. We keep a list of who we're expecting on the walk, so we can make sure they've got transport or accommodation if they need it. We tick them off when they arrive, that's all. Previous members? We tend to forget about them once they drop out and disappear. At least, I do.'

Cooper could see that last statement was likely to be true. Darius Roth would have no interest in anyone who turned their back on his group and escaped his influence. It made Cooper feel even more anxious to speak to a former member or two.

'Are there any of the current group you don't know very well?'

'Jonathan Matthew,' said Roth straight away. 'Faith's brother. She brought him into the group, for some reason.'

'Yet you had him staying at your house the night before the walk. Didn't you, sir?'

'Yes, but that's why, you see. We wanted to get to know him better. It didn't really happen, though. He said very little over supper. No, Jonathan will take a bit more work, I'm afraid.'

More work? Cooper thought that was an odd way of putting it. Jonathan Matthew had presented a bit of a challenge for Darius, then. He could expect to be worked on more.

'Do you think he'll be coming back?' asked Roth.

'Perhaps not.'

'Oh well. And there's Nick Haslam too. Nick is still a bit of an enigma to us. Sophie introduced him to the group. She used to come with her previous partner, Jake, but Nick is more recent. I don't mind that – we encourage new members, of course. But it means we don't always know much about them.'

'Does he have an interest in the history of the Mass Trespass?'

Darius shrugged. 'If he has, it isn't obvious to us. Quite the opposite, in fact. You'll have to ask Sophie about him.'

'I will.'

Something else seemed to strike Roth, and he looked towards the teddy bear again.

'Nick does have a peculiar sense of humour,' he said. 'He likes to pull my leg about the original organisers of the Kinder Mass Trespass being Communists. On Sunday, he arrived for the walk wearing a Russian Army hat. I imagine that was meant to be a joke at my expense.'

'I've seen that on the photographs,' said Cooper.

'As I say, a peculiar sense of humour.'

The steam seemed suddenly to be gone out of Darius Roth. His shoulders slumped, and a lock of hair fell over his eyes.

'What does this all mean?' he said. 'Is someone threatening me? Do they mean to do me harm?'

'I'm not sure, sir,' said Cooper. 'But if I were you, I wouldn't stand on any high places or sudden drops for a while.'

'Point taken.'

Roth produced his own set of keys to lock the chapel door.

'Will you want to examine the scene for evidence? The bear . . . ?' he said.

'Yes, we'll send someone along to check for fingerprints, which might help. We'll let you know when to expect them.'

'Very good.'

'So what will happen next to the club?' asked Cooper as he watched Roth turn the key in the lock.

'Happen? Well, we'll have to set a new date.'

'A new date? You mean you're going up onto Kinder again?'

'Of course. It'll be a way of honouring Faith.'

'I see.'

'Besides, we didn't complete the walk. We haven't fulfilled the tradition.'

That sounded honest too. But Cooper wondered how long you had to do something before it became a tradition. Was eight years enough? It was as if Roth believed he'd been doing the walk every year since 1932, a beacon of tradition for most of the last century, literally following in his ancestor's footsteps.

'Don't you think it's a good idea?' asked Roth.

'It's hard to say. Will it be the same group as before?'

'Yes. Well, with the one obvious exception. Poor Faith. So what do you think?'

Cooper hesitated. It was a strange idea. If he knew that one of his party was a killer, would he want to venture out onto the moors with them? Most people would have said no. But it didn't seem to bother the Roths.

'I can see you're a bit concerned,' said Roth. 'So here's an idea. Why don't you come with us? I take it you're a walker? Or perhaps even a hiker?'

'It depends,' said Cooper, 'on the circumstances.'

Roth smiled. 'I bet a hike across Kinder Scout is nothing to you.'

'Thank you for the invitation,' said Cooper. 'But I think I'll probably be too busy.'

As he and Villiers walked back to their car, Cooper turned to see if Darius Roth was out of earshot.

'Have you noticed how Mr Roth always talks about "us"?' he said. 'Meaning himself and his wife, as if he doesn't expect Elsa to have an opinion of her own or a different story to tell.'

'Yes, I did notice that,' said Villiers. 'And at the same time, Elsa seems content to go along with whatever Darius says.'

'That doesn't mean she doesn't have her own thoughts. She may just be reluctant to express them.'

'Do you think Elsa Roth might have a few secrets she could share with us?'

'Yes, if she could be persuaded. But that's doubtful. She has a serious vested interest in Darius. I think she might already have told me as much as she's ever going to give away. And that was intended to direct attention *away* from her husband.'

'She's the quiet one,' said Villiers. 'You know what I think.'

'And I always value your opinion, Carol.'

Villiers laughed. 'You value it but don't always take any notice of it.'

'Not quite true.'

Cooper smiled to himself. It wasn't true at all. Villiers was wrong on that subject. He always tried to take notice of everything, no matter how insignificant it might seem.

26

On the way back to Edendale, Ben Cooper tried to put out of his mind the recurring image he had of Darius Roth as a kind of charismatic cult leader, gathering loyal followers around him. It was probably unfair, though it was an image Roth himself did nothing to dispel. He might even cultivate it. Everyone had a role they tried to play, didn't they?

As he steered the Toyota across the divide between the Dark Peak and White Peak, Cooper thought of all the criminals who'd lived and died in these villages. Abney, Bradwell, Hucklow. Their histories were full of individuals who'd played their roles to the end. Murderers, thieves, conmen. They'd all thought they'd get away with their crimes. And some of them had, of course. Those were the names that didn't make it into the history books.

He turned to Carol Villiers as they were passing her home village of Tideswell.

'You know that Saturday night,' he said. 'The night before the walk. Millie Taylor and Karina Scott stayed in the Roths' guest accommodation at Trespass Lodge, didn't they?'

'Yes. Mr Roth said he didn't want them having to pay for a hotel.'

Cooper nodded. But Jonathan Matthew had been there too. The potential black sheep. Perhaps Roth had wanted Jonathan right under his roof.

'Mr Roth presents himself as a benefactor, doesn't he?' said Villiers. 'I think that's the role he aspires to. Despite his talk of working-class roots, his dream is to be a wealthy patron surrounded by grateful recipients of his generosity.'

'That's interesting too,' said Cooper.

'Is it? Why?'

'Well, if that's true – and I think you're right, Carol – then Millie Taylor and Karina Scott wouldn't be enough for him. He'd want to spread his patronage around, gain more grateful recipients who owe him a debt.'

'I see. So . . . ?'

'So who else was he a benefactor to?' said Cooper. 'Which of the walking group owed Darius Roth so much that they might kill for him?'

'Or resent their benefactor.'

'Ah, you're thinking of the crucified teddy bear. That does suggest someone who felt very bitter against Darius Roth, to say the least.'

'Whoever it was, perhaps he had something on them.'

'A kind of hold over them?' said Cooper. 'Yes. Take the Gould brothers, for example. They're the longest-standing members of the group. Why are they so loyal to Darius? What kind of hold does he have over those two?'

Villiers looked at him wide-eyed.

'You asked earlier what bound such a disparate group together,' she said, 'when it clearly isn't an interest in the Mass Trespass. Could this be it, Ben?'

'Every one of them is indebted to Darius in some way? If so, that opens up a whole new can of worms. We'll have to go back and ask them a lot more questions. The right ones this time.'

Villiers shuddered. 'Darius Roth,' she said. 'What an egotistical monster he's starting to seem.'

Cooper had to agree. He felt no satisfaction that his first instinct about Roth might have been the correct one.

Back at West Street, Millie Taylor and Karina Scott were waiting for their appointment to be interviewed. Carol Villiers collected DC Becky Hurst from the CID room and they went off to talk to the two students.

In his office, Ben Cooper studied the documents Luke Irvine had left on his desk about the Mass Trespass. Everything began somewhere. The reasons for Faith Matthew's death on Sunday might go back to 1932 – or only to the day before.

Nick Haslam had been right. Many of the organisers of the Kinder Mass Trespass were Communists. Luke Irvine's research revealed that the protest in 1932 was supported by fifteen Lancashire branches of the British Workers' Sports Federation and two branches from Sheffield.

Cooper saw that the estimates of the numbers involved in the trespass varied considerably, as they always did. Organisers claimed between six hundred and eight hundred, while a reporter for the *Manchester Guardian* guessed between four hundred and five hundred. Other claims were much lower.

The confrontation with gamekeepers and bailiffs had taken place on the slopes of Sandy Heys. As the protesters returned to the village of Hayfield, five of them were arrested by police and taken to Hayfield Lock-up, which was now the offices of the parish council on Market Street.

They joined another protester who'd been arrested at the scene of the scuffle.

The arrested ramblers were named as John Anderson, aged twenty-one; Julius 'Jud' Clyne, twenty-three; Arthur Walter 'Tona' Gillett, aged just nineteen; Harry Mendel, twenty-two; David Nussbaum, also nineteen; and the main organiser of the protest, Bernard 'Benny' Rothman, aged twenty.

After the arrests at the Mass Trespass, a group of fellow ramblers had waited outside the Hayfield Lock-up, expecting the imminent release of the prisoners. When nothing happened, a spokesman hammered on the door and offered bail for the arrested protesters. As the situation became tense, the six men were smuggled out of the lock-up and taken to New Mills Police Station, where they were kept overnight. A plaque still hung on the old police station commemorating the event.

Next day, the arrested ramblers were charged with unlawful assembly and breach of the peace. All six pleaded not guilty and were remanded for trial at Derby Assizes, sixty miles from their homes. Meanwhile, 'wanted' posters had been printed, offering a reward of five pounds for the identification of some of the ramblers who escaped arrest.

At the subsequent trial, Benny Rothman took the opportunity for some working-class rhetoric: 'We ramblers, after a hard week's work in smoky towns and cities, go out rambling for relaxation, a breath of fresh air, a little sunshine. But we find when we go out that the finest rambling country is closed to us, just because certain individuals wish to shoot for about ten days a year.'

Despite his defence, he and four other men were found guilty and given jail terms of between two and six months.

John Anderson received the longest sentence for assault on the gamekeeper. Just one, Harry Mendel, was acquitted due to a lack of evidence.

It was the severity of the sentences that unleashed a wave of public sympathy and united the cause. Even those who'd been opposed to the trespass were appalled. A few weeks later, ten thousand ramblers gathered for a rally at Winnats Pass, near Castleton, and the pressure for greater access continued to grow.

'There we are,' said Cooper when Villiers returned. 'Rothman not Roth. That's what I thought. It was niggling at the back of my mind. It's a long time since we were taught about the Mass Trespass, but I was right.'

'Mr Roth hasn't actually claimed that his grandfather was one of the men arrested, though, just that he was one of the leaders.'

'True. So you're saying the similarity of names might just be a coincidence?'

Villiers smiled. 'You've never liked coincidences, have you?'

'Not very much.'

'But they do happen,' she said.

Cooper looked at the list thoughtfully.

'Darius Roth referred to his ancestor as a "martyr". That does suggest he was one of those who were imprisoned and given heavy sentences. Suggests it without actually saying it. It would be quite enough for anyone who didn't bother to ask questions or do their own research but accepted whatever Darius said.'

Villiers shrugged. 'So he's building up his personal narrative with a bit of exaggeration. Everyone does that.'

'Mmm.'

Cooper still wasn't convinced. But there were no complete records available of who had and hadn't taken part in the trespass in 1932, so he could probably never be sure one way or the other whether Darius's tales of his grandfather were true or not. He suspected it was a fantasy.

Did it matter? Perhaps not. But it was all part of a picture that was becoming increasingly disturbing.

'Well, Becky and I have talked to Millie Taylor and Karina Scott,' said Villiers.

'Oh yes. What's your assessment?'

'We took them separately, and their stories tally in all the significant details. They say they stayed together on the walk all the time. In fact, after Mr Sharpe's accident they stuck to Darius Roth's side and never wandered off for a second. They were too scared after hearing other members of the group talking about the danger of falling off the edge near the Downfall. Millie and Karina wouldn't go near any rocks after that, let alone try to creep up on someone near a steep drop.'

'So you don't think they had the opportunity?'

'I'm sure they didn't,' she said. 'Besides, they might seem like "silly girls" to the Gould brothers, but they're actually very smart young women – and ambitious as well. They're too adult, and they have their heads screwed on too well, to play those sorts of games.'

'Do you think it's a case of Theo and Duncan being prejudiced against them?'

'Yes,' said Villiers frankly. 'Patronising at best, because of Millie and Karina's age, and their gender. "Silly girls" is something they're definitely not, Ben.'

'That's helpful, thank you.'

'By the way,' said Villiers, 'I checked online and found

Faith Matthew had both a Facebook page and a LinkedIn profile. She lists Meadow Park Hospital among her previous employers on both. Her dates working there were between nine and four years ago.'

'Good,' said Cooper. 'If only we could ask her directly what ward she was on and whether she met Darius Roth there.'

He looked at a large-scale map of the Kinder area on the wall of the CID room. The last positions of the members of the New Trespassers Walking Club on Sunday were marked on it, but only so far as they were known. There were queries on several of the names, indicating a doubt about their exact location, or the lack of definite corroboration.

The timing was confusing too. It was impossible to get a clear picture of where everyone was and when – either from the statements they'd given themselves or by working it out from other people's accounts.

Cooper recalled Pat Warburton's glasses, Theo Gould's hearing aid. Even with perfect hearing and twenty-twenty vision, the group would have been practically deaf and blind to what was going on around them in the conditions they experienced on Kinder that day. The fog had been too thick. And as far as the inquiry was concerned, it still was.

It was too soon to expect any results from a forensic examination of the threatening note received by Faith Matthew. But the crime scene examiners had preliminary reports from two other scenes.

Wayne Abbott was the senior forensic manager for North Division. He looked more like a rugby forward with his shaven head and squashed nose, but Cooper knew how capable he was at his job.

'There are no useful prints from the teddy bear in the chapel,' Abbott told him. 'That artificial fabric is the wrong kind of surface for us to take viable prints from. And the duct tape looks as though it was either wiped or handled by someone wearing gloves.'

'OK.'

'We might be able to obtain some DNA, with a bit of luck. It would take time, and it would cost you.'

'It doesn't matter,' said Cooper. 'I think I know where the teddy bear came from, and whose DNA you would find.'

Abbott looked at him in surprise but nodded without questioning him. They'd worked together before and understood each other pretty well.

'You've already got that figured out, then,' said Abbott. 'Sometimes I think you don't need us.'

'I would never say that. It's just luck.'

Cooper still had a memory stick with all the photos from Faith's phone, a Samsung Galaxy. It wasn't the poor-quality photos taken in the fog on Kinder Scout that he was interested in. He was scrolling further back, through some random pictures of people and places he didn't recognise, to some of Faith with Greg, and then . . . Yes, there it was. A selfie taken in the bedroom of Faith Matthew's house in Hayfield a few weeks ago. A selfie with a chair full of soft toys photobombing her in the background.

Most prominent among the toys was an ancient brown teddy bear wearing a red bow tie. Its glass eyes seemed to twinkle in the light from the bedside lamp. Cooper remembered that lamp from the day before, when he and Villiers had searched Faith's house for the threatening note. He recalled seeing the pile of soft toys too. But that golden teddy bear with the red bow tie? It hadn't been among them. Someone had taken it from Faith's house. And then it had turned up in that mock crucifixion at the old Methodist chapel.

'What about the scene on Kinder Scout?' he asked Abbott. 'Did you find any marks around the spot where Faith Matthew went over the edge?'

'A lot of unidentifiable shoe marks. It's a rocky surface, so it doesn't hold many usable impressions.'

Cooper grimaced impatiently. He was hearing excuses, not results. But you couldn't have it all your own way. Forensic science wasn't magic.

'There was one shoe mark you wanted us to look at in particular,' said Abbott. 'Is that right?'

'The one facing in a different direction?'

'Yes. It's oriented to about ninety degrees to the other marks. But it's only one, not a pair of impressions.'

'As if someone was turning.'

'Perhaps. I'm not sure how helpful it is. The tread on the sole is quite worn, and, as I say, the nature of the surface means it's only taken a partial impression. But we identified it as a woman's size-five walking boot, probably a Scarpa or a Garmont.'

'And?'

'That's consistent with the victim's footwear. We removed a pair of Scarpa Cyrus from the body.'

'Very good. Anything else?'

Abbott produced a set of photographic prints.

'There was just this . . . a fresh hole in the peat, no more than half an inch across, with a tapered point. I don't know what that would be.'

'It looks to me,' said Cooper, 'like the tip of a hiking pole.'

The Warburtons' caravan had gone from the campsite at Hayfield. Cooper supposed he should have checked first. But didn't Sam Warburton say the pitch was booked and paid for a week? They hadn't been in Hayfield that long.

He rang the Warburtons' number and found the couple were at home in Didsbury. He left a message to let his office know where he would be and turned the Toyota northwards.

A lot of Manchester people no longer lived in the cobbled back streets of areas like Gorton with their terraced slums but in the leafy avenues of fashionable Chorlton and Didsbury. The Warburtons' address was a pre-war detached house with mock black and white timbers, located in a cul-de-sac that ended in a turning circle against the wrought-iron fence of Didsbury Sports Ground. Cooper glimpsed the glint of the River Mersey snaking through the convoluted greens of a golf course.

The caravan was drawn onto the drive, and Pat was still unpacking some of the contents.

Sam Warburton stared at him when Cooper explained his reason for being there.

'Nonsense,' said Sam. 'A lot of people carry hiking poles.'

'The marks from the tip don't usually last very long, especially in wet weather. They get filled in, washed away or trampled on and they're no longer visible. This mark was recent.'

'Even so, it could have been anybody.'

'Including you,' said Cooper.

'If one of us was near that spot, it wasn't when Faith

fell,' said Sam. 'We were lost, remember. We could have passed the place earlier without knowing it.'

'If it was right by the drop,' added Pat, 'we could have been in danger ourselves.'

Sam began to shake his head. 'I don't think it was one of our poles. It's too much of a stretch. Detective Inspector Cooper is clutching at straws.'

'As far as we can tell, there was no one else nearby,' said Cooper.

'Apart from Liam, of course,' said Sam.

'What?'

'Liam Sharpe. He was there, obviously.'

'What do you know about Mr Sharpe?'

'More than you might think. He had quite a temper, you know.'

'Did he?'

Sam Warburton looked smug now that he sensed he had Cooper's attention.

'And Liam was . . . well, he was the only one there with Faith, after the rest of us went to get help,' he said. 'It seems fairly obvious to me, so I assume you started with him?'

Cooper didn't reply.

Sam smiled. 'After all,' he said, 'Liam Sharpe would have been the last person to see her alive.'

27

When Diane Fry had finished her interviews for the afternoon, she jumped into her car to drive to Birmingham.

She'd finally bitten the bullet and called her sister. Angie's phone was busy, so she left a brief message. Half an hour later, Angie called her back. It was always an odd sensation whenever they reconnected. It felt as though she was meeting a new person every time.

'Sis?' said Angie cautiously. 'Anything wrong?'

'Yes, I think there is.'

'And?'

'I'm coming down. I need to talk to you about it.'

'Me?'

'Yes, you. Don't try to sound so innocent.'

'It's a long while since you were so keen to talk to me about anything.'

It was true. Diane had worshipped her sister at one time. But the scales had fallen from her eyes that time in Birmingham when Angie had revealed unexpected contacts and abilities.

Diane remembered the sensation of leafing through case files, the astonishment to find herself fighting a feeling of guilt at the knowledge she was handling confidential information that she should never have had access to.

The case summary, witness statements, records of interview. And on all of the pages was the familiar black bar – RESTRICTED WHEN COMPLETE. It went against the grain even to handle something like that, when she knew it had been obtained illegitimately.

And she recalled her sister's response: 'Oh, you have got to be kidding. What – you're suddenly going to go all upright and honourable again? You don't want to put a foot wrong in case you upset your bosses? That's the old Diane. Things have changed, sis. Haven't you noticed? We're not playing this game by the rules any more. And that was your decision. Don't forget that.'

And Angie had walked out of the door, leaving her to make her own decision.

The one thing it told her was that Angie knew someone who worked at West Midlands Police headquarters in Lloyd House. She knew them pretty well, too – well enough to persuade them to break the rules.

When someone was on your side, you were supposed to feel grateful that they were willing to buck the system and help you achieve justice. Diane had never been able to figure out why that feeling of gratitude didn't come.

She'd always tried to go by the book, to follow procedures and not put a foot wrong. Yet she saw officers breaking the rules all the time. And not just back in the 1990s when she first joined up. Even now there were people willing to bend the rules, play the system or totally cross the line.

Was there some honourable justification she could claim for implicating herself in a breach of the rules? Did it really make any difference? The outcome would be the same, if she was found out.

And who had done this to her? Who was it who'd placed temptation in front of her? Her own sister.

If she couldn't trust her own sister, who could she trust?

Angie Fry had changed. She was no longer so skinny, her shoulders no longer so thin and angular. Diane knew that Angie had been fighting to control the weight she'd put on after the pregnancy, but she could see now that the battle was lost. Her habit of carrying the baby in a sling had pulled her shoulders down, making her look slow and ungainly.

And her face had changed too. It was the approach of middle age, of course. Angie had had a child relatively late, as so many women did. When Diane looked at her now, she saw a slow-moving middle-aged woman – which she would never be herself, surely? It was if an alien had taken possession of her sister's body.

Angie had a flat on the eighth floor of Inkerman House, a Birmingham City Council tower block overlooking the Aldi store at Newtown Shopping Centre and a huge Royal Mail delivery office on New Town Row. It was barely a mile from the police station in Aston where Diane had been based.

Diane stood by the window for a moment, gazing out over the familiar streets. Then she glanced down at a parking area below the tower block.

'Is that your old red Suzuki down there?' she said. 'Have you still got it?'

Angie came to stand beside her.

'The Jimny? Yes, that's mine.'

'I always thought it looked a bit odd to have a four-by-four in the middle of Birmingham.'

'I just like it. It's not too big, like some of the monsters you see on the roads.'

'And there's a baby seat for Zack, I suppose.'

'Obviously.'

Angie looked at her curiously.

'So what is it all about, Di?' she said. 'What's so urgent that it made you come all the way down here from Nottingham? It wasn't just to admire my car.'

'I want to ask you about your dealings with the National Crime Agency,' said Diane, conscious of the stiffness of the question.

Her sister picked up on the tone straight away, of course. And she wasn't the kind of person to let it go unremarked.

'Really? What is this?' she said with a laugh. 'Am I being interviewed as a suspect? Shouldn't I be given a caution? What about a lawyer?'

'I'm sorry,' said Diane. 'But I've got to ask you. There's a reason.'

Angie became more serious.

'I told you about the NCA,' she said.

'Yes, you were recruited as an informant when you were in Sheffield.'

'They've had a pretty bad rap over the years, but some of them were good to me. They were conducting a covert operation against some major drug gangs. So they approached me and made me a CHIS. Isn't that your jargon?'

'A covert human intelligence source.'

'Right. A posh name for an informant. A snitch, a nark.'

'You put yourself at risk.'

'Of course I did. I had regular contact with some dangerous people.'

'But why?'

'Why? Di, there comes a time in your life when you have to make a decision, to bite the bullet and make a major change of direction. That was the moment for me, sis. I'd been heading in the wrong direction for years. But I managed to kick the heroin and get clean. I wouldn't be here now with Zack if I hadn't made that decision at the time I did.'

'Right.'

For Diane, being a single mother saddled with a screaming child didn't seem like an objective she would aim for herself, let alone regard as some kind of dream outcome. But she'd learned to accept that Angie was different. Her sister had powerful maternal instincts that she'd searched for in her own heart and failed to locate. That was the way things were, and there was nothing to be done about it.

'My handlers got a bit nervous when you started making inquiries about me, and even more when your friend started asking questions.'

'Ben Cooper?'

'Yes, dear old Ben. He ruined things for me. They dropped me not long after that. I was too exposed, they said. My handlers said I should go back to Birmingham. So I did. And here I am. It was a pity really. The money was good.'

It was hard for Diane to imagine, even now. To be a CHIS, Angie must have signed a contract and been allocated to a handler. Diane's brain filled with extracts from the Code of Ethics relating to Section Seventy-One of the Regulation of

Investigatory Powers Act. Written authorisation from a designated authorising officer, a standard application form providing details of the purpose for which the source would be tasked, details of any confidential material that might be obtained. A risk assessment, of course.

Then someone would have kept detailed records of every task, and been prepared to account for their actions to the chief surveillance commissioner. Angie made it sound so informal. But that wasn't the way it worked any more, the street detective with his private snouts. It would all have been logged and documented.

'When you told me about your time working for the NCA, you said you were telling me because you might need my help,' said Diane. 'What did you mean by that?'

Angie shrugged. 'Down here it's different. West Midlands Police. Do I need to explain it to you?'

'You think there are some dirty cops?'

'Do I *think* so? I suppose you remember what happened to your old buddy Andy Kewley? He talked too much, that bloke. Far too much. It's not going to happen to me.'

'Have you been threatened?'

'Not directly. That wouldn't be their style. It's always just something that someone has heard and decides to pass on. You know what it's like.'

'Is that why Zack's dad got the boot?'

'He was on the way out anyway. But yeah – Craig was a remnant from an old lifestyle. I had to clear the decks. I'm with Sonny now, and I've got Zack. I'm a different person, sis.'

'Yes, I can see that.'

'So I need to know that I can rely on you if push comes

to shove. It may not happen. But I didn't want to have to start from scratch explaining it all you. So I made you aware of the situation.'

'You're worried about Zack, aren't you?' said Diane, feeling she'd experienced a sudden insight.

Her sister snapped at her impatiently, 'Of course I'm worried about Zack. Wouldn't you be?'

Diane held up a hand placatingly. 'I'm sure everything will be fine. Look, they'll have forgotten about you by now.' Then she had a sudden doubt. 'Unless there's a court case outstanding. One where your evidence will be used against someone.'

'No, I don't think so.'

'Well, then. There's no need for you to worry.'

Angie fiddled with a strand of hair. She'd dyed it a shade or two darker than it used to be. That was one thing that was making her look different.

Diane had a sense of the world having turned on its head. Here she was giving her big sister advice, reassuring her when she was worried or upset. It used to be the other way round. Surely it *should* be the other way round.

'Thanks, sis,' said Angie. 'I do feel better about it, now we've talked it through.'

'Good,' said Diane. 'Because actually, I'm the one who's in trouble right now.'

She explained to her sister about the disciplinary inquiry, repeated all the questions she'd been asked by Martin Jackson, and the concerns they'd raised in her mind over the past three days.

Even before she finished explaining, Angie had begun shaking her head.

'Di, I'm not sure there's anything I can do to help,' she

said. 'I'm out of all that now. I'm keeping my head down because—'

'Because of Zack. I get it.'

'Sorry, sis.'

Diane was silent for a few moments.

'There's someone who could help,' she said finally.

'Who do you mean?' said Angie.

'There's only one person. I hate him, but I've got to see him again.'

Angie began to shake her head. 'Not him. You can't trust him.'

'I know that. I wouldn't dream of trusting him. But he's the only one who ever seemed to know what was going on.'

'Well, he certainly knows that. He's up to his neck in it himself.'

'He always has been,' said Diane. 'That's one thing Andy Kewley told me, before he died.'

What Ben Cooper most hoped to find waiting on his desk was some results from the forensic examination of the threatening note found at Faith Matthew's house. But no such luck. Even a call to the lab failed to achieve anything. Nothing could shift their backlog, except time. Waiting didn't come easily to him.

Instead, Cooper found that Luke Irvine had left him a printout of an article from a 1922 edition of the *Sheffield Telegraph* about the death of a lone walker on Kinder Scout.

Irvine had either tried to pander to his DI's interest in Kinder or perhaps it had sparked his curiosity when he began to do the research. That was the way it got people sometimes.

The walker had set off in bad weather from the Snake Pass Inn on New Year's Day that year. Despite appalling conditions, he'd made it onto the Kinder plateau. The wind had been howling across the exposed slopes at eighty miles an hour, and the rain was described as 'falling in solid ropes'.

According to the *Telegraph*, when the man was reported missing, the opinion among experienced hill walkers was that the westerly gale would have forced him eastwards towards Grindsbrook. An extensive search on that side of Kinder had covered Golden Clough, Upper Tor, Beal Edge, the Blackden Valley and the dangerous gulleys of Fairbrook.

But the man's body was eventually found a week later just four hundred yards south of the Downfall, as if he'd been making westwards towards Hayfield in the teeth of the wind and had collapsed through exhaustion sometime during the night. Close to the Downfall, the going was hard and dangerous. There was a steep precipice, with cliffs in some places a hundred feet high.

The story ended: *All were glad that his body had been found, with the unspoken wish that he may have died quickly, and that he had not dragged himself about in agony for many hours, probably in darkness, and suffering acutely from anguish of mind and exposure. There is no worse place in England to be lost than on Kinder Scout.*

Cooper put the page aside and found another cutting. Twelve months later, a woman who wanted to visit a cairn at the site of the walker's death had slipped and fallen fifty feet from the Downfall and smashed her skull on the rocks. Her body was covered by drifting snow. It wasn't discovered until March, when the thaw came.

A commentator at the time claimed that the fact Kinder

Scout was private property, with no legal access, had made the mountain all the more attractive for ramblers who were prepared to take a risk in dangerous conditions.

Carol Villiers knocked on Cooper's office door.

'Oh, I recognise that expression,' she said. 'What are you thinking about?'

Cooper showed her the cuttings about the Kinder deaths.

'I'm thinking about the symbolism of that choice of location.'

'You mean Dead Woman's Drop?'

'Yes. It suggests someone with a poetic sense of humour, or a love of history and symbolism.'

Villiers was about to say something but seemed to change her mind.

'Carol, don't mention—' he said.

'Coincidence? I wouldn't dream of it.'

'Good.'

'You're obviously thinking of Darius Roth himself, though.'

'Is it that obvious?'

'Ben, it sounded like a perfect description of him.'

'And yet,' said Cooper, 'the Warburtons threw a subtle spanner into the works when I talked to them. They managed to cast suspicion on Liam Sharpe.'

'But he was the injured man,' protested Villiers. 'Liam Sharpe was already incapacitated, wasn't he? No broken bones, as it turns out, but he had a badly sprained ankle and torn ligaments.'

'Well, he did by the time the rescue teams got to him.'

'What do you mean?'

'Well, the timing is a bit odd. Most of the accounts are quite specific that the group split up after Mr Sharpe was

270

injured. But none of them actually witnessed his accident. They just believed what they were told.'

'They heard him cry out in pain.'

'But they didn't *see* anything,' repeated Cooper. 'Faith Matthew was probably the only one who actually examined Liam's ankle at the time. And we can't ask her about it.'

'Who was it that came and told the group he was injured?'

'Sam Warburton. But he didn't see it happen either. Nor did his wife. In their statements, they say they heard Liam cry out, found him on the ground and naturally accepted his story. That's what people do. They take in impressions and fill in the details in their own imaginations. They might have thought they'd seen him fall at the time, but when you question them thoroughly, they didn't see anything at all.'

'The other thing these accounts aren't clear about is exactly when the rest of the group lost contact with Faith Matthew. It means our timeline is just an assumption.'

'Could it be an elaborate set-up?'

'But Liam Sharpe definitely had a sprained ankle.'

'It's easy enough to do.'

'Sharpe was following up at the rear, and the Matthews dropped back to be with him. Even the Warburtons passed them, so they must have been travelling slowly.'

'Deliberately? He slowed down to lose touch with the group on purpose?'

'Maybe.'

That was odd on its own. In Cooper's experience of being part of a walking group, if one member was slow, you didn't leave them behind. Faith Matthew seemed to have been the only one who followed that principle. Had that been her mistake? Had her good nature been exploited as a weakness?

He could see Villiers thinking about it.

'So it's possible he was pretending at first,' she said. 'He was actually fit enough to push Faith Matthew off that rock. But then what? He deliberately sprained his own ankle?'

'That seems to be the suggestion.'

'It would be a good alibi.'

'Good enough that we've been discounting him from consideration so far. And that's despite the fact that he seems to have been the last person to see Faith alive, except the killer.'

'She stayed with him when the others went for help,' said Villiers. 'Liam Sharpe was alone with her all that time, while the rest of the group were wandering around the moor.'

'Remind me what his statement says.'

Villiers sorted through the pile of witness statements.

'Here it is. According to Mr Sharpe, Faith got worried that the others were taking too long to fetch help and she left him to see if she could find anyone. She told him she wouldn't go far and she'd only be a few minutes.'

'But she never came back,' said Cooper.

'Exactly. That's the precise phrase he uses.'

Villiers passed the statement back to him, and he read it through again. It was simple, unadorned. No flights of the imagination from Mr Sharpe. And it was the shortest of the twelve too. As far as Liam Sharpe was concerned, his story ended with a painful slip on a wet rock. He lay there helpless as people panicked around him, while Faith

Matthew came to sit with him, then disappeared recklessly into the fog. Left alone, he saw and heard nothing more until Dolly, the SARDA search dog, came nosing along the hillside following his scent and barked for her handler.

'His ankle was definitely injured,' said Villiers. 'The MRT had to stretcher him down off Kinder because he couldn't walk. The paramedics said it was bruised and swollen. He was transported to A and E, but he's out of hospital now, of course.'

'Have you ever sprained your ankle, Carol?'

'Several times.'

'Could you have walked on it?'

She hesitated. 'It depends. The first time I did it, I was only a child. I tried to make out it was worse than it really was.'

'Why?'

'Because I wanted sympathy, I suppose. In fact, my dad carried me back to the car. That was probably what I really wanted.'

Cooper put Liam Sharpe's statement back on the pile.

'I'll like you to interview Mr Sharpe again tomorrow. If he's out of hospital, he'll probably still be resting at home.'

'Unless he's gone back to work already. He's a check-in supervisor at Manchester Airport. He could achieve some limited mobility on crutches.'

'Make the trip to the airport if necessary. See if you can shake his story.'

Villiers raised an eyebrow. 'Do you think I was too gentle with him the first time? Too sympathetic because of his injury?'

'You *can* be sympathetic,' said Cooper. 'Sometimes.'

'Thank you.'

'But I'm thinking a second visit might take him by surprise, perhaps unsettle him enough to change his story.'

'OK, I'll try to be unsettling.' Villiers made a note. 'What did you make of the Warburtons, by the way?'

'I can't help but think they're genuine. There's no trace of a motive for them.'

'And no evidence?'

'The mark near Dead Woman's Drop? Sam Warburton was right – it could have been the tip of anyone's hiking pole that made that mark. It's forensically impossible to match the mark to a specific pole. The shape of their tips is identical, and of course there would be traces of peat on the Warburtons' poles. They were on Kinder for hours.'

'Do they go back to the bottom of your list, then?' asked Villiers.

'They were never near the top, to be honest. I think I'm just clutching at straws until a clear motive emerges, or we get an analysis back on the threatening note.'

'You're not here tomorrow, are you?'

'No, I've got a rest day due,' said Cooper. 'Make sure Dev Sharma knows where you are, though.'

Villiers was studying him curiously.

'Is there something else, Ben?' she asked.

'What do you mean?'

'Something bothering you. Only . . . we've been hearing something on the grapevine about Diane Fry. A disciplinary hearing.'

'Oh, word's gone round, has it?'

'You know what it's like.'

'Only too well.'

Cooper checked that no one else was outside his office door or passing in the corridor. He knew Carol Villiers was someone he could trust. Besides, it was pointless trying to keep secrets from her. She'd known him too long.

'I met up with her last night,' he said quietly.

'Diane?'

'Yes. She's asked me for help.'

'Well, there's a turn-up for the books.'

Cooper didn't laugh. He gave Villiers a brief outline of what Fry had told him, and she looked at him with an anxious frown when he'd finished.

'What are you going to do, Ben?' she asked.

He didn't answer for a moment. Not because he didn't know the answer but because he wasn't sure how Villiers would react. Her attitude to Diane Fry hadn't always been positive. And she knew what proper procedure was, and exactly how he should respond – co-operate with the investigation, tell the truth and do whatever Professional Standards asked, if they wanted to speak to him.

Cooper shook his head at the thought.

'I've got to help her, of course,' he said finally.

She nodded. 'That's what I thought you'd say.'

28

Diane Fry had been doing her best to rerun that meeting with Andy Kewley in her mind. She was sure there was some detail that she ought to recall that would mean more to her now than it did at the time.

That day, she'd parked her Audi on the roof level of Birmingham's Jewellery Quarter car park in Vyse Street, where she had a clear view up the street towards the exit from the Metro station.

A small trickle of people were spilling out of the station and heading off in different directions. Kewley was the last to come out, emerging onto the pavement near the old cast-iron street urinal. She recognised him even from that distance, even with the cap pulled over his eyes and a padded jacket to disguise his shape. There was something about the way people moved that made them recognisable whatever they wore.

Kewley had paused in the station entrance, looked all around him carefully, pretending to check his pockets for something. Andy was an old street cop. He'd learned to scan every doorway and corner before he made his move. It just never occurred to him to look up.

Fry looked at her watch. Kewley was bang on time for

their meeting, of course. She, on the other hand, was going to be a bit late. And that was the way she liked it.

Finally, she walked down to street level and stepped through the entrance to Warstone Lane Cemetery. She remembered some kind of white blossom on the bushes filling the air with its aroma. When she breathed it in, she felt as though she'd been punched in the nose. A certain trigger for her hay fever.

'Diane?'

Kewley had taken off the cap, revealing thinning hair streaked with grey. A warm breeze wandered through the plane trees, stirring a lock of his hair. When he raised a hand to push it back, she noticed that it wasn't as steady a hand as it once had been. The cumulative effects of thirty years in the job? Or was Andy Kewley drinking too much, like so many others?

In the middle of the cemetery, they were standing at the top of a terrace of curved brick walls. Two of the walls had rows of small, sealed-up entrances built into them, like arched doorways. Catacombs. She was surrounded by the Victorian dead.

Fry imagined Kewley using this cemetery for years to meet his informants. But it wouldn't be wise to keep coming here after he'd left the job. Too many people might remember. Too many of them might have a grievance to settle. Maybe it was just one of those eccentric fancies that overcame old coppers when they retired. Some had a hankering to run pubs, or to look for a quiet life in Northern Ireland. Others chose to hang around in Victorian grave-yards.

'I thought I might be able to help you,' he'd said.

'How?'

'Did you know there was an arrest after your assault? I was responsible for that.'

'You produced a suspect?'

'Let's say I provided intelligence. It was good intelligence too, as it turned out. This wasn't one of the primary suspects, but he knew who was involved all right, and he helped to cover it up. A real piece of work. He was as guilty as anyone I've ever met.'

'So what did you do?'

Kewley shrugged. 'We needed information, and we didn't want to spend days dragging it out of him bit by bit, with a brief at his elbow telling him to do the "no comment" stuff. So we fast-tracked the interview.'

'Fast-tracked . . . ?'

Kewley looked at her, gave her no more than a conspiratorial glance. But she understood.

'I don't want to know any more,' she said.

'No, of course you don't. You wouldn't want to be contaminated.'

Andy Kewley's career could best be described as chequered. In his early days in CID, before she'd teamed up with him at Aston, Kewley had spent some time in the West Midlands Serious Crime Squad. The squad had been disbanded, more than two decades ago now, following accusations that its members had fabricated evidence, tortured suspects and written false confessions.

For years, lawyers had been demanding fresh inquiries into the scale of corruption, claiming that dozens of innocent people had served time in jail. One had been quoted as saying that the Serious Crime Squad had operated as if they were in the Wild West: *They were out of control.*

'But you got what you wanted to know?' she said.

'Not entirely. We never got the names out of him.' Kewley smiled. 'But if we had . . . what do you reckon, Diane? Would the ends have justified the means or not?'

'What was he charged with?'

'Attempting to pervert the course of justice.'

'And what happened?'

'He got a "get out of jail free" card and a few quid in his pocket and off he went.'

'It's hardly the first time, Andy.'

'And now you're here in Birmingham again because they told you they'd opened a cold-case rape inquiry,' said Kewley. 'But they've lost a crucial witness, right?'

'You're well informed. How do you manage that?'

He ignored the question. 'The witness pulled out of the case, decided she didn't want to testify after all. The old story, eh? Someone got to her, Diane.'

'One of the suspects?'

'Or maybe their friends.' Kewley shrugged. 'Who knows?'

'She was supposed to be on witness protection,' said Fry. 'How would they have found her?'

'Information. It's easy to get hold of, if you know the right people.'

'Who?'

Again Kewley seemed to ignore the question. Fry remembered this habit of his, recalled how it had often infuriated her. He always wanted to go around the houses before he responded. But later he would drop the answer in casually, as if he'd never been asked.

She looked at the Victorian graves all around her. According to their memorials, many of them hadn't actually died but had merely 'fallen asleep'. If they woke up

279

now, they'd get a shock. And over there was another one. *Not lost but gone before.*

'Euphemisms,' said Fry. 'Don't you hate them?'

Kewley looked as though he didn't agree.

And then he mentioned a name that would come to haunt Fry. It was a name she'd never heard until that moment, but a connection that was to become much too personal.

'Have you heard of William Leeson?' he said.

Fry's ears had pricked up. This was the way it worked with Kewley. He distracted you with something irrelevant. Then the important information was dropped into the conversation like an afterthought. You had to be paying attention or you missed it.

'Leeson? No. Who is he?'

'A dodgy lawyer from Smethwick who used to practise here in the city. I thought you might have come across him.'

'I could have done,' said Fry. 'But hundreds of defence briefs come and go through interview rooms. I don't remember all their names.'

'You might want to remember this one,' said Kewley.

'Why?'

Kewley seemed to be getting more nervous now and jumped when a motorcycle with an unsilenced exhaust roared by on the Middleway.

Recalling that moment, Fry could have laughed at her own naivety. The idea that she wouldn't remember William Leeson's name for ever afterwards seemed ludicrous now.

'Leeson first came onto the scene in a big way during all that bother with the Serious Crime Squad,' said Kewley. 'He loved getting the attention, calling for public inquiries and Appeal Court hearings. "Miscarriage of justice" was practically tattooed on his forehead, he said it so often.'

'Was he the one who said you were operating like the Wild West?' asked Fry.

'No. But he would have said it, if he'd thought of it. He was always small-scale, though – and he got pushed out by the smarter, more expensive briefs who elbowed their way in when they saw a lucrative bandwagon rolling. Leeson got really pissed off about it. That was why he turned.'

'Turned?'

'He got involved in criminal activities himself. Other than as a legal representative, I mean. His money doesn't all come from legal fees.'

'I see.'

Kewley pulled his cap lower over his eyes and wiped the palms of his hands on his jacket.

'I shouldn't be telling you any of this.'

'Who says? You're retired, out of the force. You're a civilian now, Andy – as free as a bird. Get used to it.'

'I could still get myself into deep shit. You don't understand.'

Fry noticed that the memorials nearest to her had names like John Eachus and Walter Peyton Chance. Strange how names like that seemed to have died along with the Victorians themselves. She saw defaced angels, tombs blackened with soot. A statue lay broken and beheaded, an empty vodka bottle on the ground at its feet.

And there was that sickly smell again. She knew she would have to get away from the cemetery soon. It was starting to smell like the scent of death.

'I'm just telling you, Diane. There are things you need

to know. You could ask someone else, but whether you'll get the truth or not . . .'

'OK, OK.'

'I just want you to know there are political considerations at play right now. Much bigger issues than a successful conviction in any cold case – and I mean *any* case, no matter who the victim is. You understand me?'

'I'm not sure I do, Andy.'

'Damn it, I can't make it any clearer,' he said irritably. 'Look – anybody can get tossed aside, if it suits them. Justice is a slippery concept these days.'

Fry stared at him, wondering whether he'd gone completely off the rails since he retired. Leaving the job took people in different ways. It seemed as though Kewley might have developed a conspiracy obsession, or paranoid delusion. Probably he couldn't cope with the fact that he was no longer on the inside, not a member of the tribe any more. It was that primal instinct again. A desperation to belong. A craving to be part of the game.

Kewley took a breath, looked anxious at his own outburst.

'By the way,' he said, 'who's dealing with your case now?'

'Gareth Blake.'

'Blake? I remember him when he was a young DC, fresh behind the ears. Pain in the neck he was then. I don't suppose he's changed much?'

'I couldn't say. We worked together for a while, but that was years ago.'

'Gareth Blake . . . A DI now, isn't he? In fact, I hear he's well on his way to making DCI in the not-too-distant future. Yes, he's definitely got his foot on the ladder, that one. He wouldn't want anything to muck up his pristine record at this point, would he?'

Fry looked at him. 'What are you saying? Has Blake got something to hide?'

Kewley touched the side of his nose – a conspiratorial gesture that he somehow managed to make look obscene.

'You know what they say – the higher a monkey climbs up the tree, the more you see of his arse.'

He laughed and turned away. It was a signal that she wouldn't get any more out of him on that subject. Not right now, anyway. She might need some kind of pressure she could bring to bear. But that was for another day.

Angie Fry hadn't liked the idea of involving Andy Kewley, and she told her sister so after that first meeting in the cemetery.

'I didn't say I liked it either,' Diane had said. 'But he's useful. And he was my old partner. There ought to be some loyalty there still.'

When she thought back to her meeting with Kewley, Fry wondered if he'd been right, after all. Had she been sacrificed for some purpose she wasn't even aware of? *I mean any case, no matter who the victim is . . . Anybody can get tossed aside, if it suits them.* Yes, justice was a slippery concept indeed.

'I don't trust him,' Angie had said. 'I think he's dirty. I think he probably always was dirty.'

'Maybe. It doesn't matter.'

'Like hell it doesn't. I know this sort of character. He's playing both sides. If you don't watch him, he'll lead you into a trap, sis.'

'But who do we trust? Who *is* there we can trust?'

Angie had laughed. It was a short, bitter laugh that seemed to sum up decades of hard experience.

'No one,' she said. 'There's no one we can trust. That's the best advice your big sister can give you.'

'Thanks a lot. I'll treasure it.'

It was Andy Kewley who'd been late for his second meeting with Diane Fry. That was unlike him. She'd been waiting among the tiers of catacombs in Warstone Lane Cemetery, with tombs blackened with soot and that powerful, sickly sweet smell still strong on the night air.

It was very dark away from the street lights and Fry pulled a small torch from her pocket. She looked down from the top tier of the catacombs to the grass circle below, the centre of the amphitheatre.

For a moment, Fry thought the vandals had struck again since her last visit to the cemetery, that another memorial angel had been toppled to the ground. In the light of her torch, she saw blank eyes pressed into the grass, a face mottled with damp.

But when she looked again, she knew this was no angel. The face was pale, but it wasn't stone. The eyes were blank, but they were human. The mottled dampness was much too dark, as dark as clotted blood. Death had caught up with Andy Kewley.

29

Chloe Young had pitched it just right for the evening. Jeans and a white silk top that set off her dark hair, now tied up in what she described as a double-knotted pony. She looked smart, but not overdressed. Ben had emphasised that they were visiting a farm, after all. They'd be lucky if they found Matt Cooper wearing a clean pair of jeans and a shirt that wasn't ripped.

When he and Chloe entered Bridge End Farm, Ben felt ridiculously nervous, as if he were a teenager bringing his first girlfriend home to meet his parents. There was no reason to feel like that, of course. He wasn't a kid any more. He'd passed that stage a long time ago. He'd been engaged, for heaven's sake – and almost married too. If his marriage with Liz had gone ahead, he might have been a father himself by now. So his nervousness was ridiculous.

No, it was the house that made him feel like this. He couldn't escape the suspicion that the ghosts of his parents were still lurking in the dark corners of the hallway, peering out from behind the door of the snug, looking down from the banisters on the landing. Wherever he looked, his father and mother were almost there, but just out of sight. In a way, he still needed their approval, to know what they would have thought of the new woman in his life.

Chloe had raised an eyebrow in surprise when Ben led her to the back door of the farmhouse and entered without knocking. He paused for a moment, realising how odd it might look to some people. He'd never stopped thinking of Bridge End as his home, even though he'd lived in Edendale for years and now had his own house in Foolow. It would never have occurred to him to use the front door, or to knock and wait for someone to answer, the way visitors did. And he was certain Matt and Kate would have thought it very strange if he started to do that. They would take it as an insult. He'd be treating them as strangers instead of family.

'It's OK,' he said. 'This is what we do here.'

'Good job we're not burglars, then.'

'Oh, Matt would have his shotgun pointed at us by now.'

A look of concern crossed her face.

'I'm joking,' said Ben.

'Right.'

He hoped he sounded convincing. The trouble was, Chloe knew perfectly well that Matt Cooper had been involved in an incident a few years ago when a would-be burglar had been shot and wounded right here in the farmyard. Matt had faced the prospect of prosecution for a while until the CPS had taken the view that it wasn't in the public interest. There had been too many cases of that kind already, particularly in rural areas, and everyone knew what kind of outcry could be expected.

They stepped into the back hall, and Ben closed the door behind them.

'Hello!' he called. 'We're here.'

'Come on in,' answered Kate's voice from the kitchen.

Ben put his head round the door. 'Something smells good.'

Kate laughed, wiping her hands on a towel. 'That's what Matt always says.'

'This is Chloe.'

'Well, I thought it must be.'

The two women shook hands and appraised each other with that quick wordless assessment Ben had seen so often. It always made him wonder what passed between two women at a moment like this. It was as if they were communicating through some extra sense that he didn't possess, like two dogs sniffing the air and reading everything in a scent.

The test seemed to be passed on both sides. Kate and Chloe smiled at each other.

'We're so glad to meet you at last,' said Kate.

'I hope you're not going to say you've heard so much about me. I know none of it would be good.'

Ben heard an overly dramatic cough at his elbow and turned to find his niece Josie.

'Oh, and this is—' began Kate.

'I'm Josie. Are you the one who cuts up dead bodies?'

'Well, I suppose I am,' said Chloe.

'Brilliant.'

Over dinner, Josie couldn't be restrained from bombarding Chloe Young with questions about death, body parts and mortuary instruments. Matt began to look increasingly unhappy as he ate. But he'd never had much control over the females in his family.

'I blame you for this, Ben,' said Matt afterwards, when they found themselves alone in a quiet moment.

'For what?'

'First Josie said she was going to join the police, and now apparently she wants to be a pathologist.'

'She'll grow out of it. She just gets enthusiasms.'

Matt grunted. 'Always the wrong kind, though.'

'She doesn't want to come into farming, then?'

His brother's expression turned sour again.

'*Nobody* wants to come into farming,' he said. 'All everybody wants to do is get *out*.'

'But you'll never get out,' said Ben. 'Never.'

His brother scowled. 'One day,' he said, 'they'll carry out me out feet first. And what will become of Bridge End then?'

Ben couldn't answer that. There was no vision of a rosy prospect he could offer Matt. He knew what his brother said was true. Bridge End Farm would have no future without Matt Cooper.

It was one of the leafier suburbs near Solihull, a road where the trees grew denser and street signs became fewer and further between.

As Diane Fry headed out into the countryside, Angie phoned. The line was very poor, with a lot of noise in the background.

'Where are you?'

'I'm driving,' said Angie. 'Listen . . .'

'What is it?'

'I forgot to say, don't use your locker.'

'Sorry?'

'Your locker at the service station. Stay away from it for a while, that's all.'

'Why?'

But Angie had gone. Diane tried to dial again but got her recorded message. Her sister always liked to be a woman of mystery.

Fry drew her car onto the sweeping drive beyond the wrought-iron gates. The gates were open, because he was expecting her. But she knew the CCTV camera would be watching her as she approached. This was a man who didn't take risks.

Looking at his house and picturing his grey skin and skeletal hands as he sat waiting for her in his study, she couldn't help reliving for a moment her last visit here, when she was still trying to piece together what had happened the night of her rape, and why the case had collapsed so mysteriously despite a DNA match.

For some reason, within minutes of her arrival, William Leeson had been talking to her about blood.

'That's what we have to talk about, you and I,' he'd said. 'It's all about blood.'

She hadn't understood what he meant at first.

'What blood?'

'Mine,' he said. 'It was my blood at the scene of your assault. My blood the police got a DNA profile from. I pulled one of those boys off you, and he punched me in the face. I cut my hands on the fence, on the barbed wire. It was my blood, Diane. My blood was on you.'

'I don't believe you.'

'You know what they say, Diane. Blood is thicker than water. You might not believe it right at this moment. But you'll learn the truth soon enough, I think.'

'I'll tell you what I think. I think you're the cause I was sacrificed for, the reason my case will never go ahead. I think this whole charade has been about saving your pathetic skin. Well, I guess you must have the right bits of dirty knowledge about the right people in this city.'

He'd provoked her until she'd been on the verge of unacceptable violence and she'd been forced to leave the house. She'd been able to sense some awful event about to happen, something that was completely out of her control. Reluctantly, Fry got out of her Audi. The soft-topped sports car she'd glimpsed in the garage on her previous visit now stood on the gravel at the side of the house, as if for a quick getaway. A classic car, with leather seats and a noisy exhaust. Hardly inconspicuous if you wanted to disappear.

William Leeson was in his mid-sixties, but he looked a lot older. His face was gaunt and grey, and his suit jacket hung as loosely from his shoulders as it would from a wooden clothes hanger. The life had gone from his hair, which had thinned so much she could see his pale scalp, speckled with liver spots. His bony fingers moved restlessly, jerking spasmodically as if jolted by a burst of electricity.

Fry could remember picturing him as an undertaker, because of his height and cadaverous appearance. Now he looked as though he belonged in the coffin rather than driving the hearse. His skin looked so brittle, as if it might flake away at any moment and expose the bone. There was no doubt some serious illness was sapping his life away.

But Leeson knew her, of course. She hadn't changed that much.

'I didn't think I would ever see you again,' he said.

'That's the trouble with your mistakes. They keep coming back to haunt you.'

'So are you going to keep haunting me for ever, Diane?'

'I hope not. If I'm your nightmare, then you're definitely mine.'

He smiled thinly. 'Sit down. Can you at least bring yourself to do that? Would you like a drink? A gin and tonic? Or I have a nice Pinot Grigio.'

'No, thank you. I'm driving.'

'We wouldn't want to break any laws, would we?'

'It wouldn't be the first time, for some of us.'

He poured himself a large whisky. 'A fruit juice, perhaps? Something sharp but not too bad for your health.'

'All right, if you insist.'

Fry looked around the room as he opened a bottle of J2O orange and mango. She didn't know whether Leeson lived alone, if he was married or in a relationship. It was a big house for one person to live in alone. Five or six bedrooms, she imagined.

She gave an involuntary shudder. She'd just imagined William Leeson inviting her to stay overnight in one of his spare bedrooms. If she'd accepted a gin, that might have been the inevitable outcome. Her nightmare could have become a reality. What a narrow escape.

Suspiciously, Fry sniffed at the glass he gave her and took a tentative sip. It tasted OK.

Leeson was watching her expectantly.

'So I imagine this is isn't purely a social call,' he said. 'Speaking as one nightmare to another.'

'I'm not sure you'd call it social.'

'Not sure? Well, that's something.'

'I believe we have some unfinished business.'

'Really? I thought it was over and done with myself.'

'Apparently not.'

'Go on.'

'I have a problem. I think you might know something about it.'

He ran a finger round the rim of his glass. 'I know about a lot of things. You have to ask me a specific question if you want to get answers.'

'How did Professional Standards in Derbyshire get information about that time I came to Birmingham when my cold case was reopened? How did they know I met with Andy Kewley?'

He steepled his fingers. 'That's what you want to know?'

'It's what I asked.'

'One of your former colleagues,' said Leeson.

'You know that? It sounded like a guess.'

'It would seem to be a logical conclusion.'

'Why do you have to make this such hard work?'

He'd finished his whisky and poured himself another. Fry saw then how badly his hands shook. A trickle of liquid missed his glass and splashed onto the table, where it lay glistening accusingly.

'I'm sorry,' he said. 'It makes me angry.'

She watched his skeletal hands twisting and turning restlessly.

'You? What do you have to be angry about?'

'They have no right. You do what you have to do, but some of them will still pursue you out of spite.'

'Are you talking about me now? Or about yourself?'

He looked at her, his eyes cold and watery, his face an unhealthy pallor. Fry had a sudden flash of insight. She knew exactly what he was going to say next.

'I don't have much longer left to live,' he said. 'That sounds like such a cliché, doesn't it?'

'Totally. Is it true?'

'Do you want to see my medical notes? I was diagnosed—'

'I don't want to know,' interrupted Fry.

He smiled again. 'And why should you?'

'I suppose you're going to say that knowing you're dying makes you think differently about what you've achieved in your life?' she said.

'Achieved or not achieved. We all have failures. We've all made mistakes.'

'I'm not going to feel sorry for you. You're wasting your breath if that's what you're hoping for.'

'I'd be disappointed in you if you did. You wouldn't be the woman I know.'

Fry squirmed uncomfortably and put down her glass. Was it her imagination again or had he been about to say something else, use quite a different phrase to describe her? This time, he was the one who'd had a lucky escape. If he'd said those other words, the ones she never wanted to hear, she would have had no option but to punch him on the nose, sick or not. Her body had already tensed, her fist clenched instinctively. With an effort, she forced her hand to relax.

Leeson stood up, as if recognising the moment had come for her to leave. They no longer had anything left to say to each other.

'I'm glad you came, though, Diane,' he said. 'If there's one thing I can do for you, this may be it.'

Fry turned towards the door. She had no reason to feel grateful. He wasn't doing her a favour, merely going a small way towards repaying a huge debt.

'After all,' he said, 'I *am* your father.'

Fry flinched. But the moment had passed. She no longer felt like hitting anything, even him.

'Not in any meaningful sense of the term,' she said.

Leeson came to the door and watched her open her car.

'Will I see you again, Diane?' he said.

'Not if I can help it.'

'We'll speak, then?'

'I'm afraid so.'

Fry glanced in her rear-view mirror as she put her car into gear. She could see William Leeson standing in the doorway of his house, unnaturally pale and fragile. He looked nothing more than a ghost, haunting her from the past.

For a moment, she thought he would raise a hand to wave goodbye. But Leeson didn't move. And his image gradually faded away as she drove towards the gate.

It had been Ben Cooper who broke the news to her that the DNA hit from the scene of her assault had been a familial match, indicating a close relative of the victim's. A relative of *hers*.

'A brother or a son,' Cooper had said, 'or—'

'No.'

Fry shook her head, even as she thought about that moment.

A familial match. But to a family member she didn't even know existed then. Of course, she'd known she had a biological father, but not who he was, or where. And she never had any interest in finding anything out about him. She'd hated him without even knowing who he was.

And now that she'd found him, she detested him even more.

It was late when Ben Cooper returned to his home in Foolow. There were no street lights in the village, only a few windows still lit at the Bull's Head.

As he drew level with the cross on the village green, Cooper noticed the rear lights of a car pulling away from the kerb near his cottage. It looked like a small four-by-four. As it passed under his neighbour's security light, its paintwork gleamed an eerie red for a moment before it disappeared up the hill towards Grindlow. Something about the car caught his attention, but it was too far away to get a registration number. Probably he was just being paranoid. Spending too much time with Diane Fry could do that to him.

Cooper parked his Toyota behind the cottage and let himself in through the back door. He listened for the bang of the cat flap, but realised he was much later home than usual and out of routine. Hope was already curled up in her basket by the radiator. She opened one eye, gave him an accusing glare, then went back to sleep.

'Suit yourself,' he said. 'I've had a hard day too.'

He shrugged off his jacket and turned towards the kitchen to make himself a drink. When he came back, the cat was out of her bed and sitting in the middle of the rug, staring at the front door, her ears tilted forward like a pointer.

'What's up?' said Cooper. 'Mouse?'

He opened the door into the entrance hall and saw a large envelope stuck halfway through his letterbox.

'That's odd.'

He inspected the envelope carefully before sliding it clear and jumped as the letterbox sprang shut behind it with a loud clang.

It was more than just an envelope. It was quite a thick package, which had only just fit through his door. The edges were scraped and torn where it had been pushed through with some force.

Cooper glanced out of the window at the darkened village, remembering the small red car that had pulled away as he entered Foolow. The post was often delivered late in the day in these rural villages. But not this late.

He took the package back into the sitting room and laid it on the table. Slowly, he slit one end open with a knife and slid out a pile of A4 sheets fastened together with a rubber band. He looked at the title on the top page.

'Interesting,' he said.

Behind him, the cat ran a paw over her whiskers and began to purr contentedly.

30

Thursday

Ben Cooper was out and about early next morning, just after dawn. It was his official rest day, and he had a few hours to kill before an appointment at four o'clock that afternoon. The weather was fine, and there was only one place in Derbyshire he thought of going.

The roads were quiet on the way into Hayfield. The white streams lying in the hollows like trails of smoke were only an early morning mist, not a sign of returning fog. It would soon burn off when the sun reached the valley.

In Hayfield, Cooper parked at Bowden Bridge and changed into his walking boots. He set off to climb onto White Brow, having decided to avoid the path to the south, where part of the River Kinder had found its own route down the hill from the dam and was flowing over the footbridge.

Even in summer Kinder Scout was no place for a solitary rambler. Pools formed deep enough to drown in. As the New Trespassers had found to their cost, a strong walker might leap from hag to hag before finally twisting an ankle or becoming exhausted. It could be days before another rambler passed that way.

Of course, it helped to be able to read a compass. You

could get so disorientated traversing the bogs that you had no idea which direction you were heading, or where you were on the map. It was a truly unsettling feeling, especially if you were aware of the precipitous cliffs and steep drops onto shattered rocks. These days, people relied on mobile phones to get them out of trouble. But there were no phone masts on Kinder.

He passed the sheep wash at the hamlet of Booth, which would still have been in use when the mass trespassers came by in 1932, with hundreds of sheep collected from the western slopes of Kinder. Washing the sheep was regarded as a great social occasion in those decades, with shepherds standing waist-deep in the water as sheep were tossed in one by one for their fleeces to be scrubbed clean of peat before shearing, and farmers mixing their own sheep dip from soap and creosote to kill lice and ticks in the dense wool.

Cooper soon realised that he should have brought a stick or a hiking pole like the Warburtons. As soon as he stepped on the steepest stretch of cobbles beyond the entrance to the old water-treatment works, his feet slipped from underneath him. He hit the wet stones with a painful crash. For a moment, he was dazed. He sat up and rubbed his elbow where he'd scraped it on the ground. Then he got back to his feet and carried on upwards.

He passed along the edge of Kinder Reservoir, with the abandoned water-treatment works below him. The rows of arched windows on the filter house had been blocked up, and many of the skylights were smashed. The path here was scattered with dead leaves and the empty husks of acorns. A jay darted between a stand of oak trees growing along the brow.

Then the peace was shattered as an Emirates 747 roared low overhead, coming in to land at Manchester Airport, a white shape skimming in and out of the cloud. Flights passed constantly over the Kinder plateau. Where Manchester people had once fought for the right to ramble across these moors, now they flew over every week, ignoring Kinder on their way to holidays in Ibiza or Magaluf.

Above him, Cooper could see the Downfall ravine, the rocks around it like bastions and towers, broken and shattered. Water was spraying off the edge today. After heavy rain, it foamed and steamed as it cascaded off the plateau.

It was because Kinder held so much water that it was impossible to find a dry route across it. He'd heard that those streams of water removed ten thousand tons of the mountain's bulk every year. Eventually, the plateau would be flattened to the level of the surrounding river valleys. But not in his lifetime.

The whole fourteen square miles of Kinder Scout were criss-crossed with deep groughs, carved by water between the hags. Their sides were steep, spongy slopes, their bottoms filled with water that fed the Downfall. It was only by continually crossing them that it was possible to maintain a steady direction.

Some people thought this place was pretty grim, especially in the winter. The unrelenting blackness of the peat could be a bit overwhelming. It wasn't a place to wander alone if you were already depressed, or feeling despair about the futility of life. Nature could reflect your mood and exaggerate it. Half an hour of floundering through grough and bog would drain your energy and sap your will to live. And in fog? Damp, close air and reduced visibility could soon evoke sensations of isolation and fear.

So what made Kinder Scout so attractive to walkers? Well, the views were certainly extensive – Yorkshire to the north and Cheshire in the west, with the mountains of Wales visible in the distance on a clear day. This vista might not have been so clear at the time of the Mass Trespass, thanks to the smoke from mill chimneys and the coal fires of inner-city workers' homes.

For centuries the sphagnum moss binding the surface had been steadily killed off by industrial pollution, all that acid rain falling from factories in Manchester. The sphagnum was being reintroduced now, thanks to the Moors for the Future project.

After seeing its fourteen square miles of bare peat steaming with moisture, someone had once called the Kinder plateau 'land at the end of its tether, entirely covered in the droppings of dinosaurs'. It had certainly been an uncompromising landscape for generations. But now Kinder was in the throes of change. Out here on the edge of the world, two thousand feet above sea level, life was returning to this once bleak moonscape.

A grouse jumped up from the heather with a harsh cry – *Go back! Go back, back, back, back!* But Cooper continued to move onwards.

On a flattened edge of the slope below, he glimpsed the Mermaid's Pool. On the plateau itself, the rock formations were the best-known landmarks. Pym Chair, the Druid Stone, the Boxing Gloves, Madwoman's Stones, Punch's Nose, Ringing Roger.

The Woolpacks and the Mushroom Garden were names describing the appearance of many of the gritstone rocks. The Pagoda was a collection of huge flat stones laid on top of each other. The Moat Stone was named because of the shallow pool surrounding it. Some rocks resembled a frog, a fossilised giant snail or an upturned tooth.

For a moment, Cooper wondered what it was like to live in a part of the country where individual rocks weren't named on the Ordnance Survey map. Were people still as conscious of their own history, the presence of those ancestors with their dark, superstitious imaginations?

All these legends brought his thoughts back to the New Trespassers Walking Club. Their entire existence was based on a legend. Yet as a group, they seemed to have been stitched together like a kind of Frankenstein's monster.

The more Cooper thought about it, the more the Kinder Mass Trespass seemed a tenuous connection between these people. And some of them cared nothing for the significance of the 1932 trespass. One believed it was a Communist plot. So what had brought them together in the first place? Could these people be linked by something completely different?

The Mass Trespass had taken place in April. The 24th to be exact. Why was that a 'bad time' for members of the group, as Darius Roth had described it a few days ago? Cooper had assumed it was something to do with work, or school holidays: 24 April could sometimes fall during the Easter break, but not always. So was there some other significance to the choice of October? Who had chosen the date for the walk? Darius, of course.

Cooper stopped walking suddenly. He felt as though his feet had hit hidden obstacles in the wet peat; those familiar tentacles had reached out and grabbed his ankles. He was recalling his conversation with Elsa Roth about the fate of Darius's brother, Magnus, the rock climber. Didn't she say that he died six years ago? Surely that was just about the time the date of the New Trespassers' annual walk was changed. Did Darius move the date to October to mark his brother's death? Could there be some significance to that? Were they all connected through that fatal incident?

Ahead, the Swine's Back led along the southern edge of the plateau towards Grindsbrook, and Kinder itself stretched before him.

Ironically, the original trespassers had got lost on Kinder. In fact, they'd never reached the top of the hill at all but had turned left and descended to Ashop Head instead of right towards the Downfall and onto the plateau. A Sheffield group who ascended Jacob's Ladder on the other side of the moor to meet them must have been baffled to see the main party turning away and heading in the opposite direction. Like so many ramblers since, the Kinder mass trespassers had no idea where they were.

Where the restoration work was taking place, some areas of the plateau had been transformed from dark menace to a bright benevolence as the black, eroded morass was seeded over and turned green.

But here was the Kinder that he'd always known. Desolate and dangerous. A place where unwary walkers wandered lost for hours and could sink up to their waists in the bog. A path of stone slabs had been laid across a stretch of badly eroded moorland, like a causeway across a black, peaty ocean.

Cooper reached Crowden Head and for a while he sat out of the wind behind a rock, watching the clouds roll in from the south-west and taking in the silence at the summit.

To the north across the Snake Pass lay the high moors of Bleaklow and Black Hill. Along the eastern edge of the plateau, a soggy line across high ground from the Mad-woman's Stones to the cairn of Ringing Roger. The plateau today looked bleak, and dangerous.

If you were lost on Kinder, there was no safe way down unless you managed to hit one of the two main paths. Without a compass and the ability to use it, you might walk round in circles for hours. The best advice was to stay where you were until help arrived.

But the New Trespassers Walking Club hadn't done that. Why not? What had caused that division within the group and made them head off in separate directions?

Well, perhaps because they had no clear leadership. Without firm direction from Darius, there was no one able to make a decision that would be accepted by the others. That was why the group had split up. No unity, no soli-darity, no commitment to each other. They'd put their trust in Darius Roth, and he'd failed them when it came to a crisis.

That morning, Diane Fry drove under Clifton Bridge and pulled into the BP service station as usual. Another text message had arrived on her phone from InPost to alert her to a delivery, with a code to access her locker. That was odd. She wasn't expecting anything. She wracked her memory to remember what she might have ordered that hadn't already arrived, but couldn't think what it might be.

Well, she could only go and find out. All she had to do was scan the QR code or enter the number on the touch screen to open a locker. But she remembered what Angie had said in that call yesterday: *Don't use your locker.*

There was no one around the collection point. She filled up her car, bought her coffee and a packet of mints, and withdrew some money from the cash machine outside, taking her time. Then she stayed in her car for a few moments on the side of the forecourt, pretending to use her mobile phone.

A black BMW was parked across the road in the entrance to the river walk. It would be quite normal at this time of the morning. People took their dogs for exercise along the riverbank, though they rarely arrived in BMWs.

In this case, two men were sitting in the car, apparently doing nothing except admiring the scenery. They were parked so that their rear-view mirrors were angled towards the service station. Fry felt sure she was being watched. Had they been expecting her to check her locker? What would she have found inside it, if she had? Perhaps Angie's warning had meant something, after all.

Fry smiled as she put her phone away. She had at least one shot on the phone that might show up the number plate of the BMW. She wondered if it would be there again tomorrow morning, or whether they would bother to use a different car. They would have a frustrating time. She had no intention of using her locker for the foreseeable future.

As she drove northwards, Fry felt as though she'd achieved a small victory. She even smiled at the prospect of her next interview with Martin Jackson, which was scheduled for tomorrow.

Today, though, she was back at her desk at EMSOU. Fry pulled into the car park behind a building just off a junction of the M1 and keyed in the security code. She half expected the code to have been changed so that she couldn't get in. But the door opened and she walked through to her office, wondering whether she'd be able to give the appearance that everything was normal.

Everyone must know what was going on: all her colleagues would be aware of the disciplinary hearing. If not, they would naturally ask her where she'd been. But when she arrived at her desk, no one asked. She just got the usual casual greetings and a few brief nods.

Jamie Callaghan swung his chair over to speak to her.

'You OK, Diane?'

'Yes, I'm fine. Thanks.'

Callaghan smiled, but didn't say anything more.

Reports had piled up on Fry's desk during the short time she'd been gone. She checked on the progress of the Danielle Atherton murder inquiry in Edendale and frowned over an MG11 witness statement from one of the Athertons' neighbours. She made a note, wondering if DCI Mackenzie would be available to speak to her.

Then she turned to the latest briefings.

'Jamie, what's this about an unexplained death on Kinder Scout?' she said.

'Could be suspicious,' said Callaghan. 'Or maybe not. Your friend DI Cooper is dealing with it at the moment, North Division CID.'

'He won't want to pass it on to us,' said Fry.

'He'll have to, if it's confirmed as homicide.'

'Mmm. There's always a possibility that it's confirmed too late, when there's nothing left for us to do.'

Callaghan laughed. 'Well, you know him best. To be honest, I think I'd probably be the same, unless it was a high-profile case.'

Fry looked around the office to see who was missing today, who might perhaps be at Ripley being interviewed by Professional Standards. She thought Mackenzie might have wanted to welcome her back to the team, but there was no sign of him.

'Is the boss in, Jamie?' she said.

'I think he's in a meeting,' said Callaghan vaguely.

'Maybe I'll catch him later.'

Fry decided to keep her head down. DCI Mackenzie's absence from the office could be suspicious. Or maybe not.

Ben Cooper looked at his phone. There had been no signal for some time as he made his way across the plateau. But now two bars were showing on his screen, and he could see that he'd missed a call from Carol Villiers.

'I couldn't shake Liam Sharpe,' Villiers said when he called her back. 'He's at home, still with his foot up, and he can only walk with a limp. It looks genuine to me, and his account is totally consistent. He says he pleaded with Faith Matthew not to leave him alone on Kinder. Ben, he even started to look scared as he was talking about it. The memory was painful for him. I don't think he's that good an actor.'

'Did you ask him any more about Faith?'

'He says he liked her. More than he did some of the others in the group, anyway. He was glad she was the one who stayed behind. It made him feel reassured, he said. But then she left him . . . You should have heard him talking about it, Ben – it was like he'd been abandoned by his mother.'

'But why did she leave him alone?'

'She told him she'd noticed something, lights in the fog. She went up onto higher ground to see if it was a rescue party coming. It makes sense, I suppose.'

'So you don't think Mr Sharpe could have faked his injury.'

'That's my feeling.'

Cooper nodded as he listened to her account of the interview.

'Oh well. It shouldn't be possible anyway,' he said. 'Not just like that. It shouldn't have been such a simple solution, a blatant deception that no one bothered to question. Someone would have noticed something.'

'Especially when there are twelve witnesses.'

'Well, perhaps that's too many,' said Cooper.

'What?'

'Sometimes the more witnesses you have, the more difficult it is to get at the facts. Every witness sees and hears something different. We're taught that in basic training, aren't we? The skill is to look for the consistencies and inconsistencies to get at the truth hidden among all the witness statements. It can be hard, though.'

'Yes, it can.'

'Besides,' said Cooper, 'don't forget – one of those twelve people wasn't just a witness.'

'We're still struggling for a motive.'

'Speaking of which, see if someone can find out exactly when Darius Roth's brother died.'

'What was his first name?'

'Magnus. He was a rock climber. According to Elsa, he died in a fall.'

He ended the call and looked at his surroundings. He'd carried on walking while he was listening to Villiers. Now he seemed to have lost his bearings. He looked downhill and frowned at the sense of unfamiliarity as he looked in vain for signs of the River Kinder. There were two main watercourses on the plateau, fed by those thousands of small streams. The Kinder drained west to the Irish Sea, while water from Fairbrook flowed eastwards and ended up in the North Sea.

The sun was behind the clouds, but he could see from a brighter patch where the west lay and which was east. And he was facing in the wrong direction.

Cooper muttered a curse. At some point in the last few minutes, he'd unintentionally crossed the watershed in the middle of England and was heading eastwards. Kinder had performed its dangerous magic again. It had turned him round three hundred and sixty degrees, without him being aware of it. He was a long way from where he should have been. He was looking down into the valley of the Noe at Grindsbrook instead of westwards towards Hayfield.

Cooper knew he should have navigated by compass rather than relying on landscape features and his sense of direction. Because this was Kinder, and the landscape seemed to change at will, stones constantly shifting position, the groughs growing deeper, streams changing direction, paths appearing and disappearing as they petered out into nowhere. That was why Kinder Scout was impossible to map. It never stayed the same long enough. For Cooper, this mountain was a living thing.

And this must have been what happened to the New Trespassers Walking Club. In the end, none of them would have had any idea where they were, no matter what they claimed in their witness statements. Faith Matthew probably wouldn't have known she was perched on the edge of a precipice at Dead Woman's Drop.

But what about the person who pushed her over? How could he or she have known? Was there just one among the group who knew their exact position? One person who saw an opportunity to take advantage of the fear and confusion?

Cooper pictured the map showing the relative movements of the walking group that fateful day. He was remembering his interview with Jonathan Matthew. In his mind, he could hear Jonathan talking about how guilty he felt not to have been there to protect his sister when she died. Cooper had sympathised with him then, had fully understood the guilt he was experiencing.

But surely the map had been telling him quite a different story, which he'd been refusing to see. According to the MRT, only Dolly the search dog knew Jonathan's exact position when he was found. There was no evidence of where he was at the moment his sister was attacked and killed, no clear picture of where he'd gone when the party split up.

Perhaps, after all, Faith's brother *was* there when she died.

31

Derbyshire Constabulary's headquarters were tucked out of the way in the Butterley area of Ripley, accessed from an anonymous roundabout on the A610 near a McDonald's drive-through and a Sainsbury's supermarket.

It was a long while since Ben Cooper had been here, and then it was for a meeting at Operational Support in their base off Wyatt's Way. Since his last visit, the administrative departments had moved into a gleaming new building they shared with the fire service, and which seemed to be made mostly of glass.

As he drove in through the security barriers, Cooper saw the NPAS helicopter sitting on its pad behind the dog kennels at the rear of the site. He found a place in the visitors' car park backing onto the sports fields and collected an identity badge from reception. Then there was a wait before his appointment.

He took a seat in the reception area, clutching the manila folder he'd brought with him. He spent the time running back over his conversation late last night, after he'd left Bridge End Farm and parted with Chloe Young. Even now, he could hardly believe what he'd done. But if he was going to help Diane Fry, it was inevitable. He'd called

Angie, without telling Diane what he was going to do. He could just hear what she would have to say about that. She'd always hated any contact between her professional and personal lives, particularly between him and her sister. They had a history, and Diane never forgot.

'I don't think there's anyone who can be trusted,' Angie had said to him.

'Do you not trust me?'

She'd been silent for a while. Cooper had been able to hear a baby in the background, making that annoying grizzling sound babies did. He thought of suggesting to Angie that Zack was teething, but decided she wouldn't appreciate the advice. Not coming from him.

'I don't know you very well,' she'd said, 'but . . .'

'But . . . ?'

'OK. Give me your email address.'

'Great.'

Cooper jerked upright when his name was called. He was taken upstairs and ushered into a room. The Professional Standards Department investigator introduced himself as Martin Jackson. He was accompanied by a colleague, who took notes.

'Detective Inspector Cooper,' said Jackson. 'You feel you have something to contribute to this hearing?'

'Yes, sir, I do.'

'Mmm. How long have you known Detective Sergeant Fry?'

'Since she first transferred to Derbyshire from West Midlands. She was assigned to E Division, where I was based.'

'E Division.'

'Now Edendale LPU,' said Cooper. 'North Division.'

'Ah yes.'

'We were both DCs then, part of the same shift in Divisional CID. We've worked closely together a number of times since those days.'

'When Fry was promoted to detective sergeant . . . ?'

'I was still a DC, yes. So I became part of her team.'

'And now you're a DI and you're senior to her,' said Jackson. 'So you've observed her from several perspectives, serving in different roles. You've had experience of her as a colleague, a supervisor and now as a more junior officer working in a different unit.'

'Yes, sir.'

'And as a friend, would you say?'

Cooper could see he was suddenly being studied more closely for his reaction. He hesitated, though only for a second.

'She isn't an easy person to make friends with,' he said.

His interviewers exchanged glances.

'No, we've already gained that impression. So would you maintain that your opinion of Detective Sergeant Fry is purely a professional one, unbiased by personal feelings?'

'I would,' said Cooper.

That was the first lie he'd told. But exactly what feelings *were* involved? He'd be hard pressed to explain them to himself. Any attempt at explaining them to these two people would only muddy the waters and make his statement seem unreliable. Sometimes there was a necessity for reticence.

The chief inspector was nodding, as if satisfied by his replies.

'So then, Detective Inspector Cooper, would you say

that DS Fry's conduct has always been entirely professional, in your experience?'

Cooper paused again.

'No,' he said. 'Certainly not.'

Diane Fry jumped when the call came through on her mobile. She saw the number was a Birmingham code. She left her desk and walked out into the corridor as she answered it.

'Yes?'

'Diane?'

'Who else would it be?'

William Leeson laughed, but began to cough before he could speak.

'Where are you? Is anyone nearby?'

'Wait.'

Fry looked around and found a quiet spot where she couldn't be overheard.

'It's OK now.'

'I'm sending you an email,' he said. 'To your personal email address. Can you get it on your phone?'

'Yes.'

'OK, sending now.'

Fry saw an email appear in her inbox with several attachments. She opened them cautiously. You could never be too careful.

He rang off. She looked at the first one, then scrolled through the others rapidly, in increasing disbelief. He'd sent her a series of cartoons, some of which she recognised as being taken from the Police Federation magazine. There was one showing a sergeant using an e-form on a hand-held device to request a Taser during a riot and failing to get a signal. Another featured Hercule Poirot saying, 'Not now, Hastings. I'm following a suspect on Twitter.' Was she supposed to laugh?

'Bastard!' she said.

An officer passing the end of the corridor turned to stare at her in surprise. Fry realised she'd sworn much too loudly. But sometimes circumstances demanded it.

In Ripley, Martin Jackson tapped his fingers together and sat back in his chair with a hint of satisfaction at Ben Cooper's reply.

'Let's get this straight, Detective Inspector Cooper,' he said. 'You're saying that you haven't always found DS Fry to be entirely professional?'

'No,' said Cooper. 'Well, most of the time, yes.'

'Would you like to expand on that?'

'What I mean is that I've seen her go above and beyond her professional duty many times. I've seen her put herself at risk to protect both the public and her colleagues, or to apprehend a suspect. She's one of the bravest officers I know. While others might stand back and follow approved procedures, she puts herself on the line time after time. She may have made mistakes, but they've been honest ones, done with the best of intentions and a dedication to the job.'

'You have no doubts about her integrity?'

'None.'

'Her honesty?'

'No, sir.'

'Some of your colleagues might disagree.'

'She's been unfairly portrayed by some as dishonest or unprofessional. I'm here to put the record straight.'

Jackson nodded almost imperceptibly. He no longer

looked quite so satisfied. Cooper could see him preparing to change tack. It was a standard interview technique, designed to catch your interviewee off guard.

'And I believe you've met DS Fry's sister,' said Jackson. 'Is that right?'

'Angie? Yes, I have.'

'Are you familiar with her background, and her associates?'

'Some of them,' said Cooper. 'But I'm sure DS Fry made every attempt to distance herself. I'm confident she had no involvement in anything that would bring the force into disrepute.'

Then he was asking questions about an incident in Nottinghamshire that he could truthfully say he knew nothing about, and Diane Fry's visit to Birmingham when her cold case was reopened. For a while after that, Jackson repeated the same questions, phrasing them differently, probing for inconsistencies. Cooper kept to simple answers, resisting the temptation to say more than he already had.

Finally, his ordeal was over.

'Thank you for your input, Detective Inspector,' said Jackson. 'Your contribution to this inquiry is duly recorded. We'll let you go back to your duties. I'm sure you're very busy.'

From Jackson, it sounded patronising. But Cooper smiled politely and leaned over the table as he stood up.

'There's just one more thing,' he said.

'Oh?'

Cooper opened the folder he was carrying and placed a small stack of documents on the table.

'Yes, there's this.'

'What is it?'

'Evidence of a conspiracy among serving officers in West Midlands Police. Oh, only a small handful of them, it's true. But they have a long reach in these cases, don't they? They want to bring Diane Fry down because they think she has information that could compromise them. I spent all last night reading this stuff. It made me want to get outside so the fresh air could blow the stink away. It's clear to me that officers in the West Midlands undermined a witness and deliberately deterred her from testifying in DS Fry's rape case to prevent it from going to court.'

'Why would they do that?'

'So their own complicity wouldn't come to light. It was a case that could have been prosecuted successfully years ago. When DS Fry began her own inquiries in Birmingham, they were afraid she would dig up the truth. As you'll see, they've been busy trying to build a case to discredit her, clutching at any straw they could find. You've been fed the ammunition, sir.'

'But why now?' said Jackson. 'This case was some time ago.'

'I'm afraid it stems from Fry's sister.'

'Ah. Angela Jane.'

Cooper nodded. 'Angie has been speaking too freely. Her former boyfriend was pulled in for drugs offences last month, and he shared everything he'd heard, or overheard. When certain officers discovered who Fry had been talking to, they wanted to strike first. They wanted to make sure she was silenced.'

Still Jackson seemed reluctant to touch the documents.

'So where did you get these from?'

'It hardly matters, does it?' said Cooper. 'We both know that there are ways and means of getting information when it's needed. You could have got this for yourself, if you'd tried.'

He left the office without looking back, and hurried downstairs, expecting to be called back at any moment. But he handed in his visitor's pass and reached his car without anyone stopping him. He felt like a criminal leaving the scene of a crime.

As he drove out of the headquarters complex on the one-way system, Cooper gazed at the buildings he passed. He was amazed – not at the questions he'd been asked but at the answers he'd given. He'd gone to the interview without preparing what he was going to say, just knowing that he had to say something. And now he was surprised by all the things he'd come out with, the views he never knew he had.

He smiled as he put distance between himself and Ripley. There had still only been one lie too.

Another call from Carol Villiers was waiting on his phone for him to answer.

'Ben,' she said when he called back. 'We've had a report from Trespass Lodge, the Roths' property. Mrs Roth has reported her husband missing. She says she hasn't seen Darius since last night.'

32

It took Ben Cooper far longer than he would have liked to get from Ripley to Hayfield. The last thing he needed was to be pulled over for speeding by his Derbyshire road policing colleagues on his way back from a disciplinary hearing.

So a full team was already at the scene in the grounds of Trespass Lodge by the time he arrived. Cooper crossed the stretch of grass to the old Methodist chapel. Tape had been rolled out, lights were set up, and CSIs were busy in the interior of the chapel.

Carol Villiers met him at the outer cordon.

'We've found him,' she said, as he climbed into a scene suit. 'It didn't take long.'

'What exactly happened, Carol?'

'It seems Mr Roth fell from the gallery.'

'Fell?'

'I'm using the term loosely. Unlike our woman on Kinder Scout, there's no doubt about this one from the word go.'

'Let's have a look.'

Inside, Cooper could see that Darius Roth's body had landed on the flags of the chapel floor with slightly less of an impact than Faith Matthew's body had hit the rocks below Kinder Downfall. The distance of the fall wasn't so great, though the stone flags were just as hard and unyielding for a human body.

It was clear that the impact had fractured Roth's skull. A splatter of blood and cranial matter had been thrown in a bright halo round his head.

'He has cuts and abrasions on his face,' said Cooper.

'And on his hands too.'

'Defensive wounds? So there was a fight.'

'It certainly looks as though he tried to defend himself against someone. The balustrade up there is broken. Admittedly, the wood isn't in perfect condition, but he didn't just fall over it – he went through it with some force. We've found splinters of wood embedded in some of his wounds, and there are plenty of shoe marks in the dust on the floorboards of the gallery.'

'It was somebody he knew,' said Cooper.

'Well, I don't know if we can go that far. Not on the basis of the forensic evidence.'

'Think about it. Would Darius Roth go up into the gallery with a complete stranger?'

'He might already have been up there.'

Cooper nodded. Yes, he could picture that. It made a good vantage point, a balcony from where Darius Roth could look down like a king on – what? His followers, Cooper imagined.

'He would have been able to see anyone who came into the chapel from there,' said Cooper. 'Why would he let them come in and climb the steps to where he stood if it was someone he didn't know?'

'OK, so perhaps he knew his attacker.'

'And more than that – it was someone he trusted.'

'Trusted?'

Cooper thought about it. 'Or someone he felt he had a secure hold over.'

'So he was overconfident, you mean,' said Villiers. 'That fits his personality, I suppose.'

'Yes. I imagine in this case his hold on one individual wasn't secure enough. His power over them failed disastrously.'

'Do you think it was revenge for Faith Matthew's death?'

'What do you think, Carol?'

'Well, it would only make sense if Darius Roth was the one who killed her. But we have no evidence to suggest it. The accounts from our witnesses are consistent on one point at least – they show Darius to be with one of the groups who split away to try to get help.'

'With Elsa and the two students, Millie Taylor and Karina Scott. Not forgetting Nick Haslam. They were best placed to know his movements. They would have known whether he had the opportunity to kill Faith Matthew or not.'

'Could they all be lying?'

Cooper laughed. 'You and I know perfectly well that *everybody* could be lying.'

'So what then?'

'Revenge as a motive would make sense in two scenarios – if Darius Roth was the one who killed Faith or if someone had good reason to believe he did.'

'That would mean they had knowledge of the incident that we don't.'

Cooper shook his head. 'Not necessarily. Belief doesn't always need evidence.'

'Unfortunately.'

'The rest of our witnesses don't have first-hand evidence

of where Darius was, because they were in a different group and didn't see him after they split up.'

'Does that narrow it down at all?' said Villiers.

'I hope so. At least if we can get prints or DNA, we'll have some suspects for comparison. Meanwhile, let's see if we can focus our attention even more. Who actually found the body?'

'The gardener.'

'Will Sankey? You talk to him, then, Carol, and I'll deal with Mrs Roth.'

'Good luck,' said Villiers.

Elsa Roth was hugging her arms round her chest as if trying to hold in some emotion. Cooper felt immediately sorry for her. Whatever his own views of her husband, Elsa's world had just been torn apart.

'I'm sorry, Mrs Roth,' said Cooper, 'but we do need to ask some questions. Weren't you concerned that your husband was missing?'

'I don't keep track of Darius's movements,' said Elsa. 'He doesn't like it. He gets annoyed if I ask him where he's going or where he's been. So I don't ask.'

'But you must have had an idea whether he was at home or he'd gone to work.'

'He does a lot of his business from home. He has an office at the other end of the house.'

It was that phrase 'the other end of the house' that reminded Cooper he was in a different world. Back home at Tollhouse Cottage, he was aware of every sound in the house, knew which room the cat was in from the sound of her snoring or the click of her claws on the floorboards.

Here at Trespass Lodge, it was possible for Elsa Roth not

to know whether her husband was at home or not, and vice versa. They seemed to have occupied different ends of the lodge for much of the time, and the property was so large that there would be no sounds reaching from one end to the other.

He imagined they would probably have phoned each other if they needed to speak. Darius could even have got one of his cars out of the garage and driven away without Elsa knowing, if he wanted to.

'So you didn't notice your husband had gone down to the chapel?'

'No.'

'And did you see anyone else this morning?'

'Only the gardener, Will. And we have a cleaner, Milena. She was here this morning. But she's very discreet.'

'Discreet?' repeated Cooper.

Why was he interpreting that word to mean that Milena wouldn't tell him anything? Was that what Elsa intended? Perhaps. A discreet servant might notice things but wouldn't talk about them. He felt sure Elsa wouldn't refer to Milena as a servant, though. That was very Edwardian.

'Who knew about the old chapel?'

'All the members of the club, of course,' she said.

'You mean the New Trespassers Walking Club.'

'Of course.'

'And previous members too?'

'I suppose so.' She looked around vaguely, as if she couldn't remember anything before today. 'Yes, they all came here at some time.'

'Did your husband often come down to the chapel from the house at that time of night?'

'He might have done, now and then. We have separate

bedrooms. Sometimes he came home late from a meeting or a dinner, or something like that, so he arranged our rooms so that he wouldn't disturb me. But there were a few times when I was woken up by something in the early hours of the morning and thought it was Darius arriving home in his car. When I looked out of the window, though, I saw him walking up the garden from the lake, so I know he spent time down here on his own.'

'On his own?' repeated Cooper.

Elsa looked puzzled. 'Well, I assumed . . .'

'What?' said Cooper. 'What did you assume your husband was doing down here, Mrs Roth?'

She shrugged feebly. 'Just that he wanted to be on his own, and this was his place to do it. Some people are like that, aren't they?'

'Yes, it's true.'

'Well, then?'

'Did it never occur to you that Darius might not be on his own at the old chapel, that he could be meeting someone?'

'I don't know who that would be,' she said.

Again she hadn't asked questions. From what she said, it seemed Elsa hadn't even raised the possibility in her own mind. A saying of his mother's came into Cooper's head: *There are none so blind as those who will not see.* Where did that quotation come from? Or was it one of those ancient proverbs attributed to 'Anonymous', their origins lost in time? It was amazing how accurate they could still be.

Cooper went back out to his Toyota, which was parked on the gravel at the front of Trespass Lodge. Carol Villiers was waiting for him when he reached his car.

323

'I've talked to Will Sankey,' she said. 'It seems he'd worked his way down to that end of the grounds as usual by late morning and he noticed the door of the old chapel was open. He says it wasn't unknown for Darius to be down there, but he never left the door open. So Sankey went in to check. And there was the body.'

'Did he see anyone else?' asked Cooper.

'He says he didn't see anyone in the grounds or at the house this morning except Darius and Elsa Roth themselves.'

'Where did he see Elsa?'

'He spoke to her briefly in the garden room when he arrived. He parks his van at that side of the house so it isn't visible to visitors.'

Villiers raised an eyebrow at him. What did that mean?

'Do you think something is going on between Elsa and Sankey?' said Cooper.

'No. Nothing from his point of view, anyway. I have a feeling from what he said that Elsa might sometimes feel a bit . . . lonely.'

'I'm not surprised.'

'Me neither. But Will Sankey is too cautious to get involved in anything like that. I think he's in the clear.'

'Good. It would be too bad if it turned out to be the gardener who did it,' said Cooper. 'Too much of a cliché.'

'Unfortunately, we don't have anyone else in the vicinity for the time when Darius Roth was killed. Only Sankey. And Elsa, of course.'

'And you've just said Sankey is in the clear.'

'Well, all right. I don't want to jump to conclusions.'

'You don't like Elsa much, do you?' said Cooper.

'To be honest,' said Villiers, 'I haven't met one of them that I like so far.'

'And there's one other, by the way,' said Cooper.

'Who?'

'The cleaner, Milena,' he said. 'But she's too discreet.'

Villiers looked at him oddly.

'When we came here the first time, we managed to approach the chapel without passing the house,' she said. 'We reached it from the footpath through the woods. Anyone else could have done that.'

'Of course, if they knew about it.'

Cooper looked around the front of Trespass Lodge, noting the glint of lenses angled high on the walls under the eaves.

'Let's try the cameras first,' he said. 'It isn't often we get a chance to look at CCTV footage in this part of Derbyshire.'

'By the way,' said Villiers, 'the Major Crime Unit are on their way from EMSOU. DCI Mackenzie will be senior investigating officer. It's going to take them a while to get here yet, though.'

'If they can find it at all.'

'What do you mean?'

'They'll be trying to follow their satnavs,' said Cooper. 'I wish them luck with that. They'll probably end up in Stockport.'

Trespass Lodge was well equipped with security lights and cameras, of course. A computer screen in a study showed live images from the front of the property.

Cooper was able to scroll back to the previous evening. Just before it went dark and the system switched to infrared, a camera trained on the drive had recorded footage of a vehicle approaching the lodge but stopping at the gates. It stood there for a while before turning round and leaving. It was too far away for the make of the car to be established. But its colour was – what? Teal or viridian, perhaps.

'Carol, take Luke and bring in Jonathan Matthew for questioning,' Cooper said. 'Try his flat at Whalley Range, and if he's not there, he might be back at work in Manchester.'

'There's no sign of Jonathan Matthew at his home or office. His employer says he's still taking time off because of the death of his sister. So I phoned his mother. She says she spoke to Jonathan last night, and he told her he was in Manchester rehearsing with his band all evening.'

'Have we got a number for Robert Farnley?'

'Gavin should have one.'

Cooper got the number and called.

'When did you last see Jonathan Matthew, Mr Farnley?'

'He was here for rehearsals last night.'

'Until what time?'

'We worked late. There were a couple of songs we were having trouble with. We were still here at midnight.'

'Midnight?'

'Yes. Then we had to pack up and get our gear into the cars. I don't suppose we actually left the mill before half past twelve.'

If that was true, there was no way Jonathan Matthew could have got to Hayfield by the time his car was shown on the CCTV camera at Trespass Lodge. If it was true.

'Gavin, where was that place the band was rehearsing, where you talked to Robert Farnley?' he called.

'Brunswick Mill,' said Murfin. 'It's in Ancoats. One of those big old mill buildings facing onto the Ashton Canal. You can't miss it.'

*　　*　　*

Diane Fry was following DCI Alistair Mackenzie's car towards Hayfield. DC Jamie Callaghan sat in the passenger seat of the Audi, quietly texting and checking messages.

'Jamie, can you have a look at the map?' she said. 'I don't think this is right.'

Callaghan looked up. 'Where are we?'

'That's the point. I don't know.'

Callaghan opened up an app on his phone.

'It shows our present location as somewhere on the A6 near Whaley Bridge,' he said.

'I think we should have turned off at that last exit. We're almost in Greater Manchester.'

'But Mr Mackenzie—'

'He's wrong,' said Fry. 'I'm going to head back at this roundabout. Call him and tell him what we're doing?'

'Me?' protested Callaghan.

'I'm driving, in case you hadn't noticed.'

Fry swung back southwards onto the A6 as she listened to Callaghan explain to their boss. She couldn't hear what Mackenzie was saying, but she could imagine how irritable he would sound. He was probably looking at his watch too, calculating how much time they'd lost heading in the wrong direction.

They worked through Hayfield and finally found the road to Trespass Lodge. Several police vehicles were already parked in front of the house.

'How did these guys find it?' complained Mackenzie when he clambered out of his Mercedes.

'Local knowledge?' suggested Fry.

They were directed to the back of the house and across an expanse of grass until they reached the old chapel.

'Is this the crime scene?' said Mackenzie. 'Give me a nice back alley in Nottingham anytime.'

Fry couldn't argue with that. This was definitely the middle of nowhere. Ben Cooper country if ever she saw it. Murders happened here too.

But Ben Cooper himself wasn't to be found. Instead, he'd left a message for the Major Crime Unit. He was following a line of inquiry and expected to apprehend a suspect soon.

'It sounds as though we're too late,' said Mackenzie. 'I think this might be your fault, DS Fry.'

The A6 from Buxton ran straight through Stockport before it headed in towards Manchester city centre. In Gorton, a junction on Hyde Road also marked the end of the A57 from Sheffield over the Snake Pass.

Inner-city areas like Gorton were where all those young working-class men had flocked from to join the Mass Trespass on Kinder in 1932. Since then, the streets of terraced houses had disappeared in Manchester's slum clearances, entire communities moved to new estates in Wythenshawe and Hattersley.

Cooper recalled that in the early 1960s, the Moors Murderers, Ian Brady and Myra Hindley, had been inconspicuous clerks working in a Gorton chemical factory. In their case, they'd driven out of the city on summer evenings for the purpose of murdering children and disposing of their victims' bodies on Saddleworth Moor.

Then the factories themselves had closed and Gorton itself had died. So now the descendants of those factory workers lived miles out of the city in Hayfield and Glossop.

Cooper turned off the A6 and went through Ardwick

towards Ancoats, glimpsing the stands of the Etihad Stadium, where Manchester City played.

He recognised Brunswick Mill straight away from Gavin Murfin's description. Ancoats had been described as the world's first industrial suburb, one of the cradles of the Industrial Revolution – and Brunswick Mill was a huge relic of that industrial past. Boarded-up windows overlooked Bradford Road, where the mill's seven storeys loomed over rows of modern townhouses.

But Gavin was wrong about one thing. The mill wasn't 'backing onto' the Ashton Canal. The mill's loading bays all *faced* the canal. That was where the raw materials had come in and the finished products had gone out.

He found Robert Farnley in one of the practice rooms, just as Murfin had said he would be. Farnley had two other musicians with him, but there was no sign of Jonathan Matthew.

'He hasn't turned up,' said Farnley when Cooper asked. 'It's a real nuisance at this stage. And you can tell him that from me if you find him.'

'Do you have any idea where he might be, Mr Farnley?'

'He lives in Whalley Range.'

'We've tried there.'

'Or he might be at work. He has a job—'

'We've tried there too. He told his mother he'd be here rehearsing.'

'Well, we haven't seen him today, have we?'

The other musicians muttered their agreement.

'He's missing,' said Cooper.

'I hope this isn't going to affect the band,' said Farnley. 'We've got a gig coming up next week in Stockport.'

'I'm afraid Jonathan Matthew won't be playing with you, sir.'

'That's a real shame.'

'I'm sure there are plenty of session guitarists hanging around Brunswick Mill.'

'You don't know much about music, do you? You can't just turn up and do a gig without putting in some rehearsal time together. Jonno is an important part of the band. When will we get him back?'

Cooper smiled. 'By the time you see him again, Mr Farnley, I'm afraid he'll be long out of practice.'

'It's a shame,' said Farnley. 'I liked Jonathan. But the truth is, bass players are always a bit unreliable. Temperamental. It's a complication for us, though. Jonno was putting up the money for promotion and to make a proper demo. That's why we let him join the band in the first place. He's not a brilliant bass player, to be honest. I could have got someone better.'

'But he wasn't going to be able to provide the money, was he?'

'Oh yes, he did. Just this week. He came through on his promise.'

'Really? Did he tell you where he got it from?'

'No. And I didn't ask him.' Farnley laughed. 'Wait – you're the cops. He hasn't robbed a bank or something, has he?'

'Well, it wasn't Jonathan's money anyway,' said Cooper. 'And we believe he may have killed his benefactor.'

'Oh well. He wouldn't be the first person to think there's something more important than money.' Then Farnley stopped laughing. 'You're not kidding with me, are you?'

'Hardly, Mr Farnley. This is a murder inquiry.'

'Darn. That puts a different light on things.'

330

'Oh? Do you want to change your story, sir?'

Farnley shifted uneasily on his stool.

'All right. Jonathan wasn't here at all last night,' he said. 'He asked me to say he was, if anyone asked. But I wasn't expecting it to be *you* asking. I never thought . . . Well, Jonno said his mother might call, and he'd told her he was here rehearsing.'

'His mother?'

'Mrs Matthew is a bit of a dragon, apparently. She doesn't approve of him being in a band. She rang here once before trying to get hold of him, so I didn't think too much of it when he asked me to do him a favour.'

'If he wasn't here, then where was he?' said Cooper. 'Did he tell you?'

'Again I didn't ask.' Farnley smiled and almost winked. 'I thought it was probably a private matter. Something he didn't want his old mother to find out about, if you understand me.'

Cooper heaved another sigh. Keeping secrets became so natural to people that it made his job very difficult sometimes. But there were secrets and secrets. This was on a different level to anything Robert Farnley might have been imagining.

'This, sir,' he said, 'is definitely something Jonathan Matthew wouldn't want his mother to find out about.'

33

Fog returned to the Peak District that evening. As dusk began to fall, it rolled down from the hills and filled the valleys, swallowing villages and turning the roads into treacherous grey funnels where headlights bounced back against a dense wall of murk.

But Ben Cooper and his team were in Manchester, conducting a search of Jonathan Matthew's flat in Whalley Range. He and Luke Irvine were examining Jonathan's computer and CD collection.

'He's really into horror films,' said Cooper. 'Look at all these DVDs: *Friday the 13th*, *The Texas Chainsaw Massacre*, *Dawn of the Dead*.'

'And some more recent stuff. *Jigsaw*. That's very nasty.'

'How nasty?'

'Very. Torture, dismemberment, that sort of thing.'

'Mmm.'

'Do you ever think there's a connection between people watching these things and going on to commit violent crime?' said Irvine.

'I think the latest theories are against it.'

'They do tend to stay in the mind, though. Some of the images . . .'

Cooper wasn't convinced by Irvine's generalisation. But then, he wasn't au fait with the horror-film genre the way Luke was. The titles Irvine had mentioned were familiar, of course. He might have watched many of them himself. But they'd blurred in his mind, become one long sequence of crazed killers and screaming victims, accompanied by dramatic music. He couldn't recall the plot of any of them – if they had a plot.

Cooper looked at Irvine's expression and realised he was afraid of being made fun of. Well, other members of the team would have scoffed. Gavin Murfin certainly. Becky Hurst too, if she was having a bad day.

'So what are you suggesting, Luke?' he said. 'Do you think Jonathan Matthew had some obsession with graphic violence and finally acted it out in real life?'

Irvine looked relieved. 'Well, it's possible, isn't it?'

'Everything's possible when it comes to the reasons people commit murder.'

Then Irvine gave a low whistle.

'There's an envelope here with a cheque in it,' he said. 'A pretty large cheque too. More than my monthly salary, anyway.'

'Jonathan doesn't have any money,' said Cooper. 'So who was he sending a cheque to?'

'No, he was receiving the money, not sending it. And take a look who it came from.'

Irvine passed him the cheque. Cooper took it carefully between his gloved fingers. The flamboyant signature might have been enough to give him a clue. But the sender's name was printed clearly on the bottom of the cheque.

'Darius A. Roth,' said Cooper. 'So that was where Jonathan was getting the money from for his band.'

They met up with Carol Villiers and Gavin Murfin in the hallway of the flat.

'What are we going to do next, Ben?' asked Villiers.

'We'll wait. Jonathan will come back when he thinks it's gone quiet.'

'Why are you so sure?'

'Look, he's left his guitar here. But we won't all wait here. We'll leave Gavin on surveillance.'

'You think I'll look inconspicuous around here,' said Murfin. 'As though I might be a devotee of Krishna Consciousness.'

'No,' said Cooper, 'because you'll recognise Jonathan Matthew when you see him.'

It was an hour later when Gavin Murfin phoned. Ben Cooper was already on his way to Hayfield with Carol Villiers when he took the call.

'An old Subaru Impreza has arrived,' said Murfin. 'Colour, er . . . unidentifiable.'

'That's him. Don't lose him, Gavin.'

Murfin kept them updated as Jonathan Matthew's car headed across South Manchester to reach the A6.

'He's going out of town,' said Murfin. 'I've still got him in sight.'

'Where do you think he's going?' Villiers asked Cooper.

'If he's southbound on the A6, I'll bet he's going to his parents' house in Stockport.'

'I thought Jonathan didn't get on with his parents. He didn't even want to speak to his mother the day after his sister was killed.'

'True,' said Cooper. 'But where else is he going to go when he knows he's in trouble? He must be aware that we're looking for him, but he doesn't know what to do. He can't escape, so he'll head for a sanctuary.'

'He'll go home to Mum.'

'Exactly.'

Murfin reported that the Subaru had left the A6 at the turning for Stockport Crematorium.

'There he goes,' said Cooper. 'His parents live in Heaviley, Gavin. He'll be home in a few minutes.'

'Oh, hold on,' said Murfin. He swore under his breath. 'Damn, I think he's spotted me. He must have seen me following him from Whalley Range. It was too obvious when I turned off to the crematorium right behind him.'

'What's he doing?' demanded Cooper.

'He's turning round. Heading straight back onto the A6 again.'

'Still southbound?'

'Yes. Sorry, Ben.'

'Don't worry. Let me know straight away if he turns off again.'

Cooper parked his Toyota in a layby on the A6 and watched for Jonathan Matthew's Subaru to come by. Then he fell in behind Murfin's green Skoda a couple of vehicles back. When they hit Hazel Grove, he rang Murfin.

'You can drop out now, Gavin.'

'Will do.'

Ten miles later, Jonathan's car left the A6 at the Blackbrook exit near Chapel-en-le-Frith and turned onto Sheffield Road. Once they were in Derbyshire, the rising altitude was evident from the banks of mist rolling down from the hills. At a few hundred feet above sea level, the climate was completely different. It could be inches deep in snow here while Manchester barely experienced a drizzle.

'He's stopped,' said Villiers after another mile or two.

'The Chestnut Centre,' said Cooper. 'What does he want there?'

But he stopped for only a moment, as if to get his bearings. He set off again, driving up the hill at Slackhall from the Chestnut Centre and taking the back road to Sparrowpit to reach the A623.

'Do you think he's lost?' said Villiers.

'I don't know. But if he stays on these roads, we'll have to call in a Road Traffic unit for a pursuit.'

Cooper knew the narrow back lanes were dangerous at the best of times if you were travelling at speed, but the thickening fog would make anyone think twice. You had no idea what might be coming round the next bend until their headlights were in front of your bonnet and there was no room to pass.

But Jonathan seemed to have ceased to care. Instead of staying on the main road, he swung north again at Peak Forest and followed the winding lanes round the Limestone Way and Hucklow Moor.

The Eden Valley railway line emerged from a tunnel here on its way from Edendale to the junction at Doveholes. Straight ahead was a level crossing on a lane that led from Hucklow and climbed over the moor towards the furthest edges of the town. Visibility was growing worse, the isolated farmsteads on the lower slopes sinking into mist like ships disappearing under the waves.

Then red brake lights flared ahead.

'He's slowing down,' said Villiers. 'Is he stopping again?'

'I think the crossing gates are down.'

'We've got him, then.'

But instead of stopping, Jonathan Matthew's car swung suddenly to the right and the brake lights went out.

'No. He's going round the gate,' said Villiers.

'Idiot. He can't see anything in this fog. There could be—'

But it was too late to complete the sentence. The front end of a diesel locomotive emerged from the fog, the beams of its lights briefly catching Jonathan Matthew's shocked face through the window of his Impreza.

A mournful horn blasted out. But there was no time for the train driver to brake. Cooper heard a smash and a screeching of metal as the locomotive struck the car and pushed it along the track until it lurched sideways and began to slide down the banking. It came to a halt with a loud thump and a shattering of glass.

'It sounds as though it's hit a tree.'

'Let's see if he's still alive.'

They got out of the car. As they crossed the line, Cooper saw movement in the fog. Something falling from above. But they were just leaves, wafting slowly down from the trees and settling onto the wet track.

34

Diane Fry walked into the police station at West Street. She'd almost forgotten what a dump it was. It was hard to think that she'd worked here for years and had put up with these conditions. She hoped she never had to come here again.

She went straight to Ben Cooper's office and walked in with a perfunctory tap on the door.

Cooper looked up.

'Diane?' he said. 'What is it?'

'DCI Mackenzie wants to know what's happening with the Darius Roth murder inquiry. He thinks you might be taking matters into your own hands.'

'Tell Mr Mackenzie it's all under control. We already have a suspect in custody.'

'I know that. Have you interviewed him yet?'

'We're just about to. Do you want to sit in?'

Fry hesitated. 'No. But keep us informed.'

'Of course.'

Without waiting for an invitation, she sat down on a chair in front of his desk, suddenly feeling weary.

'And have you sorted out the problem with the Atherton case?' she asked.

Cooper raised an eyebrow. 'What do you know about that?'

'A conflict in a witness statement from the neighbour, isn't there? The timing of a phone call.'

'Yes, but—'

'It's probably quite simple,' she said.

'It may look simple to you, Diane, but it isn't so easy when you've got a witness to interview who might be mistaken about what happened.'

'I don't think she's mistaken,' said Fry. 'I think you are.'

'What?'

'You've been trusting Gary Atherton to tell the truth.'

'He's confessed to killing his wife. He was still there holding the murder weapon when the FOSAs arrived. He says he made the call when he realised what he'd done.'

'According to the files, there's a teenage son,' said Fry.

'So?'

'Why don't you ask him if *he* made the call?'

'And his father is covering for him? It's a hell of a risk for Gary Atherton. He'll get a life sentence if he's convicted.'

'But he won't if there's a flaw in your evidence,' said Fry. 'The timing of that 999 call. I spotted it myself.'

'It was you who kicked the file back?'

'I took it to Mr Mackenzie anyway. I'm sorry if it reflected badly on you.'

Cooper thought of poor old Dev Sharma's disappointment that a hole had been poked in his case so easily. But of course he could never mention Sharma's role. Cooper was the DI in this department. It was his team. It was part of the job to take the responsibility when things went wrong.

'Sometimes it just needs a fresh pair of eyes to see where

someone has made an assumption or accepted a statement on trust,' said Fry. 'That's often where it all goes off the rails, isn't it? Trusting the wrong person.'

'Yes,' said Cooper. 'You're right again.'

They had Jonathan Matthew waiting in Interview Room 1. He'd been treated for his injuries and released into custody. The fact that he hadn't suffered any broken bones or internal injuries was down to a combination of seat belt, air bag and a lot of good luck. His ancient Subaru was a write-off, of course.

'Jonathan, why did you try to run?' asked Ben Cooper.

'I've never trusted the cops,' he said. 'Once you fix on someone as a suspect, you never change your minds. You'll have me in court without any proper evidence and there'll be nothing I can do about it.'

'Evidence of what?'

'Of—' Jonathan stopped and scowled suspiciously. 'Of whatever you're arresting me for.'

Cooper couldn't help but laugh. He'd never heard it put quite like that before.

'You're here for questioning in connection with the murder of Mr Darius Roth,' he said.

Jonathan lowered his head. Was this as far as he'd planned? An attempted escape with his guitar in the back of the Subaru, like a hippy on a road trip? But he hadn't even worked that out properly. He'd left his guitar behind at his flat in his haste to get away.

'Faith was behaving oddly. It was so obvious,' said Jonathan.

'What was?'

'Her relationship with Darius.'

'Are you sure about that?' said Cooper.

'Of course.'

'Did Greg suspect?'

'She'd finished with Greg Barrett.'

'Mr Barrett doesn't seem to be aware of that.'

'Well, I'm sure she was intending to finish it. She'd developed other interests.'

'With Darius?'

'Yes.'

'Did Elsa know?'

'I think she knew everything about Darius that she wanted to,' said Jonathan. 'Anything she didn't want to know she just ignored, pretended it didn't exist or that it never happened. She lives in her own world, that one. And it's partly a fantasy.'

Cooper remembered his earlier conversation with Elsa Roth. Elsa herself had said, *It's like a fantasy.* And perhaps it was, even more than she understood.

'Well, what would you have done?' said Jonathan.

His question and his suddenly penetrating stare caught Cooper off guard. He remembered Jonathan talking about the feeling of guilt at not being able to protect Faith. He'd empathised with that feeling. He'd felt the guilt himself, wondered what he might do if he got the opportunity for revenge on the person responsible. What *would* he have done?

'You took the teddy bear from Faith's house on Monday evening, didn't you?' said Cooper. 'So it must have been sometime during that day, after you'd heard she was dead. You spoke to somebody then.'

'Teddy Bear,' said Jonathan. 'That's what Elsa called him. I hope he got the message.'

But Cooper wasn't sure Darius did get the message. If his relationship with Faith had been as close as Jonathan suggested, he might have recognised the teddy bear by its red bow tie.

'Jonathan, who told you Darius Roth killed your sister?'

'It doesn't matter.'

'I think it does.'

Jonathan's face set into a stubborn mask. He had a cut below his eye and his cheekbone was bruised. It would be difficult to tell now which injuries he'd sustained in the crash and which were inflicted by Darius Roth as he defended himself from attack on that gallery in the old chapel.

'Did you actually see Darius push your sister off that rock?' asked Cooper.

'He was there,' repeated Jonathan. 'Who else could it have been?'

Cooper sat back. There was nothing he could say to that.

'The perfect murder,' said Jonathan. 'That's what Darius would have called it. But he made a mistake. There was a witness.'

'Who?'

'I can't say. But I couldn't let him get away with it, could I?'

'A lot of people who commit murder think they're doing the right thing,' said Cooper. 'But almost all of them are mistaken.'

Jonathan continued to look stubborn. 'Still, there *was* a witness.'

'Not really,' said Cooper. 'Unfortunately.'

An hour or two hitting the phones got Ben Cooper the answers he needed. When you were able to ask exactly

342

the right question, people were much more likely to tell you the truth.

'We've spoken to all the members of the New Trespassers now,' said Villiers. 'It's the same with almost every one of them.'

And there was the connection. Darius Roth had a financial hold on all of them – he'd bailed out the Goulds' nursery when their lease ran out, bought their land and leased it back to them. He was subsidising the two students through college so they didn't have to get jobs working in bars in the evenings. He'd rescued the Warburtons when they had a pension disaster. He'd set Liam up in a nice apartment near Manchester Airport so he could move in with the Hungarian chef.

And what about Nick Haslam? He'd been facing a drink-driving charge and was likely to get banned. Roth had paid for good lawyers to save his licence. And of course he was paying for the promotion of Jonathan Matthew's band.

Then there was Elsa herself. She was much younger than Darius, but she wasn't the typical trophy wife. He'd married a waitress, not a catwalk model. Cooper suspected a large part of Elsa's appeal had been her submissiveness. Men like Darius Roth seemed to like that. Cooper had never been able to see the attraction of it himself. In his opinion, if you wanted slavish devotion, you'd be better off getting a dog.

'You'd think people would be grateful for being financially supported. But often they're not. They hate the feeling of being dependent and they become resentful about it. Patronage, it's called. Artists used to thrive on it. Now they're too independent. That's why Jonathan came to hate Darius. He longed to bite the hand that fed him. He'd become a bit unstable anyway. Darius had told him to stay off the drugs if he wanted the money to keep coming in. And he was trying. But when Jonathan felt really bad, who do you think he focused the blame on for his torment?'

'Darius.'

'But somebody used Jonathan, didn't they? They made him suspect that Darius had killed Faith. They channelled his anger.'

Cooper was still thinking about Darius Roth. Many psychopaths were very charming and adept at manipulating people around them. They could pass as perfectly normal in society, even appear convincingly successful and affluent. But it was all a façade. Underneath, there was a seriously disturbed personality.

'None of the walking-club members ever thought to question his façade as a wealthy property developer. Why should they? And Elsa certainly didn't care. She had no curiosity about his business dealings as long as the money was coming in to support their lifestyle. She knew he went off to meetings and had business calls in his office at home, but she never inquired what they were about.'

'I'm sure he would have discouraged her from inquiring if she ever showed an interest. The one thing Elsa Roth was good at – doing what Darius wanted. She would have avoided anything that might annoy him.'

'She must have felt in a very precarious position, I suppose.'

'But she was his wife. Even if he divorced her, she would have been in line for a handsome settlement.'

'I think it was more than just financial self-preservation. I believe she was very afraid of him. She must have sensed something in Darius that the others didn't.'

344

'What a pity she didn't tell us before it was too late.'

So there were only two people in that group Darius didn't have a financial hold over. Faith Matthew and Sophie Pullen. One of them was dead. And perhaps he'd been right to trust what the other was saying.

'Any one of them might have killed Faith to protect Darius. I wonder what story he told them in the clubhouse that night.'

'Whatever it was, I'm sure he was very convincing.'

So Darius had bought their loyalty. He'd paid for their friendship. And with Elsa it was more than just friendship. Perhaps it was with the students too. Which one of them had been willing to go even further for him and commit murder?

What about previous members? Had they angered him in some way and had their financial support withdrawn? Or did they just have enough? They'd been forced to pander to his obsessions. Yet they were all just part of his façade, an elaborate role play that must have gone some way to satisfy his ego.

'What about Faith, though?' said Cooper.

'There's no financial connection with Darius Roth that we can see.'

Cooper considered that for a moment.

'Carol, I need you to go to that hospital where Faith Matthew worked,' he said.

'Meadow Park?'

'Yes. See if you can find out why she left. We know Darius was a patient there. I want to establish if there's a previous connection between them. If so, it might have begun at the hospital.'

'I'll get straight on to it in the morning.'

345

'It was all about to come to an end anyway,' said Irvine.

'What do you mean?'

'Look at the figures.'

Cooper's ability to read spreadsheets was a recently acquired skill. Some of it meant little to him, but he recognised a downward trend, knew what figures meant when they were printed in red or placed in brackets.

Irvine's inquiries into his company showed it to be on the verge of collapse. Darius had been syphoning off the profits and selling assets until the business was on its knees. The money was about to run out. Within months he would be bankrupt. Liam Sharpe's rent wouldn't be paid, the Goulds' land would be sold off, and the students' allowances stopped.

Did Jonathan Matthew find out there was no money? Did he confront Darius Roth, furious to find himself indebted to his sister's killer? Maybe Roth had lorded it over him, as just another beneficiary of his patronage. But if so, he'd chosen the wrong person to patronise. The life of Jonathan's sister had meant more to him than money or music.

But someone else had used Jonathan Matthew to target Darius. Was it another member of the group who got wind of the problem? Had their funding failed? It was interesting to speculate what might have happened next time the walking group met in that clubhouse in the old chapel.

'You see, Darius inherited control of the businesses when his brother died six years ago,' said Irvine. 'In October.'

'And the date of the Kinder walk was changed to mark the anniversary of Magnus's death.'

'Yes.'

'So it's some kind of memorial to his brother,' said Villiers. 'Perhaps they were very close.'

'I think there's more to it than that,' said Irvine. 'It was Magnus who quickly built up the business. As the older son, he took it over when their father died. By all accounts, he made a big success of it. That was when the money really started to roll in.'

'But when Magnus was killed—'

'Darius inherited.'

'Yes, but it seems Darius wasn't as good a businessman as his brother. He's drained the companies of profit. There's a massive mortgage on Trespass Lodge too, which he would have been defaulting on very soon.'

Cooper nodded. That made sense. Darius had failed to live up to his brother. And he lost all the money trying. The company he inherited had declined rapidly under Darius's leadership. He'd made bad decisions, poor investments, trusted the wrong people, all while spending extravagantly on vanity projects.

He'd ruined the business Magnus and their father had built up, wrecked the Roth empire. He must have been glad that Magnus wasn't around to see it.

Diane Fry called that afternoon. Ben Cooper wasn't as surprised as he might have been at any other time. She'd wanted something from him, after all.

'They've called off the disciplinary hearing,' she said without any preamble or small talk.

Cooper breathed a sigh of relief. It had been weighing on his mind ever since his visit to Ripley.

'Good,' he said. 'I'm pleased to hear it.'

'They must have found out something that undermined the case they thought they had against me.'

'Yes, I'm pretty sure that's what happened,' said Cooper.

'I know you did something. But maybe I shouldn't ask what it was.'

He laughed. 'Well, whatever it was, I'm glad it helped.'

'You know, I think they were watching me,' said Fry. 'They had me under surveillance. Can you believe it?'

'How do you know that?'

'I've seen them,' she said. 'Sitting in a black BMW watching for me to use my InPost locker at the service station by Clifton Bridge. They must know I use that terminal regularly to receive packages.'

'Do you think they sent something to your locker and were waiting for you to pick it up?'

'Yes. Something incriminating, I imagine. I bet they planned to catch me opening the locker and taking delivery.'

'But you never went to your locker?'

'No.'

'Why not?'

'Angie warned me not to.'

'I guess she was the one who saved your bacon, then.'

'Maybe.'

'You said you receive regular packages at the InPost terminal,' said Cooper. 'Were they . . . ?' He left the question hanging.

Then it was Fry's turn to begin laughing.

'I order Whole Earth organic no-caffeine coffee alternative and vegetarian tofu ragout from Holland and Barrett,' she said. 'And occasionally some moringa powder and cacao nibs.'

Cooper laughed too. And it wasn't just relief. It seemed so out of character with the Diane Fry he knew.

'Well, I just never get time to go into Nottingham to visit their store,' she said defensively.

'I thought you were more of a chocolate and wine woman. What's with all the healthy foodstuffs?'

'They give me energy. That's better than cocaine any day, Ben.'

Cooper was trying to readjust his mental image of Diane Fry to some kind of health-food fanatic. It wasn't really working.

'So nothing suspicious,' he said.

'People can see anything as suspicious,' said Fry. 'It depends on your perspective. It depends what you want to believe – or what you want others to believe.'

There was another important question on Ben Cooper's mind. He called his brother as soon as he got home that night. He had just had one question to ask him after the previous evening.

'So what do you reckon, Matt?' he said.

Matt breathed noisily down the line for a moment. Ben pictured him looking round at Kate, seeking her approval or agreement. There was no doubt they would have discussed the subject at length after Ben and Chloe had left Bridge End Farm last night.

'All right, we reckon,' said Matt finally.

Ben breathed a sigh of relief. 'Good.'

There was another pause, longer this time, then a deep breath from Matt.

'And I think Mum would have approved too.'

35

Friday

Next morning, Ben Cooper had a copy of the post-mortem report on his desk. Chloe Young and her colleagues at the mortuary had worked overnight to conduct the examination so that he had the results in his hands first thing. And he was grateful for it. He must remember to tell her that. He suspected DCI Mackenzie wouldn't.

Cooper looked through the report. It was pretty much as he'd expected. Roth had died from head injuries sustained in the fall. Much like Faith Matthew, in fact.

Then one apparently irrelevant detail caught his eye.

He picked up the phone. 'Carol? Are you free? Can you pop in?'

Villiers pushed open the door a moment later. 'What is it? I'm just on my way to Meadow Park Hospital.'

'Do you remember what Elsa said was wrong with him?' asked Cooper.

'Sorry?'

'Darius Roth. Why he was being treated at Meadow Park?'

'She said he had appendicitis.'

'Right. An appendectomy, then? That's what they would have done, isn't it?'

'Of course. Why?'

Cooper tapped the post-mortem report on Roth.

'This body in the mortuary. Dr Young says the dead man had an enlarged appendix.'

'Interesting.'

'It's more than interesting. It makes all the difference. If this body was Darius Roth's, he shouldn't have an appendix at all.'

Elsa Roth was sitting in her enormous sitting room, a tiny figure in the midst of all that space and expensive furniture.

'Mrs Roth, you told me your husband went into hospital for appendicitis,' said Cooper.

'What? What does that have to do—'

'Bear with me, please. It was just before your marriage, wasn't it? You had to postpone the wedding for six months.'

'That's right. I told you.'

'Yes, you did tell me that. But it can't be true. Mr Roth has never had an appendectomy. He never had appendicitis.'

'How do you know something like that? Oh, I see. A post-mortem.'

'I'm sorry,' said Cooper. 'I know it's distressing. But the fact is, I think Darius went into Meadow Park Hospital for an entirely different reason. It doesn't take six months to recover from an appendectomy anyway. I should have seen that straight away.'

'I have no idea about these things,' said Elsa. 'Why should I have?'

'No reason,' said Cooper, 'if you're prepared to accept everything you're told.'

'I had no cause to doubt Darius,' she said loyally.

But Cooper could see she was wondering now. What

else could her future husband have gone into hospital for? If he left her wondering for long enough, what interpretation might she come up with? How much imagination did Elsa Roth have?

Finally, Cooper took pity on her.

'Did you know that Meadow Park also has a rehabilitation unit?' he said.

'Rehabilitation?'

'Drugs,' said Cooper. 'Alcohol too. But I think your husband was a drug addict. Probably cocaine. It's not unusual among businessmen, I'm told. It's the pressure of the work. I remember your husband talking about how hard his father worked.'

'What you're saying can't be true.'

'We can establish it for definite. But if it helps, I think Mr Roth decided to get clean before your wedding.'

As Cooper watched her face, he saw her put two and two together, then snatch them apart again just as quickly. Sometimes people didn't want to believe what was right in front of their noses.

Elsa stared at him. 'I'm going to miss him so much,' she said.

Cooper was sure that was true, at least.

'Unfortunately, Mrs Roth,' he said, 'it gives your husband a motive for the murder of Faith Matthew. Faith worked at Meadow Park Hospital as a nurse at the time Darius was admitted. I wonder if she threatened to tell what she knew. Did Darius do something to her that made her threaten him? Or that made him threaten her? Would he take the trouble to write a note telling her to "fall down dead"?'

'Of course not.'

'Or,' said Cooper, 'was that you, Mrs Roth? You were

352

always very defensive of your husband. I think if you believed Faith was a threat, you'd do anything to frighten her off. Sending a note. Perhaps even pushing her off Dead Woman's Drop.'

'I have no idea what you're talking about. I don't understand any of this,' she said.

'Jonathan Matthew certainly believes your husband killed his sister on Kinder Scout last Sunday. Somebody told him so.'

'Darius was with me all the time,' said Elsa.

'Or you were with him.'

'What's the difference?'

'Quite a bit. Are you sure he even noticed you were there?'

She flushed. She knew exactly what he meant. She must have put up with Darius's lack of attention often enough that she took it for granted. But there was a difference.

Elsa was too loyal, though. She wouldn't have told him what Darius did even if she'd seen it with her own eyes. She would have rationalised it to herself, figured that he must have had a good reason for it. And she would be willing to protect him even now he was dead. Perhaps especially now.

'Are you aware of the state of Darius's businesses?'

'What do you mean?'

'Mrs Roth, there's no money left. Darius would have been bankrupt within the next six months. He wouldn't have been able to pay the mortgage on this house much longer.'

'Mortgage?'

Cooper looked at her pityingly. Had she taken so little interest that she didn't know there was a huge mortgage to pay on the lodge? Had she taken it for granted that Darius owned the property outright? She was in for a horrible shock.

He let the thought sink in for a moment.

'You'll have a lot of things to deal with, Mrs Roth,' he said. 'Contact me if you decide there's anything you want to tell me.'

The French bulldogs were missing from the front lawn when they left the house. Whose job was it to care for them? he wondered. Elsa didn't look up to it at the moment.

'Jonathan Matthew was dead set on revenge,' said Villiers as they got in the car. 'He didn't plan it very well, though. He would never have got away with it. He must have been too consumed with hatred.'

Cooper started the ignition and drove out of the gates towards Hayfield.

'I understand why he would feel like that if Jonathan believed Darius Roth killed his sister,' he said. 'The trouble is, I don't think Darius was a killer.'

When Diane Fry passed the service station that morning, she saw the BMW in position again. Had no one told them the disciplinary hearing was over? That would be normal. Lines of communication could be slow, especially through official channels. For a moment, she felt sorry for the two men sitting in the car. But the feeling didn't last long.

She circled the roundabout and came back to the service station, pulling onto the forecourt. She imagined her watchers sitting up, suddenly alert.

Fry opened her glove compartment and opened a packet of latex gloves. Then she got out of her car and checked her phone for the email giving her a code for her InPost locker. She pulled on the gloves, keyed in the number and a door popped open. A yellow box sat innocently inside. She drew it out, closed the door and walked casually across the road.

As she walked up to the rear of the BMW, she thought she heard muffled cursing from inside. But what could they do? They weren't even supposed to be here.

Fry tapped on the driver's window. After a moment, the window slid down. She didn't recognise either of the faces of the two men, but she knew them by their suspicious manner, their wary expressions.

The driver looked at her, saying nothing.

'I think this is for you,' she said.

'I think you've—'

But he didn't have time to finish the sentence. Fry tossed the box through the window onto the floor of the car and watched them scramble to avoid it, as if afraid it might contaminate them. A corner of the box split open and a puff of white dust hit the driver's trouser leg.

'Enjoy yourselves,' she said.

She peeled off the gloves as she walked back across the road and couldn't resist a satisfied smile at the sound of the cursing and the bouncing of the BMW on its springs. She contemplated making an anonymous call to Nottinghamshire Police reporting suspected drug dealers operating on the Trent River Walk. She pictured the arrival of the Armed Response Unit, the sniffer dogs, the lengthy awkward explanations that would follow.

But no. It was enough to imagine them fearing it. They would be back on the M1 headed south as fast as their BMW could go.

36

Sometimes a solution was all about knowing where you were, and where everyone else was too. Ben Cooper realised he had never known that in this case.

He went back to study the satellite view of the Kinder Scout plateau on Google Maps. The peat groughs feeding into the River Kinder showed as meandering reddish-brown streaks like rivulets of dried blood. Eroded tracks were visible in a way they wouldn't have been for walkers on the ground, and the Mermaid's Pool was no more than a dark blob on the greenish-brown of the western slopes.

But the Downfall stood out as an eruption of broken rock, twisted and spattered on the hillside, the abandoned shell of a reptile skin. It was shadowed by a darker outline, the deeper chasm where water blew over the edge, where Faith Matthew had fallen from Dead Woman's Drop.

Cooper printed out a new copy of the image and laid it on his desk. Thoughtfully, he took a yellow marker and tried again to locate the position of each of the members of the New Trespassers Walking Club at the time Faith had died.

Several times he had to refer back to the statements made by the group. He marked some of the positions with queries, crossed them out and started again from scratch, trying to get all the conflicting accounts to make coherent sense. After a lot of trial and error, he ended up with eleven markers identifying specific walkers, and one he placed roughly in the area where the search dog Dolly had located Jonathan Matthew. Finally, he took a red pen and drew a cross on the location of Dead Woman's Drop.

As he stared at his map, Cooper became aware of Carol Villiers looking over his shoulder. He wasn't sure how long she'd been standing there watching him at work. He could see from her face that she had something to tell him.

'I'm just back from Meadow Park Hospital,' she said.

'Success?'

'I knew there was no point in trying the official channels, so I sniffed around and found some staff who've worked there for a while and remember her. One or two of them were willing to talk. Hospitals are a hotbed of gossip.'

'And?'

'Well, the talk is that Faith had an affair with one of the junior hospital doctors. He was working there as part of his training – they get assigned to different hospitals and various specialties. The trouble was, this junior doctor was married, and when it all came out, it wrecked his marriage. Faith was asked to leave, and that was when she took up agency nursing work.'

'Did you get the doctor's name?'

'Yes. Dr Jake Gooding.'

Cooper wrote the name down and looked at it for a long moment. It meant something, didn't it? There was a connection, he was sure of it.

'Is this accurate?' asked Villiers, looking at the map.

'As near as I can make it, given the contradictions in the witness statements.'

'If that's where everyone was at the time, it only leaves one possibility,' she said.

'Yes, when you look at it this way, it seems obvious,' said Cooper.

Yes, it was obvious. But perhaps too obvious? If you were planning to commit a murder, surely you would take more effort not to be the obvious suspect. Everything else had been planned. So why not this detail? It didn't make sense. It was like presenting yourself on a plate as a prime suspect.

And yet he had rejected that obvious suspect.

And then he remembered. He heard Darius Roth's smooth voice in his head, as clear as a bell. He was talking about Sophie Pullen bringing Nick Haslam to the walking group. *She used to come with Jake.* So who was Jake? Not just a previous boyfriend, as he'd assumed, but—

'Sophie Pullen was married, wasn't she?' said Cooper. 'It was in your summary, Carol.'

'Yes, she divorced and reverted to her maiden name.' Villiers looked at him with her mouth open. 'So—'

Cooper held up his hand. 'Let's not be too hasty. We need to find out her ex-husband's name first.'

'Oh yes,' said Villiers. 'Just in case it's a coincidence.'

But this wasn't a coincidence, and he knew it.

The perfect murder. Cooper recalled Sophie Pullen telling him that story about Darius Roth. The idea had been in Darius's mind for some time, and the opportunity had arisen on Kinder. He thought the fog would mean no witnesses. Had he really believed he could get away with it? It seemed such a risk for a man like Darius Roth to take.

But what actual evidence had there ever been that Darius killed Faith Matthew? It all came down to one confused witness account. One that Cooper himself had insisted must be mistaken. But one that he'd believed nevertheless.

He remembered what Diane Fry had said to him. *That's often where it all goes off the rails, isn't it? Trusting the wrong person.*

'Faith,' he said. 'It's an interesting name. Faith. That's what it's been about all along.'

Villiers looked up. 'What do you mean, Ben?'

'I mean I can't believe I had faith in the wrong person.'

It was the end of the school day in Buxton. Pupils at St Anselm's were looking forward to the weekend. The teachers too, no doubt. Though one teacher might have to change their plans.

Ben Cooper and Carol Villiers were sitting in Cooper's Toyota on the street watching the gates as parents collected their children. For a while, the road was choked with vehicles, with cars on the pavement, parked on double yellow lines, leaving barely enough space for traffic to pass.

'You never saw Darius Roth as a murderer, did you?' said Villiers.

'No,' said Cooper. 'He was all façade. If his businesses went bankrupt, he might have been capable of killing himself – an overdose, a pipe from his car exhaust – but not someone else. It wasn't part of the image he worked so hard on.'

'And I was wrong too,' said Villiers.

'Were you?'

'I said the quiet ones were the worst. But there are some who talk and talk, and say all the right things, so that you believe them even when they're lying.'

'You're right, Carol,' said Cooper. 'That's exactly what I did.'

'It isn't like you.'

'Thanks. But it doesn't make me feel any better about it. I failed on this one. Well, almost.'

'What was it that misled you?' she asked.

'Sophie Pullen said she followed someone wearing a blue jacket to the Downfall, right to the rock where Faith Matthew fell from. There was no other member of the party wearing a blue jacket apart from Sophie herself. So it seemed to me that it could only have been Darius Roth she saw – he had a long blue scarf. In the fog, Sophie could easily have been mistaken about the item of clothing, while the colour would have been obvious.' Cooper sighed. 'But Darius couldn't have been there – all the members of his group are adamant that he never left them during that time. And I believe them.'

'It's unlikely for them all to agree on the point unless it was true.'

'Not just because of that. Darius was the sort of person who liked to be the centre of attention. He would have been leading the way, giving instructions, chivvying his followers along. He would have been very much *present*.'

'So there's no way he could have just sneaked off for a few minutes without them noticing.'

'No. On the other hand, there are some people you might not notice very much, so you wouldn't realise if they'd slipped away. Then you couldn't really be sure if they were there or not when you were asked later on.'

'So it must have been someone else that Sophie Pullen was following,' said Villiers. 'Could she have been so easily mistaken?'

Cooper was shaking his head. 'No, you're still not getting it, Carol. We only have Miss Pullen's word that she followed anybody.'

'Oh.'

'And yet, and yet . . . we *do* have her own testimony that she left her group. She told us that herself. She volunteered the information but misdirected us by claiming she'd followed someone. She cast suspicion onto someone else even as she drew it to herself. So clever. I should have known. She was always the smartest of the group. I recognised that and took notice of everything she said, all the details she claimed to have observed. I thought she was my most valuable witness. Now she's made me feel an idiot.'

'Was it Sophie who told Jonathan that Darius Roth killed his sister, then?'

'Yes. I think he'll confirm it now, when we put it to him.'

'How do you know?'

'When we interviewed him, Jonathan referred to Darius's story about getting away with the perfect murder. Sophie Pullen told me about that story. But Sophie said only she and Elsa were present when Darius told it. That was a giveaway. Sophie must have passed it on to Jonathan in her efforts to persuade him of Darius's guilt.'

'Was it true? Did Darius tell that story?'

'I don't know. We can ask Elsa if she remembers it, but Sophie might have made it up. It didn't really matter, as long as Jonathan believed her.'

'All that stuff about the blue jacket . . .' said Villiers.

'She forced me to put two and two together and make five,' said Cooper. 'She led me by the nose, and I did exactly what she wanted me to do.'

Cooper groaned quietly. He could hear her now. Sophie Pullen had insisted it was a blue jacket that she'd seen near Dead Woman's Drop. She'd listened politely as he contradicted her several times, told her it was impossible, that she

361

must have made a mistake. She was the only person wearing a blue jacket that day, he'd said. Perhaps it was a blue hat or a scarf she'd seen. And she'd shaken her head at that.

To Cooper, it had seemed clear that she was wrong. Not lying, just mistaken. Sophie had seen things wrong in that fog, jumped to an inaccurate conclusion. In fact, he had been feeling frustrated that she couldn't recognise her own mistake. She was such a good observer of the details in other ways. He'd so wanted her to admit it was a blue scarf, the kind that Darius was wearing. He'd almost tried to persuade her of the fact. That was a fatal flaw in his interview technique. It filled him with anger at himself that he'd made such an error.

He just hadn't put two and two together properly. What should he have done? He should have pointed out to Sophie Pullen that if someone in a blue jacket was near that rock, then it must have been her.

It seemed so obvious now. At the time, it had been too obvious. Sophie Pullen had put the simple fact there, lain it right out on the table in front of him and watched him look the other way. How often had he seen stage magicians pull off that trick? It was the old distraction technique.

Sophie had known that another member of the group might have seen her, at least recognised the jacket through the fog.

She already had her explanation on record.

When she left St Anselm's Primary School for that last time, Sophie Pullen seemed unsurprised to see Cooper and Villiers waiting for her at the gate.

'You're parked on the "no waiting" signs,' she said.

'I think we'll get away with it this once.'

362

Sophie looked around at the school gates and the empty yard.

'We waited until the children had all gone,' said Cooper. 'We thought it would be better that way.'

'Thank you,' she said. 'That's very considerate.'

They put her in the back of the car. Cooper looked at Sophie for a moment. She looked so composed, as if this was nothing unusual or unexpected. Perhaps it had been part of her planning. Option B: co-operate if arrested by the police.

'Faith deserved to die, you know,' said Sophie Pullen. 'I knew it from the start that day. Right at the beginning of the walk. I could see what was going to happen. I could see what I was going to do. And I didn't want to stop it from happening.'

She was in the same interview room that Jonathan Matthew had sat in the day before. Looking across the table at her, Ben Cooper thought she seemed a different woman from the one he'd admired for her power of observation, the detailed recollections she had of the walk on Kinder Scout. Apparently she'd reported everything she could remember, apart from the one most significant incident of all, the act of murder.

'She wanted to take Nick off me,' said Sophie. 'It was so obvious that day on Kinder. It was the final straw.'

'Were Nick Haslam and Faith Matthew having an affair behind your back?' asked Cooper.

'I don't know that I'd call it that. They were certainly becoming closer. Faith knew things about me that I didn't tell her myself, like my new job teaching at St Anselm's. She must have got that from Nick. It explains why he was so awkward around her on the walk. He didn't know how to behave towards her in front of me, couldn't even make a joke of it. Nick was always such a joker.'

'He doesn't come across as a joker to me. Bad-tempered and sarcastic maybe.'

'He wasn't always like that,' said Sophie, suddenly keen to defend him. 'He's changed recently. *She* did that.'

'So it became obvious on the walk.'

'She was more blatant, of course. But poor old Nick tried to hide their relationship and pretend he didn't like her. He tried too hard, though. He always does. I saw straight through him.'

'Miss Pullen, do you feel so strongly about Mr Haslam that you'd kill for him?'

She hesitated, taken aback at the direction of the question.

'No, of course you don't,' continued Cooper. 'But that's not the point, is it?'

'What do you mean?'

'I think we should talk about someone else entirely. About Dr Jake Gooding. That is your ex-husband, isn't it?'

She shrank a little, deflated by his mention of the name.

'You obviously know.'

'Tell me about him.'

'I met Jake Gooding through my father. He's a GP, you know,' said Sophie.

'Yes.'

'Well, I fell for Jake straight away. He was so good-looking, confident and charming. I was a complete pushover. We married within a couple of years. Perhaps it was too soon.'

'And then you heard about his affair.'

'Yes.'

She pursed her lips, as if she didn't want to say any

more, as though her ex-husband's affair was the one subject she'd been hoping to avoid. If that was the case, it was the one subject Cooper was going to press her on.

'You heard it involved a nurse at the hospital where Jake was working,' he said. 'Someone tipped you off, I suppose. They thought you ought to know about it?'

'I dare say it sounds so mundane to you. You must hear this sort of thing every day.'

'Quite often,' said Cooper. 'But it doesn't always lead to such a tragic outcome.'

Sophie looked down at the table.

'I never knew who the nurse was at the time,' she said. 'In every story you read, the wronged wife always demands the name of the other woman, doesn't she? But it was one of those things I didn't want to know, the sort of detail I would have felt tainted by. It was such a betrayal. Jake agreed to a divorce without a murmur. I thought he'd gone straight to *her*, you know. He was certainly living with someone soon after – everyone told me that. But it turns out it was a different woman. There could have been more of them when we were together, I suppose.'

'Did you never meet her?'

'No. I only saw her once, in the distance. I was so angry that I went to Meadow Park Hospital to confront him. I wanted to embarrass him at work. I suppose everyone knew what was going on anyway. He was frantic when I turned up. A nurse was just leaving the doctors' office on the ward, and the guilt was written all over his face. I hardly needed to ask him if it was true.'

'So when did you realise who Faith was?'

'During the walk on Kinder Scout on Sunday.'

'Actually *during* the walk?'

'Yes. It was after we'd stopped, in fact. When were lost in the fog and Liam Sharpe fell and injured his leg. Everyone else went off to call for help, but Faith stayed with him. It was seeing her bending over Liam to tend to his injury, and someone saying, "Of course. You're a nurse, aren't you?" Just in that moment, I had a vivid flashback. It was like that figure I described to you, the monstrous shadow in the fog. I suddenly saw her in her nurse's uniform walking down the ward and leaning over a patient. It's the way someone moves that gives them away, isn't it? Their walk, the angle they hold their head. With Faith, it was the way she pushed back that red woollen hat from her face. I'd seen her straightening her nurse's cap and it was exactly the same gesture. That memory made such a lasting impression on me that I knew it was her. I was a hundred per cent certain. I could picture her with Jake and imagine what they might have been doing. The image hit me so hard I thought my legs would give way.'

Cooper let her replay the memory for a moment. It was ironic that Sophie Pullen's imagination and her power of observation, which he'd valued so much before, appeared to have been too sharp for her own good. It would have been much better if she'd taken no notice of Faith Matthew at the hospital and had never recognised her on Kinder Scout. Better not just for Faith but for both of them.

'I loved Jake,' she said. 'I still love him now. It was the biggest mistake I ever made, letting him go like that. If only I could have just let it pass.'

Sophie began to cry, the tears creeping slowly down her cheeks. Cooper had seen a lot of suspects burst into tears in the interview room. Sometimes it was through remorse at what they'd done. Often, though, it was out of pity for themselves. Even the most intelligent person could cling to a conviction that they were the victim. Sophie's life had been destroyed, but largely through her own decisions. Faith Matthew had become the target for all her bitterness.

'I couldn't let her escape justice,' Sophie said through her tears.

'Justice is a subjective concept,' said Cooper. 'When we take it personally, we can get it very wrong.'

Sophie glowered at him.

'She deserved to die a hundred times.'

'That's been said before, Miss Pullen.'

'Because it's true.'

'Perhaps. But murder is still murder.'

She tossed her head dismissively.

'And justice is still justice.'

Half an hour later, after Sophie Pullen had been returned to a cell, Nick Haslam slumped in the same chair. He looked a beaten man. There was no effort at a joke, sarcastic or otherwise.

'Yes, it felt uncomfortable on the walk,' he said when Cooper asked him about the day on Kinder Scout. 'She was pestering me, playing some kind of game.'

'She?'

'Faith, of course. I knew Sophie would be jealous, so I tried to ignore Faith and pretend it was nothing.'

'Sophie saw straight through it, you know.'

Nick cursed under his breath.

'I should have known she would. She tends to over-imagine things at the best of times. But throw in a bit of jealousy and well . . .' He gestured with his hands as if describing an uncontrollable explosion. 'The fact is, though,

Faith was just a nuisance. It would never have come to anything. I really like Sophie. I just have trouble saying it. I suppose I've completely messed everything up now.'

'You would have been better telling her the truth from the start,' said Cooper. 'It could have saved a lot of trouble. It might even have saved two people's lives.'

'Yes, you're right.'

Haslam looked even more dejected. But would this knowledge change his behaviour in the future? Cooper doubted it.

Back in his office, Ben Cooper reviewed the evidence on his desk. What had he missed? Sophie Pullen's prints had been taken and matched those finally retrieved in the lab from the threatening note. FALL DOWN DEAD, she'd written. So how long had Sophie been planning the murder of Faith Matthew? Was it longer than she said, her plan conceived well before the walk? More questioning was needed. It seemed Sophie was still lying, even now.

Well, the photographs taken on Kinder Scout had been pretty accurate, anyway. They showed a fog of confusion. Most of the witness statements had been truthful too, as far as they could be. But the group had been prone to visual and auditory hallucinations, illusionary memories that would be hard to get rid of. In the intricate structures of the human brain, the imagination lay next to the memory. It only took a single misfiring synapse for one to intrude on the other.

Sophie Pullen had no need to be too secretive about her movements. Nobody had any idea where they were.

And there had been no scream when Faith Matthew fell from Dead Woman's Drop. It was one sound the walking group hadn't heard on that foggy moor. Faith would have been too surprised to react as she made that half-turn and saw Sophie behind her.

Even the Kinder Mass Trespass was nothing more than a smokescreen. There was no connection to the death of Darius Roth's brother. It wasn't even linked to the imminent collapse of Roth's businesses. At the end of the day, it was nothing to do with politics or principles, or even money. It was a much, much simpler story than that. A tale as ancient as time. It came down to one of the age-old reasons for murder. This was a story of jealousy.

He imagined the fall had been too sudden. The cold air would have snatched the breath from her throat as she fell. The impact on the rocks had been instantly fatal. Yet it, too, had been muffled by the fog, her body shrouded from sight by the dank miasma.

Cooper put the papers away in a box file and slid it onto the shelf of his office with the others. Yes, Faith Matthew's ending was sad, rather than dramatic. She went with hardly a whimper, let alone a bang. And that was the way it usually happened. It was so simple to make one slip. So easy to meet your downfall.

37

Saturday

A meeting at West Street had just finished. Three murder cases concluded and the files finalised for the CPS. DCI Alistair Mackenzie from the Major Crime Unit made a quick exit with the excuse that he had another meeting to get to back at EMSOU.

But Ben Cooper noticed that Diane Fry seemed in no rush to leave.

'Do you want to get a coffee?' he asked. 'We can drink it in my office.'

'Oh, your office,' said Fry. 'One of the privileges of being an inspector.'

'Pretty much the only one.'

Fry sat hunched in a chair on the other side of his desk, clutching a plastic cup as if she needed its warmth to thaw out her frozen hands.

'Diane, have you heard the news?' said Cooper.

'I don't watch the news,' she said. 'What's happened? Another politician kicked out on his arse?'

'No, I mean the news from Birmingham.'

Fry looked up at him suddenly.

'What?' she demanded.

'It's William Leeson,' said Cooper. 'He's dead.'

'How did you hear that?'

'Angie told me. She sent me a text. I checked, though. He's definitely dead, Diane.'

She seemed to slip into a trance as she gazed into the distance. Cooper wondered what was going through her head. Memories from her childhood? If so, he knew from her face that none of the memories were good ones.

'Well, I'm glad,' she said.

'Was he ill?' asked Cooper.

'I think he had cancer. Is that what he died from?'

'Angie didn't know. Apparently, he was found collapsed at home. There will have to be a post-mortem, I suppose.'

'Yes, I suppose.'

'You don't seem too bothered.'

'I'm not. In fact, I don't even want to think about him. Talk to me about something else.'

'Right.'

Cooper wondered what it was she wanted him to say. Should he mention the weather, the latest office gossip? Fry had never enjoyed small talk. She despised it, in fact. But there was that one question he'd been burning to ask all week.

'So what about the promotion?' he said. 'There's a vacancy for a DI at EMSOU, isn't there?'

Fry shook her head. 'Not for me. It was never going to be my job.'

'Really? I'm sorry.'

'It's not a problem. I didn't expect it. They already had someone lined up.'

'Anyone I know?'

'Actually, yes,' she said. 'But I don't suppose I should tell you. You'll be officially informed in due course.'

There was no need for her to say any more. Cooper didn't know why it should come as a surprise to him. He had had the feeling it would happen for a long time, almost as soon as Dev Sharma came to Edendale as his sergeant.

'Will you be working with him?' he asked, deliberately not mentioning a name.

'I have no idea. Who knows what will happen in the future? There hardly seems any point in planning anything.'

'I know what you mean.'

A silence settled between them as they drank their coffee. Cooper looked at his phone, expecting it to ring and break the silence. But, for once, it didn't. He raised his head and met Fry's eyes. She blinked, apparently embarrassed.

'I owe you, by the way,' she said, looking away. 'For the favour you did me.'

'That's OK. I'm glad it helped.'

'I'm sure it did.'

'I owe you quite a lot too, in a sense,' said Cooper.

'Oh?'

She didn't ask for an explanation, and Cooper was glad of it. He wasn't sure he could have explained it himself.

'That's funny,' she said.

It was odd how so much could be left unspoken between them. He'd only ever experienced that with his brother. As far as Fry was concerned, the silence had always seemed more like a lack of communication rather than any level of understanding. What had changed? Could it possibly be Diane herself?

'I'm not sure I did much for you anyway,' said Cooper.

'No, really. You helped a lot,' she said.

'Me and your biological father, apparently. The man you hate most in the world.'

'No, not him,' she said bitterly. 'He did nothing.'

'Actually, he did,' said Cooper. 'He sent the information to me, and I gave it to Professional Standards.'

'Sent it to you how?'

Cooper shrugged. 'It was delivered anonymously to my house.'

'When did you get it?'

'Wednesday night.'

'That was while I was talking to him in Solihull. He must already have given it to someone.'

'Yes, he must have.'

Fry stared at him. 'That doesn't make any sense. Why would Leeson do it that way? Why wouldn't he send it directly to me, when I'd taken the trouble to go there and ask him?'

Cooper thought he knew the explanation for that. He wasn't sure whether Fry would want to hear it, though. But what else could he tell her? He certainly couldn't mention the message that Leeson had included with the package, because he'd been asked not to. He couldn't say that it was her own sister who'd delivered it. People were on her side, taking risks and working on her behalf. But it hurt him not to be able to tell her. He had to give her something.

'If you ask me,' he said, 'he didn't want you to feel indebted to him. He wasn't going to put that onto you right at the end of his life. After your visit, he decided to do what he could, but not to shake your antipathy. He knew how much you hated him, Diane. He didn't want you to feel guilt or obligation as well.'

'What? You're saying he was thinking of me?'

'In the last few months and weeks before he died, yes.

The approach of death makes people think about everything differently.'

Fry took a moment to digest this, her mouth twisting in disgust as if she was tasting something particularly bitter.

'So why did *you* tell me?' she said. 'Why have you stuck your oar into my life again, Ben?'

'I just had to tell you the truth.'

'Truth?' said Fry. 'Truth is vastly overrated.'

'Well, they wouldn't have got anywhere with a disciplinary hearing,' said Cooper. 'They didn't have a proper case. They were just fishing, you know. You weren't guilty of anything, so you could tell the truth. That's always the best thing.'

Fry didn't reply. Cooper studied her face.

'You weren't guilty of anything,' he repeated. 'Were you, Diane?'

'The truth?' she said.

He hesitated, but only for a moment.

'Yes, please.'

'You say that's always for the best?'

'If you want people to trust you.'

Fry was silent for much longer.

'I don't agree,' she said. 'The truth can destroy everything.'

She drained her cup and dropped it into his waste-paper bin. She nodded to him as she walked to the door. Cooper watched her go, a sour taste bubbling in the back of his throat. So that was the way it ended here too. With no more than a whimper.

Fry had been right when she said to him, years ago, *The people who you think are on your side always turn round and betray you.*

And that was the real truth.

*   *   *

374

That afternoon, Chloe Young accompanied Ben Cooper on his visit to check on Bridge End Farm.

'How long are Matt and Kate away for?' she asked as he unlocked the front door and turned off the alarm.

'Just a week. Matt would never last longer than that. In fact, I imagine he'll be getting withdrawal symptoms by now.'

'Withdrawal symptoms?'

'From the farm. This place is Matt's drug. He's totally dependent on Bridge End. And it's dependent on him too, of course.'

They stepped into the hallway, a place filled with memories for Ben.

'The Coopers seem to be a close family,' said Chloe.

'I suppose we are. Matt and Kate particularly.'

'Twenty years, eh? It's quite a wedding anniversary.'

Cooper looked at her. What did that mean? Was the tone of her voice admiring, envious even? Or did she sound faintly horrified? Was Chloe Young yearning for that sort of lasting relationship, one that would still be secure in twenty years' time? Or was she appalled at the prospect of being tied to the same person for so long? Some people said it was a life sentence. Murderers got out of prison in less time than that.

He checked the back door and examined the porch for leaks, though there had been very little rain. Then he went into the kitchen and opened a tin of dog food for Jess.

'You're really at home here, aren't you?' said Chloe.

'It was my home for over twenty-five years.'

'No, I mean *really* at home, not just in a place where you used to live.'

'It does mean something special,' admitted Cooper. 'So many memories, I suppose.'

'Good and bad?'

'You can't separate them, can you?' he said. 'Well, I can't anyway.'

Even as he said it, the memories came crowding round him, reminding him of all those years he'd spent growing up here. His father was there in the sitting room, occupying his favourite armchair, still in his uniform shirt and trousers, his sleeves rolled up on muscular arms, and his tunic hanging on a hook in the hall, where his sergeant's stripes always seemed to gleam as they caught the light. His mother was in the kitchen, humming to herself in a cloud of steam and there was the aroma of roast beef, which always seemed to ooze through the door when he came home from school. He saw his grandfather there too, out in the yard at the back in his flat cap and tweed jacket, whistling for his dog, while Matt followed behind him, trying to copy the way Granddad walked, splashing through a cowpat in his wellies, so that he'd come in smelling of manure again and get shouted at by Dad.

Cooper felt dizzy for a moment under the barrage of memories, until Chloe put a hand gently on his arm.

'So,' she said, 'there's something that's been puzzling me. You avoided giving me an answer.'

'An answer to what?'

'It's probably not important.'

'No, go on.'

'Well, you never finished telling me about the cat. You didn't say what name she originally had at the rescue centre when you collected her.'

'Oh, that. You're right – it's not important.'

She laughed. 'Now I really want to know.'

Cooper hesitated. But he knew she wouldn't give up on the subject now.

376

'The cat was called Diane,' he said.

'Diane? Are you kidding?'

'No, it's true.'

Chloe let her head fall back. 'Yes, I see. There's no way you could have lived with a cat called Diane. Imagine you going outside and shouting for Diane to come home. She would never have done what you told her.'

'She doesn't now,' said Cooper. 'She just carries on doing exactly what she wants and gets herself into all kinds of trouble.'

Chloe glanced at him, still smiling. 'Now I'm not sure which one you're talking about.'

'Me neither,' he said. 'I'll just check upstairs.'

'I'll come with you.'

He turned on the bottom step. 'There's no need.'

She held his eye and smiled again. Cooper suddenly realised what she meant.

'I'll come with you,' she repeated.

He took her hand and they walked upstairs together. Cooper pushed open the door of the spare bedroom, the room he'd once slept in as a teenager. Sunlight streamed in through the window. In the distance, the Peak District hills shone like precious stones.

Well, that was one way to dispel old ghosts. The best way to wipe out old memories, and to replace them with entirely new ones.

ACKNOWLEDGEMENTS

Many thanks to my editor Ed Wood, all the team at Little, Brown, and everyone who helped to bring *Fall Down Dead* to fruition. A special mention must go to a wonderful surgeon, Mr Keshev Nigam, who got me back in action so quickly when the book was delayed by my illness last year (you can hardly see the scars!). Thanks particularly to my agent Teresa Chris, who has been such a champion of the Cooper and Fry series from the start.

In 2017, following the tragic fire at Grenfell Tower in London, which claimed seventy-one lives, a group called Authors for Grenfell ran an online auction to raise money for bereaved and homeless families. Canadian reader (and former Manchester musician) Robert Farnley was the winning bidder to appear as a character in *Fall Down Dead*. I hope he enjoys his appearance! Many thanks to Robert for his generosity, and to everyone else who made bids in the auction.

A big 'thank you' also to everyone whose donations helped to fund the vet bills for Dolly, the Kinder Mountain Rescue Team's search and rescue dog, who should now be back in action saving lives in the Peak District.